The Hand
of Chaos

Bantam Spectra Books
by Margaret Weis and Tracy Hickman

THE DARKSWORD TRILOGY
Forging the Darksword
Doom of the Darksword
Triumph of the Darksword

DARKSWORD ADVENTURES

ROSE OF THE PROPHET
The Will of the Wanderer
The Paladin of the Night
The Prophet of Akhran

THE DEATH GATE CYCLE
Dragon Wing
Elven Star
Fire Sea
Serpent Mage
The Hand of Chaos

and by Margaret Weis

STAR OF THE GUARDIANS
The Lost King
King's Test
King's Sacrifice

A DEATH GATE NOVEL

The Hand of Chaos

MARGARET WEIS
AND
TRACY HICKMAN

BCA

LONDON NEW YORK SYDNEY TORONTO

This edition published 1993
by BCA
by arrangement with Bantam Press Ltd

Copyright © 1993 by Margaret Weis and Tracy Hickman

Book design by Robin Hessel-Hoffmann
Technical illustrations by GDS/Jeffrey L. Ward
Illustrations in the Introduction by Tom Canty

CN 1148

Printed and bound in Great Britain by
Mackays of Chatham PLC, Chatham, Kent

This my son was dead,

and is alive again;

he was lost, and is found.

♦

Luke 15:24

INTRODUCTION

TO THE

FOUR REALMS

◆

I AM CALLED HAPLO.

My name means single, alone. It was given to me by my parents as a sort of prophecy, for they knew they would not survive the prison into which my people, the Patryns, had been cast—the prison of dark and terrible magics known as the Labyrinth.

I became a Runner—one who fights the Labyrinth. I was one of the lucky ones. I made it through the Final Gate, though I very nearly perished in the attempt. If it had not been for this sausage-stealing dog who sits here beside me, I would not be here, penning this account. The dog gave me the will to live when I would have given up and died. He saved my life.

The dog gave me the will to live, but my lord Xar gave me a *reason* to live, a purpose.

Xar was the first Patryn to escape the Labyrinth. He is old and powerful, highly skilled in the rune-magic that gives both the Patryns and our enemies, the Sartan, our strength. Xar escaped the Labyrinth, then immediately went back into it. No other has ever had the courage to do so, and even now *he* risks his life daily to rescue us.

Many of us have emerged from the Labyrinth. We live in the Nexus, which we have made into a beautiful city. But have we been rehabilitated as our captors had intended?

An impatient people, we learned patience in that hard school. A selfish people, we learned self-sacrifice, loyalty. Above all, we learned to hate.

It is my lord Xar's goal—our goal—to take back the world that was snatched from us, to rule it as we were always meant to rule, and to inflict dire punishment on our enemies.

The realms used to be but one world, one beautiful green-blue world. It belonged to us and the Sartan, for our rune-magic made us powerful. The other, *lesser* races, whom we call mensch—the humans, elves, and dwarves—worshiped us as gods.

But the Sartan thought we Patryns were gaining too much control. The balance of power started to shift in our favor. Furious, the Sartan did the only thing they could to stop us. Using their rune-magic—the magic based on probabilities—the Sartan sundered the world and cast us into prison.

They formed four new worlds out of the rubble of the old, each from an element of the original: air, fire, stone, water. The four are connected by the magical Death's Gate—conduits through which those possessing the rune-magic may safely travel. The four worlds should have worked to support each other: Pryan, the world of fire, would supply energy to Abarrach, the world of stone. Abarrach would supply ores and minerals to Chelestra, world of water, and so forth. All was to be coordinated and fueled by a wondrous machine, the Kicksey-winsey, which the Sartan constructed on Arianus.

But the plans of the Sartan went awry. Their populations on each of the worlds began to mysteriously dwindle and die out. The Sartan on each world called for help from the others, but their pleas went unanswered. Each world had its own troubles.

I discovered this, you see, because it was my task—assigned to me by Xar—to travel to each of the worlds. I was to spy them out and discover what had happened to our ancient enemy. And so, I visited each realm. The complete record of my adventures can be found in my journals, which have come to be known as *The Death Gate Cycle*.

What I learned was a complete surprise. My discoveries changed my life—and not for the better. When I set forth, I had all the answers. Now, I am left only with questions.

My lord blames my unsettled state of mind on a Sartan I met during my travels. A Sartan who calls himself by a mensch name —Alfred Montbank. And at first, I agreed with my lord. I blamed Alfred, I was convinced he was tricking me.

But now, I am not so certain. I doubt everything—myself . . . my lord.

Let me try to tell you—in brief—what happened to me.

ARIANUS

The first world I visited was the world of air, Arianus. It is made up of floating continents that exist on three levels. The Low Realm is the home of the dwarves, and it is here, on Drevlin, that the Sartan built the great and wondrous machine, the Kicksey-winsey. But before the Sartan could get the machine working, they began to die. Panic-stricken, they placed their young people into a state of suspended animation, hoping that when they awoke, the situation would have stabilized.

But only one of the Sartan survived—Alfred. He awoke to find himself the only one of his friends and family still alive. The knowledge appalled him, terrified him. He felt responsible for the chaos into which his world had fallen—for the mensch were, of course, on the brink of all-out war. Yet he was afraid of revealing the truth about himself. His rune-magic would give him the power of a demigod over the mensch. He feared that the mensch would try to force him to use his magic for their own destructive ends. And so Alfred hid his power, refused to use it even to save himself. Today, whenever he is threatened, instead of fighting back with his strong magic, Alfred faints.

The dog and I crash-landed on Arianus and nearly died. We were rescued by a dwarf named Limbeck. The dwarves on Arianus are slaves to the Kicksey-winsey, serving it mindlessly as it works away mindlessly, lacking any direction. But Limbeck is a revolutionary, a freethinker. The dwarves were, at that time, under the thumb of a strong nation of elves, who had set up a dictatorship on the Mid Level of Arianus. The elves therefore control the only supply of fresh water in the world, water that comes from the Kicksey-winsey.

The humans, who also dwell in the Mid Realm, have been at war with the elves over water for most of the history of Arianus. The war raged on during my time there, and the battle continues now—with one significant difference. An elven prince has arisen who wants peace, unity among the races. This prince has started a

rebellion against his own people, but the only result, so far, has been to cause more chaos.

I managed to assist Limbeck, the dwarf, in leading his people in a revolt against both the humans and elves. And when I left, I brought with me a human child—a changeling named Bane— who had figured out the secret to the Kicksey-winsey. Once the machine is up and running, as the Sartan intended it to be, then my lord will use its power to begin his conquest of the other worlds.

I would have liked to have brought another mensch back with me—a human named Hugh the Hand. A highly skilled assassin, Hugh was the one of the few mensch I've met whom I could have accepted as a trusted ally. Unfortunately, Hugh the Hand died fighting Bane's father, an evil human wizard. And who did *I* get for a traveling companion?

Alfred.

But that is skipping ahead.

While I was on Arianus, I came across Alfred, who was acting as a servant to the child Bane. I am ashamed to admit it, but Alfred discovered I was a Patryn long before I knew he was a Sartan. When I found out, I intended to kill him, but, at the moment, I had enough to do to save my own life. . . .

But that is a long story.[1] Suffice it to say, I was forced to leave Arianus without settling my score with the one Sartan who had fallen into my grasp.

PRYAN

The next world the dog and I visited was Pryan, world of fire. Pryan is a gigantic world, a hollow sphere of rock, its size nearly incomprehensible to the mind. Its sun burns in the center. Life and vegetation exist on the rock's inner crust. Because the world does not rotate, Pryan's sun shines continually—there is no night. Consequently, Pryan is a world of jungle life so thick and heavy that few who live on the planet have ever seen the ground. Entire cities are built in the limbs of huge trees, whose strong branches support lakes, even oceans.

[1] *Dragon Wing*, vol. 1 of *The Death Gate Cycle*.

One of the first people I met on Pryan was a daft old wizard and the dragon who appears to be the old man's keeper. The wizard calls himself Zifnab (when he can remember to call himself anything at all!), and gives every indication of being a raving lunatic. Except that there are times when his madness is all too sane. He knows too much, this befuddled old fool; knows too much about me, about the Patryns, about the Sartan, about everything. He knows too much, yet tells exactly nothing.

Here on Pryan, as on Arianus, the mensch are at war with each other. Elves hate the humans, the humans mistrust the elves, the dwarves hate and mistrust everybody. I should know. I traveled with a bunch of humans, elves, and a dwarf. You never saw such quarreling and bickering and fighting. I grew sick of them and left. I have no doubt that they've all probably killed each other by now. That, or the tytans have slaughtered them.

The tytans.

I encountered many fearsome monsters in the Labyrinth, but few equaled the tytans. Gigantic humanoids, blind, with limited intelligence, the tytans are magical creations of the Sartan, who used them as overseers for the mensch. So long as the Sartan survived, they kept the tytans under control. But on Pryan, as on Arianus, the Sartan race mysteriously began to dwindle. The tytans were left without instruction, without supervision. Now they wander Pryan in large numbers, asking all the mensch they meet these strange questions:

"Where are the citadels? What is our purpose?"

When they receive no answer, the tytans fly into a rage and beat the wretched mensch to death. Nothing, no one, can withstand these terrible creatures, for they possess a rudimentary form of Sartan rune-magic. They came very close to destroying me, in fact, but that too is another tale.[2]

And what is the answer to their question? *Where* are the citadels? *What* are the citadels? This became my question as well. And I found at least part of the answer.

The citadels are shining cities, built by the Sartan upon their arrival on Pryan. As near as I can determine from records the Sartan left behind, the citadels were intended to gather energy

---

[2] *Elven Star*, vol. 2 of *The Death Gate Cycle*.

from Pryan's constantly burning sun and transmit that energy to the other worlds, through Death's Gate, via the power of the Kicksey-winsey. But Death's Gate remained closed; the Kicksey-winsey didn't work. The citadels are empty, deserted. Their lights shine feebly, if at all.

ABARRACH

I traveled next to Abarrach, world of stone.

And it was on this journey I picked up my unwanted traveling companion: Alfred, the Sartan.

Alfred had been navigating Death's Gate in a futile attempt to locate Bane, the child I'd taken from Arianus. Alfred bungled it, of course. The man can't walk without falling over his own shoelaces. He missed his destination and landed in my ship.

At this point, I made a mistake. Alfred was now my captive. I should have returned him immediately to my lord. Xar would have been able to elicit, painfully, all the secrets of this Sartan's soul.

But my ship had just entered Abarrach. I was loath to leave it, loath to travel back through Death's Gate—a fearsome, disturbing journey. And, to be honest, I wanted to keep Alfred around awhile. Passing through Death's Gate, we had—quite unintentionally—switched bodies. For a short while, I found myself in Alfred's mind, with his thoughts, fears, memories. He found himself in mine. Each of us returned to his own body, but I know I was not quite the same—though it was long before I could admit it to myself.

I had come to know and understand my enemy. And that made it difficult to continue to hate him. Besides, as it turned out, we needed each other for our very survival.

Abarrach is a terrible world. Cold stone on the outside, molten rock and lava on the inside. The mensch the Sartan brought here could not long live in its hellish caverns. It took all our magical strength—both Alfred's and mine—to survive the blistering heat rising from the molten oceans, the poisonous fumes that fill the air. But people live on Abarrach.

And so do the dead.

It was here, on Abarrach, that Alfred and I discovered debased descendants of his race—the Sartan. And it was here we found the tragic answer to what had happened to his people. These Sartan on Abarrach had begun to use the forbidden art of necromancy. The Sartan were raising the dead, giving them a semblance of cursed life, using the corpses of their own people as slaves. According to Alfred, this arcane art was prohibited anciently because it was discovered that whenever one of the dead is brought back to life, one of the living will die untimely. Either the Sartan on Abarrach had forgotten the prohibition—or were ignoring it.

Having survived the Labyrinth, I thought myself hardened, inured to the sight of almost any atrocity. But the walking dead of Abarrach still haunt my darkest dreams. I tried to convince myself that necromancy would prove a most valuable skill to my lord. An army of the dead is indestructible, invincible, undefeatable. With such an army, my lord could easily conquer the other worlds, without the tragic waste of the lives of my people.

I very nearly ended up a corpse myself, on Abarrach. The thought of my body continuing to live on in mindless drudgery horrified me. I could not bear the thought of this happening to others. I resolved, therefore, not to tell my lord that the art of necromancy was being practiced by the Sartan on that wretched world. That was my first act of rebellion against my lord.

It was not to be my last.

Another experience happened to me on Abarrach, one that is painful, perplexing, irritating, confusing, yet inspires me with awe whenever I recall it.

Fleeing pursuit, Alfred and I stumbled into a room known as the Chamber of the Damned. Through the magic of that chamber I was transported back in time, thrust again into another body, the body of a Sartan. And it was then, during this strange and magical experience, that I encountered a higher power. I was given to know that I was *not* a demigod, as I had always believed, that the magic I controlled was not the strongest force in the universe.

Another, stronger force exists, a benevolent force, a force that seeks only goodness and order and peace. In the body of this unknown Sartan, I longed to contact this force, but before I could, other Sartan—fearful of our newfound truth—swept into the chamber and cut us down. Those of us gathered in that chamber died there. All knowledge of us and our discovery was lost, except for a mysterious prophecy.

When I awoke, in my own time, in my own body, I could only imperfectly remember what I had seen and heard. And I tried very hard to forget even that much. I didn't want to face the fact that—compared to this power—I was as weak as any mensch. I accused Alfred of attempting to trick me, of creating this illusion himself. He denied it, of course. He swore that he had experienced exactly the same thing that I did.

I refused to believe him.

We barely escaped Abarrach with our lives.[3] When we left, the Sartan on that dreadful world were busy destroying each other, turning the living into lazar—dead bodies whose souls are eternally trapped inside their lifeless shells. Different from the ambulating corpses, the lazar are far more dangerous, for they have minds and purpose—dark and dread purpose.

I was glad to leave such a world. Once inside Death's Gate, I let Alfred go his way, as I went mine. He had, after all, saved my life. And I was sick of death, of pain, of suffering. I'd seen enough.

I knew well what Xar would do to Alfred, if my lord got hold of him.

CHELESTRA

I returned to the Nexus, made my report on Abarrach to my lord in the form of a message, for I feared that if I had to face Xar, I could not hide the truth from him. But Xar knew I lied. He sought me out before I had a chance to escape from the Nexus. He chastised me, very nearly killed me. I deserved the punishment. The physical pain I endured was far easier to bear than the pain of my guilt. I ended up telling Xar everything I had found on Abarrach. I told him about the art of necromancy, about the Chamber of the Damned, about the higher power.

My lord forgave me. I felt cleansed, whole. All my questions had been answered. I once more knew my purpose, my goal. They were Xar's. I was Xar's. I traveled to Chelestra—the world of water—strong in my resolve to renew my lord's faith in me.

And here an odd circumstance occurred. The dog—my constant companion ever since he saved my life in the Labyrinth—

[3] *Fire Sea*, vol. 3 of *The Death Gate Cycle*.

disappeared. I searched for the beast, for though he is a nuisance sometimes, I'd grown used to having him around. He was gone. I felt bad about this, but only for a while. I had more important matters on my mind.

Chelestra is a world comprised solely of water. Drifting in the cold depths of space, its outer surface is made up of solid ice. But inside Chelestra, the Sartan placed a sun that burns magically in the water, lights and warms the world's interior.

The Sartan intended to control the sun, but they discovered that they lacked the power. And so the sun drifts freely through the water, warming only certain areas of Chelestra at one time, leaving others to freeze until the sun's return. Mensch live on Chelestra, on what are known as seamoons. Sartan live on Chelestra, as well, although I did not know this at first.

My arrival on Chelestra was not propitious. My ship plunged into the water and instantly began breaking apart. The destruction was astonishing, since my ship was protected by rune-magic on the outside and very few forces—certainly not ordinary seawater —could break down the powerful runes.

Unfortunately, this was not ordinary seawater.

I was forced to abandon my vessel and found myself swimming in a vast, unending ocean. I knew I must surely drown, but I discovered—to my pleasure and amazement—that I could breathe the water as easily as I breathed air. I also discovered—with far less pleasure—that the water had the effect of completely destroying my rune-magic, leaving me powerless, helpless as a mensch.

On Chelestra, I uncovered additional evidence of a higher power. However, this power is not working for good, but for evil. It thrives on fear, feeds on terror, delights in inflicting pain. It lives only to promote chaos, hatred, destruction.

Embodied in the forms of enormous dragon-snakes, the evil power very nearly seduced me into serving it. I was saved by three mensch children, one of whom later died in my arms. I saw the evil for what it was. I came to understand that it was intent on destroying everything—including my people.

I determined to fight it, though I knew I could not win against it. This power is immortal. It lives within each of us. We created it.

At first, I thought I fought alone, but someone joined me in the battle—my friend, my enemy.

Alfred, too, had arrived on Chelestra, at about the same time I did, although we landed in far different places. Alfred found himself in a crypt similar to the one where most of his people lay dead on Arianus. But the people in the crypt on Chelestra were alive—the Sartan Council, those who had been responsible for the sundering of the world centuries ago.

Threatened by the evil dragon-snakes, unable to fight them due to the fact that the seawater nullified their magic, the Sartan sent out a call for help to their brethren. Then they placed themselves in suspended animation to await the coming of other Sartan.

The only one who came—and he did so by accident—was Alfred.

Needless to say, he was not quite what the Council expected.

The head of the Council, Samah, is a mirror image of my lord, Xar (though neither would thank me for the comparison!). Both are proud, ruthless, ambitious. Both believe that they wield the ultimate power in the universe. The thought that there might be a stronger force, a higher power, is anathema to both of them.

Samah discovered that Alfred not only believed in this higher power, but that he had actually come close to contacting it. Samah considered this open rebellion. He attempted to break Alfred, destroy his faith. It was rather like trying to break bread dough. Alfred meekly absorbed every punch, every blow. He refused to recant, refused to accept Samah's dictates.

I must admit I almost felt sorry for Alfred. At last he had found the people he so longed to find, only to discover that he couldn't trust them. Not only that, he came to learn a terrible truth about the Sartan's past.

With the help of an unlikely confederate (my very own dog, to be exact), Alfred accidentally stumbled (literally) into a secret Sartan library. Here he discovered that Samah and the Council had discovered the existence of this higher power. The Sundering had not been necessary. With the help of this power, the Sartan could have worked for peace.

Samah did not want peace, however. He wanted the world his way—and only his way. And so he broke the world apart. Unfortunately, when he tried to put it back together, the world crumbled into smaller and smaller pieces, began to slip through his fingers.

Alfred now knew the truth. Alfred became a threat to Samah.

But it was Alfred—meek, bumbling Alfred, who fainted at the very mention of the word "danger"—who joined my fight against the dragon-snakes.[4] He saved my life, the lives of the mensch, and very probably the lives of his own ungrateful people.

Despite this—or perhaps because of it—Samah sentenced Alfred to a dire fate. Samah cast Alfred and Orla, the woman who loves him, into the Labyrinth.

Now I am the only one left who knows the truth about the danger we face. The evil forces embodied in the dragon-snakes do not seek to rule us—they desire nothing that constructive. Suffering, agony, chaos, fear—this is their goal. And they will attain it, unless we all join together to find some way to stop them. For the dragon-snakes are powerful, far more powerful than any of us. Far more powerful than Samah. Far more powerful than Xar.

I must convince my lord of this—a task that will not be easy. He already suspects me of being a traitor. How can I prove to him that my loyalty to him, to my people, was never greater than it is now?

And Alfred, what do I do about Alfred? The kind, vague, and bumbling Sartan will not long survive the Labyrinth. I could return there to save him . . . if I dared.

But—I must admit to myself—I am afraid.

I am more afraid now than I have ever been in my life. The evil is very great, very powerful, and I face it alone, as my name foretold.

Alone, except for a dog.

---

[4] *Serpent Mage*, vol. 4 of *The Death Gate Cycle*.

REALM
OF
FIRE
(Pyran)

Power and
Agriculture
for all
Realms

ENERGY

ENERGY

WATER

WATER AND
MANUFACTURED
GOODS

MANUFACTURED
GOODS

AGRICULTURE

LABYRINTH

REALM
OF
WATER
(Chelestra)

Chemicals and
Biological
elements for
manufacture

THE
NEXUS

REALM
OF
STONE
(Abarrach)

Raw metals
and elements
prepared for
manufacture

MANUFACTURED
GOODS

AGRICULTURE
AND WATER

MINERALS AND
MANUFACTURED
GOODS

MINERALS

ORGANIC
MATERIALS

INORGANIC
MATERIALS

REALM
OF
AIR
(Arianus)

Industry and
Manufacture
of all goods
required by
the Realms

PROLOGUE

I WRITE THIS AS I SIT IN A SARTAN PRISON CELL, AWAITING MY FREEDOM.[1] IT will be a long time coming, I think, for the level of the seawater that will free me is rising very slowly. Undoubtedly the water level is being controlled by the mensch, who do not want to harm any of the Sartan, but merely rid them of their magic.[2] The seawater of Chelestra is breathable as air, but a wall of water sent crashing through the land would cause a considerable amount of destruction. Remarkably practical-minded of the mensch to think of such an angle. I wonder, though, how they have managed to force the dragon-snakes—the serpents—to cooperate.

The serpents[3] of Chelestra . . .

I knew evil before them—I was born in, survived, and escaped the Labyrinth. But I have *never* known evil like *them*. It is these creatures who have taught me to believe in a higher power —a power over which we have little control, a power that is inherently evil.

[1] Written in the human language, in Haplo's hand, the entry can be found in the back of the journal left the Patryn by the dwarf maid, Grundle. Patryns typically use mensch language to record events and thoughts, considering their own magical rune language far too powerful to be used indiscriminately.

[2] Reference to the fact that the seawater on the world of Chelestra nullifies the powerful magics of both Sartan and Patryn. See *Serpent Mage*, vol. 4 of *The Death Gate Cycle*.

[3] "Dragon-snake" is a mensch term, coined by Grundle. The Sartan word for the creature is "serpent." Haplo adopts the Sartan word used in this volume, a change from his previous work. Why he made the change is unclear. One reason suggests itself—he did not want to confuse these false "dragons" with the true dragons who inhabit the worlds. Haplo used a Sartan word because the Patryns, having never encountered this evil, have no word for it.

Alfred, my old nemesis, you would be horrified, reading that statement. I can almost hear you stuttering and stammering in protest.

"No, no! There is a corresponding power for good. We've seen it, you and I." That is what you would tell me.

Did you see it, Alfred? And if so, where? Your own people denounced you as a heretic, sent you to the Labyrinth, or so they threatened. And Samah doesn't seem to me to be the type who makes threats lightly. What do you think of your power for good now, Alfred? . . . as you fight for your life in the Labyrinth.

I'll tell you what *I* think of it. I think it's a lot like you—weak and bumbling. Although I must admit that you came through for us in our fight against the serpents—if that *was* you who turned into the serpent mage, as Grundle claimed.

But when it came to standing up for yourself against Samah (and I'll lay odds that you could have taken the bastard), you "couldn't remember the spell." You let yourself and the woman you love be led meekly away, sent to a place where, if you *are* still alive, you probably wish you weren't.

The seawater is starting to seep under the door now. Dog doesn't know what to make of it. He's barking at it, trying to convince it to turn around and leave. I know how he feels. It is all I can do to sit here calmly and wait, wait for the tepid liquid to creep over the toe of my boot, wait for the terrible feeling of panic that comes when I feel my magic start to dissolve at the water's touch.

The seawater is my salvation. I have to remind myself of that. Already, the Sartan runes that keep me prisoner in this room are beginning to lose their power. Their red glow fades. Eventually it will wink out altogether and then I will be free.

Free to go where? Do what?

I must return to the Nexus, warn my lord of the danger of the serpents. Xar will not believe it; he will not *want* to believe. He has always held himself to be the most powerful force in the universe. And, certainly, he had every reason to think that was true. The dark and dreadful might of the Labyrinth could not crush him. Even now, he defies it daily to bring more of our people out of that terrible prison.

But against the magical power of the evil serpents—and I begin to think they are only evil's minions—Xar must fall. This dread, chaotic force is not only strong, it is cunning and devious. It works its will by telling us what we want to hear, by pandering to us and fawning on us and serving us. It does not mind demeaning itself, it has no dignity, no honor. It uses lies made powerful because they are lies we tell ourselves.

If this evil force enters Death's Gate, and nothing is done to stop it, I foresee a time when this universe will become a prison house of suffering and despair. The four worlds—Arianus, Pryan, Abarrach, and Chelestra—will be consumed. The Labyrinth will not be destroyed as we had hoped. My people will emerge from one prison only to find themselves in another.

I must make my lord believe! But how, when at times I am not certain that I truly believe myself. . . .

The water is up to my ankle. Dog has given up barking. He is eyeing me with reproach, demanding to know why we don't leave this uncomfortable place. He tried lapping the water and got it up his nose.

No Sartan are visible on the street beneath my window, where the water now flows in a wide and steady river. I can hear, in the distance, horn calls—the mensch, probably, moving onto the Chalice, as the Sartan call this haven of theirs. Good, that means there will be ships nearby—mensch submersibles. My ship, the dwarven submersible I magically altered to take me through Death's Gate, is moored back on Draknor, the isle of the serpents.

I don't look forward to going back there, but I have no choice. Rune-enhanced, that ship is the only vessel on this world that can carry me safely through Death's Gate. I have only to glance down at my legs, now wet with seawater, to see the blue runes tattooed on my skin fading. It will be a long time before I will be able to use my magic to alter another ship. And I am running out of time.

My people are running out of time.

With luck, I can slip into Draknor unnoticed, steal back my ship, and leave. The serpents must all be intent on assisting the attack on the Chalice, although I think it is odd, and perhaps a bad sign, that I've seen nothing of them. But, as I said, they are devious and cunning and who knows what they are plotting?

Yes, dog, we're going. I trust dogs can swim. It seems to me I remember hearing somewhere that all the lower forms of animals can swim enough to keep themselves afloat.

It is man who thinks and panics and drowns.

CHAPTER ♦ 1

SURUNAN

CHELESTRA

♦

THE SEAWATER RAN SLUGGISHLY THROUGH THE STREETS OF SURUNAN, THE CITY built by the Sartan. The water rose slowly, flowed through doors and windows, eased over low rooftops. Fragments of Sartan life floated on the water's surface—an unbroken pottery bowl, a man's sandal, a woman's comb, a wooden chair.

The water seeped into the room of Samah's house used by the Sartan as a prison cell. The prison room was located on an upper floor and was, for a time, above the rising tide. But, eventually, the seawater slid under the door, flowed across the floor, crept up the room's walls. Its touch banished magic, canceled it, nullified it. The dazzling runes, whose flesh-searing heat kept Haplo from even approaching the door, sizzled and went out. The runes that guarded the window were the only ones yet left unaffected. Their bright glow was reflected in the water below.

Prisoner of the magic, Haplo sat in enforced idleness watching the runes' reflections in the rising seawater, watched them move and shift and dance with the water's currents and eddies. The moment the water touched the base of the runes on the window, the moment their glow began to glimmer and fade, Haplo stood up. The water came to his knees.

The dog whined. Head and shoulders above the water, the animal was unhappy.

"This is it, boy. Time to leave." Haplo thrust the book in which he'd been writing inside his shirt, secured it at his waist, tucked it between pants and skin.

He noticed, as he did so, that the runes tattooed on his body had almost completely faded. The seawater that was his blessing, that was allowing him to escape, was also his curse. His magical power gone, he was helpless as a newborn child, and had no mother's comforting, protecting arms to cradle him.

Weak and powerless, unsettled in mind and in soul, he must leave this room and plunge into the vast sea whose water gave him life as it washed away his life, and it would carry him on a perilous journey.

Haplo thrust open the window, paused. The dog looked questioningly at its master. It was tempting to stay here, to stay safe in his prison. Outside, somewhere beyond these sheltering walls, the serpents waited. They would destroy him, they *must* destroy him; he knew the truth. Knew them for what they were—the embodiment of chaos.

This knowledge of the truth was the very reason he had to leave. He had to warn his lord. An enemy greater than any they'd yet faced—more cruel and cunning than any dragon in the Labyrinth, more powerful than the Sartan—was poised to destroy them.

"Go on," Haplo said to the dog, and gestured.

Cheered at the prospect of finally leaving this soggy, boring place, the dog leapt gleefully out the window, splashed into the water in the street below. Haplo drew in a deep breath—an instinctive reaction, not really necessary, for the seawater was breathable as air—and jumped in after.

The Chalice was the only stable land mass in the water world of Chelestra. Built by the Sartan to more closely resemble the world they had sundered and fled, the Chalice was encased in its own protective bubble of air. The water that surrounded it gave the illusion of sky, through which Chelestra's water-bound sun shone with a rippling brightness. The serpents had broken through the barrier and now the Chalice was flooding.

Haplo found a piece of wood, caught hold of it, used it to keep himself afloat. He paddled in the water, stared around, attempted to get his bearings, and saw, with relief, the top of Council Hall. It stood on a hill and would be the last place to be submerged by the rising tides. There, undoubtedly, the Sartan had taken refuge. He squinted in the sunlight that sparkled off the water, thought he could detect people on the roof. They would keep themselves dry, free of the magic-debilitating seawater as long as possible.

"Don't fight it," he advised them, though they were much too far away to hear him. "It only makes it worse, in the end."

At least now he had some idea where he was. He propelled himself forward, heading for the tops of the city walls that he could see thrusting up out of the water. The walls divided the Sartan portion of the city from what had once been the mensch portion. And beyond that lay the shoreline of the Chalice; the shoreline and mensch landing parties and a ship to carry him to Draknor. On that tortured seamoon was moored his own dwarven submersible, altered with the magic of the runes, strengthened to carry him through Death's Gate. His only hope of escape.

But also, on Draknor, the serpents.

"If so," he said to the dog, who was paddling along valiantly, front paws working like a small machine, back legs not quite certain what to make of this strange swimming business but doing their best to hold up their end, "this is going to be one short trip."

His plans were vague, couldn't be formed until he knew where the snakes were . . . and how to avoid them.

He pushed forward, balanced on the wood, kicking through the water. He could have abandoned the plank and given himself to the sea, breathing it as effortlessly as air. But he detested those first few moments of terror that came with purposefully drowning oneself, the body refusing to accept the mind's reassurance that it was only returning to the womb, to a world it had once known. He clung to the plank, kicked until his legs ached.

It occurred to him suddenly that this plank was an ominous sign. Unless he was much mistaken, it had come from one of the wooden dwarven submersibles, and it had been broken, both ends splintered.

Had the serpents become bored with this peaceful takeover of Surunan, then turned on and butchered the mensch?

"If so," Haplo muttered, "I've got myself to blame for it."

He kicked harder, faster, needing desperately to find out what was happening. But he soon tired, his muscles burned and cramped. He was swimming against the tide, against the flow of the seawater that was being channeled into the city. The loss of his magic made him feel unusually weak; he knew that from past bitter experience.

The tide carried him up against the city walls. He caught hold of a turret, climbed up the side, planning not only to rest but to reconnoiter, to try to catch a glimpse of what lay ahead on the shore. The dog attempted to stop, but the current carried it on past. Haplo leaned out at a perilous angle, caught hold of the dog by the scruff of its neck. He hauled it in—the animal's back legs scrabbling for purchase—and heaved it up onto the balustrade with him.

From this vantage point, he had an excellent view of the harbor of Surunan, the shoreline beyond that. Haplo looked out, nodded grimly.

"We needn't have worried, boy," he said, smacking the dog's wet and shaggy flank. "At least they're safe."

The animal grinned, shook itself.

The fleet of mensch submersibles was drawn up in a more or less orderly line in the harbor. The sun-chasers bobbed on the surface. Mensch lined the bows, pointing and shouting, leaning over the rails, jumping into the water. Numerous small boats plied back and forth between ship and shore, probably ferrying the dwarves, who could not swim. The humans and elves—far more at home in the water—were directing the work of several huge whales, pushing crudely built, heavily loaded rafts into the harbor.

Eyeing the rafts, Haplo glanced down at the wooden plank that he'd dragged up with him. That's why they'd broken up the submersibles. The mensch were moving in.

"But . . . where are the serpents?" he asked the dog, who lay, panting, at his feet.

Nowhere in sight, apparently. Haplo watched as long as he could, driven by the need to escape this world and return to the Nexus and his lord, yet constrained by the equal need to reach that world alive. Patience, caution—hard lessons to learn, but the Labyrinth was an excellent teacher.

He saw no sign of serpent heads looming out of the water. Perhaps they were all under the surface, boring the holes into the foundation of the Chalice through which the seawater was pouring.

"I need to find out," Haplo said to himself in frustration. If the snakes knew he was free and was planning to flee Chelestra, they'd stop him, if they could.

He weighed the alternatives. Taking time to talk to the mensch meant delay, risked revealing his presence to them. They'd welcome him with joy, want to hang on to him, use him. He didn't have time to fool with the mensch. But *not* taking the time to find out what was going on with the serpents might mean an even greater delay—perhaps a deadly one.

He waited several moments, hoping for some sign of the snakes.

Nothing. And he couldn't stay on this damn wall forever.

Deciding to trust to opportunity, Haplo plunged back into the water. The dog, with a wild bark, splashed in beside him.

Haplo swam into the harbor. Hanging on to the wood, he kept himself low in the water, steered clear of the flow of traffic. He was well known by sight among the mensch and wanted to avoid them as much as possible. Clinging to his plank, he peered closely into the dwarven boats. It was in his mind to talk to Grundle, if he could find her. She had more sense than most mensch, and, though she would undoubtedly make a fuss over him, he figured he could extract himself from her affectionate clutches without too much difficulty.

He didn't find her, however. And still no sign of any serpents. But he did come across a small submersible—used to rescue dwarves who had the mischance to fall into the water—secured to a post. He drifted near, eyeing it intently. No one was around; it appeared to have been abandoned.

A whale-driven raft had just arrived on shore. Numerous dwarves were gathered around, preparing to unload its cargo. Haplo guessed that the crew of this submersible were among them.

He swam over to it. This was too good to pass up. He'd steal it, sail to Draknor. If the serpents were there . . . well . . . he'd deal with that when the time came. . . .

Something large and alive and slick-skinned bumped into him. Haplo's heart lurched. He gulped in his breath and a mouthful of water at the same time, started to choke and cough. Kicking himself backward, away from the creature, he struggled to breathe and readied himself to fight.

A shining head with two beady eyes and a wide-open, laughing mouth popped out of the water directly in front of him. Two more heads shot up on either side of him, four swam about him in rollicking delight, nosing him and prodding him.

Dolphins.

Haplo gasped, spit out water. The dog attempted a furious bark, which proceeding highly amused the dolphins and nearly drowned the dog. Haplo dragged its forelegs up onto the plank, where the animal lay panting and glaring.

"Where are the dragon-snakes?" Haplo demanded, speaking in the human tongue.

Previously, the dolphins had refused to talk to him or have anything to do with him. But that was when they'd assumed him to be—rightly enough—on the side of the serpents. Now their attitude toward him had changed. They began to squeak and whistle in excitement and a few started to swim off, eager to be the first to spread the news around the mensch that the mysterious man with the blue-tattooed skin had reappeared.

"No! Wait, don't go. Don't tell anyone you've seen me," he said hastily. "What's going on here? Where are the dragon-snakes?"

The dolphins squeaked and gabbled. In seconds, Haplo heard everything he wanted to know and quite a lot that he didn't.

"We heard that Samah took you prisoner . . ."

"The snakes brought poor Alake's body back to . . ."

"Parents prostrate with grief . . ."

"Snakes said you . . ."

". . . and the Sartan . . ."

"Yes, you and the Sartan were responsible . . ."

"You double-crossed . . ."

"Betrayed your friends . . ."

"Coward . . ."

"No one believed . . ."

"Yes, they did . . ."

"No, they didn't. Well, maybe for a moment . . ."

"Anyway, the snakes used their magic to bore holes in the Chalice . . ."

"Gigantic holes!"

"Huge!"

"Immense!"

"Floodgates."

"Opened at once . . . a wall of water . . ."

"Tidal wave . . ."

"Nothing survive . . . Sartan crushed!"

"Flattened . . ."

"City destroyed . . ."

"*We* warned the mensch about the dragon-snakes and their bore holes . . ."

"Grundle and Devon returned . . ."

"Told the *true* story. You are a hero . . ."

"No, he isn't. That was the one called Alfred."

"I was only being polite . . ."

"Mensch were worried . . ."

"They don't want to kill the Sartan . . ."

"They're afraid of the dragon-snakes. Dwarven ships went to investigate . . ."

"But the snakes are nowhere in sight . . ."

"The dwarves opened the floodgates just a crack and . . ."

"Stop! Shut up!" Haplo shouted, managing at last to make himself heard. "What do you mean 'the snakes are nowhere in sight'? Where are they?"

The dolphins began to argue among themselves. Some said the serpents had returned to Draknor, but the general consensus seemed to be that the snakes had swum through the holes and were attacking the Sartan in Surunan.

"No, they're not," said Haplo. "I just came from Surunan, and the city's quiet. The Sartan are, as far as I know, safely inside their Council Chamber, trying to keep dry."

The dolphins looked rather disappointed at this news. They meant no harm to the Sartan, but it had been such a great story. They were now all in agreement.

"The dragon-snakes must have gone back to Draknor."

Haplo was forced to agree himself. The serpents had returned to Draknor. But why? Why had they left Surunan so abruptly? Why had they abandoned the chance to destroy the Sartan? Abandoned their plans to foment chaos among the mensch, turn them against each other?

Haplo couldn't answer the questions, supposed bitterly it didn't matter. What mattered was that the serpents were on Draknor and so was his ship.

"I don't suppose any of you have been to Draknor to find out?" he asked.

The dolphins squealed in alarm at the thought, shook their heads emphatically. None would get near Draknor. It was a terrible place of great sadness and evil. The water itself was poison, killed anything that swam in it.

Haplo forwent mentioning that he himself had swum in the water and survived. He couldn't blame these gentle creatures for not wanting to go near Draknor. He wasn't pleased at the prospect of returning to that tortured seamoon himself. But he had no choice.

Now his main problem was ridding himself of the dolphins. Fortunately, that was simple. They loved to feel important.

"I need you fish to carry a message from me to the mensch leaders, to be delivered to every member of the royal family in person, in private. Understand? It's extremely important."

"We'll be only too glad . . ."

"You can trust . . ."

"Implicitly . . ."

"Tell every person . . ."

"No, not every . . ."

"Just the royal . . ."

"Every person, I tell you . . ."

"I'm sure that's what he said . . ."

Once he got them quiet long enough to hear, Haplo imparted the message, taking care that it was complicated and involved.

The dolphins listened intently and swam off the moment Haplo shut his mouth.

When he was certain that the dolphins' attention was no longer on him, he and the dog swam to the submersible, climbed aboard, and sailed off.

CHAPTER ♦ 2

DRAKNOR

CHELESTRA

♦

HAPLO HAD NEVER COMPLETELY MASTERED THE DWARVEN SYSTEM OF NAVIGA-
tion, which, according to Grundle, relied on sounds emitted by
the seamoons themselves. At first he was concerned about being
able to find Draknor, but he soon discovered that the seamoon
was easy to find . . . too easy. The serpents left a trail of foul
ooze in their wake. The path led to the murky black waters surrounding the tormented seamoon.

Darkness swallowed him. He had sailed into the caverns of
Draknor. He could see nothing and, fearful of running aground,
slowed the submersible's forward progress until it barely moved.
He could swim through the foul water, if he had to; he'd done it
before. But he hoped swimming wouldn't be necessary.

His hands were dry, and his lower arms where he'd rolled up
the wet sleeves. The runes were extremely faint, but they were
visible. And though they gave him the magical power of a child of
two, the faint blue of the sigla was comforting. He didn't want to
get wet again.

The submersible's prow scraped against rock. Haplo steered it
swiftly upward, breathed a sigh when it continued on, unim-
peded. He must be nearing the shore. He decided to risk bringing
the vessel to the surface . . .

The runes on his hands! Blue. *Faint* blue.

Haplo brought the ship to a full stop, stared down at the sigla.
Faint blue color, not nearly as blue as the veins beneath his skin
on the back of his hands. And that was odd. Damn odd!

Weak as they were, the sigla should have been glowing—his body's reaction to the danger of the serpents. But the sigla weren't reacting as they had in the past and, he realized, neither were his other instincts. He'd been too preoccupied piloting the submersible to notice.

Before, when he'd come this close to the snakes' lair, he could scarcely move, scarcely think for the debilitating fear that flowed from the monsters.

But Haplo *wasn't* afraid; at least, he amended, he wasn't afraid for himself. His fear ran deeper. It was cold and twisted him inside.

"What's going on, boy?" he asked the dog, who had crowded near him and was whimpering against his leg.

Haplo patted the animal reassuringly, though he himself could have used reassurance. The dog whined and edged closer.

The Patryn started the vessel again, guided it toward the surface, his attention divided between the gradually brightening water and the sigla on his skin. The runes did not alter in appearance.

Judging by the evidence of his own body, the serpents were no longer on Draknor. But if they weren't on Draknor and they weren't with the mensch and they weren't battling the Sartan, where were they?

The submersible surfaced. Haplo scanned the shoreline rapidly, found his ship, smiled in satisfaction to see it whole, undamaged. But his fear grew stronger, though the sigla on his skin gave him no reason to be afraid.

The body of the king serpent, slain by the mysterious "serpent mage" (who might or might not have been Alfred), lay on the cliffs above. No sign of living serpents was visible.

Haplo beached the submersible. Cautious, wary, he opened the hatch, climbed up onto the top deck. He carried no weapons, though he'd found a cache of battle-axes inside the ship. Only blades enhanced by magic would bite through the flesh of the serpents, and Haplo was too weak in his own magic now to impart its power to metal.

The dog followed him, growled a warning. Its legs stiffened, its hackles rose. Its gaze was fixed on the cave.

"What is it, boy?" Haplo asked, tensing.

The dog quivered all over, looked at its master, pleading permission to race to the attack.

"No, dog. We're heading for our own ship. We're getting out of here."

Haplo jumped off the deck, landed on the foul, slime-covered sand, began to edge his way along the shoreline toward his rune-inscribed ship. The dog continued to growl and bark and came along with Haplo only reluctantly and after repeated commands.

Haplo was within arm's length of reaching his vessel when he caught a glimpse of movement near the cavern's entrance.

He waited, watching. He was cautious, but not particularly worried. He was now close enough to his ship to seek the safety of its protective runes. The dog's growl became a snarl; its upper lip curled, revealing sharp teeth.

A man emerged from the cave.

Samah.

"Easy, boy," said Haplo.

The leader of the Sartan Council walked with the bowed head and listless tread of someone deep in thought. He had not come by boat; no other submersibles were moored along the shore. He had come by magic, then.

Haplo glanced at the sigla on his hands. The runes were a little darker in color, but they did not glow, were not warning him of the advance of an enemy. By this and by logical deduction, Haplo guessed that Samah's magic, like Haplo's own, must be spent. Probably waterlogged. The Sartan was waiting, resting, to regain strength enough for his return journey. He posed no threat to Haplo. Just as Haplo posed no threat to him.

Or did he? All things equal, both bereft of their magic, Haplo was the younger of the two, the stronger. The fight would be crude, undignified, menschlike—two men rolling about on the sand, pummeling each other. Haplo thought it over, sighed, shook his head.

He was just too damn tired.

Besides, Samah looked to have suffered a beating already.

Haplo waited quietly. Samah did not glance up from his troubled musings. He might conceivably have walked past the Patryn without seeing him. The dog, unable to contain itself, remembering past wrongs, barked a sharp warning—the Sartan had come close enough.

Samah raised his head, startled at the sound but not, apparently, startled to see either the dog or its master. The Sartan's lips tightened. His gaze shifted from Haplo to the small submersible floating behind him.

"Returning to your lord?" Samah asked coldly.

Haplo saw no need to reply.

Samah nodded; he hadn't expected a response. "You'll be glad to know your minions are already on their way. They have preceded you. No doubt a hero's welcome awaits you." His tone was bitter, his gaze dark with hatred and, lurking beneath, fear.

"On their way . . ." Haplo stared at the Sartan, then, suddenly, he understood. Understood what had happened, understood the reason for his seemingly unreasonable fear. Now he knew where the serpents were . . . and why.

"You bloody fool!" Haplo swore. "You opened Death's Gate!"

"I warned you we would do so, Patryn, if your mensch lackeys attacked us."

"*You* were warned, Sartan. The dwarf told you what she overheard. The serpents *wanted* you to open Death's Gate. That was their plan all along. Didn't you listen to Grundle?"

"And so now I should be taking advice from mensch?" Samah sneered.

"They have more sense than you do, seemingly. You opened Death's Gate, intending to do what? Flee? No, that wasn't your plan. Help. You sought help. After what Alfred told you. You still don't believe him. Nearly all your people are gone, Samah. You few on Chelestra are all that's left, except for a couple of thousand animated corpses on Abarrach. You opened the Gate, but it was the serpents who passed through it. Now they'll spread their evil throughout the four worlds. I hoped they stopped long enough to thank you!"

"The power of the Gate should have stopped the creatures!" Samah replied in a low voice. His fist clenched. "The serpents should *not* have been able to enter!"

"Just as mensch can't enter without your help? You still don't understand, do you, Sartan? These snakes are more powerful than you or I or my lord or maybe all of us put together. They don't *need* help!"

"The serpents had help!" Samah retorted bitterly. "Patryn help."

Haplo opened his mouth to argue, decided it wasn't worth it. He was wasting time. The evil was spreading. It was now even more imperative that he return to warn his lord.

Shaking his head, Haplo started for his ship. "C'mon, dog."

But the animal barked again, refused to budge. The dog looked at Haplo, ears cocked.

Don't you have something you want to ask, master?

A thought did occur to Haplo. He turned back.

"What happened to Alfred?"

"Your friend?" Samah mocked. "He was sent to the Labyrinth —the fate of all who preach heresy and conspire with the enemy."

"You know, don't you, that he was the one person who might have stopped the evil."

Samah was briefly amused. "If this Alfred is as powerful as you claim, then he could have prevented us from sending him to prison. He didn't. He went to his punishment meekly enough."

"Yes," said Haplo softly. "I'll bet he did."

"You value your friend so dearly, Patryn, why don't you go back to your prison and try to get him out?"

"Maybe I will. No, boy," Haplo added, seeing the dog's gaze go longingly to Samah's throat. "You'd be up sick half the night."

He returned to his ship, cast off the moorings, dragged the dog—who was still growling at Samah—inside, slammed the hatch shut behind him. Once on board, Haplo hastened to the window in the steerage compartment to keep an eye on the Sartan. Magic or no magic, Haplo didn't trust him.

Samah stood unmoving on the sand. His white robes were damp and bedraggled, the hem covered with slime and the blood of the dead serpents. His shoulders sagged; his skin was gray. He looked exhausted to the point of falling, but—probably aware that he was under scrutiny—he remained standing upright, jaw thrust out, arms folded across his chest.

Satisfied that his enemy was harmless, Haplo turned his attention to the runes burned into the wooden planks of the ship's interior. He traced each one again in his mind—runes of protection, runes of power, runes to take him once again on the strange and terrifying journey into Death's Gate, runes to ensure his safety until he reached the Nexus. He spoke a word, and the sigla began to glow soft blue in response.

Haplo breathed a deep sigh. He was guarded, protected. He allowed himself to relax for the first time in a long, long while. Making certain his hands were dry, he placed them on the ship's wheel. It, too, had been enhanced by runes. The mechanism wasn't as powerful as the steering stone he'd used aboard *Dragon Wing*. But *Dragon Wing* and the steering stone were now at the bottom of the sea—if Chelestra's sea had a bottom. The rune-magic on the wheel was crude, it had been hurriedly done. But it would take him through Death's Gate and that was all that mattered.

Haplo guided his ship away from the shoreline. He glanced back at the Sartan, who seemed to dwindle in size as the expanse of black water separating them grew larger.

"What will you do now, Samah? Will *you* enter Death's Gate, search for your people? No, I don't think so. You're scared, aren't you, Sartan? You know you made a terrible mistake, a mistake that could mean the destruction of all you've worked to build. Whether you believe the serpents represent a higher, evil power or not, they're a force you don't understand, one you can't control.

"You've sent death through Death's Gate."

CHAPTER ◆ 3

THE NEXUS

◆

Xᴀʀ, ʟᴏʀᴅ ᴏғ ᴛʜᴇ ɴᴇxᴜs, ᴡᴀʟᴋᴇᴅ ᴛʜᴇ sᴛʀᴇᴇᴛs ᴏғ ʜɪs ǫᴜɪᴇᴛ, ᴛᴡɪʟɪɢʜᴛ ʟᴀɴᴅ, a land built by his enemy. The Nexus was a beautiful place, with rolling hills and meadows, verdant forests. Its structures were built with soft, rounded corners, unlike the inhabitants, who were sharp-edged and cold as steel. The sun's light was muted, diffused, as if it shone through finely spun cloth. It was never day in the Nexus, never quite night. It was difficult to distinguish an object from its shadow, hard to tell where one left off and the other began. The Nexus seemed a land of shadows.

Xar was tired. He had just emerged from the Labyrinth, emerged victorious from a battle with the evil magicks of that dread land. This time, it had sent an army of chaodyn to destroy him. Intelligent, giant, insectlike creatures, the chaodyn are tall as men, with hard black-shelled bodies. The only way to destroy a chaodyn utterly is to hit it directly in the heart, kill it instantly. For if it lives, even a few seconds, it will cause a drop of its blood to spring into a copy of itself.

And he'd faced an army of these things, a hundred, two hundred; the numbers didn't matter for they grew the moment he wounded one. He had faced them alone, and he'd had only moments before the tide of bulbous-eyed insects engulfed him.

Xar had spoken the runes, caused a wall of flame to leap up between him and the advance ranks of the chaodyn, protecting him from the first assault, giving him time to extend the wall.

The chaodyn had attempted to outrun the spreading flames that were feeding off the grasses in the Labyrinth, springing to magical life as Xar fanned them with magical winds. Those few chaodyn who ran through the fire, Xar had killed with a rune-inscribed sword, taking care to thrust beneath the carapace to reach the heart below. All the while, the wind blew and the flames crackled, feeding off the shells of the dead. The fire jumped from victim to victim now, decimating the ranks.

The chaodyn in the rear watched the advancing holocaust, wavered, turned, and fled. Under cover of the flames, Xar had rescued several of his people, Patryns, more dead than alive. The chaodyn had been holding them hostage, using them as bait to lure the Lord of the Nexus to do battle. The Patryns were being cared for now by other Patryns, who also owed their lives to Xar.

A grim and stern people, unforgiving, unbending, unyielding, the Patryns were not effusive in their gratitude to the lord who constantly risked his life to save theirs. They did not speak of their loyalty, their devotion—they showed it. They worked hard and uncomplaining at any task he set them. They obeyed every command without question. And each time he went into the Labyrinth, a crowd of Patryns gathered outside the Final Gate, to keep silent vigil until his return.

And there were always some, particularly among the young, who would attempt to enter with him; Patryns who had been living in the Nexus long enough for the horror of their lives spent in the Labyrinth to fade from their minds.

"I will go back," they would say. "I will dare it with you, my Lord."

He always let them. And he never said a word of blame when they faltered at the Gate, when faces blanched and the blood chilled, legs trembled and bodies sank to the ground.

Haplo. One of the strongest of the young men. He'd made it farther than most. He'd fallen before the Final Gate, fear wringing him dry. And then he'd crawled on hands and knees, until, shuddering, he shrank back into the shadows.

"Forgive me, Lord!" he'd cried in despair. So they all cried.

"There is nothing to forgive, my child," said Xar, always.

He meant it. He, better than anyone, understood the fear. He faced it every time he entered and every time it grew worse. Rarely was there a moment, outside the Final Gate, that his step did not hesitate, his heart did not shiver. Each time he went in, he knew with certainty that he would not return. Each time he came back out, safely, he vowed within himself that he would never go back.

Yet he kept going back. Time and again.

"The faces," he said. "The faces of my people. The faces of those who wait for me, who enclose me in the circle of their being. These faces give me courage. My children. Every one of them. I tore them out of the horrible womb that gave them birth. I brought them to air and to light.

"What an army they will make," he continued, musing aloud. "Weak in numbers, but strong in magic, loyalty, love. What an army," he said again, louder than before, and he chuckled.

Xar often talked to himself. He was often alone, for the Patryns tend to be loners.[1] And so he talked to himself, but he never chuckled, never laughed.

The chuckle was a sham, a crafty bit of play-acting. The Lord of the Nexus continued to talk, as might any old man, keeping company with himself in the lonely watches of the twilight. He cast a surreptitious glance at his hand. The skin showed his age, an age he could not calculate with any exactness, having no very clear idea when his life began. He knew only that he was old, far older than any other who had come out of the Labyrinth.

The skin on the back of his hand was wrinkled and taut, stretched tight, revealing clearly beneath it the shape of every tendon, every bone. The blue sigla tattooed on the back of the hand were twisted and knotted, but their color was dark, not faded by the passage of time. And their magic, if anything, was stronger.

These tattooed sigla had begun to glow blue.

Xar would have expected the warning inside the Labyrinth, his magic acting instinctively to ward off attack, alert him to danger. But he walked the streets of the Nexus, streets that he had always known to be safe, streets that were a haven, a sanctuary.

---

[1] Those whom the Patryns accept into the circle of their being are few. They are fiercely loyal to these they term "family" either by blood or by vow. These circles of loyalty (Patryns would scorn to call it affection) are generally kept to the death. Once broken, however, the circle can never be mended.

The Lord of the Nexus saw the blue glow that shone with an eerie brightness in the soft twilight, he felt the sigla burn on his skin, the magic burn in his blood.

He kept walking as if nothing were amiss, continued to ramble and mutter beneath his breath. The sigla's warning grew stronger, the runes shone more brightly still. He clenched his fist, hidden beneath the flowing sleeves of a long black robe. His eyes probed every shadow, every object.

He left the streets of the Nexus, stepped onto a path that ran through a forest surrounding his dwelling place. He lived apart from his people, preferring, *requiring* quiet and peace. The trees' darker shadows brought a semblance of night to the land. He glanced at his hand; the rune's light welled out from beneath the black robes. He had not left the danger behind, he was walking straight toward its source.

Xar was more perplexed than nervous, more angry than afraid. Had the evil in the Labyrinth somehow seeped through that Final Gate? He couldn't believe it was possible. Sartan magic had built this place, built the Gate and the Wall that surrounded the prison world of the Labyrinth. The Patryns, not particularly trusting an enemy who had cast them inside that prison, had strengthened the Wall and the Gate with their own magic. No. It was not possible that anything could escape.

The Nexus was protected from the other worlds—the worlds of Sartan and mensch—by Death's Gate. So long as Death's Gate remained closed, no one could leave or enter who had not mastered the powerful magic required to travel it. Xar had mastered the secret, but only after eons of long and difficult study of Sartan writings. He had mastered it and passed his wisdom on to Haplo, who had ventured forth into the universe.

"But suppose," Xar said to himself beneath his breath, his eyes darting side to side, attempting to pierce the darkness that had always before been restful, was now ominous, "suppose Death's Gate were opened! I sensed a change when I came out of the Labyrinth—as if a breath of air stirred suddenly within a house long closed up and sealed shut. I wonder . . ."

"No need to wonder, Xar, Lord of Patryns," came a voice from out of the darkness. "Your mind is quick, your logic infallible. You are correct in your assumption. Death's Gate has been opened. And by your enemies."

Xar halted. He could not see the speaker, hidden in shadows, but he could see eyes, flickering with a strange red light, as if they reflected a distant fire. His body warned him that the speaker was powerful and might prove dangerous, but Xar heard no note of threat or menace in the sibilant voice. The speaker's words were respectful, even admiring, and so was his tone.

Yet Xar remained on his guard. He had not grown old in the Labyrinth by falling victim to seductive voices. And this speaker had already committed a grave error. He had somehow penetrated into the lord's head, descried his thoughts. Xar had been talking beneath his breath. No one, standing at that distance from him, could have overheard.

"You have the advantage of me, sir," said Xar calmly. "Come closer, that these aged eyes of mine, which are easily confused in the shadows, can see you."

His eyesight was sharp, sharper than it had been in his youth, for now he knew what to look for. His hearing was excellent. The speaker didn't need to know that, however. Let him think he faced a frail old man.

The speaker was not fooled. "Your aged eyes see clearer than most, I'll wager, Lord. But even they can be blinded by affection, misplaced trust."

The speaker walked out of the forest, onto the path. He came to stand directly in front of the Lord of the Nexus, spread his hands to indicate he carried no weapon. Torchlight flared, a burning brand materialized in the speaker's hands. He stood in its light, smiling with quiet confidence.

Xar stared at the man, blinked. Doubt crept into his mind, increased his anger.

"You look like a Patryn. One of my people," he said, studying the man. "Yet I don't know you. What trick is this?" His voice hardened. "You had best speak quickly. The breath won't be in your body long."

"Truly, Lord, your reputation has not been exaggerated. No wonder Haplo admires you, even as he betrays you. I am *not* a Patryn, as you have surmised. I appear in this guise in your world in order to maintain secrecy. I can appear in my true form, if such is your pleasure, my lord Xar, but my true form is somewhat daunting. I deemed it best for you to decide if you wanted to reveal my presence to your people."

"And what is your true form, then?" Xar demanded, ignoring, for the moment, the accusation regarding Haplo.

"Among the mensch, we are known as 'dragon,' my lord."

Xar's eyes narrowed. "I have dealt with your species before and I see no reason why I should let you live any longer than I let them. Particularly as you stand in my homeland."

The false Patryn smiled, shook his head. "Those whom you refer to by that appellation are not true dragons, merely distant cousins.[2] Much as the ape is said to be a distant cousin of the human. We are far more intelligent, far more powerful in magic."

"All the more reason you should die . . ."

"All the more reason we should live, especially since we live only to serve you, Lord of the Patryns, Lord of the Nexus, and, shortly, Lord of the Four Worlds."

"You would serve me, eh? You say 'we'? How many of you are there?"

"Our numbers are enormous. They've never been counted."

"Who created you?"

"You did, Patryn, long ago," said the serpent, softly hissing.

"I see. And where have you been all this time?"

"I will tell you our story, Lord," answered the serpent coolly, ignoring the sarcastic tone. "The Sartan feared us, feared our power, just as they feared you Patryns. The Sartan cast your people into prison, but—since we are of a different species—they determined to exterminate us. The Sartan lulled us into a false sense of security by pretending to make peace with our kind. When the Sundering came, we were caught completely off guard, defenseless. We barely escaped with our lives. To our grief, we were powerless to save your people, who had always been our friends and allies. We fled to one of the newly created worlds and hid there to nurse our wounds and regain our strength.

"It was our intent to seek out the Labyrinth and attempt to free your people. Together, we could rally the mensch, who were left dazed and helpless by their terrible ordeal, and we could defeat the Sartan. Unfortunately, the world in which we chose to live—Chelestra—was also the choice of the Sartan Council. The

---

[2] The serpent is, of course, lying to Xar. Since this evil has no true form of its own, it borrows any form that suits its needs.

mighty Samah himself established his city, Surunan, populated it with thousands of enslaved mensch.

"He soon discovered us and our plans to overthrow his tyrannical rule. Samah vowed that we would never leave Chelestra alive. He closed and sealed Death's Gate, dooming himself and the rest of the Sartan on other worlds to isolation—only for a short time, or so he thought. He meant to make quick work of us. But we proved stronger than he'd anticipated. We fought back, and, though many of our kind gave up their lives, we forced him to free the mensch and at length drove him to seek the safety of the Sartan stasis chamber.

"Before the Sartan abandoned their world, they had their revenge on us. Samah cut adrift the seasun that warms the water of Chelestra. We could not escape; the bitter chill of the ice surrounding this world of water overtook us. Our body temperatures dropped, our blood grew cold and sluggish. It was all we could do to manage to return to our seamoon and take refuge inside its caverns. Ice locked us in, sent us into an enforced hibernation that lasted centuries.[3]

"At length, the seasun returned and brought with it warmth and renewed life for us. With it came a Sartan, one who is known as Serpent Mage, a powerful wizard who has been traveling Death's Gate. He awoke the Sartan and freed them from their long sleep. But by now, you, Lord, and some of your people had also attained your freedom. We sensed it, far away as we were. We felt your hope shine on us and it was warmer than the sun. And then Haplo came to us and we bowed to him and pledged him our help to defeat the Sartan. Defeat Samah, the ancient enemy."

The serpent's voice dropped low. "We admired Haplo, trusted him. Victory over Samah was within our grasp. We intended to bring the Sartan leader to you, Lord, as proof of our devotion to your cause. Alas, Haplo betrayed us, betrayed you. Samah fled, as did the Serpent Mage—the Sartan responsible for poisoning

---

[3] Again, the serpent is relating its own version of the truth, which is considerably different from the story told by the Sartan, found in *Serpent Mage*, vol. 4 of *The Death Gate Cycle*. It is interesting to note, as does Haplo, in his somewhat bitter commentary on this section of Xar's journal, that the serpents are adept at telling people exactly what they want to hear.

Haplo's mind. The two Sartan escaped, but not before Samah had been driven by his fear of us and his fear of you, great Xar, to open Death's Gate!

"The Sartan can no longer stop us from returning to assist you. We entered Death's Gate and we present ourselves to you, Xar. We would call you 'Lord.'" The serpent bowed.

"And what is the name of this 'powerful' Sartan to whom you keep referring?" Xar asked.

"He calls himself by the mensch name 'Alfred,' Lord."

"Alfred!" Xar forgot himself, lost his composure. His hand beneath the black robe clenched into a fist. "Alfred!" he repeated beneath his breath. He glanced up, saw the eyes of the serpent glint red. Xar quickly regained his calm.

"Haplo was with this Alfred?"

"Yes, Lord."

"Then Haplo will bring him to me. You need not fear. You have obviously misunderstood Haplo's motives. He is cunning, is Haplo. Intelligent and clever. He may not be a match for Samah— if this is truly the same Samah, which I much doubt—but Haplo is more than a match for this Sartan with the mensch name. Haplo will be here shortly. You will see. And he will have Alfred with him. And then all will be explained.

"In the meantime," Xar added, cutting short the serpent, who would have spoken, "I am very tired. I am an old man and old men need their rest. I would invite you to my house, but I have a child staying with me. A very sharp child, quite intelligent for a mensch. He would ask questions that I would prefer not to answer. Keep hidden in the forest. Avoid going around my people, for they will react to you as I have." The Lord of the Nexus held forth his hand, exhibited the runes that glowed a vibrant blue. "And they might not be as patient as I have been."

"I am honored by your concern, my lord. I will do as you command."

The serpent bowed again. Xar turned to take his leave. The serpent's words followed him.

"I hope that this Haplo, in whom my lord has placed such faith, will be found worthy of it." *But I most sincerely doubt it!*

Unspoken words whispered from the twilight shadows. Xar heard them plainly, or perhaps he was the one who gave them utterance in thought, if not aloud. He glanced back over his shoulder, irritated at the serpent, but the serpent was gone. It had apparently slunk into the woods without a sound, without the rustle of a leaf, the cracking of a twig. Xar was further irritated, then angered at himself for having let the serpent upset him.

"A lack of confidence in Haplo is a lack of confidence in myself. I saved his life. I brought him out of the Labyrinth. I raised him up, trained him, assigned him this most important task, to travel Death's Gate. When he first had doubts, I chastised him, cleansed him of the poison inflicted by the Sartan, Alfred. Haplo is dear to me. To discover that he has failed me is to discover that *I* have failed!"

The glow of the sigla on Xar's skin was beginning to fade, though it still gleamed brightly enough to light the lord's path through the fringes of the forest. He irritably forbore the temptation to look backward again.

He didn't trust the serpent, but then he trusted very few. He would have liked to have said "none." He trusted no one. But that would have been wrong.

Feeling older and wearier than usual, the lord spoke the runes and summoned out of the magical possibilities an oaken staff, strong and sturdy, to aid his tired steps.

"My son," he whispered sadly, leaning heavily on the staff. "Haplo, my son!"

CHAPTER ✦ 4

DEATH'S GATE

✦

THE JOURNEY THROUGH DEATH'S GATE IS A TERRIBLE ONE—A FRIGHTENING collision of contradictions slamming into the consciousness with such force that the mind blacks out. Haplo had once attempted to remain conscious during the journey[1]; he still shuddered when he recalled that frightful experience. Unable to find refuge in oblivion, his mind had jumped into another body, the nearest body—that of Alfred. He and the Sartan had exchanged consciousness, relived each other's most profound life experiences.

Each had learned something about the other then; neither could quite view the other the same as before. Haplo knew what it was like to believe yourself to be the last member of your race, alone in a world of strangers. Alfred knew what it was like to be a prisoner in the Labyrinth.

"I guess Alfred knows firsthand now," Haplo said, settling down beside the dog, prepared to sleep as he always did now before entering Death's Gate. "Poor bastard. I doubt if he's still alive. He and the woman he took with him. What was her name? Orla? Yes, that was it. Orla."

The dog whimpered at the mention of Alfred's name, laid its head in Haplo's lap. He scratched the dog's jowls. "I guess the best to hope for Alfred would be a quick death."

The dog sighed and gazed out the window with sad, hopeful

---

[1] *Fire Sea*, vol. 3 of *The Death Gate Cycle*.

eyes, as if expecting to see Alfred bumble his way back on board any moment.

Guided by the rune-magic, the ship left behind the waters of Chelestra, entered the huge pocket of air that surrounded Death's Gate. Haplo roused himself from musings that weren't offering either help or consolation, checked to make certain that the magic was working as it should, keeping his ship protected, holding it together, propelling it forward.

He was astounded to notice, however, that his magic was doing remarkably little. The sigla were inscribed on the inside of the ship, not the outside, as he'd always done before, but that should not make a difference. If anything, the runes should be working harder to compensate. The cabin should be lit with a bright blue and red light, but the interior was only suffused with a pleasant glow that had a faint purplish tinge.

Haplo fought down a brief moment of panicked doubt, carefully went over every rune structure inscribed on the interior of the small submersible. He found no flaw and he wouldn't, he knew, because he'd gone over it twice previously.

He hurried over to the window in the steerage, stared out. He could see Death's Gate, a tiny hole that looked much too small for a ship of any size larger than a . . .

He blinked, rubbed his eyes.

Death's Gate had changed. Haplo couldn't think why, couldn't understand for a moment. Then he had the answer.

Death's Gate was open.

It had not occurred to him that opening the Gate would make any difference. But it must, of course. The Sartan who designed the Gate in the beginning would have provided themselves with quick, easy access to the other three worlds. It was logical, and Haplo berated himself for being thickheaded, for not having thought of this before. He could probably have saved himself time and worry.

Or could he?

He frowned, considering. Entering Death's Gate might be easier, but what would he do once he was inside? How was it controlled? Would his magic even work? Or would his ship come apart at the seams?

"You'll have your answer soon enough," he told himself. "You can't very well go back."

He controlled an urge to pace nervously about the small cabin, focused his attention on Death's Gate.

The hole that had previously appeared too small for a gnat to pass through now loomed large. No longer dark and forbidding, the entrance was filled with light and color. Haplo couldn't be certain, but he thought he caught glimpses of the other worlds. Quick impressions slid into his mind and then out, moving too rapidly for him to focus on any in particular, like images seen in a dream.

The steamy jungles of Pryan, the molten-rock rivers of Abarrach, the floating islands of Arianus passed swiftly before his eyes. He saw, too, the soft shimmering twilight of the Nexus. This faded and from it emerged the stark and terrifying wasteland of the Labyrinth. Then, very briefly—gone so fast that he wondered if he'd truly seen it—he caught a glimpse of another place, a strange place he didn't recognize, a place of such peace and beauty that his heart constricted with pain when the vision vanished.

Dazed, Haplo watched the images shift rapidly from one to the other, was reminded of an elven toy[2] he'd seen on Pryan. The images began to repeat themselves. Odd, he thought, wondering why. They went through his mind again, in the same order, and he finally understood.

He was being given a choice: destination. Where did he want to go?

Haplo knew where he wanted to go. He just wasn't certain how to get there anymore. Before, the decision had been locked into his magic—he sorted through the possibilities and selected a site. The rune structure necessary to effect such a determination had been complex, extremely difficult to devise. His lord had spent innumerable hours studying the Sartan books[3] until he learned the key, then spent additional time translating

---

[2] Undoubtedly an elven "collide-a-scope." One looks down a hollow wooden tube at the end of which is a glass ball containing bits of different colored glass. When the ball is rotated, the glass pieces "collide" to form a variety of shapes, visible to the viewer.

[3] Xar discovered in the Nexus a small library of Sartan books written on various topics, including: a history of the Sundering, incomplete descriptions of the four worlds, and details on how to travel through Death's Gate. The

the Sartan language into Patryn in order to teach it to Haplo.

Now everything had changed. Haplo was sailing closer and closer to the Gate, his ship moving faster and faster, and he had no idea how to control it.

"Simplicity," he told himself, fighting his rising panic. "The Sartan would have made it simple, easy to travel."

The images flashed past his vision again, whirling faster and faster. He had the horrible sensation of falling, as one does in a dream. Pryan's jungles, Arianus's islands, Chelestra's water, Abarrach's lava—all spun around him, beneath him. He was tumbling into them, he couldn't stop himself. Nexus twilight . . .

Desperately, Haplo latched onto that image, grabbed hold of it, clung to it in his mind. He thought of the Nexus, remembered it, summoned images of its twilight forests and ordered streets and people. He closed his eyes, to concentrate better, and to blot out the terrifying sight of spinning into chaos.

The dog began to yelp, not with warning, but with glad excitement and recognition.

Haplo opened his eyes. The ship was flying peacefully over a twilight land, illuminated by a sun that never quite rose, never quite set.

He was home.

Haplo wasted no time. On landing his ship, he traveled directly to his lord's dwelling place in the forest to give his report. He walked rapidly, abstracted, absorbed in his thoughts, paying very little attention to his surroundings. He was in the Nexus, a place that held no danger for him. He was considerably startled, therefore, to be roused out of his musings by the dog's angry growl.

---

books are written in the Sartan rune language. Xar taught himself to read the language—a laborious task that took him many years.

Haplo writes: "We assumed that the Sartan left the books behind to taunt us, never thinking that we would have the patience or the desire to learn to read and make use of them. But now, knowing that Sartan were once in the Labyrinth, I wonder if we are wrong. Perhaps Xar was not the first one to escape the Labyrinth. Perhaps a Sartan emerged and left these books—not for us—but for those of his people he hoped would follow."

The Patryn glanced instinctively at the sigla on his skin, saw, to his surprise, that they gave off a faint blue glow.

Someone stood on the path before him.

Haplo quieted the dog with a hand on its head, a hand whose sigla were glowing brighter every moment. The runes tattooed on his skin itched and burned. Haplo waited, unmoving, on the path. No use hiding. Whatever was in the forest had already seen him and heard him. He would remain and find out what danger lurked so near his lord's mansion, deal with it if necessary.

The dog's growl rumbled in its chest. Its legs stiffened, the hackles rose on the back of its neck. The shadowy figure came closer, not bothering to hide, but taking care to keep out of the few patches of light that filtered through open places amid the thick leaves. The figure had the form and height of a man, moved like a man. Yet it wasn't a Patryn. Haplo's defensive magic would have never reacted so to any of his own kind.

His puzzlement increased. The idea that a foe of any sort should exist in the Nexus was untenable. His first thought was Samah. Had the head of the Sartan Council entered Death's Gate, found his way here? It was possible, though not very likely. This would be the last place Samah would come! Yet Haplo could think of no other possibility. The stranger drew nearer and Haplo saw, to his astonishment, that his fears had been groundless. The man *was* a Patryn.

Haplo didn't recognize him, but this was not unusual. Haplo had been gone a long while. His lord would have rescued many Patryns from the Labyrinth during the interim.

The stranger kept his gaze lowered, glancing at Haplo from beneath hooded eyelids. He nodded a stern, austere greeting— customary among Patryns, who are a solitary and undemonstrative people—and appeared likely to continue on his way without speaking. He was traveling the opposite direction from Haplo, heading away from the lord's dwelling.

Ordinarily Haplo would have responded with a curt nod of his own and forgotten the stranger. But the sigla on his skin itched and crawled, nearly driving him frantic. The blue glow illuminated the shadows. The other Patryn's tattoos had not altered in appearance, remained dark. Haplo stared at the stranger's hands. There was something odd about those tattoos.

The stranger had drawn level with him. Haplo had hold of the dog, forced to drag the excited animal back or it would have gone for the man's throat. Another oddity.

"Wait!" Haplo called out. "Wait, sir. I don't know you, do I? How are you called? What is your Gate?"[4]

Haplo meant nothing by the question, was hardly aware of what he asked. He wanted only to get a closer look at the man's hands and arms, the sigla tattooed on them.

"You are wrong. We have met," said the stranger, in a hissing voice that was familiar.

Haplo couldn't recall where he'd heard it and was now too preoccupied to think about it. The sigla on the man's hands and arms were false; meaningless scrawls that not even a Patryn child would have drawn. Each individual sigil was correctly formed, but it did not match up properly to any other.

The tattoos on the man's arms should have been runes of power, of defense, of healing. Instead, they were mindless, a jumble. Haplo was suddenly reminded of the rune-bone game played by the Sartan on Abarrach, of the runes tossed at random on a table. This stranger's runes had been tossed at random on his skin.

Haplo jumped forward, hands reaching, planning to seize the false Patryn, find out who or what was attempting to spy on them.

His hands closed over air.

Overbalanced, Haplo stumbled, fell onto his hands and knees. He was up instantly, looking in all directions.

The false Patryn was nowhere in sight. He had vanished without a trace. Haplo glanced at the dog. The animal whimpered, shivered all over.

Haplo felt like doing the same. He poked halfheartedly

---

[4] Reference to the number of Gates in the Labyrinth through which a Patryn has passed. The number of Gates gives a fair indication of what type of life the person led. A Squatter, for example, would have passed through relatively few Gates compared to a Runner. The Lord of the Nexus standardized the classification process in terms of age, using the runes tattooed on a person's body combined with cycles discovered in the Labyrinth to judge a Patryn's true age.

The question Haplo has asked would be the equivalent of one mensch asking another about his occupation.

among the trees and brush lining the path, knowing he wouldn't find anything, not certain he wanted to find anything. Whatever it was, it was gone. The sigla on his arms were starting to fade, the burning sensation of warning cooled.

Haplo continued on his way, not wasting further time. The mysterious encounter gave him all the more reason to hurry. Obviously, the stranger's appearance and the opening of Death's Gate were not coincidence. Haplo knew now where he'd heard that voice, wondered how he could have ever forgotten.

Perhaps he had wanted to forget.

At least now he could give the stranger a name.

CHAPTER ♦ 5

THE NEXUS

♦

"Serpents, lord," said Haplo. "But not serpents as we know them. The most deadly snake in the Labyrinth is a worm compared to these! They are old, old as man himself, I think. They have the cunning and the knowledge of their years. And they have a power, Lord, a power that is vast and . . . and . . ." Haplo paused, hesitated.

"And what, my son?" encouraged Xar gently.

"Almighty," answered Haplo.

"An omnipotent force?" Xar mused. "You know what you are saying, my son?"

Haplo heard the warning in the voice.

Be very careful of your thoughts, your surmises, your deductions, my son, the tone cautioned. *Be careful of your facts, your judgment. For by acknowledging this power* almighty, *you place it above me.*

Haplo was careful. He sat long without answering, staring into the fire that warmed the lord's hearth, watched its light play over the blue sigla tattooed on his hands and arms. He saw again the runes on the arms of the false Patryn: chaotic, unintelligible, without meaning, without order. The sight brought back the wrenching, debilitating fear he'd experienced in the serpents' lair on Draknor.

"I've never felt fear like that," he said suddenly, speaking aloud the thoughts in his mind.

Though he came in on the middle of Haplo's mental conversation, Xar understood. The lord always understood.

"The fear made me want to crawl into some dark hole, Lord. I wanted to curl up and lie there cowering. I was afraid . . . of my fear. I couldn't understand it, couldn't overcome it."

Haplo shook his head. "And I was born in fear, raised with fear, in the Labyrinth. What was the difference, Lord? I don't understand."

Xar did not respond, sat unmoving in his chair. He was a quiet, attentive listener. He never betrayed any emotion, his attention never wandered, his interest was always completely focused on the speaker. People talk to such a rare type of listener; they talk eagerly, oftimes incautiously. Their thoughts are focused on what they are saying, not on the person listening. And so Xar, with his magical power, was often able to hear the unspoken, as well as the spoken. People poured their minds into the lord's empty well.

Haplo clenched his fist, watched the sigla stretch smoothly, protectively over the skin of his hand. He answered his own question.

"I knew the Labyrinth could be defeated," he said softly. "That's the difference, isn't it, Lord. Even when I thought I would die in that place, I knew in my hour of dying a bitter triumph. I had come close to defeating it. And though I had failed, others would come after me and succeed. The Labyrinth, for all its power, is vulnerable."

Haplo raised his head, looked at Xar. "You proved that, Lord. You defeated it. You have defeated it, time and again. I defeated it, finally. With help." He reached down his hand, scratched the dog's head.

The animal lay snoozing at his feet, basking in the warm glow of the fire. Occasionally, it opened its eyes a glittering slit, fixed their gaze on Xar.

Just checking, the dog seemed to say.

Haplo did not notice, from where he was sitting, his dog's wary, watchful observation. Xar, seated opposite, did.

Haplo fell silent again, stared into the fire, his expression grim and dark. He had no need to continue. Xar understood completely.

"You are saying that this power cannot be defeated. Is that it, my son?"

Haplo stirred restlessly, uncomfortably. He cast the lord a troubled glance, shifted his gaze swiftly back to the fire. His face flushed, his hand unclenched, clenched again on the arm of the chair.

"Yes, Lord. That is what I am saying." He spoke slowly, heavily. "I think this evil power may be checked, halted, driven back, controlled. But never beaten, never ultimately destroyed."

"Not by us, your people, as strong and powerful as we are?" Xar put the question mildly, not arguing, merely requiring additional information.

"Not by us, Lord. As strong and powerful as we are." Haplo smiled at some inner thought, a sardonic smile.

The Lord of the Nexus was angered by this, although, to the casual observer, his expression appeared as placid and calm as before. Haplo did not notice, he was lost in a tangle of dark thoughts. But one other person was watching their conversation, eavesdropping on it. And this person was not a casual observer. He knew well what the lord was thinking.

This person, hidden away in a dark room, doted on the lord and thus had come to know every fleeting expression on the man's face. The unseen watcher now saw, illuminated by the firelight, the narrowing of Xar's eyes, the minute darkening of certain lines amidst the cobweb of wrinkles on Xar's forehead. The unseen observer knew his lord was angry, knew that Haplo had made a mistake, and the observer reveled in the knowledge.

The observer was so elated that he injudiciously wriggled at the thought, with the result that the stool on which he was seated scraped across the floor. The dog's head lifted instantly, ears pricked.

The observer froze. He knew the dog, remembered it, respected it. Wanted it. He did not move again, held still to the point of holding his breath, afraid even breathing might give him away.

The dog, hearing nothing further, apparently concluded it was a rat, and resumed its fitful nap.

"Perhaps," said Xar casually, making a small movement with his hand, "you think that the Sartan are the ones who are capable of defeating this 'almighty power.' "

Haplo shook his head, smiled into the fire's dying blaze. "No, Lord. They are as blind as—" He checked the words, afraid of what he'd been about to say.

"—as I am," Xar finished dryly.

Haplo looked up swiftly, the flush in his cheeks darkened. It was too late to recall the thought, too late to deny it. Any attempt at explanation would make him sound like a whining child, trying to weasel out of just punishment.

Haplo rose to his feet, faced the Lord of the Nexus, who remained seated, gazing up at him with dark, unfathomable eyes.

"Lord, we *have* been blind. And so have our enemies. The same things have blinded us both: hatred and fear. The serpents— or whatever force they are or represent—have taken advantage of it. They have grown strong and powerful. 'Chaos is our life's blood,' the serpents said. 'Death our meat and drink.' And now that they have entered Death's Gate, they can spread their influence throughout the four worlds. They want chaos, they want bloodshed, they *want* us to go to war, Lord!"

"And thus you counsel we should not, Haplo? You say we should not seek revenge for the centuries of suffering inflicted on our people? Not avenge the deaths of your parents? Not seek to defeat the Labyrinth, free those still left trapped within? Should we let Samah pick up where he left off? He will, you know that, my son. And this time, he will not imprison us. He will destroy us, if we let him! And is it your counsel, Haplo, that we let him?"

Haplo stood before the lord, staring down at him.

"I don't know, Lord," he said brokenly, fists clenching, unclenching. "I don't know."

Xar sighed, lowered his eyes, rested his head in his hand. If he had been angry, if he had railed and shouted, accused and threatened, he would have lost Haplo.

Xar said nothing, did nothing but sigh.

Haplo fell to his knees. Grasping the lord's hand, he pressed it to his lips, clasped it, held it fast. "Father, I see hurt and disappointment in your eyes. I beg your forgiveness if I've offended you. But the last time I was in your presence, the time before I sailed to Chelestra, you showed me that my salvation lay in telling you the truth. I have done so, Father. I've bared my soul to you, though it shames me to reveal my weakness.

"I don't offer counsel, Lord. I'm quick-thinking, quick to act. But I'm not wise. You are wise, Father. That is why I bring this very great dilemma to you. The serpents are here, Father," Haplo added in grim, dark tones. "They are here. I've seen one of them.

He has disguised himself as one of our people. But I knew him for what he was."

"I am aware of this, Haplo." Xar clasped the hand that held his.

"You know?" Haplo sat back on his haunches, expression startled, wary.

"Of course, my son. You say I am wise, but you must not think I am very bright," Xar said with some asperity. "Do you imagine that I do not know what is happening in my own homeland? I have met the serpent and talked with him, both last night and today."

Haplo stared, silent, stunned.

"He is, as you say, powerful." Xar bestowed the compliment magnanimously. "I was impressed. A contest between we Patryns and these creatures would be interesting, though I have no doubt who would be the victor. But such a contest is not to be feared. It will never come about, my son. The serpents are our allies in this campaign. They have pledged their allegiance to me. They have bowed before me and called me Master."

"So they did with me," said Haplo in a low voice. "And they betrayed me."

"That was *you*, my son," said Xar, and the anger was back, this time visible to both the seen and the unseen observers. "This time they bowed to *me*."

The dog jumped to its feet with a "whuff," glared about fiercely.

"Easy, boy," Haplo said absently. "It was just a dream."

Xar glanced at the animal with displeasure. "I thought you got rid of that creature."

"He came back," Haplo replied, troubled, uneasy. He rose to his feet from where he knelt beside his lord, remained standing, as if thinking the interview might be at an end.

"Not precisely. Someone brought the dog back to you, didn't he?" Xar stood up.

A tall man, the lord was easily Haplo's equal in height, very probably his match in physical strength, for Xar had not permitted age to soften his body. He was more than Haplo's equal in magical prowess. Xar had taken the younger Patryn apart once, the time of which Haplo spoke, the time he'd lied to his lord. Xar could have killed Haplo then, but the lord chose to let him live.

"Yes, Lord," Haplo said. He stared down at the dog, at the floor. "Someone did bring him back to me."

"The Sartan called Alfred?"

"Yes, Lord," Haplo answered without voice.

Xar sighed. Haplo heard the sigh, closed his eyes, bent his head. The lord rested his hand on the younger man's shoulder.

"My son, you have been deceived. I know it all. The serpents told me. They did not betray you. They saw your danger, sought to help you. You turned on them, attacked them. They had no choice but to defend themselves . . ."

"Against mensch children?" Haplo lifted his head, his eyes flashed.

"A pity, my son. They said you were fond of the girl. But you must admit, the mensch acted as mensch always do: recklessly, foolishly, without thinking. They aspired too high, meddled in affairs they could not possibly understand. In the end, as you well know, the dragons were forgiving. They helped the mensch defeat the Sartan."

Haplo shook his head, turned his gaze from his lord to the dog.

Xar's frown deepened. The hand on Haplo's shoulder tightened its grip. "I have been extremely lenient with you, my son. I have listened patiently to what some might term fantastic metaphysical speculations. Do not mistake me," he added, when Haplo would have spoken. "I am pleased that you brought these thoughts to me and shared them. But, once having answered your doubts and questions—as I believe I have—I am displeased to see you continue in your wrong-thinking.

"No, my son. Let me finish. You claim to rely on my wisdom, my judgment. And once you used to do so, Haplo, implicitly. This was the main reason I chose you for these delicate tasks which, up to now, you have performed satisfactorily. But do you now rely on me, Haplo? Or have you come to rely on another?"

"If you mean Alfred, Lord, you're wrong!" Haplo snorted derisively, made a swift, negating gesture with his hand. "He's gone now, anyway. Probably dead."

He stood staring down at the fire or the dog or both for long moments. Then suddenly, resolutely, he raised his head, looked directly at Xar.

"No, Lord, I do not rely on any other. I am loyal to you. That is why I came to you, brought you this information. I will be only too glad to be proven wrong!"

"Will you, my son?" Xar studied Haplo searchingly.

Seeming satisfied with what he saw, the lord relaxed, smiled, clapped Haplo affectionately on the shoulder. "Excellent. I have another task for you. Now that Death's Gate is opened and our enemies the Sartan are aware of us, we must move swiftly, more swiftly than I had intended. Within a short time, I leave for Abarrach, there to study the art of necromancy . . ."

He paused, cast a sharp glance at Haplo. The younger Patryn's expression did not alter; he made no opposition to this plan. Xar continued.

"We do not have sufficient numbers of Patryns to form an army, as I had hoped. But, if we have armies of the dead to fight for us, then we do not need to waste our people. It is imperative, therefore, that I go to Abarrach, imperative that I go now, for I am *wise*"—dry emphasis on the word—"enough to know that I must study long and hard before I can master the art of raising the dead.

"But this trip poses a problem. I must go to Abarrach but, at the same time, it is imperative that Bane returns to Arianus, the Realm of Air. Let me explain. It involves the great machine of Arianus. The machine the mensch call, somewhat fancifully, the Kicksey-winsey.

"In your report, Haplo, you stated you found information left by the Sartan which indicated that they built the Kicksey-winsey in order to bring the floating islands of Arianus into alignment."

Haplo nodded. "Not only bring the islands into line, Lord, but then shoot a geyser of water up to those that are now dry and barren."

"Whoever rules the machine, rules the water. And whoever rules the water, rules those who must drink it or perish."

"Yes, Lord."

"Review for me the political situation as it was when you left Arianus."

Xar remained standing. This summary was obviously meant to be brief, and was probably for Haplo's benefit more than the lord's own. Xar had read Haplo's report many times, knew it from memory. Haplo, however, had visited three other worlds since he'd been to Arianus. He spoke hesitantly, trying to refresh his memory.

"The dwarves—known on Arianus as Gegs—live in the lower isles, down in the Maelstrom. They are the ones who run the machine, or rather they serve it, for the machine runs itself. The elves discovered that the machine could supply water for their empire, located in the Mid Realm of Arianus. Neither the humans nor the elves, who live in the Mid Realm, are able to collect water in any amount, due to the porous nature of the continents.

"The elves traveled into the lower realms in their magical dragonships, took the water from the dwarves, paid them in worthless trinkets and refuse left over from the elven kingdoms. A dwarf named Limbeck discovered the elven exploitation of the dwarven people. He is now—or he was when I left—leading the rebellion against the elven empire by, as you say, cutting off their water supplies.

"The elves have other problems, as well. An exiled prince is leading his own rebellion against the tyrannical regime currently in power. The humans, led by a strong king and queen, are themselves uniting and fighting against the elven rule."

"A world in chaos," said Xar, with satisfaction.

"Yes, Lord," responded Haplo, face flushing, wondering if this was, perhaps, a subtle rebuke for words spoken earlier, a reminder that the Patryns wanted worlds in chaos.

"The child Bane must go back to Arianus," Xar repeated. "It is vital that we take control of the Kicksey-winsey before the Sartan can return and claim it. Bane and I have undertaken a lengthy study of the machine. He will put the Kicksey-winsey into operation, start the process to realign the islands. This will, no doubt, further disrupt the lives of the mensch, causing terror, panic. In the midst of the turmoil, I will enter Arianus with my legions, restore order. I will be looked upon as a savior."

Xar shrugged. "Conquering Arianus—the first world to fall to my might—will be easy."

Haplo started to ask a question, paused, checked himself. He stared moodily into the flickering embers.

"What is it, my son?" Xar urged gently. "Speak freely. You have doubts. What are they?"

"The serpents, Lord. What about the serpents?"

Xar pursed his lips. His eyes narrowed alarmingly. His long, thin, strong hands clasped behind his back, maintaining the calming circle of his being. He had rarely been so angry.

"The serpents will do what I tell them to do. As will you, Haplo. As will all my subjects."

He had not raised his voice, nor altered its gentle modulations. But the unseen observer in the back room shivered and scrunched together on his stool, thankful that he wasn't the one shriveling in the heat of the old man's ire.

Haplo knew he had displeased his lord. He recalled a time of punishment. His hand went instinctively to the name-rune tattooed over his heart—the root and source of all his magical power, the starting of the circle.

Xar leaned forward, suddenly, laid his hand over Haplo's, laid his gnarled old hand over Haplo's heart.

The Patryn flinched, drew in a quick breath, but otherwise held still. The unseen observer ground his teeth. Much as he was gleefully enjoying Haplo's downfall, the observer was also bitterly jealous of Haplo's obvious closeness to his lord—a closeness the observer could never hope to share.

"Forgive me, Father," Haplo said simply, speaking with dignity, out of sincere contrition, not out of fear. "I will not fail you. What is your command?"

"You will escort the child Bane to Arianus. Once there, you will assist him in the operation of the Kicksey-winsey. You will do whatever else you need to do in order to foment chaos and turmoil in the world. That should be easy. This dwarven leader, this Limbeck, likes and trusts you, doesn't he?"

"Yes, Lord." Haplo had not stirred beneath the lord's touch on his heart. "And when that is accomplished?"

"You will wait on Arianus for my instructions."

Haplo nodded in silent acquiescence.

Xar held him a moment longer, feeling Haplo's life beating beneath his fingers, knowing he could end that life in a second, if he chose; knowing that Haplo knew it, as well.

Haplo gave a great, shuddering sigh, bowed his head.

The lord pressed him close. "My son. My poor troubled son. You bear my touch with such courage . . ."

Haplo lifted his head. His face was flushed, he spoke savagely. "Because, my lord, there is no pain you or anyone could inflict on me worse than the pain I bear within myself."

Wrenching free of the lord's hold, Haplo walked abruptly from the room, from his lord's presence. The dog jumped to its feet, hurried after him, paws pattering quietly across the floor. There came the sound of a door slamming shut.

Xar stared after him, not greatly pleased. "I grow tired of these doubts, this whining. You will have one more chance to prove yourself loyal . . ."

The observer left his stool, slid out into the room, which was now dark with shadows. The fire had almost completely died.

"He didn't ask leave to go, Grandfather," noted the observer in a shrill voice. "Why didn't you stop him? I would have had him whipped."

Xar glanced about. He was not startled at the child's presence, or by the fact that he'd been listening. Xar was even somewhat amused at the vehemence in the tone.

"Would you, Bane?" Xar asked, smiling at the boy fondly, reaching out a hand to ruffle the fair hair. "Remember something, child. Love breaks a heart. Hatred strengthens it. I want Haplo broken, contrite, repentant."

"But Haplo doesn't love you, Grandfather," cried Bane, not completely understanding. He crowded close to the old man, looking up at him with adoring eyes. "I'm the only one who loves you. And I'll prove it. I will!"

"Will you, Bane?" Xar patted the boy approvingly, caressed him fondly.

A Patryn child would have never been encouraged to feel such affection, much less permitted to reveal it. But Xar had taken a fancy to the human child. Having lived a solitary life, the lord enjoyed the boy's company, enjoyed teaching him. Bane was bright, intelligent, and extraordinarily skilled in magic—for a mensch. Besides all this, the Lord of the Nexus found it rather pleasant to be worshiped.

"Are we going to study the Sartan runes tonight, Grandfather?" Bane asked eagerly. "I learned some new ones. I can make them work. I'll show you . . ."

"No, child." Xar withdrew his hand from the boy's head, his body from the child's clinging grasp. "I am weary. And there is study I must undertake before I journey to Abarrach. You run along and play."

The boy looked downcast. He kept silent, however, having learned the hard lesson that arguing with Xar was both futile and dangerous. Bane would remember the rest of his life the first time he'd thrown a floor-kicking, breath-holding tantrum in an effort to get his way. The ploy had always worked around other adults. It didn't work with the Lord of the Nexus.

The child's punishment had been swift, hard, severe.

Bane had never respected any adult until that moment. From then on, he respected Xar, feared him, and came to love him with all the passion of an affectionate nature granted him from his mother's side, darkened and corrupted by his evil father.

Xar left for his library, a place Bane was not permitted to enter. The child returned to his room to draw again the elementary Sartan rune-structure that he had finally, after much exhaustive toil, managed to reproduce and make functional. Once alone in his room, Bane paused. An idea had come to him.

He examined the idea to make certain it had no flaw, for he was a shrewd child and had learned well the lord's lessons in proceeding on any venture cautiously and with forethought.

The scheme appeared flawless. If Bane was caught, he could always whine or cry or charm his way out. Such tricks didn't work with the man he'd adopted as Grandfather, but Bane had never known them to fail with other adults.

Including Haplo.

Snatching up a dark cloak, throwing it over his thin shoulders, Bane slipped out of the lord's house, and merged with the twilight shadows of the Nexus.

CHAPTER ♦ 6

THE NEXUS

♦

Troubled, Haplo left his lord's house and walked without any very clear idea where he was going. He wandered the forest paths; there were several, crisscrossing, leading to different parts of the Nexus. Most of his mental processes were given to reconstructing the conversation with his lord, trying to find in it some hope that Xar had heeded his warning and would be on his guard against the serpents.

Haplo wasn't very successful in finding hope. He couldn't blame his lord. The serpents had seduced Haplo with their flattery, their attitude of abject debasement and fawning servility. They had obviously fooled the Lord of the Nexus. Somehow, Haplo had to convince his lord that it was the serpents, not the Sartan, who were the real danger.

Most of his mind running on this worrisome topic, Haplo watched for any sign of the serpent, thinking vaguely that he might catch the creature in an unguarded moment, force it to confess its true purpose to Xar. Haplo saw no false Patryn, however. Probably just as well, he admitted to himself morosely. The creatures were cunning, highly intelligent. Little chance one would permit itself to be coerced.

Haplo walked and considered. He abandoned the forest and headed across twilit meadows for the city of the Nexus.

Now that Haplo had seen other Sartan cities, he knew the Nexus for one of theirs.

A towering, pillared, crystal spiral balanced on a dome

formed of marble arches in the city's center. The center spire was framed by four other spires, matching the first. On a level beneath stood eight more gigantic spires. Large marble steppes flowed between the spires. Here, on the steppes, were built houses and shops, schools and libraries—those things the Sartan considered necessary to civilized living.

Haplo had seen this identical city standing on the world of Pryan. He had seen one very similar on Chelestra. Studying it from a distance, looking at the city with the eyes of one who has met its siblings and sees a disconcerting family resemblance, Haplo thought he could at last understand why his lord did not choose to live within the marble walls.

"It is just another prison, my son," Xar had told him. "A prison different from the Labyrinth and, in some ways, far more dangerous. Here, in their twilight world, they hoped we would grow soft as the air, become as gray as the shadows. They planned for us to fall victim to luxury and easy living. Our sharp-edged blade would turn to rust in their jeweled scabbard."

"Then our people should not live in the city," Haplo had said. "We should move from these buildings, dwell in the forest." He had been young and full of anger then.

Xar had shrugged. "And let all these fine structures go to waste? No. The Sartan underestimate us, to think we would be so easily seduced. We will turn their plan against them. In these surroundings that they provide, our people will rest and recover from their terrible ordeal and we will grow strong, stronger than ever, and ready to fight."

The Patryns—the few hundred who had escaped the Labyrinth—lived in the city, adapted it to their own use. Many found it difficult, at first—coming from a primitive, harsh environment—to feel settled and comfortable inside four walls. But Patryns are practical, stoic, adaptable. Magical energy once spent fighting to survive was now being channeled into more constructive uses: the art of warfare, the study of controlling weaker minds, the building up of supplies and equipment necessary to carrying a war into vastly differing worlds.

Haplo entered the city, walked its streets, which glimmered like pearl in the half-light. He had always before experienced a pride and fierce exultation when he traveled through the Nexus.

The Patryns are not like the Sartan. The Patryns do not gather on street corners to exchange high-minded ideals or compare philosophies or indulge in pleasant camaraderie. Grim and dour, stern and resolute, occupied on important business that is one's own concern and no other's, Patryns pass each other in the street swiftly, silently, with sometimes a nod of recognition.

Yet there is a sense of community about them, a sense of familial closeness. There is trust, complete and absolute.

Or at least there had been. Now he looked around uneasily, walked the streets warily, with caution. He caught himself staring hard at each of his fellow Patryns, eyeing them suspiciously. He'd seen the serpents as gigantic snakes on Arianus. He'd seen one as one of his own people. It was obvious to him now that the creatures could take on any form they chose.

His fellow Patryns began to notice Haplo's odd behavior, cast him dark, puzzled glances that instinctively shifted to the defensive if his suspicious stares appeared about to invade personal boundaries.

It seemed to Haplo that there were a lot of strangers in the Nexus, more than he'd remembered. He didn't recognize half the faces he saw. Those he thought he should know were altered, changed.

Haplo's skin began to glow faintly, the sigla itched and burned. He rubbed his hand, glared furtively at everyone passing by him. The dog, pattering along happily, noticed the change in its master and was instantly on guard itself.

One woman, wearing long, flowing sleeves that covered her arms and wrists, passed by too closely, or so Haplo thought.

"What are you doing?" He reached out, grabbed her arm roughly, shoved the fabric up to see the sigla beneath it.

"What the hell do you think *you're* doing?" The woman glared at him, broke his grip on her arm with a practiced, easy twist of her wrist. "What's wrong with you?"

Other Patryns halted in their pursuit of private affairs, banded instantly and instinctively together against the possible threat.

Haplo felt foolish. The woman was, indeed, a Patryn.

"I'm sorry," he said, lifting empty hands, bare and unprotected palms facing out, the sign of harmless intent, a sign that he would not use his magic. "Hush, dog. I—I thought maybe . . ."

He couldn't tell them what he'd thought, couldn't tell them what he'd feared. They wouldn't believe him, any more than Xar had believed him.

"Labyrinth sickness," said another, older woman in flat, practical tones. "I'll take care of him."

The others nodded. Her diagnosis was likely correct. They had seen this type of reaction often, especially to those newly come from the Labyrinth. A mindless terror takes possession of the victim, sends him racing into the streets, imagining he is back in that dread place.

The woman reached to take Haplo's two hands in her own, to share the circle of their beings, restore his confused and wandering senses.

The dog glanced up at its master questioningly. *Should I allow this? Or not?*

Haplo caught himself staring fixedly at the sigla on the woman's hands and arms. Did they make sense? Was there order, meaning, purpose in them? Or was she a serpent?

He backed away a step, shoved his hands in his pockets.

"No," he mumbled. "Thank you, but I'm all right. I'm . . . I'm sorry," he repeated again, to the first woman, who was regarding him with cool pity.

Hunching his shoulders, keeping his hands in his pockets, Haplo strode away rapidly, hoping to lose himself in the winding streets. The dog, confused, fell into step behind him, its unhappy gaze fixed on its master.

Alone and unseen, Haplo leaned against a building and tried to stop his body's trembling.

"What *is* wrong with me? I don't trust anyone—not even my own people, my own kind! The serpents' doing! They've put this fear in me. Every time I look at anyone from now on, I'll wonder: Is he an enemy? Is she one of them? I won't be able to trust anyone anymore! And soon, everyone in all the worlds will be forced to live like this! Xar, my lord," he cried in agony, "why can't you see?

"I have to make him understand!" Haplo muttered feverishly. "I have to make my people understand. How? How can I convince them of something I'm not certain I understand? How can I convince myself?"

♦

He walked and walked, not knowing where, not caring. And then he found himself standing outside the city, on a barren plain. A wall, covered with Sartan runes of warding, blocked his way. Strong enough to kill, these sigla prohibited anyone coming near the wall on either side. There was only one passageway through the wall. This was the Final Gate.

The Gate led out of . . . or into . . . the Labyrinth.

Haplo stood before the Gate, without any very clear idea why he was here, why he'd come. He stared at it, experiencing the mingled sensations of horror and fear and dread that always assailed him whenever he ventured near this place.

The land around him was silent, and he imagined he could hear the voices of those trapped inside, pleading for help, shouting in defiance, screaming curses with their dying breaths on those who had locked them in this place.

Haplo felt wretched, as he always did whenever he came here. He wanted to go in and help, wanted to join the fight, wanted to ease the dying with promises of vengeance. But his memories, his fear were strong hands holding him, keeping him back.

Yet he'd come here for a reason, and certainly not to stand staring at the Gate.

The dog pawed at his leg and whined, seemed to be trying to tell him something.

"Hush, boy," Haplo ordered, shoving the dog away.

The dog became more frantic. Haplo looked around, saw nothing, no one. He ignored the animal, stared at the Gate, feeling increasingly frustrated. He'd come here for a reason, but he hadn't the slightest idea what that reason was.

"I know what it's like," someone commiserated, a voice booming right behind him. "I know just how you feel."

Haplo had been quite alone. At the sudden utterance, spoken directly in his ear, he sprang back, instantly on the defensive, runes tingling, this time with a welcome sensation of protection.

He faced nothing more alarming than a very old man with a long scraggly beard, dressed in mouse-colored robes and wearing an extremely disreputable-looking pointed hat. Haplo couldn't speak for astonishment, but his silence didn't bother the old man, who carried on with his conversation.

"Know exactly how you feel. Felt that way myself. I recall once walking along, thinking of something extremely important.

It was, let me see, ah, yes! The theory of relativity. 'E equals mc squared.' By George, I've got it! I said to myself. I saw the Whole Picture, and then, the next moment, bam! it was gone. No reason. Just gone."

The old man looked aggrieved. "Then some wiseacre named Einstein claimed *he'd* thought of it first! Humpf! I always wrote things down on my shirtsleeves after that. Didn't work either, though. Best ideas . . . pressed, folded, and starched." He heaved a sigh.

Haplo recovered himself. "Zifnab," he said in disgust, but he didn't relax his defensive posture. The serpents could take any form. Though this was not, on second thought, exactly the form he would have chosen.

"Zifnab, did you say? Where is he?" the old man demanded, extremely irate. Beard bristling, he whirled around. "This time I'll 'nab' you!" he shouted threateningly, shaking his fist at nothing. "Following me again, are you, you—"

"Cut the crazy act, old man," Haplo said. Putting a firm hand on a thin and fragile-feeling shoulder, he twisted the wizard around to face him, stared intently into the old man's eyes.

They were bleary, rheumy, and bloodshot. But they did not glint red. The old man may not be a serpent, Haplo said to himself, but he certainly isn't what he passes himself off as, either.

"Still claim to be human?" Haplo snorted.

"And what makes you think I'm not?" Zifnab demanded, highly insulted.

"Subhuman, perhaps," rumbled a deep voice.

The dog growled. Haplo recalled the old man's dragon. A true dragon. Perhaps not as dangerous as the serpents, but dangerous enough. The Patryn glanced quickly at his hands, saw the sigla on his skin begin to glow a faint blue. He searched for the dragon, but could see nothing clearly. The tops of the wall and the Final Gate itself were shrouded in pink-tinged gray mist.

"Shut up, you obese frog," shouted Zifnab. He was talking, apparently, to the dragon, but he eyed Haplo uneasily. "Not human, eh?" Zifnab suddenly put his wizened fingers to the corners of his eyelids, pulled his eyes into a slant. "Elf?"

The dog cocked its head to one side. It appeared to find this highly diverting.

"No?" Zifnab was deflated. He thought a moment, brightened. "Dwarf with an overactive thyroid!"

"Old man—" Haplo began impatiently.

"Wait! Don't tell me! I'll figure it out. Am I bigger than a bread box? Yes? No? Well, make up your mind." Zifnab appeared a bit confused. Leaning close, he whispered loudly, "I say, you wouldn't happen to know what a bread box is, would you? Or the approximate size?"

"You're Sartan," stated Haplo.

"Oh, yes. I'm certain." Zifnab nodded. "Quite certain. What I'm certain of, I can't remember at the moment, but I'm definitely certain—"

"Not 'certain'! Sartan!"

"Sorry, dear boy. Thought you came from Texas. They talk like that down there, you know. So you think I'm Sartan, eh? Well, I must say, I'm extremely flattered, but I—"

"Might I suggest that you tell him the truth, sir?" boomed the dragon.

Zifnab blinked, glanced around. "Did you hear something?"

"It might be to his advantage, sir. He knows now, anyway."

Zifnab stroked his long, white beard, regarded Haplo with eyes that were suddenly sharp and cunning. "So you think I should tell him the truth, eh?"

"What you can remember of it, sir," the dragon remarked gloomily.

"Remember?" Zifnab bristled. "I remember any number of things. And you'll be sorry when I do, lizard lips. Now, let's see. Berlin: 1948. Tanis Half-Elven was taking a shower, when—"

"Excuse me, but we haven't got all day, sir." The dragon sounded stern. "The message we received was quite specific. *Grave danger! Come immediately!*"

Zifnab was downcast. "Yes, I s'pose you're right. The truth. Very well. You've wrung it out of me. Bamboo sticks beneath the fingernails and all that. I"—he drew a deep breath, paused dramatically, then flung the words forth—"I *am* Sartan."

His battered pointed hat toppled off, fell to the ground. The dog walked over, sniffed at it, gave a violent sneeze. Zifnab, miffed, snatched the hat away.

"What do you mean?" he demanded of the dog. "Sneezing on my hat! Look at this! Dog snot—"

"And?" prodded Haplo, glaring at the old man.

"—and dog germs and I don't know what else—"

"You're Sartan *and* what else? Hell, I knew you were Sartan. I guessed that on Pryan. And now you've proved it. You would have to be, in order to travel through Death's Gate. Why are you here?"

"Why am I here?" Zifnab repeated vaguely, glancing up at the sky. "Why *am* I here?"

No help from the dragon.

The old man folded his arms, placed one hand on his chin. "Why am I here? Why are any of us here? According to the philosopher Voltaire, we are—"

"Damn it!" Haplo exploded. He grabbed hold of the old man's arm. "Come with me. You can tell the Lord of the Nexus all about Voltaire—"

"Nexus!" Zifnab recoiled in alarm. Clasping his heart, he staggered backward. "What do you mean—Nexus? We're on Chelestra!"

"No, you're not," Haplo said grimly. "You're in the Nexus. And my lord—"

"You!" Zifnab shook his fist at the heavens. "You sorry excuse for an omnibus! You've brought us to the wrong place!"

"No, I did not," retorted the dragon, indignant. "You said we were to stop here first, *then* proceed to Chelestra."

"I said that, did I?" Zifnab looked extremely nervous.

"Yes, sir, you did."

"I didn't happen to say *why* I wanted to come here, did I? Didn't happen to suggest that it was a great place for barbecued chaodyn carapace? Anything of that sort?"

The dragon sighed. "I believe you mentioned, sir, that you wanted to speak to this gentleman."

"Which gentleman?"

"The one to whom you are currently speaking."

"Aha! *That* gentleman," Zifnab cried triumphantly. He reached out, wrung Haplo's hand. "Well, my boy, nice seeing you again. Sorry to run, but we really must be going. Glad you got your dog back. Give my regards to Broadway. Remember me to

Harold Square. Nice chap, Harold Square. Used to work in a deli on Fifth. Now, where's my hat—"

"In your hand, sir," observed the dragon with long-suffering patience. "You have just turned it inside out."

"No, this isn't mine. Positive. Must be yours." Zifnab attempted to hand the hat to Haplo. "Mine was much newer. Better condition. This one's all covered with hair tonic. Don't try to switch hats on *me*, sonny!"

"You're going to Chelestra?" Haplo asked, casually accepting the hat. "What for?"

"What for? Sent for!" Zifnab stated importantly. "Urgent call. All Sartan. *Grave danger! Come immediately!* I wasn't doing anything else at the time, and so— I say," he said, eyeing Haplo anxiously. "Isn't that my hat you're holding?"

Haplo had turned the hat right side out again, was keeping it just out of the old man's reach. "Who sent the message?"

"It wasn't signed." Zifnab kept his gaze on the hat.

"Who sent the message?" Haplo began revolving the hat round and round.

Zifnab stretched out a trembling hand. "Mind you don't crush the brim . . ."

Haplo drew the hat back.

Zifnab gulped. "Sam-hill. That was it. As in 'What the Sam-hill are you doing with my hat?' "

"Sam-hill . . . You mean 'Samah'! Gathering his forces. What's Samah intend to do, old man?"

Haplo lowered the hat until it was about level with the dog's nose. The animal, sniffing at it cautiously this time, began to nibble at the already shapeless point.

Zifnab gave a sharp cry. "Ah! Oh, dear! I—I believe he said something . . . No, don't drool on it, there's a good doggie! Something about . . . Abarrach. Necromancy. That's . . . that's all I know, I'm afraid." The old man clasped his hands, cast Haplo a pleading glance. "May I have my hat now?"

"Abarrach . . . Necromancy. So Samah's going to Abarrach to learn the forbidden art. That world could get rather crowded. My lord will be quite interested in this news. I think you'd better come—"

"*I* think not."

The dragon's voice had altered, rolled on the air like thunder. The sigla on Haplo's skin flared bright. The dog leapt to its feet, teeth bared, looking all around for the unseen threat.

"Give the doddering old fool his hat," commanded the dragon. "He's told you all he knows anyway. This lord of yours wouldn't get anything else out of him. You don't want to fight me, Haplo," the dragon added, tone stern and serious. "I would be forced to kill you . . . and that would be a pity."

"Yes," agreed Zifnab, taking advantage of Haplo's preoccupation with the dragon to make a deft grab. The wizard retrieved his hat, began to sidle backward, heading in the direction of the dragon's voice. "It would be a pity. Who would find Alfred in the Labyrinth? Who would rescue your son?"

Haplo stared. "What did you say? Wait!" He lunged out after the old man.

Zifnab shrieked, clutched his hat protectively to his chest. "No, you can't have it! Get away!"

"Damn your hat! My son . . . What do you mean? Are you saying I have a son?"

Zifnab regarded Haplo warily, suspecting designs on the hat.

"Answer him, fool," snapped the dragon. "It's what you came to tell him in the first place!"

"I did?" The old man cast a deprecating glance upward, then, blushing, said, "Oh, yes. Quite."

"A son," Haplo repeated. "You're certain?"

"No, I'm Sartan. Hah! Caught you!" Zifnab cackled. "Well, yes, you have a son, dear boy. Congratulations." He reached out, shook Haplo's hand again. "Unless, of course, it's a daughter," the old man added, after giving the matter some thought.

Haplo waved that aside impatiently. "A child. You're saying a child of mine was born and . . . that child is trapped in there." He pointed at the Final Gate. "In the Labyrinth."

"I'm afraid so," said Zifnab, voice softening. He was suddenly serious, grave. "The woman, the one you loved . . . She didn't tell you?"

"No." Haplo had little idea what he was saying, to whom he was saying it. "She didn't. But I guess I always knew. . . . Speaking of knowing, how the hell do *you* know, old man?"

"Ah, he's got you there," said the dragon. "Explain that, if you can!"

Zifnab appeared rather flustered. "Well, you see, I once . . . That is to say, I ran into a chap, who knew a chap, who'd once met . . ."

"What am I doing?" Haplo demanded of himself. He wondered if he were going mad. "How would *you* know anything? It's a trick. That's it. A trick to force me into going back into the Labyrinth—"

"Oh, dear, no! No, my boy," said Zifnab earnestly. "I'm trying to keep you out of it."

"By telling me that a child of mine is trapped inside?"

"I'm not saying you shouldn't go back, Haplo. I'm saying that you shouldn't go back *now*. It isn't time. You have much to do before then. And, above all, you shouldn't go back alone."

The old man's eyes narrowed. "That is, after all, what you were thinking about when we found you here, wasn't it? You were going to enter the Labyrinth, search for Alfred?"

Haplo frowned, made no response. The dog, at the sound of Alfred's name, wagged its tail and looked up hopefully.

"You were going to find Alfred and take him to Abarrach with you," Zifnab continued in a soft voice. "Why? Because there, on Abarrach, in the so-called Chamber of the Damned, there's where you'll find the answers. You can't get into the chamber on your own. The Sartan have it well guarded. And Alfred's the only Sartan who would dare disobey the orders of the Council and unlock the runes of warding. That's what you were thinking, wasn't it, Haplo?"

Haplo shrugged. He was staring moodily at the Final Gate. "What if it was?"

"It isn't time, yet. You must get the machine working. Then the citadels will begin to shine. The durnai will awaken. When all that happens—*if* all that happens—the Labyrinth will start to change. Better for you. Better for them." Zifnab gave the Gate an ominous nod.

Haplo glared at him. "Do you ever make sense?"

Zifnab looked alarmed, shook his head. "I try not to. Gives me gas. But now you've interrupted. What else was I going to say?"

"He is not to go alone," intoned the dragon.

"Ah, yes. You're not to go alone, my boy," said Zifnab brightly, as if he'd just thought of it himself. "Not into the Labyrinth, not into the Vortex. Certainly not into Abarrach."

The dog barked, deeply wounded.

"Oh, I beg your pardon," said Zifnab. Reaching out, he gave the animal a timid pat. "Sincere apologies and all that. I know *you'll* be with him, but that won't be enough, I'm afraid. I was thinking more in terms of a group. Commando squads. *The Dirty Dozen. Kelly's Heroes. The Seven Samurai. Debbie Does Dallas.* That sort of thing. Well, perhaps not Debbie. Wonderful girl, Debbie, but—"

"Sir," said the dragon, exasperated, "need I remind you that we are in the *Nexus. Not* exactly the place *I'd* choose to indulge in prepubescent fantasies."

"Ah, yes. Perhaps you're right." Zifnab clutched his hat, glanced about nervously. "Place has changed a lot since I was here last. You Patryns have done wonders. I don't suppose I'd have time to pop over and look at—"

"No, sir," said the dragon firmly.

"Or maybe—"

"Nor that either, sir."

"I suppose not." Zifnab sighed, pulled the shapeless and battered hat over his eyes. "Next time. Good-bye, dear boy." Groping about blindly, the old man solemnly shook hands with the dog, apparently mistaking it for Haplo. "Best of luck. I'll leave you with the advice Gandalf gave Frodo Baggins. 'When you go, go as Mr. Underhill.' Worthless bit of advice, if you ask me. As a wizard, Gandalf was highly overrated. Still, it must have meant something, else why would they have bothered to write it down. I say, you should really consider clipping your nails—"

"Get him out of here," Haplo advised the dragon. "My lord could be along any moment."

"Yes, sir. I believe that would be the best idea."

An enormous green-scaled head swooped out of the clouds.

Haplo's sigla flared, he backed up until he stood against the Final Gate. The dragon ignored the Patryn, however. Huge fangs, protruding from lower and upper jaws, caught hold of the wizard by the back of his mouse-colored robes and, none too gently, heaved the old man off his feet.

"Hey, let go of me, you twisted toad!" Zifnab shouted, flailing about wildly in midair. He began to wheeze and cough. "Ugh! Your breath is enough to flatten Godzilla. Been in the cat's tuna again, haven't you? I say, put me down!"

"Yes, sir," the dragon said through clenched teeth. He was holding the wizard about twenty feet off the ground. "If that's *really* what you want, sir."

Zifnab lifted the brim of his hat, peered out from underneath. Shuddering, he pulled the hat back over his eyes.

"No, I've changed my mind. Take me . . . where is it Samah said we were to meet him?"

"Chelestra, sir."

"Yes, that's the ticket. Hope it isn't one-way. To Chelestra, there's a good fellow."

"Yes, sir. With all dispatch, sir."

The dragon, carrying the wizard, who looked, from this distance, very much like a limp mouse, disappeared into the clouds.

Haplo waited tensely to be certain the dragon was gone. Slowly, the blue light of the sigla faded. The dog relaxed, sat down to scratch.

Haplo turned to face the Final Gate. He could see, through the iron bars, the lands of the Labyrinth. Barren plains, without a tree, shrub, bush, or any type of cover, stretched from the Gate to dark and distant woods.

The last crossing, the most deadly crossing. From those woods, you can see the Gate, see freedom. It seems so close.

You start to run. You dash into the open, naked, exposed. The Labyrinth allows you to get halfway across, halfway to freedom, then sends its foul legions after you. Chaodyn, wolfen, dragons. The grasses themselves rise up and trip you, vines entangle you. And that was getting out.

It was far worse, going back in.

Haplo knew, he'd watched his lord battle it every time he entered the Gate. The Labyrinth hated those who had escaped its coils, wanted nothing more than to drag its former prisoner back behind the wall, punish him for his temerity.

"Who am I kidding?" Haplo asked the dog. "The old man's right. Alone, I'd never make it alive to the first line of trees. I wonder what the old man meant about the Vortex? I seem to recall hearing my lord mention something about that once. Supposedly the very center of the Labyrinth. And Alfred's there? It'd be just like Alfred to get himself sent to the very center of the Labyrinth!"

Haplo kicked at a pile of broken stone, rubble. Once, long ago, the Patryns had attempted to tear down the wall. The lord had stopped them, reminded them that though the wall kept them out, it also kept the evil in.

Perhaps it's the evil in us, she'd said, before she left him.

"A son," said Haplo, staring through the Gate. "Alone, maybe. Like I was. Maybe he saw his mother die, like I did. He'd be what—six, seven, now. If he's still alive."

Picking up a large, jagged-edged chunk of rock, Haplo threw it into the Gate. He threw it as hard as he could, wrenching his arm, nearly dislocating his shoulder. Pain flashed through his body, felt good. At least better than the bitter aching in his heart.

He watched to see where the stone landed—a far distance inside. He had only to walk in the Gate, walk as far as the stone. Surely, he had that much courage. Surely, he could do that much for his son. . . .

Haplo turned, abruptly walked away. The dog, caught flat-footed by his master's sudden move, was forced to run to catch up.

Haplo berated himself for a coward, but the accusation was halfhearted. He knew his own worth, knew that his decision wasn't based on fear but on logic. The old man had been right.

"Getting myself killed won't help anyone. Not the child, not his mother—if she's still alive—not my people. Not Alfred.

"I will ask my lord to come with me," Haplo said, walking faster, his excitement, determination mounting. "And my lord *will* come. He'll be eager to, when I tell him what the old man said. Together, we'll go deep into the Labyrinth, deeper than he's ever gone. We'll find this Vortex, if it exists. We'll find Alfred and . . . whoever else. Then we'll go to Abarrach. I'll take my lord to the Chamber of the Damned and he will learn for himself—"

"Hullo, Haplo. When did you get back?"

Haplo's heart lurched. He looked down.

"Oh, Bane," he muttered.

"I'm glad to see you, too," said Bane, with a sly smile that Haplo ignored.

He was back in the Nexus, he'd entered the city without even knowing it.

After his greeting, Bane raced off. Haplo watched him go. Running through the streets of the Nexus, Bane dodged the Patryns, who regarded him with patient tolerance. Children were rare and precious beings—the continuation of the race. Haplo was not sorry to see the boy leave. He needed to be alone with his thoughts.

He recalled vaguely that he was supposed to take Bane back to Arianus, start the machine working.

Start the machine working.

Well, that could wait. Wait until he came back out of the Labyrinth . . .

You must get the machine working. Then the citadels will begin to shine. The durnai will awaken. When all that happens—if all that happens—the Labyrinth will start to change. Better for you. Better for them.

"Oh, what do you know, old man?" Haplo muttered. "Just another crazy Sartan . . ."

CHAPTER ♦ 7

THE NEXUS

♦

Bᴀɴᴇ ʜᴀᴅ ꜱᴛᴜᴅɪᴇᴅ ʜᴀᴘʟᴏ ᴄʟᴏꜱᴇʟʏ ꜰᴏʀ ꜱᴇᴠᴇʀᴀʟ ᴍᴏᴍᴇɴᴛꜱ ᴀꜰᴛᴇʀ ʜɪꜱ
greeting, noted that the man was paying more attention to inward
musings than outward influences.

Excellent, the child thought and dashed on ahead. It doesn't
matter if Haplo sees me now. Probably wouldn't have mattered if
he'd noticed me watching him earlier.

Adults have a tendency to overlook the presence of a child, to
treat a child as if it were a dumb animal and could not possibly
understand what was going on, what was being said. Bane had
discovered this tendency early in his short life, had used it often
to his own advantage.

But Bane had learned to be careful around Haplo. Although
Bane despised the man, as he despised nearly every adult, the
child had been forced to concede Haplo grudging respect. He
wasn't as stupid as most adults. Therefore, Bane had taken extra
precautions. But now the need for caution was ended, the need
for haste urgent.

Bane ran through the forest, nearly knocking over a Patryn,
lounging along the path, who gazed after the child with eyes that
glinted red in the twilight. Reaching the lord's house, Bane hurled
open the door and dashed into the study.

The lord was not there.

For an instant, Bane panicked. Xar had left for Abarrach already! Then he paused a moment to catch his breath, consider.

No, that couldn't be possible. The lord had not given Bane his final instructions, nor said good-bye. Bane breathed easier and, his head clear, he knew where he would find his adopted "grandfather."

Proceeding through the large house, Bane walked out a door at the back, emerged onto a broad expanse of smooth green lawn. A ship, covered with runes, stood in the lawn's center. Haplo would have recognized the ship—it was similar in almost every detail to the one he'd flown through Death's Gate to Arianus. Limbeck, the Geg on Arianus, would have recognized the ship, for it was similar to the vessel he had discovered wrecked on one of the isles of Drevlin in Arianus.[1]

The ship was perfectly round and had been wrought of metal and of magic. The outside hull was covered with sigla that wrapped the ship's interior in a sphere of protective power. The ship's hatch stood open, bright light streamed out. Bane saw a figure moving within.

"Grandfather!" the child shouted, and ran toward the ship.

The Lord of the Nexus paused in whatever it was he was doing, glanced out the hatch. Bane couldn't see the lord's face, silhouetted against the bright light, but the child knew by the rigidity of the stance and the slight hunching of the shoulders that Xar was irritated at the interruption.

"I will be in presently, child," Xar told him, going back to his duties, disappearing into the depths of the ship. "Return to your lessons—"

"Grandfather! I followed Haplo!" The child gasped for breath. "He was going to enter the Labyrinth, only he met a Sartan who talked him out of it."

Silence within the ship, all movement had ceased. Bane hung onto the doors of the hatch, sucking in great quantities of breath, excitement and lack of oxygen combining to make him lightheaded. Xar came back, a figure of darkness against the bright interior light.

"What are you talking about, child?" Xar's voice was gentle,

---

[1] *Dragon Wing*, vol. 1 of *The Death Gate Cycle*. Haplo flew the ship to Arianus. Having underestimated the magical power of Death's Gate, Haplo had not prepared his ship properly, with the result that it crash-landed. The Geg, Limbeck, discovered the downed ship, rescued Haplo and the dog.

soft. "Calm down. Don't get yourself so worked up." The lord's hand, callused, hard, stroked Bane's golden curls, damp with sweat.

"I was . . . afraid you would leave . . . without hearing . . ." Bane gulped air.

"No, no, child. I am making last-minute adjustments, seeing to the placement of the steering stone. Come, what is this about Haplo?" Xar's voice was mild, but the eyes were hard and chill.

Bane wasn't frightened by the cold. The ice was meant to burn another.

"I followed Haplo, just to see where he was going. I told you he didn't love you, Grandfather. He wandered around the forest a long time, looking for someone. He kept talking to that dog of his about serpents. Then he went into the city. He almost got into a fight." Bane's eyes were round, awed.

"Haplo?" The lord sounded disbelieving.

"You can ask anyone. Everyone saw." Bane was not above slight exaggeration. "A woman said he had some sort of sickness. She offered to help him, but he shoved her away and stalked off. I saw his face. It wasn't nice."

"Labyrinth sickness," Xar said, his expression softened. "It happens to us all—"

Bane understood that he'd made a mistake in mentioning the sickness, given his enemy a way out. The child hastened to shut off that escape route.

"Haplo went to the Final Gate. I didn't like that, Grandfather. What reason did he have to go there? You told him he was to take me to Arianus. He should have been back at his ship, getting it ready to go. Shouldn't he?"

Xar's eyes narrowed, but he shrugged. "He has time. The Final Gate draws many back to it. You would not understand, child—"

"He was going to go inside, Grandfather!" Bane insisted. "I know. And that would have been defying you, wouldn't it? You don't want him to go inside, do you? You want him to take me to Arianus."

"How do you know he was going inside, child?" Xar asked, voice soft, tone dangerous.

"Because the Sartan told him he was. And Haplo didn't say he wasn't!" Bane said triumphantly.

"What Sartan? A Sartan in the Nexus?" Xar almost laughed. "You must have been dreaming. Or making this up. Are you making this up, Bane?" The lord said the last sternly, stared at Bane intently.

"I'm telling you the truth, Grandfather," Bane averred solemnly. "A Sartan appeared out of nowhere. He was an old man with gray robes and an old, stupid-looking hat—"

"Was his name Alfred?" Xar interrupted, frowning.

"Oh, no! I know Alfred, remember, Grandfather? This wasn't him. Haplo called this man 'Zifnab.' He said that Haplo was going into the Labyrinth to look for Alfred and Haplo agreed. At least he didn't disagree. Then the old man told Haplo that going into the Labyrinth alone was a mistake, that Haplo would never reach Alfred alive. And Haplo said he had to reach Alfred alive, because he was going to take Alfred to the Chamber of the Damned on Abarrach and prove you wrong, Grandfather."

"Prove me wrong," Xar repeated.

"That's what Haplo said." Bane did not allow himself to be inconvenienced by the truth. "He was going to prove you wrong."

Xar shook his head slowly. "You must have been mistaken, child. If Haplo had discovered a Sartan in the Nexus, he would have brought the enemy to me."

"*I* would have brought the old man to you, Grandfather," said Bane. "Haplo could have, but he didn't." No mention of the dragon. "He warned the Sartan to leave quickly, because you might be coming."

Xar's breath hissed through clenched teeth, the gnarled hand that had been stroking Bane's curls jerked spasmodically, accidentally pulling the child's hair. Bane winced from the pain, inwardly reveled in it. He guessed that Xar was hurting far worse than Bane himself and that Haplo would be the one to suffer for it.

Xar suddenly grasped hold of Bane's hair, jerked his head back, forced the blue eyes to meet Xar's black ones. The lord held the child in his daunting gaze long, searching, penetrating to the bottom of Bane's soul—not a very far drop.

Bane looked back unblinking, unflinching in Xar's rough grip. Xar knew Bane for what he was—a skilled and cunning liar—and Bane knew Xar knew. The child had floated enough truth on the surface to conceal the lies beneath. And, with that uncanny insight into adults gained from long and lonely hours when he had nothing to do except study them, Bane guessed that Xar would be too hurt by Haplo's betrayal to probe deeper.

"I told you, Grandfather," Bane said earnestly, "Haplo doesn't love you. I'm the only one."

The hand holding Bane went suddenly nerveless. Xar released the boy. The lord stared out into the twilight, his pain raw and visible in the ravaged face, in the sudden sagging of the shoulders, the limpness of the hand.

Bane had not expected this, was displeased, jealous of Haplo's ability to cause such pain.

Love breaks the heart.

Bane flung his arms around Xar's legs, hugged him close.

"I hate him, Grandfather! I hate him for hurting you. He should be punished, shouldn't he, Grandfather? You punished me, the time I lied to you. And Haplo's done worse than that. You told me about the time you punished him before he went to Chelestra, how you could have killed him, but you didn't, because you wanted him to learn from his punishment. You must do that again, Grandfather. Punish him like that again."

Annoyed, Xar started to try to free himself from Bane's clinging grasp, then stopped. Sighing, the lord again fondled the boy's hair, stared out into the twilight. "I told you about that time, Bane, because I wanted you to understand the reason for your punishment and for his. I do not inflict pain wantonly. We learn from pain, that's why our bodies feel it. But some, apparently, choose to ignore the lesson."

"And so you'll punish him again?" Bane peered upward.

"The time for punishment is past, child."

Though Bane had been waiting for a year to hear those words, spoken in that tone, he couldn't help but shudder.

"You're going to kill him?" Bane whispered, overawed.

"No, child," said the Lord of the Nexus, twisting the golden curls. "You are."

Haplo arrived back at the lord's house. Entering, he crossed the living area, heading for Xar's library.

"He's gone," said Bane, seated cross-legged on the floor, his elbows on his knees, his chin on his hands. He was studying Sartan runes.

"Gone." Haplo stopped, stared at Bane, frowning, then looked back at the doorway leading to the library. "Are you sure?"

"See for yourself." Bane shrugged.

Haplo did. He walked into the library, glanced around, then returned. "Where did Lord Xar go? To the Labyrinth?"

Bane held out a hand. "Here, dog. Here, boy."

The dog pattered over, sniffed warily at the Sartan book of runes.

"Grandfather went to that world—the one made of stone. The one where the dead bodies walk." Bane looked up, blue eyes large and glittering. "Will you tell me about that world? Grandfather said you might—"

"Abarrach?" Haplo asked in disbelief. "He's gone already. Without—" The Patryn stalked out of the room. "Dog, stay," he ordered as the animal started to follow.

Bane heard the man banging doors in the back part of the dwelling. Haplo was going outside to look for Xar's ship. Bane grinned, wriggled in delight, then quickly sobered, continued to pretend to study his runes. The child cast a surreptitious glance beneath his long lashes at the dog, who had flopped down on its belly and was watching him with friendly interest.

"You'd like to be *my* dog, wouldn't you?" Bane asked softly. "We'd play together all day and *I'll* give you a name—"

Haplo returned, walking slowly. "I can't believe he left. Without saying . . . anything to me."

Bane looked at the runes, heard Xar's voice.

It is clear to me that Haplo has betrayed me. He is in league with my enemies. I think it best that I do not meet him again, face to face. I am not certain I could control my anger.

"Grandfather had to leave in a hurry," said Bane. "Something came up. New information."

"What new information?"

Was it wishful thinking on Bane's part, or did Haplo look guilt-ridden, uneasy? Bane buried his chin in his hands again, to keep his grin from showing.

"I don't know," he mumbled, shrugging again. "It's grown-up stuff. I didn't pay any attention."

I must allow Haplo to live awhile longer. An unfortunate necessity, but I need him and so do you, child. Don't argue with me. Haplo is the

only one among our people who has been to Arianus. This Geg, Limbeck,
who is in control of the great machine, knows Haplo and trusts him. You
will need the dwarves' trust, Bane, if you are to gain control of them, the
Kicksey-winsey, and, eventually, the world.

"Grandfather said he gave you your orders already. You're
supposed to take me to Arianus—"

"I know," Haplo interrupted impatiently. "I know."

Bane risked a glance. The man was not looking at the child,
not paying him any attention. Haplo, dark, brooding, was staring
at nothing.

Bane felt a twinge of alarm. What if Haplo refused to go?
What if he'd made up his mind to enter the Labyrinth, search for
Alfred? Xar had said Haplo wouldn't, that Haplo would obey his
command. But Xar himself had proclaimed Haplo a traitor.

Bane didn't want to lose him. Haplo was his. The child decided to take action on his own. Jumping to his feet, eager and
excited, Bane came over to stand in front of Haplo.

"I'm ready to go. Anytime you say. Won't it be fun? To see
Limbeck again. And the Kicksey-winsey. I know how to make it
work. I've studied the Sartan runes. It will be glorious!" Bane
waved his arms with calculated childish abandon. "Grandfather
says that the effects of the machine will be felt on all the worlds,
now that Death's Gate is open. He says that every structure the
Sartan built will likely come alive. He says that *he'll* feel the effects, even as far away as Abarrach."

Bane watched Haplo closely, tried to guess what the man was
thinking. It was difficult, practically impossible. The man's face
was impassive, expressionless; he might not have been listening.
But he had been. Bane knew.

Haplo hears everything, says little. That is what makes him good.
That is what makes him dangerous.

And Bane had seen the man's eyelids flicker, ever so slightly,
when the child mentioned Abarrach. Was it the idea of the Kicksey-winsey affecting something on Abarrach that had caught the
man's interest? Or was it the reminder that, even on Abarrach,
Xar would be aware of what his servant was—or was not—doing?
Xar would know when the Kicksey-winsey came to life. And if it
didn't, he would start to wonder what had gone wrong.

Bane flung his arms around Haplo's waist. "Grandfather said

to give you his embrace. He said to tell you he trusted you, relied on you completely. He knows you won't fail him. Or me."

Haplo put his hands on Bane's arms, pulled the boy loose as the man might have pulled loose a leech.

"Ouch, you're hurting me," Bane whimpered.

"Listen, kid," said Haplo grimly, not relaxing his hold. "Let's get one thing straight. I know you. Remember? I know you for the scheming, conniving, manipulative little bastard that you are. I'll obey my lord's command. I'll take you to Arianus. I'll see to it that you have a chance to do whatever it is you need to do to that damn machine. But don't think you're going to blind me with the light from your halo, kid, because I've seen that halo, close-up."

"You don't like me," said Bane, crying a little. "No one likes me, except Grandfather. No one ever did like me."

Haplo grunted, straightened. "Just so we understand each other. And another thing. I'm in charge. What I say goes. Got that?"

"I like *you*, Haplo," said Bane, with a snivel.

The dog, feeling tenderhearted, came over and licked the child's face. Bane threw his arm around the animal's neck.

I'll keep you, he promised the dog silently. When Haplo's dead, you'll be my dog. It will be fun.

"At least *he* likes me," Bane said aloud, pouting. "Don't you, boy?"

The dog wagged its tail.

"The damn dog likes everyone," Haplo muttered. "Even Sartan. Now go to your room, pack up your things. I'll wait here until you're ready."

"Can the dog come with me?"

"If it wants. Go on, now. Hurry up. The sooner we get there, the sooner I'll be back."

Bane left the room with a show of quiet obedience. It was fun, playacting; fun to fool Haplo. Fun to pretend to obey a man whose life you hold in your small hands. Bane hugged to himself a conversation—almost the last conversation—he'd had with Xar.

When your task is completed, Bane, when the Kicksey-winsey is in operation and you have taken control of Arianus, Haplo will then become expendable. You will see to it that he is killed. I believe you knew an assassin on Arianus . . .

Hugh the Hand, Grandfather. But he's not alive anymore. My father killed him.

There will be other assassins for hire. One thing is most important. One thing you must promise me to do. You must keep Haplo's corpse preserved until my arrival.

You're going to resurrect Haplo, Grandfather? Make him serve you after he's dead, like they do with the dead men on Abarrach?

Yes, child. Only then will I be able to trust him. . . .

Love breaks the heart.

"Come on, boy!" Bane cried, suddenly. "Race you!"

He and the dog dashed madly for the child's bedroom.

CHAPTER ◆ 8

WOMBE, DREVLIN

LOW REALM

◆

THE TRIP THROUGH DEATH'S GATE WAS UNEVENTFUL. HAPLO CHARMED BANE TO sleep almost immediately after they departed the Nexus. It had occurred to Haplo that the passage into Death's Gate had become so simple a skilled mensch wizard might attempt it. Bane was observant, intelligent, and the son of a skilled wizard. Haplo had a sudden vision of Bane flitting from one world to another. . . . Nope. Nap time.

They had no difficulty reaching Arianus, World of Air. The images of the various worlds flashed past Haplo; he found the floating isles of Arianus with ease. But before he concentrated on it, he spent a few moments watching the other worlds drift before him, shining in rainbow hues like soap bubbles, before bursting and being replaced by the next. All of them were places he recognized except one. And that one—the most beautiful, the most intriguing.

Haplo stared at the vision as long as he could, which was only a matter of fleeting seconds. He had intended to ask Xar about it, but the lord had left before Haplo had a chance to discuss it.

Was there a fifth world?

Haplo rejected that notion. No mention of a fifth world had ever been made in any of the ancient Sartan writings.

The old world.

Haplo thought this much more probable. The flashing image he saw of it accorded with descriptions of the old world. But the old world no longer existed; a world torn apart by magic. Perhaps this was nothing more than a poignant memory, kept around to remind the Sartan of what had once been.

But, if that were so, why should it be presented as an option? Haplo watched the possibilities sparkle before his eyes again and again. Always in the same order: the strange world of blue sky and bright sun, moon, and stars, boundless ocean and broad vistas; then the Labyrinth, dark and tangled; then the twilight Nexus, then the four elemental worlds.

If Haplo had not had Bane with him, he would have been tempted to explore, to select the image in his mind and see what happened. He glanced down at the child, slumbering peacefully, his arm around the dog; both of them sharing a cot Haplo had dragged onto the bridge in order to keep an eye on the kid.

The dog, sensing its master's gaze, opened its eyes, blinked lazily, yawned widely, and, seeing no action was imminent, gave a contented sigh and crowded closer to the child, nearly pushing Bane off the cot. Bane muttered something in his sleep, something about Xar, and suddenly clutched the dog's fur with pinching hands.

The dog gave a pained yelp, reared its head, and looked at the child with a bemused expression, wondering what it had done to deserve such rough treatment, uncertain how to extricate itself. The dog looked up at Haplo, asking for help.

Haplo, smiling, uncurled the sleeping child's fingers from the dog's fur, petted the dog's head in apology. The dog gave Bane a distrustful glance, jumped off the cot, and curled up safely on the deck at Haplo's feet.

Haplo looked back at the visions, concentrated on Arianus, put the others out of his mind.

The first time Haplo had traveled to Arianus had nearly been his last. Unprepared for both the magical forces of Death's Gate and the violent physical forces existent in the Realm of Air, he had been forced to crash-land his ship on what he had later learned were a series of small floating isles known as the Steps of Terrel Fen.

He was prepared, now, for the terrible effects of the ferocious storm that raged perpetually in the Lower Realms. The protective sigla that had only glowed faintly during their passage through Death's Gate flared a vibrant blue when the first blast of wind smote the vessel. Lightning was almost continual, brilliant, blinding. Thunder crashed around them, the wind buffeted them. Hail battered the wooden shell, rain lashed against the window, forming a solid sheet of water, making it impossible to see.

Haplo brought the ship to a standstill, kept it floating in mid-air. Having spent time on Drevlin—the principal isle of the Lower Realm—he had learned that these storms swept through in cycles. He had only to wait for this one to pass; then would come a period of relative calm before the next one. During that calm, he would find a place to land, make contact with the dwarves.

Haplo considered keeping Bane asleep, decided to allow the boy to wake up. He might as well make himself useful. A quick brush of Haplo's hand wiped away the rune he'd traced on the child's forehead.

Bane sat up, blinked dazedly around for a moment, then glared at the Patryn accusingly.

"You put me to sleep."

Haplo saw no need to verify, comment on, or apologize for his action. Keeping watch as best he could out the rain-smeared window, he flicked a glance at the boy.

"Go through the ship, see if there are any leaks or cracks in the hull."

Bane flushed angrily at the Patryn's offhand, commanding tone. Haplo watched the crimson wave spread from the fair neck to the cheeks. The blue eyes flashed in rebellion. Xar had not spoiled the child, who had been in the lord's care over a year now. The lord had done much to improve Bane's temper, but the boy had been raised a prince in a royal household and was accustomed to giving orders, not taking them.

Especially not from Haplo.

"If you've done your magic right, there shouldn't be any cracks," said Bane petulantly.

We might as well get settled now who's boss, Haplo thought. He shifted his gaze back to the window, watching for the first signs that the storm was about to subside.

"I did the magic right. But you've worked with the runes. You know how delicate the balance is. One tiny sliver could start a crack that would end up breaking apart the entire ship. Best to make sure, to stop it now before it gets wider."

A moment's silence, which Haplo assumed was spent in internal struggle.

"Can I take the dog with me?" Bane asked in sullen tones.

Haplo waved a hand. "Sure."

The child seemed to cheer up. "Can I feed him a sausage?"

The dog, at the sound of its favorite word, was on its feet, tongue lolling, tail wagging.

"Only one," said Haplo. "I'm not sure how long this storm's going to last. We may need to eat the sausages ourselves."

"You can always conjure up more," said Bane happily. "C'mon, dog."

The two clattered away, heading for the ship's stern.

Haplo watched the rain slide down the windowpane, thought back to when he'd first brought the boy to the Nexus . . .

. . . "The kid's name is Bane, Lord," said Haplo. "I know," he added, seeing Xar's frown, "it's a strange name for a human child, but, once you know his history, the name makes sense. You'll find an account of him there, Lord, in my journal."

Xar fingered the document but did not open it. Haplo remained standing in respectful silence, waiting for his lord to speak. The lord's next question was not entirely unexpected.

"I asked you to bring me a disciple from this world, Haplo. Arianus is, as you describe it, a world in chaos: elves, dwarves, humans all fighting each other, the elves fighting among themselves. A serious shortage of water, due to the failure of the Sartan to align the floating islands and make their fantastic machine operational. When I begin my conquest, I will need a lieutenant, preferably one of the mensch, to go to Arianus and gain control over the people in my name while I am busy elsewhere. And for this purpose you bring me . . . a ten-year-old human child?"

The child under discussion was asleep in a back bedroom in Xar's dwelling. Haplo had left the dog with him, to give its master notice if Bane woke. Haplo did not flinch beneath his lord's stern gaze. Xar was not doubting his minion; the lord was puzzled, perplexed—a feeling Haplo could well understand. He'd been prepared for the question, he was prepared with the answer.

"Bane is no ordinary mensch child, Lord. As you will note in the journal[1]—"

"I will read the journal later, at my leisure. I would be much interested to hear your report on the child now."

Haplo bowed in compliance, sat down in the chair Xar indicated with a wave of his hand.

"The boy is the son of two humans known among their people as mysteriarchs—powerful wizards, by mensch standards, at least. The father called himself Sinistrad, the mother's name is Iridal. These mysteriarchs with their great skill in magic considered the rest of the human race barbaric boors. The mysteriarchs left the fighting and chaos in the Mid Realms, traveled up to the High Realms. Here they discovered a land of beauty that, unfortunately for them, turned out to be a death trap.

"The High Realms had been created by the rune-magic of the Sartan. The mysteriarchs had no more idea how to read Sartan magic than a toddler can read a treatise on metaphysics. Their crops withered in the fields, water was scarce, the rarefied air was difficult to breathe. Their people began to die out. The mysteriarchs knew they had to flee this place, return to the Mid Realms. But, like most humans, they feared their own kind. They were afraid to admit their weakness. And so they determined that when they went back, it would be as conquerors, not as suppliants.

"The boy's father, Sinistrad, devised a remarkable plan. The human king of the Mid Realms, one Stephen, and his wife, Anne, had given birth to an heir to the throne. At about that same time, Sinistrad's own wife, Iridal, gave birth to their son. Sinistrad switched the babies, taking his own child down to the Mid Realms and bringing Stephen's son back to the Upper Realms. It was Sinistrad's intent to use Bane—as heir to the throne—to gain control of the Mid Realms.

"Of course, everyone in the Mid Realms knew the babies had been switched, but Sinistrad had cleverly cast a charm upon his son that made everyone who looked on the child dote on him. When Bane was a year old, Sinistrad came to Stephen and informed the king of his plan. King Stephen was powerless to fight

[1] Haplo, *Arianus, World of Air,* vol. 1 of *Death Gate Journal.*

the mysteriarch. In their hearts, Stephen and Anne loathed and feared the changeling—that was why they named him Bane—but the enchantment around him was so strong that they could do nothing themselves to get rid of him. Finally, in desperation, they hired an assassin to take Bane away and kill him.

"As it turned out, Lord,"—Haplo grinned—"Bane almost assassinated the assassin."

"Indeed?" Xar appeared impressed.

"Yes, you'll find the details there." Haplo indicated the journal. "Bane wore an amulet, given to him by Sinistrad, that transmitted the wizard's commands to the boy, transmitted whatever the boy heard back to Sinistrad. Thus the mysteriarchs spied on the humans, knew every move King Stephen made. Not that Bane needed much guidance in intrigue. From what I've seen of the kid, he could have taught his father a thing or two.

"Bane's quick-witted, intelligent. He's a clairvoyant, and skilled in magic, for a human, though he's untrained. It was Bane who figured out how the Kicksey-winsey works, what it's intended to do. That's his diagram I've included in there, Lord. And he's ambitious. When it became clear to Bane that his father did *not* intend for them to rule the Mid Realms as a father and son team, Bane determined to get rid of Sinistrad.

"Bane's plot succeeded, though not quite as he'd planned it. The boy's life was saved, ironically enough, by the man who'd been hired to kill him. A waste, that," Haplo added thoughtfully. "Hugh the Hand was an interesting human, a skilled and able fighter. He was exactly what you were seeking in a disciple, Lord. I had planned bringing him to you, but, unfortunately, he died battling the wizard. A waste, as I said."

The Lord of the Nexus was only half listening. Opening the journal, he'd discovered the diagram of the Kicksey-winsey. He studied it carefully.

"The child did this?" he asked.

"Yes, Lord."

"You're certain."

"I was spying on them when Bane showed this to his father. Sinistrad was as impressed as you are."

"Remarkable. And the child *is* charming, winning, comely. The enchantment his father cast over him would have no effect on us, certainly, but does it still work upon the mensch?"

"Alfred, the Sartan, was of the opinion that the enchantment had been dispelled. But"—Haplo shrugged—"Hugh the Hand was under this boy's spell—whether by magic or merely pity for an unloved child who had been nothing but a pawn all his life. Bane is clever and knows how to use his youth and his beauty to manipulate others."

"What of the child's mother? What did you say her name was, Iridal?"

"She could be trouble. When we left, she was searching for her son in company with the Sartan, Alfred."

"She wants the boy for her own purposes, I presume."

"No, I think she wants him for himself. She never went along with her husband's plan, not really. Sinistrad had some sort of terrible hold over her. She was afraid of him. And, with his demise, the courage of the other mysteriarchs collapsed. There was talk when I left that they were abandoning the High Realms, planning to move down among the other humans."

"The mother could be disposed of?"

"Easily, Lord."

Xar smoothed the pages of the journal with his gnarled fingers, but he wasn't looking at it any longer, nor paying attention to it.

" 'A little child shall lead them.' An old mensch saying, Haplo. You have acted wisely, my son. I might go so far as to say that your choice was inspired. Those mensch who would feel threatened by an adult coming to lead them will be completely disarmed by this innocent-seeming child. The boy has the typical human faults, of course. He is hotheaded, lacks patience and discipline. But with the proper tutelage, I believe he can be molded into something quite extraordinary for a mensch. I begin, already, to see the vague outline of my plan."

"I am glad to have pleased you, Lord," said Haplo.

"Yes," murmured the Lord of the Nexus, " 'a little child shall lead them . . .' "

The storm abated. Haplo took advantage of the relative calm to fly over the isle of Drevlin, searching for a place to land. He had come to know this area quite well. He'd spent considerable time here on his last visit, preparing his elven ship for its return through Death's Gate.

The continent of Drevlin was flat and featureless, a hunk of what the mensch called "coralite" floating in the Maelstrom. One could judge landmarks, however, by the Kicksey-winsey, the gigantic machine whose wheels and engines and gears and pulleys and arms and claws spread out over Drevlin's surface, delved deep into the island's interior.

Haplo was searching for the Liftalofts, nine huge mechanical arms made of gold and steel that thrust up into the swirling storm clouds. These Liftalofts were the most important part of the Kicksey-winsey, at least as far as the mensch on Arianus were concerned, for it was the Liftalofts that provided water to the dry realms above. The Liftalofts were located in the city of Wombe, and it was in Wombe that Haplo hoped to find Limbeck.

Haplo had no idea how the political situation might have changed during his absence, but when he'd last left Arianus, Limbeck had made Wombe his power base. It was necessary that Haplo find the leader of the dwarves, and he judged that Wombe would be as good a place to start searching as any.

The nine arms, each with an outstretched golden hand, were easy to spot from the air. The storm had died down, though more clouds were massing on the horizon. Lightning reflected off the metal, the frozen hands were silhouetted against the clouds. Haplo landed on a patch of empty ground, bringing the ship down in the shadow of an apparently abandoned portion of the machine. At least he assumed it was abandoned, no light shone from it, no gears were grinding, no wheels turning, no "'lectricity," as the Gegs termed it, was rivaling the lightning with its blue-yellow voltage.

Once safely on the ground, Haplo noticed that there were no lights anywhere. Puzzled, he peered out the rain-streaked window. As he recalled, the Kicksey-winsey turned the storm-ridden darkness of Drevlin into artificial, perpetual day. Glimmerglamps shone everywhere, 'lectric zingers sent jagged bolts sparking into the air.

Now, the city and its surroundings were lit only by the light of the sun, which, by the time it had been filtered down through the clouds of the Maelstrom, was leaden and sullen and more depressing than darkness.

Haplo stood staring out the window, recalling his last visit here, trying to remember if there had been lights on this part of the Kicksey-winsey, or if he was, in fact, thinking about another portion of the great machine.

"Maybe that was in Het," he muttered, then shook his head. "No, it was here. I definitely remember—"

A thump and a warning bark jolted him out of his reverie.

Haplo walked back to the ship's stern. Bane was standing beside the hatch, holding a sausage just out of the dog's reach.

"You can have this," he was promising the dog, "but only if you quit barking. Let me get this open. All right? Good dog."

Bane shoved the sausage in a pocket, turned to the hatch, and began to fumble with the sliding latch that would, ordinarily, have opened the door.

The latch remained stuck firmly in place. Bane glared at it, beat on it with his small fists. The dog kept its eyes fixed intently on the sausage.

"Going somewhere, Your Highness?" Haplo asked, leaning casually against one of the bulkheads. He had decided, in the interests of portraying Bane as rightful heir to the Volkaran throne, to use the title due to a human prince. He supposed he might as well get used to it now, before they appeared in public. Of course, he'd have to blunt the ironic edge.

Bane glanced reproachfully at the dog, gave the recalcitrant latch one final, futile push with his hands, then looked up coolly at Haplo.

"I want to go outside. It's hot and stuffy in here. And it smells of dog," he added scornfully.

The animal, hearing its name and thinking it was being referred to in a friendly manner—perhaps in regard to the sausage —wagged its tail and licked its chops.

"You used magic on it, didn't you," Bane continued accusingly, giving the latch another push.

"The same magic I've used throughout the ship, Your Highness. I had to. It wouldn't do to let one part remain unprotected, just as it wouldn't do to ride to battle with a gaping hole in your armor. Besides, I don't think you want to go outside just yet. There's another storm coming. You remember the storms on Drevlin, don't you?"

"I remember. I can see when a storm's coming, same as you.

And I wouldn't have stayed out that long. I wasn't going that far."

"Where were you going, Your Highness?"

"Nowhere. Just for a walk." Bane shrugged.

"Not thinking of trying to contact the dwarves on your own, eh?"

"Of course not, Haplo," Bane said, eyes round. "Grandfather said I was to stay with you. And I always obey *Grandfather*."

Haplo noticed the emphasis on the last word, smiled grimly. "Good. Remember, I'm here for your protection, as much as anything. It's not very safe on this world. Not even if you *are* a prince. There are those who would kill you just for that alone."

"I know," said Bane, looking subdued, somewhat ashamed. "The elves almost killed me last time I was here. I guess I didn't think about that. I'm sorry, Haplo." Clear blue eyes gazed upward. "It was very wise of Grandfather to give you to me for a guard. You always obey Grandfather, too, don't you, Haplo?"

The question caught Haplo by surprise. He glanced swiftly at Bane, wondering what—if anything—the child meant by it. For an instant, Haplo thought he saw a glitter of cunning, sly and malevolent, in the wide blue eyes. But Bane stared at him guilelessly, a child asking a childish question.

Haplo turned away. "I'm going back up front, to keep watch."

The dog whined, looked pathetically at the sausage, still in Bane's pocket.

"You didn't ask me about the leaks," Bane reminded Haplo.

"Well, were there any?"

"No. You work the magic pretty good. Not as good as Grandfather, but pretty good."

"Thank you, Your Highness," Haplo said, bowed, and walked off.

Bane took the sausage out of his pocket, smacked the dog lightly and playfully on the nose with it. "That's for giving me away," he said, in mild reproof.

The dog slavered, regarded the sausage hungrily.

"Still, I guess it was for the best." Bane frowned. "Haplo's right. I'd forgotten about those damn bastard elves. I'd like to meet the one who threw me off the ship that time. I'd tell Haplo to throw that elf into the Maelstrom. And I'd watch him fall, all the way down. I'll bet you could hear him scream a long, long time. Yes, Grandfather was right. I see that now. Haplo will be useful to me, until I can find someone else.

"Here you go." Bane handed over the sausage. The dog snapped it up, swallowed it in a gulp. Bane petted the silky head fondly. "And then you'll be mine. You and me and Grandfather. We'll all live together and we won't let anyone hurt Grandfather anymore ever. Will we, boy?"

Bane laid his cheek on the dog's head, cuddled the warm body.

"Will we?"

CHAPTER ◆ 9

WOMBE

LOW REALM, ARIANUS

◆

The great Kicksey-winsey had stopped.

Nobody on Drevlin knew what to do. Nothing like this had ever happened before in all the history of the Gegs.

As long as the Gegs could remember—and because they were dwarves, that was a long time indeed—the wondrous machine had been at work. It worked and it worked. Feverishly, serenely, frantically, obtusely—it worked. Even when parts of the Kickseywinsey broke down, it worked; other parts worked to repair those that didn't. No one was ever quite certain what work the Kickseywinsey did, but all knew, or at least suspected, that it worked well.

But now it had stopped.

The 'lectriczingers no longer zinged, they hummed—ominously, some thought. The whirly-wheels neither whirled nor wheeled. They held perfectly still, except for a slight quivering. The flashrafts halted, disrupting transportation throughout the Low Realm. The metal hands of the flashraft that grabbed the overhead cable and—with the help of the 'lectriczingers—pulled the flashraft along were stilled. Palms open, the metal hands reached futilely out to heaven.

The whistle-toots were silent, except for a sigh that escaped them now and then. The black arrows inside the glass boxes—arrows that must never be allowed to point to red—had sagged clear down to the bottom half of the boxes and now pointed at nothing.

When it first quit, there had been immediate consternation. Every Geg man, woman, and child—even those off duty, even those involved in the guerrilla action against the Welves—had left his or her post and run to stare at the great—now inactive—machine. There were some who thought that it would start again. The assembled Gegs had waited hopefully . . . and waited and waited. Scrift-change had come and gone. The marvelous machine had continued to do nothing.

And it was still doing it.

Which meant that the Gegs did nothing. Worse still, it appeared as if they were going to be forced to do nothing without heat and without light. Due to the constant, ferocious storms of the Maelstrom that sweep continually across their isles, the Gegs lived underground. The Kicksey-winsey had always provided heat from the bubble-boils and light from the glimmerglamps. The bubble-boils had stopped bubbling almost at once. The glamps had continued to burn for some time following the shutdown of the machine, but now their flames were fading. Lights all over Drevlin were flickering, going out.

And all around, a terrible silence.

The Gegs lived in a world of noise. The first sound a baby heard was the comforting whump, bang, slam of the Kickseywinsey at work. Now it was no longer working and it was silent. The Gegs were terrified of the silence.

"It's died!" was the wail that went up simultaneously from a thousand Geg throats, across the isle of Drevlin.

"No, it hasn't died," stated Limbeck Bolttightner, peering grimly at one portion of the Kicksey-winsey through his new spectacles. "It's been murdered."

"Murdered?" Jarre repeated in an awed whisper. "Who would do such a thing?" But she knew, before she asked.

Limbeck Bolttightner took off his spectacles and wiped them carefully on a clean white handkerchief, a habit he'd formed recently. Then he put his spectacles back on, stared at the machine by the light of a torch (made from a rolled-up sheaf of paper containing one of his speeches). He'd lit it by holding it to the sputtering flame of the fast-fading glimmerglamp.

"The elves."

"Oh, Limbeck, no," cried Jarre. "You can't be right. Why, if the Kicksey-winsey's stopped working, then it's stopped producing water, and the Welves—elves—need that water for their people. They'll die without it. They need the machine just as much as we do. Why would they shut it down?"

"Perhaps they've stockpiled water," said Limbeck coldly. "They're in control up there, you know. They have armies ringed round the Liftalofts. I see their plan. They're going to shut the machine down, starve us, freeze us out."

Limbeck shifted his gaze to Jarre, who immediately looked away.

"Jarre!" he snapped. "You're doing it again."

Jarre flushed, tried very hard to look at Limbeck, but she didn't like looking at him when he wore his spectacles. They were new, of an original design, and—so he claimed—improved his sight immeasurably. But, due to some peculiarity in the glass, the spectacles had the effect of making his eyes appear small and hard.

Just like his heart, Jarre thought to herself sadly, trying her best to look Limbeck in the face and failing miserably. Giving up, she fixed her gaze on the handkerchief that was a glaring patch of white poking out through the dark mass of long, tangled beard.

The torch burned low. Limbeck gestured to one of his bodyguards, who immediately grabbed another speech, rolled it up, and lit it before the last one could go out.

"I always said your speeches were inflammatory." Jarre attempted a small joke.

Limbeck frowned. "This is no time for levity. I don't like your attitude, Jarre. I begin to think that you are weakening, my dear. Losing your nerve—"

"You're right!" Jarre said suddenly, talking to the handkerchief, finding it easier to talk to the handkerchief than to its owner. "I *am* losing my nerve. I'm afraid—"

"I can't abide cowards," remarked Limbeck. "If you're so scared of the elves that you can no longer function in your position of WUPP Party Sectrary—"

"It's not the elves, Limbeck!" Jarre clasped her hands tightly together to keep them from yanking off his spectacles and stomping all over them. "It's us! I'm afraid of us! I'm afraid of you and . . . and you"—she pointed at one of the Geg bodyguards, who appeared highly flattered and proud of himself—"and you and you! And me. I'm afraid of myself! What have we become, Limbeck? What have we become?"

"I don't know what you mean, my dear." Limbeck's voice was hard and sharp as his new spectacles, which he took off once again and started to clean.

"We used to be peace-loving. Never in the history of the Gegs did we ever kill anyone—"

"Not 'Gegs'!" said Limbeck sternly.

Jarre ignored him. "Now we *live* for killing! Some of the young people, that's all they think about now. Killing Welves—"

"Elves, my dear," Limbeck corrected her. "I've told you. The term 'welves' is a slave word, taught to us by our 'masters.' And we're not Gegs, we're dwarves. The word 'Gegs' is derogatory, used to keep us in our place."

He put the spectacles back on, glared at her. The torchlight shining from beneath him (the dwarf holding the torch was unusually short) sent the shadows cast by the spectacles swooping upward, giving Limbeck a remarkably sinister appearance. Jarre couldn't help looking at him now, stared at him with a terrible fascination.

"Do you want to go back to being a slave, Jarre?" Limbeck asked her. "Should we give in and crawl to the elves and grovel at their feet and kiss their little skinny behinds and tell them we're sorry, we'll be good little Gegs from now on? Is that what you want?"

"No, of course not." Jarre sighed, wiped away a tear that was creeping down her cheek. "But we could talk to them. Negotiate. I think the Wel—elves—are as sick of this fighting as we are."

"You're damn right, they're sick of it," said Limbeck, with satisfaction. "They know they can't win."

"And neither can we! We can't overthrow the whole Tribus empire! We can't take to the skies and fly up to Aristagon and do battle."

"And they can't overthrow us either! We can live for generations down here in our tunnels and they'll never find us—"

"Generations!" Jarre shouted. "Is that what you want, Limbeck? War that will last generations! Children who will grow up never knowing anything but hiding and running and fear?"

"At least they'll be free," Limbeck said, hooking his spectacles back over his ears.

"No, they won't. So long as you're afraid, you're never free,"
Jarre answered softly.

Limbeck didn't respond. He was silent.

The silence was terrible. Jarre hated the silence. It was sad
and mournful and heavy and reminded her of something, some-
place, someone. Alfred. Alfred and the mausoleum. The secret
tunnels beneath the statue of the Manger, the rows of crystal
coffins with the bodies of the beautiful young dead people. It
had been silent down there, too, and Jarre had been afraid of the
silence.

Don't stop! she'd told Alfred.

Stop what? Alfred had been rather obtuse.

Talking! It's the quiet! I can't stand listening to it!

And Alfred had comforted her. *These are my friends. . . . Nobody here can harm you. Not anymore. Not that they would have anyway—at least, not* intentionally.

And then Alfred had said something that Jarre had remembered, had been saying to herself a lot lately.

But how much wrong have we done unintentionally, *meaning the
best.*

"Meaning the best," she repeated, talking to fill the dreadful
silence.

"You've changed, Jarre," Limbeck told her sternly.

"So have you," she countered.

And after that, there wasn't much to say, and they stood there,
in Limbeck's house, listening to the silence. The bodyguard shuffled his feet and tried to look as if he'd gone deaf and hadn't
heard a word.

The argument was taking place in Limbeck's living quarters—
his current dwelling in Wombe, not his old house in Het. It was a
very fine apartment by Geg standards, suited to be the dwelling
place of the High Froman,[1] which is what Limbeck now was.
Admittedly, the apartment was not as fine as the holding tank
where the previous High Froman, Darral Longshoreman, used to
live. But the holding tank had been too near the surface—and
consequently too near the elves, who had taken over the surface
of Drevlin.

---

[1] Ruler of the Gegs of Drevlin of the Low Realm of Arianus.

Limbeck, along with the rest of his people, had been forced to delve far beneath the surface, seek shelter down below. This had been no hardship for the dwarves. The great Kicksey-winsey was constantly delving and drilling and boring. Hardly a cycle passed without a new tunnel being discovered somewhere in Wombe or Het or Lek or Herot or any of the other Geg towns on Drevlin. Which was fortunate, because the Kicksey-winsey, for no apparent reason that anyone could see, would often bury, crush, fill up, or otherwise destroy previously existing tunnels. The dwarves[2] took this philosophically, burrowing out of collapsed tunnels and trudging off to seek new ones.

Of course, now that the Kicksey-winsey had stopped working, there would be no more collapses, no more new tunnels either. No more light, sound, heat. Jarre shivered, wished she hadn't thought about heat. The torch was starting to fizzle and die. Swiftly, Limbeck rolled up another speech.

Limbeck's living quarters were located far below the surface, one of the lowest points on Drevlin, directly beneath the large building known as the Factree. A series of steep, narrow stairs led down from a hallway to another hallway, which led to the hallway in front of Limbeck's apartment.

The steps, the hall, the apartment were not carved out of the coralite, as were most of the other tunnels made by the Kicksey-winsey. The steps were made of smooth stone, the hall had smooth walls, the floor was smooth, as was the ceiling. Limbeck's apartment even had a door, a real door, with writing on it. None of the dwarves could read the writing and accepted Limbeck's pronouncement—that BOILER ROOM meant HIGH FROMAN—without question.

Inside the apartment, things were a bit cramped, due to the presence of a large and extremely imposing-looking part of the Kicksey-winsey. The gigantic contraption, with its innumerable

---

[2] Haplo, in this and future accounts, uses the term "dwarves" as opposed to "Gegs," as he used in the account of his first trip to Arianus. Haplo doesn't give a reason for this change, but it is probable that he agreed with Limbeck that "Geg" was a demeaning term. Haplo includes a notation in this manuscript defining the word "Geg" as a short version of the elven word "gega'rega," a slang term for an insect.

pipes and tanks, no longer worked and had not worked for a long, long time, just as the Factree itself had not worked for as long as the dwarves could remember. The Kicksey-winsey had moved on, leaving this part of itself behind.

Jarre, not wanting to look at Limbeck in the spectacles, fixed her gaze on the contraption, and she sighed.

"The old Limbeck would have taken the thing apart by now," she said to herself, whispering, to fill up the silence. "He would have spent all his time hammering this and unscrewing that and all the time asking why, why, why. Why is it here? Why did it work? Why did it stop?

"You never ask 'why' anymore, do you, Limbeck?" Jarre said aloud.

"Why what?" Limbeck muttered, preoccupied.

Jarre sighed again. Limbeck either didn't hear her, or ignored her.

"We've got to go to the surface," he said. "We've got to find out how the elves managed to shut down the Kicksey-winsey—"

The sound of footsteps, shuffling and slow—those made by a group trying to descend a steep staircase in pitch darkness, punctuated by an occasional crash and muffled curse—interrupted him.

"What's that?" asked Jarre, alarmed.

"Elves!" said Limbeck, looking fierce.

He scowled at the bodyguard, who was also looking alarmed, but—at the sight of his leader's frown—altered his expression to look fierce, as well.

Shouts of "Froman! High Froman!" filtered through the closed door.

"Our people," said Limbeck, annoyed. "They want me to tell them what to do, I suppose."

"You *are* the High Froman," Jarre reminded him with some asperity.

"Yes, well, I'll tell them what to do," Limbeck snapped. "Fight. Fight and keep on fighting. The elves have made a mistake, shutting down the Kicksey-winsey. Some of our people weren't too keen on bloodshed before, but now they will be! The elves will rue the day—"

"Froman!" Several voices howled at once. "Where are you?"

"They can't see," said Jarre.

Taking the torch from Limbeck, she flung open the door, trotted out into the hallway.

"Lof?" she called, recognizing one of the dwarves. "What is it? What's wrong?"

Limbeck came to stand next to her. "Greetings, Fellow Warrior in the Battle to End Tyranny."

The dwarves, shaken from their perilous trip down the stairs in the darkness, looked startled. Lof glanced around nervously, searching for such a fearsome-sounding personage.

"He means you," said Jarre curtly.

"He does?" Lof was impressed, so impressed that he forgot momentarily why he'd come.

"You were calling me," said Limbeck. "What do you want? If it's about the Kicksey-winsey stopping work, I'm preparing a statement—"

"No, no! A ship, Yonor," answered several at once. "A ship!"

"A ship has landed Outside." Lof waved a hand vaguely upward. "Yonor," he added belatedly and somewhat sullenly. He had never liked Limbeck.

"An elf ship?" Limbeck asked eagerly. "Crashed? Is it still there? Can you see any elves moving about? Prisoners," he said in an aside to Jarre. "It's what we've been waiting for. We can interrogate them and then use them for hostages—"

"No," said Lof, after some thought.

"No what?" demanded Limbeck, irritated.

"No, Yonor."

"I mean, what do you mean, by saying no."

Lof considered. "No the ship hasn't crashed and no it's not a Welf ship and no I didn't see anyone."

"How do you know it's not a Wel—elf ship? Of course, it has to be an elf ship. What other kind of ship could it be?"

" 'Tisn't," stated Lof. "I should know a Welf ship when I see one. I was on one once." He glanced at Jarre, hoping she'd be impressed. Jarre was the main reason Lof didn't like Limbeck. "Leastwise, I was close to one, the time we attacked the ship at the Liftalofts. This ship doesn't have wings, for one thing. And it didn't fall out of the skies, like the Welf ships do. This one sort of floated down gently, like it meant it. And," he added, eyes still on

Jarre, having saved the best for last, "it's all covered with pictures."

"Pictures . . ." Jarre glanced at Limbeck uneasily. His eyes, behind his glasses, had a hard, bright gleam. "Are you sure, Lof? It's dark Outside and there must have been a storm—"

"'Course I'm sure." Lof wasn't to be denied his moment of glory. "I was standing in the Whuzel-wump, on watch, and the next thing I know this ship that looks like a . . . like a . . . well, like him." Lof pointed at his exalted leader. "Kind of round in the middle and sawed off at both ends."

Fortunately, Limbeck had removed his spectacles and was thoughtfully polishing them again, and so missed the comparison.

"Anyway," Lof continued, swelling with importance, noting that everyone, including the High Froman, was hanging on every word, "the ship sailed right smack out of the clouds and plunked itself down and sat there. And it's all covered with pictures, I could see 'em in the lightning."

"And the ship wasn't damaged?" Limbeck asked, replacing his spectacles.

"Not a bit of it. Not even when the hailstones the size of you, Yonor, came smash down onto it. Not even when the wind was tossing pieces of the Kicksey-winsey up into the air. The ship just sat there, snug as could be."

"Maybe it's dead," said Jarre, trying hard not to sound hopeful.

"I saw a light inside and someone moving around. It's not dead."

"It isn't dead," said Limbeck. "It's Haplo. It has to be. A ship with pictures, just like the ship I found on the Terrel Fen. He's come back!"

Jarre walked over to Lof, grabbed hold of his beard, sniffed at him and wrinkled her nose. "Like I thought. He's had his head in the ale barrel. Don't pay any attention to him, Limbeck."

Giving the astounded Lof a shove that sent him rolling backward into his fellows, Jarre took hold of Limbeck's arm and attempted to turn him around, drag him back inside his quarters.

Once his feet were planted, Limbeck, like all dwarves, was not easily moved. (Jarre had caught Lof off guard.) Limbeck shook Jarre loose, brushing her off his arm as if she were a bit of lint.

"Did any of the elves sight the ship, Lof?" Limbeck asked. "Make any attempt to contact it or see who was inside?"

Limbeck was forced to repeat his questions several times. The puzzled Lof, reestablished on his feet by his comrades, was staring in hurt bewilderment at Jarre.

"What'd I do?" he demanded.

"Limbeck, please—" Jarre begged, tugging again on Limbeck's arm.

"My dear, leave me be," said Limbeck, staring at her through the glittering spectacles. His tone was stern, even harsh.

Jarre slowly dropped her hands. "Haplo did this to you," she said softly. "Haplo did this to all of us."

"Yes, we owe him a great deal." Limbeck turned away from her. "Now, Lof. Were there any elves around? If so, Haplo might be in danger—"

"No Welves, Yonor." Lof shook his head. "I haven't seen a Welf since the machine stopped running. I— Ouch!"

Jarre had kicked him hard in the shins.

"What'd you go and do that for?" Lof roared.

Jarre made no response, marched on past him and the rest of the dwarves without a glance at any of them.

Returning to the BOILER ROOM, she whipped around, pointed a quivering finger at Limbeck. "He'll be the ruin of us! You'll see!"

She slammed the door shut.

The dwarves stood perfectly still, afraid to move. Jarre had taken the torch with her.

Limbeck frowned, shook his head, shrugged, and continued the sentence that had been so violently interrupted. "Haplo might be in danger. We don't want the elves to capture him."

"Anyone got a light?" ventured one of Lof's companions.

Limbeck ignored this question as unimportant. "We'll have to go rescue him."

"Go Outside?" The dwarves were aghast.

"*I've* been Outside," Limbeck reminded them tersely.

"Good. You go Outside and get him. We'll watch," said Lof.

"Not without light we won't," muttered another.

Limbeck glared angrily at his compatriots, but the glare was rather ineffective since no one could see it.

Lof, who had apparently been giving the matter thought, piped up. "Isn't this the Haplo who's a god—"

"There are no gods," Limbeck snapped.

"Well, then, Yonor"—Lof was not to be deterred—"the Haplo who battled that wizard you're always talking about?"

"Sinistrad. Yes, that's Haplo. Now you see—"

"Then he won't need rescuing!" Lof concluded in triumph. "He can rescue himself!"

"Anyone who can fight a wizard can fight elves," said another, speaking with the firm conviction of one who had never seen an elf up close. "They're not so tough."

Limbeck checked an impulse to strangle his Fellow Warriors in the Battle to End Tyranny. He took off his spectacles, polished them on the large white cloth. He was quite fond of his new spectacles. He could see through them with remarkable clarity. Unfortunately, the lenses were so thick that they slid down his nose, unless held on by strong wire bows wrapped tightly about his ears. The bows pinched him painfully, the strong lenses made his eyeballs ache, the nosepiece dug into his flesh, but he could see quite well.

At times like this, however, he wondered why he bothered. Somehow or other, the revolution, like a runaway flashraft, had veered off the track and been derailed. Limbeck had tried backing it up, had tried turning it around, but nothing had worked. Now, at last, he saw a glimmer of hope. He wasn't derailed, after all. Merely sitting on a siding. And what he'd first considered a terrible disaster—the demise of the Kicksey-winsey—might well work to get the revolution going again. He put his spectacles back on.

"The reason we don't have any light is because—"

"Jarre took the torch?" inserted Lof helpfully.

"No!" Limbeck sucked in a deep breath, clenched his hands to fists to keep his fingers from Lof's throat. "The elves shut down the Kicksey-winsey."

Silence. Then, "Are you sure?" Lof sounded dubious.

"What other explanation could there be? The elves have shut it down. They plan to starve us, freeze us out. Maybe use their magic to come on us in the dark and kill us all. Are we going to just sit here and take it or are we going to fight?"

"Fight!" shouted the dwarves, anger rumbling through the darkness like the storms that swept the land above.

"That's why we need Haplo. Are you with me?"

"Yes, Yonor!" cried the Fellow Warriors.

Their enthusiasm was considerably dampened when two of them started to march off and ended up nose-first against a wall.

"How can we fight what we can't see?" Lof grumbled.

"We *can* see," said Limbeck, undaunted. "Haplo told me that once long ago dwarves like us lived all their lives underground, in dark places. And so they learned to see in the dark. We've been dependent on light. Now that the light is gone, we'll have to do like our ancestors and learn to see and fight and live in darkness. Gegs couldn't manage. Gegs couldn't do it. But dwarves can. Now"—Limbeck drew a deep breath—"everyone forward. Follow me."

He advanced a step and another and another. He didn't run into anything. And he realized that he *could* see! Not very clearly; he couldn't have read one of his speeches, for example. But it seemed as if the walls had absorbed some of the light that had been shining on the dwarves for as long as they could remember and that light, out of gratitude, was giving some of itself back. Limbeck could see the walls and the floor and the ceiling shining faintly. He could see the silhouettes of his Fellow Warriors stand out black against the light. Moving on, he could see the break in the walls made by the staircase, could see the stairs running upward, a pattern of darkness and faint, eerie light.

Behind him, he heard the other dwarves gasp in awe, knew that he wasn't alone. They could see, too. His heart swelled with pride for his people.

"Things will change now," he said to himself, marching up the stairs, hearing the bold footsteps marching right behind. The revolution was back on track, and, if not exactly rushing along, at least it was rolling.

He could almost have thanked the elves.

Jarre wiped away a few tears, stood with her back planted against the door, waiting for Limbeck to knock, meekly request the torch. She'd give it to him, she decided, and give him a piece of her mind as well. Listening to the voices, she heard what sounded like Limbeck, launching into a speech. She sighed gustily, tapped her foot on the floor.

The torch had nearly burned out. Jarre grabbed another sheaf of speeches, set them ablaze. She heard "Fight!" in a loud roar, then a thud against the wall. Jarre laughed, but her laugh was bitter. She put her hand on the doorknob.

Then, inexplicably, she heard the sound of marching feet, felt the heavy vibrations of many pairs of thick dwarven boots clumping down the hall.

"Let them bang their fool heads on the wall a couple of times," she muttered. "They'll be back."

But there was only silence.

Jarre opened the door a crack, peeped out.

The hallway was empty.

"Limbeck?" Jarre cried, flinging the door wide. "Lof? Anyone?"

No response. Far away, she heard the sound of boots thumping determinedly up the stairs. Bits of Limbeck's speech, turned to glowing ash, drifted down from the torch, fell on the floor at her feet.

CHAPTER ♦ 10

WOMBE, DREVLIN

LOW REALM

♦

Haplo had often used the dog to listen in on the conversations of others, hearing their voices through the animal's ears. It never occurred to him, however, to listen to conversations anyone might be having *with* his dog. The animal had been ordered to keep an eye on the boy, alert Haplo to any misdeed—as in the case of the attempt to open the hatch. Beyond that, Haplo didn't care what Bane said or thought.

Though he had to admit that Bane's innocent-seeming question about obedience to the Lord of the Nexus had disturbed him. There had been a time—and Haplo knew it well—when he would have answered such a question immediately, without reservation, with a clear conscience.

Not now. Not anymore.

It was useless to tell himself that he'd never actually gone so far as to disobey his lord. True obedience is in the heart, as well as the mind. And in his heart, Haplo had rebelled. Evasions and half-truths were not as bad as outright refusals and lies, but they were not as good as open honesty, either. For a long time now, ever since Abarrach, Haplo had not been honest with his lord. The knowledge had once made him feel guilty, uncomfortable.

"But now," Haplo said to himself, staring out the window into the rapidly intensifying storm, "I begin to wonder. Has my lord been honest with me?"

The storm broke over the ship. The vessel rocked on its moorings in the violent wind, but otherwise held fast, secure. The con-

stantly flashing lightning lit the landscape brighter during the
height of the storm than the sun did during the calm. Haplo put
his questions about his lord out of his mind. That was not his
problem, at least not now. The Kicksey-winsey was. He walked
from window to window, studying what he could see of the great
machine.

Bane and the dog wandered onto the bridge. The dog smelled
strongly of sausage. Bane was obviously bored and out of sorts.

Haplo ignored them both. He was certain now that his memory was not playing him false. Something was definitely
wrong. . . .

"What are you looking at?" Bane demanded, yawning, plunk-
ing himself down on a bench. "There's nothing out there except—"

A jagged bolt of lightning struck the ground near the ship,
sending rock fragments exploding into the air. Heart-stopping
thunder crashed around them. The dog cowered down against the
floor. Haplo instinctively fell back from the window, though he
was in his place again an instant later, staring out intently.

Bane ducked his head, covered it with his arms. "I hate this
place!" he yelled. "I— What was that? Did you see that?"

The child jumped to his feet, pointing. "The rocks! The rocks
moved!"

"Yeah, I saw it," Haplo said, glad to have confirmation. He'd
been wondering if the lightning had affected his vision.

Another near strike. The dog began to whimper. Haplo and
Bane pressed their faces close to the glass, stared out into the
storm.

Several coralite boulders were behaving in a most extraordinary manner. They had detached themselves from the ground,
seemingly, and were trundling across it at a great rate, heading
straight—there could be no mistaking that now—for Haplo's ship.

"They're coming to us!" Bane said in awe.

"Dwarves," Haplo guessed, but why dwarves should risk
coming Outside, particularly Outside during a storm, was difficult to fathom.

The boulders were beginning to circle the ship, searching for a
way to enter. Haplo ran back to the hatch, Bane and the dog at his
heels. He hesitated a moment, reluctant to break the rune-magic's
protective seal. But if the mobile rocks were really dwarves, they

were in danger of being struck by lightning every second they were out in the storm.

Desperation drove them to this, Haplo decided. Something, he guessed, to do with the change in the Kicksey-winsey. He placed his hand on a sigil drawn in the center of the hatch, began tracing it backward. Immediately, its glowing blue fire started to fade and darken. Other sigla touching it began to darken as well. Haplo waited until those runes on the hatch had dwindled to almost nothing, then he threw the bolt and flung the door wide.

A blast of wind nearly knocked him down. Rain drenched him instantly.

"Get back!" he shouted, flinging an arm up to protect his face from slashing hailstones.

Bane had already scrambled backward, out of the way, nearly falling over the dog in the process. The two huddled a safe distance from the open door.

Haplo braced himself, peered out into the storm. "Hurry!" he cried, though he doubted if anyone could hear him above the boom of the thunder. He waved his arm to attract attention.

The blue glow that illuminated the inside of the vessel was still shining brightly, but Haplo could see it starting to grow dim. The circle of protection was broken. Before long, the sigla guarding the entire ship would weaken.

"Hurry!" he shouted again, this time remembering to speak dwarven.

The lead boulder, coming around the ship a second time, saw the blue light shining from the open hatchway and headed straight for it. The other two boulders, catching sight of their leader, scurried after. The lead boulder slammed against the side of the hull, went through a few moments' wild gyrating, then the rock was suddenly flung upward and over and the bespectacled face of Limbeck, panting and flushed, emerged.

The ship had been built to sail in water, not through the air, and the hatch, therefore, was located some distance off the ground. Haplo had added a rope ladder for his own convenience, and he tossed this out to Limbeck.

The dwarf, nearly flattened against the hull by the wind, began to clamber up, glancing down worriedly at two other boulders, which had crashed into the ship's side. One dwarf managed to extricate himself from his protective shell, but the other was apparently having difficulty. A piteous wail rose above the roar of the wind and the crashing thunder.

Limbeck, looking extremely irritated, checked an impatient exclamation and started back down, moving slowly and ponderously, to rescue his fellow warrior.

Haplo glanced around swiftly; the blue glow was growing dimmer every moment.

"Get up here!" he called to Limbeck. "I'll take care of it!"

Limbeck couldn't hear the words, but he caught the meaning. He began to climb again. Haplo jumped lightly to the ground. The sigla on his body flared blue and red, protecting him from the cutting hailstones and—he hoped fervently—from the lightning.

Half blinded by the rain in his face, he studied the contraption in which the dwarf was trapped. Another dwarf had his hands under the bottom of the thing and was obviously, from the puffing and grunting, attempting to raise it. Haplo added his strength —enhanced by his magic—to the dwarf's. He heaved the boulder up into the air with such force that the dwarf lost his grip and fell flat on his face in a puddle.

Haplo jerked the Geg to his feet, to keep him from drowning, and caught hold of the trapped dwarf, who was staring about dazedly, awestruck by his sudden deliverance. Haplo hustled the two up the ladder, cursing the slowness of the thick-legged dwarves. Fortunately, an extremely close lightning strike impelled all of them to faster action. Thunder rumbling around them, they scaled the ladder in record time, tumbled headfirst inside the ship.

Haplo brought up the rear, shut the hatch, and sealed it swiftly redrawing the sigla. The blue glow began to brighten. He breathed easier.

Bane, with more thoughtfulness than Haplo would have credited the boy with, arrived with blankets, which he distributed to the dripping dwarves. Out of breath from exertion and fright and amazement at seeing Haplo's skin shining blue, none was able to talk. They wrung water from their beards, sucked in deep breaths, and stared at the Patryn in considerable astonishment. Haplo wiped water from his face, shook his head when Bane offered a blanket to him.

"Limbeck, good to see you again," Haplo said, with a quiet friendly smile. The warmth of the sigla was rapidly causing the rain water on his body to evaporate.

"Haplo . . ." said Limbeck, somewhat dubiously. His spectacles were covered with water. Taking them off, he started to dry them on his white handkerchief, only to pull a sodden mass out of his pocket. He stared at the sopping wet handkerchief in dismay.

"Here," said Bane helpfully, offering his shirttail, which he tugged out of leather breeches.

Limbeck accepted the assistance, carefully cleaned his spectacles on Bane's shirt. Putting them on, he took a long look at the child, then at Haplo, then at the child again.

It was odd, but Haplo could have sworn that Limbeck was seeing them both for the first time.

"Haplo," said Limbeck gravely. He glanced again at Bane, hesitated, seemed uncertain how to address the boy who had been presented to the Geg as first a god, then a human prince, then the son of an extremely powerful human wizard.

"You remember Bane," said Haplo easily. "Crown prince and heir to the throne of the Volkaran Isles."

Limbeck nodded, an expression of extreme cunning and shrewdness on his face. The great machine outside may have been at a standstill, but wheels were turning inside the dwarf's head. His thoughts were so obvious on his face that Haplo could have spoken them aloud.

So this is the story, is it? and *How will this affect me?*

Haplo, accustomed to the vague, impractical, idealistic dwarf he'd left behind, was surprised at this change in Limbeck, wondered what it portended, didn't particularly like it. Any type of change, even change for the good, was disruptive. Haplo saw in these first few moments of their meeting that he was going to have to deal with a completely new and different Limbeck.

"Your Highness," said Limbeck, having apparently, by the crafty smile on his face, come to the conclusion that this situation would suit him fine.

"Limbeck is *High Froman*, Your Highness," said Haplo, hoping Bane would take the hint and treat Limbeck with the respect he deserved.

"High Froman Limbeck," said Bane, in a tone of cool politeness used by one royal ruler to an equal. "I am pleased to see you once again. And who are these other Gegs you have brought with you?"

"Not *Gegs*!" said Limbeck sharply, his face darkening. " 'Geg' is a slave word. An insult! Demeaning!" He slammed his clenched hand into his fist.

Taken aback by the dwarf's vehemence, Bane looked swiftly to Haplo for an explanation. Haplo himself was startled, but, remembering some of his conversations with Limbeck in the past, thought he understood what was going on. Indeed, Haplo might even be held partially accountable.

"You must understand, Your Highness, that Limbeck and his people are dwarves—a proper and ancient term for their race, just as you and your people are known as humans. The term 'Gegs'—"

"—was given to us by the elves," said Limbeck, tugging at his spectacles, which were starting to steam over due to the moisture rising from his beard. "Pardon me, Your Highness, but might I— Ah, thank you."

He wiped his spectacles again on Bane's proffered shirttail.

"I'm sorry I snapped at you, Your Highness," Limbeck said coolly, placing the spectacles around his ears and staring at Bane through them. "You, of course, had no way of knowing that this word has now become a deadly insult to us dwarves. Hasn't it?"

He looked to his fellows for support. But Lof was gaping at Haplo, whose blue glow was just beginning to fade. The other dwarf was staring nervously at the dog.

"Lof," Limbeck snapped. "Did you hear what I just said?"

Lof jumped, looked extremely guilty, nudged his companion.

Their leader's voice was stern. "I was saying that the term 'Geg' is an insult to us."

Both dwarves instantly attempted to appear mortally offended and deeply wounded, though it was quite obvious that they didn't have slightest idea what was going on.

Limbeck frowned, seemed to start to say something, then sighed and fell silent.

"May I talk to you? Alone?" he asked Haplo suddenly.

"Sure," said Haplo, shrugging.

Bane flushed, opened his mouth. Haplo forestalled him with a look.

Limbeck eyed the boy. "You're the one who came up with a diagram on the Kicksey-winsey. You figured out how it worked, didn't you, Your Highness?"

"Yes, I did," said Bane, with a becoming modesty.

Limbeck took off his spectacles, reached absently for the handkerchief. Pulling it out, he rediscovered the sodden mass. He shoved the spectacles back on his nose. "You come along, too, then," he said.

Turning to his compatriots, he issued orders. "You stay here, keep watch. Let me know when the storm starts to lift."

The two nodded solemnly, moved to stand by the window.

"It's the elves I'm worried about," Limbeck explained to Haplo. They were walking toward the front of the ship and Haplo's living quarters. "They'll spot your ship and come out to investigate. We'll need to be getting back to the tunnels before the storm ends."

"Elves?" Haplo repeated in astonishment. "Down here? On Drevlin?"

"Yes," said Limbeck. "That's one of the things I need to talk to you about." He settled himself on a stool in Haplo's cabin, a stool that had once belonged to the dwarves on Chelestra.

Haplo almost said something to that effect, checked himself. Limbeck wasn't worried about dwarves on other worlds. He was having trouble enough with this one, apparently.

"When I became High Froman, the first thing I ordered done was to shut the Liftalofts down. The elves came for their water shipment . . . and didn't get any. They decided to fight, figured they'd scare us with their bright steel and magic.

" 'Run, Gegs,' they yelled at us, 'run away before we step on you like the bugs you are!'

"They played right into my hands," Limbeck said, removing his spectacles and twirling them about by the ear bow. "Quite a few dwarves didn't agree with me that we should fight. Especially the clarks. They didn't want to upset things, wanted our lives to go on as before. But when they heard the elves call us 'bugs' and speak to us as if we truly had no more brains or feelings than insects, even the most peace-loving graybeard was ready to gnaw on elf ears.

"We surrounded the elves and their ship. There were hundreds, maybe a thousand dwarves there that day." Limbeck looked back with a dreamy, wistful expression, and Haplo saw, for the first time since he'd met the dwarf, a hint of the idealistic Limbeck of old acquaintance.

"The elves were mad, frustrated, but there was nothing they could do. We outnumbered them and they were forced to surrender to us. They offered us money.

"We didn't want their money[1]—what was that to us? And we didn't want any more of their castoffs and garbage."

"What did you want?" Haplo asked, curious.

"A city," said Limbeck with pride. His eyes shone. He appeared to have forgotten about the spectacles that dangled loosely from his hand. "A city up there, in the Mid Realms. Above the storm. A city where our children could feel sunshine on their faces and see trees and play Outside. And elven dragonships to take us there."

"Would your people like that? Wouldn't they miss . . . er . . . this?" Haplo waved vaguely at the lightning-blasted landscape, the shining skeletal arms of the Kicksey-winsey.

"We don't have much choice," said Limbeck. "There are far too many of us crowded down here. Our population is growing, but the tunnels are not. Once I began studying the matter, I found out that the Kicksey-winsey has been destroying more housing than it's been providing. And there are mountain ranges, up there in the Mid Realms. Our people could tunnel and build. In time they'd learn to be happy there."

He sighed and fell silent, staring at the floor that he couldn't see without his spectacles.

"What happened? What did the elves say?"

Limbeck stirred restlessly, glanced up. "They lied to us. I suppose it was my fault. You know how I was then—trusting, naive."

Limbeck put his spectacles back on, glared at Haplo as if daring him to argue. He didn't.

"The elves promised that they would agree to all our terms," Limbeck went on. "They would come back, they said, with ships ready to take our people to the Mid Realms. They came back, all right." His voice was bitter.

---

[1] Due to the severe water shortage in the Mid Realms, water is an extremely valuable commodity. Both human and elven monetary systems are based on water. In human lands, 1 barl is equivalent to 1 barrel of water and may be exchanged for such at the king's treasury or on any of the royal waterfarms scattered throughout the Volkaran and Uylandian isles.

"With an army."

"Yes. Fortunately, we were forewarned. Do you remember that elf who brought you from High Realm? Captain Bothar'el?"

Haplo nodded.

"He's joined up with the rebel elves; I forget the name of their leader. Anyway, Bothar'el came down here to warn us that the Tribus elves were setting sail in force to crush our resistance. I don't mind telling you, my friend, that I was devastated.

"What could *we* do"—Limbeck thumped himself on the chest —"against the might of the elven empire? We knew nothing about fighting. It was our numbers alone forced them to surrender the first time. We were just lucky they didn't attack us then or about half the dwarves would have run off.

"No dwarf living had ever raised a weapon in anger against a fellow being. It seemed we didn't have a chance, we must surrender. But Bothar'el said no, we must not surrender. He showed us the way.

"Of course"—Limbeck's eyes glittered behind the thick glass with sudden, hard cunning—"this Bothar'el and that rebel leader of his have their own reasons for wanting us to fight. I soon figured *that* out. Instead of concentrating all their forces on the rebel elves, the Tribus elves are forced to split their army, send half of it down here to fight us. The Tribus figured it would be a short war, then they'd be back to fighting their own people and maybe the humans, too. So, you see, my friend, it paid Bothar'el and his rebels to help us keep the Tribus army occupied.

"When the Tribus elves arrived in their huge dragonships, we were nowhere to be seen. They took over the Liftalofts—there was no help for that. Then they tried to come down into the tunnels, but they soon found out that was a mistake.

"Up until then, most of my people didn't care whether or not the elves took over. They had their jobs on the Kicksey-winsey and their families to care for. The clarks, in fact"—Limbeck sneered—"tried to make peace with the elves! The clarks sent out a delegation to meet them. The elves murdered them, every one. Then we got angry."

Haplo, having seen dwarves fight on other worlds, could well imagine what happened after that. Dwarves are fiercely bound to one another. *What happens to one dwarf happens to all* is the dwarven philosophy.

"Those elves who were left alive fled," Limbeck continued, with a dour smile. "I thought at first that they might leave Drevlin altogether, but I should have known better. They made a stand around the Liftalofts. Some of my people wanted to continue fighting, but Bothar'el warned that this was just what the elves wanted us to do, to come out in the open, where we'd be at the mercy of their ships' wizards and their magical weapons. So we let them have the Liftalofts and the water. They've taken over the Factree, too. But they don't come down into the tunnels anymore."

"I'll bet not," Haplo agreed.

"And we've made life difficult for them ever since," continued Limbeck. "We sabotaged so many of their dragonships that they don't dare land them on Drevlin. They have to transport their people down here through the Liftalofts. They're forced to keep a large army down here, to protect their water supply, and they have to replace their soldiers pretty often, though I think that has more to do with the Maelstrom than with us.

"The elves hate the storm, so Bothar'el told us. They hate being cooped up inside, and the constant noise of both the storm and the Kicksey-winsey drives some of them crazy. They have to keep sending in new men. They've brought in slaves—captured rebel elves, with their tongues cut out,[2] or any of our people they can catch—to operate their part of the Kicksey-winsey.

"We attack them in small groups, harry them, make nuisances of ourselves, force them to keep a lot of elves down here, instead of the small, skeleton force they planned. But now . . ."

Limbeck frowned, shook his head.

"But now you're at a standstill," Haplo filled in. "You can't retake the Liftalofts, the elves can't ferret you and your people out. Both sides are dependent on the Kicksey-winsey, so both must keep it going."

"True enough," said Limbeck, taking off his spectacles, rub-

---

[2] A magical song, sung by the rebel elves, has the effect of causing those elves who hear it to remember long-forgotten values once honored by all elves. Those who hear this song come to see the corruption of the Tribus empire and it causes them to renounce their allegiance, join the rebellion. Thus rebel elves, captured alive, have their tongues cut out or are otherwise silenced.

bing the red marks, where the nosepieces pinched. "That's how it's *been*."

"Been?" said Haplo, noting the emphasis on the word. "What's changed?"

"Everything," said Limbeck grimly. "The elves have shut off the Kicksey-winsey."

CHAPTER ♦ 11

WOMBE, DREVLIN

LOW REALM

♦

"Shut it off!" Bane blurted. "The whole machine!"

"It's been seven cycles now," said Limbeck. "Look out there. You can see it. Dark, silent. Nothing moves. Nothing works. We have no light, no heat." The dwarf heaved a frustrated sigh. "We never knew, until now, how much the Kicksey-winsey did for us. Our fault, of course, because no dwarf ever wondered why it did anything at all.

"Now that the pumps have quit, many of the tunnels far below the surface are filling up with water. My people had homes down there. They've been forced to leave or drown. What dwellings we had were already overcrowded.

"There were special caves in Herot where we grew our food. Glimmerglamps that shone like the sun gave us light for our crops. But when the Kicksey-winsey shut down, the glimmerglamps went out and now the light's gone. The crops are starting to wilt and will soon die.

"But aside from all of that," said Limbeck, rubbing his temples, "my people are terrified. They weren't afraid when the elves attacked them. But now they're scared silly. It's the quiet, you see." He gazed about, blinking his eyes. "They can't stand the quiet."

Of course, it's more than that, thought Haplo, and Limbeck knows it. For centuries, the lives of the dwarves had revolved around their great and beloved machine. They served it faithfully, devotedly, never bothering to ask how or why. Now the master's heart has stopped beating and the servants have no idea what to do with themselves.

"What do you mean, High Froman, when you say 'the elves shut it down'? How?" Bane wondered.

"I don't know!" Limbeck shrugged helplessly.

"But you're sure it was the elves?" Bane persisted.

"Pardon me, Your Highness, but what difference does it make?" the dwarf asked bitterly.

"It could make a big difference," said Bane. "If the elves shut down the Kicksey-winsey, it could be because they've discovered how to start it up."

Limbeck's expression darkened. He fumbled at his spectacles, ended up with one side dangling from one ear at a crazed angle. "That would mean they would control our lives! This is intolerable! We *must* fight now!"

Bane was watching Haplo from out of the corners of the blue eyes, a faint smile on the sweetly curved lips. The boy was pleased with himself, knew he was one up on the Patryn in whatever game they were playing.

"Keep calm," Haplo cautioned the dwarf. "Let's think about this a minute."

If what Bane said was right, and Haplo was forced to admit that the kid made sense, then the elves *had* very probably learned how to operate the Kicksey-winsey, something no one else had been able to do since the Sartan mysteriously abandoned their great machine centuries ago. And if the elves knew how to work it, then they knew how to control it, control its actions, control the alignment of the floating isles, control the water, control the world.

Whoever rules the machine, rules the water. And whoever rules the water, rules those who must drink it or perish.

Xar's words. Xar expected to come to Arianus a savior, bringing order to a world in chaos. Xar did not expect to arrive and find a world choked into submission by the iron fist of the Tribus elves, who would not easily loosen their grasp.

But I'm as bad as Limbeck, Haplo told himself. Getting worked up over what might be nothing. The first thing I have to do is discover the truth. It's possible the damn machine simply broke; although the Kicksey-winsey was, as he knew from Limbeck's past explanations, quite capable of repairing itself and had done so all these many years.

But there is one other possibility. And if I'm right and that's the real reason, then the elves must be as puzzled and worried over the shutdown of the Kicksey-winsey as the dwarves.

He turned to Limbeck. "I take it you move about Outside only during the times when it's storming, use the storm for cover?"

Limbeck nodded. He'd finally managed to adjust his spectacles. "And it won't last much longer," he said.

"We have to find out the truth about the machine. You don't want to commit your people to a bloody war that may be all for nothing. I need to get inside the Factree. Can you manage it?"

Bane nodded eagerly. "That's where the central control must be located."

Limbeck frowned. "But there's nothing in the Factree, now. There hasn't been for a long time."

"Not *in* the Factree. Underneath it," Haplo amended. "When the Sartan—the Mangers, as you call them—lived on Drevlin, they built a system of underground rooms and tunnels that were hidden away, protected by their magic, so that no one could ever find them. The controls for the Kicksey-winsey aren't anywhere on Drevlin's surface, are they?" He glanced at Bane.

The child shook his head. "It wouldn't make sense for the Sartan to put them out in the open. They would want to protect them, keep them safe. Of course, the controls could be located anywhere on Drevlin, but it's logical to assume that they'd be in the Factree, which is where the Kicksey-winsey was born—so to speak. What is it?"

Limbeck was looking extremely excited. "You're right! There *are* secret tunnels down there! Tunnels protected by magic! Jarre saw them. That . . . that other man who was with you. His Highness's servant. The one who kept falling over his own feet—"

"Alfred," said Haplo with a quiet smile.

"Yes, Alfred! He took Jarre down there! But"—Limbeck looked gloomy again—"she said all she saw were dead people."

So that's where I was! Haplo said to himself.[1] And he didn't particularly relish the thought of going back.

"There's more down there than that," he said, hoping he spoke the truth. "You see, I—"

"Froman! High Froman!" Shouts, accompanied by a bark, came from the front of the ship. "The storm's ending!"

"We have to go." Limbeck stood up. "Do you want to come with us? It won't be safe here on this ship, once the elves see it. Though they'll probably destroy it. Either that, or their wizards will try to take it—"

"Don't worry," Haplo said, grinning. "I have magical powers myself, remember? No one will get near this ship if I don't want them to. We'll come with you. I need to talk to Jarre."

Haplo sent Bane off to gather up his bundle of clothes and, most important, the diagram the child had made of the Kicksey-winsey. Haplo buckled on a rune-inscribed sword, thrust a similarly inscribed dagger inside the top of his boot.

He looked down at his hands, the blue tattoos vivid on his skin. Last time he'd come to Arianus, he had concealed the tattoos —and the fact that he was a Patryn—beneath bandages. No need to conceal his true identity now. The time for that was past.

He joined Limbeck and the other dwarves near the ship's hatch.

The storm still raged as fiercely as ever, as far as Haplo could determine, though he thought it barely possible that the hurricane had dwindled to a torrential downpour. Giant hailstones continued pounding the ship's hull and the lightning blasted three holes in the coralite during the brief time Haplo stood and watched. He could use his magic to instantly transport himself and Bane, but in order for the magic to work, he had to be able to visualize exactly where it was he wanted to go, and the only place on Drevlin he could clearly remember was the Factree.

He had a sudden vision of appearing in a circle of blue flame smack in the middle of the elven army.

He studied, as best he could through the rain-smeared win-

---

[1] During a journey through Death's Gate, on their way to Abarrach, Alfred and Haplo fell into each other's consciousness, lived each other's most vivid and painful memory. *Fire Sea*, vol. 3 of *The Death Gate Cycle*.

dow, the contraptions the dwarves used to travel through the storm.

"What are those things?"

"Carts from the Kicksey-winsey," said Limbeck. He took off his spectacles, smiled a vague smile reminiscent of the old Limbeck. "My idea. You probably don't remember, but we carried you in one when you were hurt, the time the dig claws brought us up. Now we've turned the carts upside down and put the wheels on the top instead of the bottom and covered them over with coralite. You'll fit inside one, Haplo," he added reassuringly, "though it will be tight and not too comfortable. I'll go with Lof. You can have mine—"

"I wasn't worried about the fit," interrupted Haplo grimly. "I was thinking about the lightning." His magic would protect him, but not Bane or the dwarves. "One bolt hits that metal and—"

"Oh, no need to worry about that," said Limbeck, his chest swelling with pride. He gestured with the spectacles. "Note the metal rods on top of each cart. If lightning strikes, the rods carry the charge down the side of the cart, through the wheels and into the ground. I call them ' 'lectricity rods.' "

"They work?"

"Well," Limbeck conceded reluctantly, "they've never really been tested. But the theory is sound. Someday," he added, hopeful, "we'll get struck and then I'll see."

The other dwarves looked extremely alarmed at this prospect. Apparently they didn't share Limbeck's enthusiasm for science. Neither did Haplo. He would take Bane along in his cart, use his magic to cast a shell over the two of them that would keep them both from harm.

Haplo opened the hatch. Rain blew inside. The wind howled, thunder set the ground vibrating beneath their feet. Bane, now able to view the full fury of the storm, was pale and wide-eyed. Limbeck and the dwarves dashed out. Bane hung back in the open hatchway.

"I'm not afraid," he said, though his lips quivered. "My father could make the lightning stop."

"Yeah, well, Daddy's not here. And I'm not sure even Sinistrad would have had much control over this storm."

Haplo caught hold of the boy around the waist, lifted him bodily, and ran to the first cart, the dog bounding along behind.

Limbeck and his fellow warriors had already reached theirs. The dwarves lifted the contraptions, scooted underneath them with remarkable speed. The carts dropped down on top of them, hiding the dwarves from view, protecting them from the fierce storm.

The sigla on Haplo's skin glowed bright blue, formed a protective shield around him that kept the rain and hail from hitting him. Wherever the Patryn's arm or other part of his body contacted Bane, the boy, too, was protected, but Haplo couldn't hold him close and still get him inside the cart.

Haplo fumbled at the contraption in the darkness. The sides of the cart were slippery, he couldn't get his fingers beneath the metal edge. Lightning lit the sky, a hailstone struck Bane on the cheek. The boy clapped his hand over the bleeding cut, but didn't cry out. The dog barked back at the thunder, as if it were a living threat the animal could chase away.

Finally, Haplo managed to raise the cart high enough to thrust Bane inside. The dog slithered in with the boy.

"Stay put!" Haplo ordered, and ran back to his ship.

The dwarves were already trundling over the ground, heading toward safety. Haplo marked the direction they were taking, turned back to his business. Swiftly, he traced a sigil on the ship's outer hull. It flared blue, other sigla caught the magical fire. Blue and red light spread in patterns over the ship's hull. Haplo stood in the driving rain, watched carefully to make certain the magic covered the ship completely. A soft blue light gleamed from it. Nodding in satisfaction, certain now that no one—elf, human, or dwarf—could harm his vessel, Haplo turned and ran back to the cart.

Lifting it up, he crawled inside. Bane was huddled in the center, his arms around the dog.

"Go on, get out," Haplo told the animal, who vanished.

Bane looked around in astonishment, forgot his fear. "What happened to the dog?" he cried shrilly.

"Shut up," Haplo grunted. Hunched almost double, he planted his back against the top of the cart. "Get underneath me," he told Bane.

The child wriggled his way awkwardly under Haplo's outspread arms.

"When I crawl, you crawl."

Moving clumsily, with many halts and starts, falling over each other, they lumbered along. A hole cut into the side of the cart allowed Haplo to see where they were going, and it was a lot farther off than he'd imagined. The coralite, where it was hard, was slick from the water; in other places they sank elbow deep in mud, floundered through puddles.

Rain beat down, hailstones clattered on top of the metal cart, making a deafening racket. Outside, he could hear the dog bark back at the thunder.

"'Lectricity rods," muttered Haplo.

CHAPTER ◆ 12

WOMBE, DREVLIN

LOW REALM

◆

"I'M NOT GOING TO TELL YOU ANYTHING ABOUT THE STATUE!" STATED JARRE. "It will only cause more trouble, I'm sure of it!"

Limbeck flushed in anger, glowered at her through his spectacles. He opened his mouth to deliver a pronouncement on Jarre, a pronouncement that would have not only ended their relationship but got his spectacles smashed in the bargain. Haplo trod discreetly on the dwarf's foot. Limbeck understood, subsided into a smoldering silence.

They were back in the BOILER ROOM, Limbeck's apartment, now lit by what Jarre called a "glampern." Tired of burning Limbeck's speeches, and equally tired of hearing that she could see in the dark, if only she put her mind to it, she had gone off, after Limbeck's departure, and appropriated the glampern from a fellow warrior, stating it was for the High Froman's use. The fellow warrior, as it turned out, hadn't much use for the High Froman, but Jarre was stoutly built and could add muscle to her political clout.

She walked off with the glampern—a castoff of the elves, left over from the days when they paid for water with their refuse. The glampern, hanging on a hook, served well enough, once one got used to the smoky flame, the smell, and the crack down the side that allowed some sort of obviously highly flammable substance to drip out onto the floor.

Jarre cast them all a defiant glance. Her face, in the glampern light, hardened into stubborn lines. Haplo guessed that Jarre's anger was a mask for affectionate concern, concern for her people and for Limbeck. And maybe not in that order.

Bane, catching Haplo's attention, raised an eyebrow.

I can handle her, the child offered. *If you'll give me permission.*

Haplo shrugged in answer. It couldn't hurt. Besides being unusually intuitive, Bane was clairvoyant. He could sometimes see the innermost thoughts of others . . . other mensch, that is. He couldn't worm his way inside Haplo.

Bane glided to Jarre, took hold of her hands. "I can see the crystal crypts, Jarre. I can see them and I don't blame you for being frightened of going back there. It truly is very sad. But dear, dear Jarre, you *must* tell us how to get into the tunnels. Don't you want to find out if the elves have shut down the Kicksey-winsey?" he persisted in wheedling tones.

"And what will you do if they have?" Jarre demanded, snatching her hands away. "And how do you know what I've seen? You're just making it all up. Or else Limbeck told you."

"No, I'm not," Bane sniveled, his feelings hurt.

"See what you've done now?" Limbeck asked, putting a comforting arm around the boy.

Jarre flushed in shame.

"I'm sorry," she mumbled, twisting the skirt of her dress around her stubby fingers, "I didn't mean to yell at you. But what will you do?" Raising her head, she stared at Haplo, her eyes shimmered with tears. "We can't fight the elves! So many would die! You know that. You know what would happen. We should just surrender, tell them we were wrong, it was all a mistake! Then maybe they'll go away and leave us alone and everything will be like it was before!"

She buried her face in her hands. The dog crept over, offered silent sympathy.

Limbeck swelled up until Haplo thought the dwarf might explode. Giving him a cautionary sign with an upraised finger, Haplo spoke quietly, firmly.

"It's too late for that, Jarre. Nothing can ever be like it was. The elves won't go away. Now that they have control of the water supply on Arianus, they won't give it up. And sooner or later they'll get tired of being harassed by your guerrilla tactics. They'll send down a large army and either enslave your people or wipe them out. It's too late, Jarre. You've gone too far."

"I know." Jarre sighed, wiped her eyes with the corner of her skirt. "But it's obvious to me that the elves have taken over the machine. I don't know what you think you can do," she added in dull, hopeless tones.

"I can't explain now," said Haplo, "but there's a chance the elves may *not* have shut down the Kicksey-winsey. They may be more worried about this than you are. And if that's true, and if His Highness can start it up again, then you can tell the elves to go take a flying leap into the Maelstrom."

"You mean, we'll have the Liftalofts back under our control?" Jarre asked dubiously.

"Not only the Liftalofts," said Bane, smiling through his tears, "but everything! All of Arianus! All of it, all the people—elves and humans—under your rule."

Jarre looked more alarmed than pleased at this prospect, and even Limbeck appeared somewhat taken aback.

"We don't really want them under our rule," he began, then paused, considering. "Or do we?"

"Of course we don't," Jarre said briskly. "What would we do with a bunch of humans and elves on our hands? Always fighting among each other, never satisfied."

"But, my dear . . ." Limbeck seemed inclined to argue.

"Excuse me"—Haplo cut in swiftly—"but we're a long way from that point yet, so let's not worry about it."

Not to mention the fact, the Patryn added silently, that Bane was lying through his small, pearl-white teeth. It would be the Lord of the Nexus who ruled Arianus. Of course, his lord *should* rule Arianus, that wasn't the point. Haplo disliked deceiving the dwarves, urging them to take risks by giving them false hopes, making false promises.

"There's another point you haven't considered. If the elves didn't shut down the Kicksey-winsey, they probably think that you dwarves did. Which means that they're probably more worried about you than you are about them. After all, with the machine not working, they haven't got water for their people."

"Then they might be preparing to attack us right now!" Limbeck glowered.

Haplo nodded.

"You truly think the elves may not have taken control of it?" Jarre was wavering.

"We'll never know until we see for ourselves."

"The truth, my dear," said Limbeck in a softened tone. "It's what we believe in."

"What we *used* to believe in," murmured Jarre. "Very well." She sighed. "I'll tell you what I can about the statue of the Manger. But I'm afraid I don't know much. It was all so confused, what with the fighting and the coppers and—"

"Just tell us about the statue," suggested Haplo. "You and the other man who was with us, the clumsy one, Alfred. You went inside the statue and down into the tunnels below."

"Yes," said Jarre, subdued. "And it was sad. So sad. All the beautiful people lying dead. And Alfred so sad. I don't like to think about it."

The dog, hearing Alfred's name, wagged its tail and whined. Haplo petted it, counseling silence. The dog sighed and flopped down, nose on paws.

"Don't think about it," Haplo said. "Tell us about the statue. Start from the beginning."

"Well"—Jarre's brow furrowed in thought, she chewed on her side whiskers—"the fight was going on. I was looking around for Limbeck and I saw him standing next to the statue. The High Froman and the coppers were trying to drag him off. I ran over to help him, but by the time I got there, he was gone.

"I looked around and I saw that the statue had opened up!" Jarre spread her hands wide.

"What part of the statue?" Bane asked. "The body, the whole thing?"

"No, only the bottom part, the base, under the Manger's feet. That's where I saw *his* feet—"

"Alfred's feet." Haplo smiled. "They'd be hard to miss."

Jarre nodded vigorously. "I saw feet sticking up out of a hole underneath the statue. Stairs ran down into the hole and Alfred was lying on his back on the stairs with his feet in the air. At that moment, I saw more coppers coming and I knew that I better hide or they'd find me. I popped into the hole and then I was afraid they'd see Alfred's feet. So I dragged Alfred down the stairs with me.

"Then a strange thing happened." Jarre shook her head. "When I pulled Alfred down into the hole, the statue started to slide shut. I was so frightened I couldn't do anything. It was all dark, down there, and quiet." Jarre shivered, glanced around. "Horribly quiet. Like it is now. I . . . I began to scream."

"What happened then?"

"Alfred woke up. He'd fainted, I think—"

"Yes, he has a habit of that," Haplo said grimly.

"Anyway, I was terrified and I asked him if he could open the statue. He said he couldn't. I said he must be able to, he'd opened it once, hadn't he? He said no, he hadn't meant to. He'd fainted and fallen onto the statue and could only suppose that it had opened by accident."

"Liar," muttered Haplo. "He knew how to open it. You didn't see him do it?"

Jarre shook her head.

"You didn't see him anywhere near it? During the fight, for example?"

"I couldn't have. I'd gone over to where our people were hiding in the tunnels and told them to come up and attack. By the time I came back, the fighting had started and I couldn't see anything."

"But I saw him!" said Limbeck suddenly. "I remember now! That other man, the assassin—"

"Hugh the Hand?"

"Yes. I was standing with Alfred. Hugh ran toward us, crying out that the coppers were coming. Alfred looked sick and Hugh shouted at him not to faint but Alfred did anyway. He fell right across the statue's feet!"

"And it opened!" Bane shouted excitedly.

"No." Limbeck scratched his head. "No, I don't think so. I'm afraid things get rather muddled after that. But I remember seeing him lying there and wondering if he was hurt. I think I would have noticed if the statue had been open."

Not likely, Haplo thought, considering the dwarf's poor eyesight.

The Patryn attempted to put himself into Alfred's overlarge shoes, tried to re-create in his mind what might have happened. The Sartan, fearful as always of using his magical power and revealing himself, is caught up in the midst of battle. He faints— his normal reaction to violent situations—falls over the statue's feet. When he wakes, battle swirls around him. He must escape.

He opens the statue, intending to enter and vanish, but some-

thing else frightens him and he ends up fainting and falls inside
. . . either that or he was hit on the head. The statue stays open,
and Jarre stumbles across it.

Yes, that's probably what occurred, reasoned Haplo, for all the
good it does us. Except for the fact that Alfred was groggy and
not thinking clearly when he opened the statue. A good sign. The
device must not be too difficult to open. If it is guarded by Sartan
magic, the rune-structure must not be too complex. The tricky
part will be finding it . . . and evading the elves long enough to
open it.

Haplo gradually became aware that everyone had stopped
talking, was staring at him expectantly. He wondered what he'd
missed.

"What?" he asked.

"What happens once we get down into the tunnels?" asked
Jarre practically.

"We look for the controls for the Kicksey-winsey," answered
Haplo.

Jarre shook her head. "I don't remember seeing anything that
looked like it belonged to the Kicksey-winsey." Her voice softened. "I just remember all the beautiful people . . . dead."

"Yeah, well, the controls have to be down there somewhere,"
said Haplo firmly, wondering just who he was trying to convince.
"His Highness will find them. And once we're down there, we'll
be safe enough. You said yourself the statue closed behind you.
What we need is some sort of diversion, to get the elves out of the
Factree long enough for us to get in. Can your people supply it?"

"One of the elven dragonships is anchored at the Liftalofts,"
Limbeck suggested. "Perhaps we could attack it . . ."

"No attacking!"

Jarre and Limbeck launched into a discussion that almost instantly turned into an argument. Haplo sat back, let them thrash it
out, glad to have changed the subject. He didn't care what the
dwarves did, as long as they did it. The dog, lying on its side, was
either dreaming of chasing or of being chased. Its feet twitched, its
flanks heaved.

Bane, watching the sleeping dog, stifled a yawn, tried to look
as though he wasn't in the least bit sleepy himself. He dozed off
and nearly fell over on his nose. Haplo shook him.

"Go to bed, Your Highness. We won't do anything until morning."

Bane nodded, too tired to argue. Staggering to his feet, bleary-eyed, he stumbled over to Limbeck's bed, fell on it, and was almost instantly asleep.

Haplo, watching him idly, felt a sharp, strange pain in his heart. Asleep, his eyelids closed over the glitter of adult cunning and guile, Bane looked like any other ten-year-old child. His sleep was deep and untroubled. It was for others, older and wiser, to look after his well-being.

"So might a child of mine be sleeping, right this moment," said Haplo to himself, the pain almost more than he could bear. "Sleeping where? In some Squatters' hut, left behind in safety—as safe as one can be in the Labyrinth—by his mother before she moved on. Or is he with his mother, provided she's still alive. Provided the child's still alive.

"He's alive. I know he is. Just as I knew he'd been born. I've always known. I knew when she left me. And I didn't do anything. I didn't do a damn thing, except try to get myself killed so I wouldn't have to think about it anymore.

"But I'll go back. I'll come for you, kid. The old man's right, maybe. It isn't time yet. And I can't do it alone." He reached out, stroked back one of Bane's wet curls. "Just hold on a little longer. Just a little longer . . ."

Bane huddled up in a ball on the bed. It was cold down in the tunnels, without the heat from the Kicksey-winsey. Haplo rose to his feet. Picking up Limbeck's blanket, the Patryn placed it over the boy's thin shoulders, tucked it around him.

Returning to his chair, listening to Limbeck and Jarre arguing, Haplo drew his sword from its scabbard and began to retrace the sigla inscribed on the hilt. He needed something else to think about.

And something occurred to him as he laid the sword carefully on the table before him.

I'm not in Arianus because my lord sent me. I'm not here because I want to conquer the world.

I'm here to make the world safe for that child. My child, trapped in the Labyrinth.

But that's why Xar's doing this, Haplo realized. He's doing

this for his children. All his children, trapped in the Labyrinth.

Comforted, feeling at last reconciled with himself and his
lord, Haplo spoke the runes, watched the sigla on his blade catch
fire, outshining the dwarf's glampern.

CHAPTER 13

WOMBE, DREVLIN

LOW REALM

♦

"ACTUALLY, THIS NEED FOR A DIVERSION COULDN'T COME AT A BETTER TIME," stated Limbeck, peering at Haplo through the spectacles. "I've developed a new weapon and I've been wanting to test it."

"Humpf!" Jarre sniffed. "Weapons," she muttered.

Limbeck ignored her. The argument over plans for the diversion had been long and bitter and occasionally dangerous to bystanders, Haplo having narrowly missed being struck by a thrown soup pan. The dog had wisely retreated under the bed. Bane slept through the entire discussion.

And Haplo noted that, though Jarre had no compunction about hurling kitchen utensils, she was careful to keep them clear of the High Froman and august leader of WUPP. She seemed nervous and uneasy around Limbeck, watched him out of the corner of her eye with an odd mixture of frustration and anxiety.

In the early days of the revolution, she had been accustomed to smacking Limbeck on both cheeks or tugging playfully, if painfully, at his beard to bring him back to reality. Not any longer. Now she appeared reluctant to come near him. Haplo saw her hands twitch, more than once, during the argument, and guessed that she would have liked nothing better than to give her leader's side whiskers a good tweak. But her hands always ended up twisting her own skirts instead, or mangling the forks.

"I designed this weapon myself," said Limbeck proudly. Rummaging under a pile of speeches, he produced it, held it to the flickering light of the glampern. "I call it a flinger."

Haplo would have called it a toy. The humans in the Mid Realms would have called it a slingshot. The Patryn said nothing disparaging about it, however, but duly admired it and asked how it worked.

Limbeck demonstrated. "When the Kicksey-winsey made new parts for itself, it used to turn out quite a lot of these things." He held up a particularly wicked-looking, sharp chunk of metal. "We used to throw them into the helter-melter, but it occurred to me that one of these, flung at the wings of the elves' dragonships, would tear a hole in the skin. I learned from my own experience that an object cannot travel through the air with holes in its wings.[1] Fill it full of enough holes, and it seems to me logical that the dragonships will not be able to fly."

Haplo had to admit that it seemed logical to him, too. He regarded the weapon with more respect. "This would do a fair bit of damage to someone's skin," he said, picking up the razor-sharp metal chunk gingerly. "Elf skin included."

"Yes, I thought of that, too," remarked Limbeck with satisfaction.

An ominous clanging came from behind him. Jarre was banging an iron skillet in a threatening manner against the cold stove. Limbeck turned around, stared at her through his spectacles. Jarre dropped the skillet on the floor with a bang that caused the dog to scoot as far back beneath the bed as possible. Head high, Jarre stalked toward the door.

"Where are you going?" Limbeck demanded.

"For a walk," she said haughtily.

"You'll need the glampern," he advised.

"No, I won't," she mumbled, one hand wiping her eyes and nose.

"We need you to come with us, Jarre," Haplo said. "You're the only one who's been down in the tunnels."

"I can't help you," she said, her voice choked. She kept her back turned. "I didn't do anything. I don't know how we got

---

[1] Undoubtedly a reference to a previous adventure, when Limbeck was made to "walk the Steps of Terrel Fen"—a form of execution. Feathered wings are strapped to the arms of the accused and he is pushed off the floating isle of Drevlin into the Maelstrom. *Dragon Wing*, vol. 1 of *The Death Gate Cycle*.

down there or how we got back out. I just went where that man Alfred told me to go."

"This is important, Jarre," Haplo said quietly. "It could mean peace. An end to the fighting."

She glanced at him over one shoulder, through a mass of hair and side whiskers. Then, tight-lipped, she said, "I'll be back," and walked out, slamming the door shut behind her.

"I'm sorry for that, Haplo," said Limbeck, cheeks flushed in anger. "I don't understand her anymore. In the early days of the revolution, she was the most militant among us." He took off his spectacles, rubbed his eyes. His voice softened. "She was the one who attacked the Kicksey-winsey! Got *me* arrested and nearly killed." He smiled wistfully, gazing back into the past with his fuzzy vision. "She was the one who wanted change. Now, when change is here, she . . . she throws soup pans!"

The concerns of the dwarves are not mine, Haplo reminded himself. Stay out of it. I need them to take me to the machine, that's all.

"I don't think she likes the killing," he said, hoping to mollify Limbeck, end the disruption.

"I don't like the killing," Limbeck snapped. He put his spectacles back on. "But it's them or us. We didn't start it. They did."

True enough, Haplo thought, and put the matter aside. After all, what did he care? When Xar came, the chaos, the killing would end. Peace would come to Arianus. Limbeck continued planning the diversion. The dog, after making certain Jarre was gone, came out from under the bed.

Haplo snatched a few hours' sleep himself, woke to find a contingent of dwarves milling about in the hallway outside the BOILER ROOM. Each dwarf was armed with his or her own flinger and metal chunks, carried in strong canvas bags. Haplo washed his hands and face (which reeked of glampern oil), watched, and listened. Most of the dwarves had become quite adept at using the flingers, to judge from what he saw of their crude target practice taking place in the corridor.

Of course, it was one thing to shoot at a drawing of an elf scrawled on the wall, quite another to shoot at a live elf who is shooting back at you.

"We don't want *anyone* to get hurt," Jarre told the dwarves. She had returned and had, with her characteristic briskness, taken control. "So keep under cover, stay near the doors and entrances to the Liftalofts, and be ready to run if the elves come after you. Our objective is to distract them, keep them busy."

"Shooting holes in their dragonship should do that!" Lof said grinning.

"Shooting holes in them would do it better," added Limbeck, and there was a general cheer.

"Yes, and then they'll shoot holes in you and where will you be?" Jarre said crossly, casting Limbeck a bitter glance.

The dwarf, not at all perturbed, nodded and smiled, his smile seeming grim and cold, topped by the glittering spectacles.

"Remember this, Fellow Warriors," he said, "if we manage to bring the ship down, we will have scored a major victory. The elves will no longer be able to moor their dragonships on Drevlin; they will be reluctant to even fly near it. Which means that they may think twice about keeping troops stationed down here. This could be our first step toward driving them off."

The dwarves cheered again.

Haplo left to ascertain that his own ship was safe.

He returned, satisfied. The runes he'd activated not only protected his ship, but also created a certain amount of camouflage, causing it to blend in with objects and shadows around it. Haplo could not make his ship invisible—that was not within the spectrum of probable possibilities and, as such, could not be contrived by his magic. But he could make it extremely difficult to see, and it was. An elf would have to literally walk into it to know it was there, and that in itself was not possible, since the sigla created an energy field around the ship that would repel all attempts to get near it.

He returned to find the dwarves marching off to attack the Liftalofts and the elven ship that was moored there, floating in the air, attached to the arms by cables. Haplo, Bane, Limbeck, Jarre and the dog headed off in the opposite direction, to the tunnels that ran beneath the Factree.

Haplo had traveled this route once before, the last time they'd sneaked into the Factree. He could not have remembered the way, however, and was glad to have a guide. Time and wonders witnessed on other worlds had blurred the wonder of the Kicksey-winsey. His awe returned at the sight of it, however; awe tinged now with a sense of unease and disquiet, as if he were in the presence of a corpse. He remembered the great machine pounding with life: 'lectric zingers zapping, whirly-wheels whirling, iron hands smashing and molding, dig claws digging. All still now. All silent.

The tunnels led him past the machine, beneath it, over it, around it, through it. And the thought came to him suddenly that he'd been wrong. The Kicksey-winsey wasn't a corpse. The machine was not dead.

"It's waiting," said Bane.

"Yes," said Haplo. "I think you're right."

The boy edged nearer, looking at him through narrowed eyes. "Tell me what you know about the Kicksey-winsey."

"I don't know anything."

"But you said there was another explanation—"

"I said there could be. That's all." He shrugged. "Call it a guess, a hunch."

"You won't tell me."

"We'll see if my guess is right when we get there, Your Highness."

"Grandfather put me in charge of the machine!" Bane reminded him, scowling. "You're only here to protect me."

"And I intend to do just that, Your Highness," Haplo replied.

Bane darted him a sullen, sidelong glance, but said nothing. He knew it would be useless to argue. Eventually, however, the boy either forgot his grievance or decided it wasn't suited to his dignity to be caught sulking. Leaving Haplo's side, Bane ran up to walk with Limbeck. Haplo sent the dog along, to keep an ear on both of them.

As it was, the dog heard nothing interesting. In fact, it heard very little at all. The sight of the Kicksey-winsey motionless and quiet had a depressing effect on all of them. Limbeck stared at it through his spectacles, his face grim and hard. Jarre regarded the machine she had once attacked with fond sadness. Coming to a part she had worked on, she would sidle close and give it a comforting pat, as though it were a sick child.

They passed numerous dwarves standing about in enforced idleness, looking helpless and frightened and forlorn. Most had been coming to their work every day since the machine quit running, though there was now no work to do.

At first they'd been confident that this was all a mistake, a fluke, a slipped cog of monumental proportions. The dwarves sat or stood about in the darkness, lit by whatever source of light they could manufacture, and watched the Kicksey-winsey expectantly, waiting for it to roar to life again. When their scrift ended, the dwarves went home and another scrift took their place. But by now, hope was beginning to dim.

"Go home," Limbeck kept telling them as they walked along. "Go to your homes and wait. You're only wasting light."

Some of the dwarves left. Some of the dwarves stayed. Some left, then came back. Others stayed, then left.

"We can't go on like this," said Limbeck.

"Yes, you're right," said Jarre, for once agreeing with him. "Something terrible will happen."

"A judgment!" called out a deep and ragged voice from the too-quiet darkness. "A judgment, that's what it is! You've brought the wrath of the gods upon us, Limbeck Bolttightner! I say we go to the Welves and surrender. Tell the gods we're sorry. Maybe they'll turn the Kicksey-winsey back on."

"Yes," muttered other voices, safely hidden by the shadows. "We want everything back the way it was."

"There, what did I tell you?" Limbeck demanded of Jarre. "This kind of talk is spreading."

"They surely can't believe the elves are gods?" Jarre protested, glancing behind her to the whispering shadows, her face drawn in concern. "We've seen them die!"

"They don't," Limbeck answered gloomily. "But they'll be ready enough to swear they do if it means heat and light and the Kicksey-winsey working once again."

"Death to the High Froman!" came the whispers.

"Give him to the Welves!"

"Here's a bolt for you to tighten, Bolttightner."

Something whizzed out of the darkness—a bolt, big around as Bane's hand. The chunk of metal didn't come anywhere near its target, clunked harmlessly into the wall behind them. The dwarves were still in awe of their leader, who had, for a brief time, given them dignity and hope. But that wouldn't last long. Hunger and darkness, cold and silence bred fear.

Limbeck didn't say anything. He didn't flinch or duck. His lips pressed together grimly, he kept walking. Jarre, face pale with worry, posted herself at his side and flashed defiant glances at every dwarf they passed. Bane skipped hastily back to walk near Haplo.

The Patryn felt a prickling of his skin, glanced down, saw the sigla tattooed on his arms start to glow a faint blue—a reaction to danger.

Odd, he thought. His body's magic wouldn't react that way in response to some frightened dwarves, a few muttered threats, and a thrown piece of hardware. Something or someone truly menacing was out there, a threat to him, to them all.

The dog growled, its lip curled.

"What's wrong?" asked Bane, alarmed. He had lived among Patryns long enough to know the warning signs.

"I don't know, Your Highness," said Haplo. "But the sooner we get that machine started again, the better. So just keep walking."

They entered the tunnels, which, as Haplo remembered from his last journey, bisected, dissected, and intersected the ground underneath the Kicksey-winsey. No dwarves lurked down here. These tunnels were customarily empty, since they led nowhere anyone had any reason to go. The Factree had not been used in eons, except as a meeting place, and that had ended when the elves took it over and turned it into a barracks.

Away from the whispers and the sight of the corpselike machine, everyone relaxed visibly. Everyone except Haplo. The runes on his skin glowed only faintly, but they still glowed. Danger was still present, though he couldn't imagine where or how. The dog, too, was uneasy and would occasionally erupt with a loud and startling "whuff" that made everyone jump.

"Can't you get him to stop doing that?" complained Bane. "I almost wet my pants."

Haplo placed a gentle hand on the dog's head. The animal quieted, but it wasn't happy and neither was Haplo.

Elves? Haplo couldn't recall a time his body had ever reacted to a danger from mensch, but then—as he recalled—the Tribus elves were a cruel and vicious lot.

"Why, look!" exclaimed Jarre, pointing. "Look at that! I never saw that before, did you, Limbeck?"

She pointed to a mark on the wall, a mark that was glowing bright red.

"No," he admitted, removing his spectacles to stare at it. His voice was tinged with the same childlike wonder and curiosity that had brought him to first question the whys of Welves and the Kicksey-winsey. "I wonder what it is?"

"I know what it is," cried Bane. "It's a Sartan rune."

"Shush!" Haplo warned, catching hold of the boy's hand and squeezing it tightly.

"A what?" Limbeck peered round at them. Eyes wide, he had forgotten, in his curiosity, the reason for their being down here, or their need for haste.

"The Mangers made marks like that. I'll explain later," said Haplo, herding everyone on.

Jarre kept walking, but she wasn't watching where she was going. She was staring back at the rune. "I saw some of those funny glowing drawings when that man and I were down in the place with the dead people. But those I saw shone blue, not red."

And why were these sigla gleaming red? Haplo wondered. Sartan runes were like Patryn runes in many ways. Red was a warning.

"The light's fading," said Jarre, still looking back. She stumbled over her feet.

"The sigil's broken," Bane told Haplo. "It can't do anything anymore—whatever it was that it was supposed to do."

Yes, Haplo knew it was broken. He could see that for himself. Large portions of the wall had been covered over, either by the Kicksey-winsey or by the dwarves. The Sartan sigla on the walls were obscured, some missing entirely, others—like this one— cracked and now rendered powerless. Whatever it was they had been supposed to do—alert, halt, bar entry—they had lost the power to do.

"Maybe it's you," Bane said, looking up at him with an impish grin. "Maybe the runes don't like you."

Maybe, thought Haplo. But the last time I came down here, no runes glowed red.

They continued walking.

"This is it," stated Jarre, stopping beneath a ladder, shining her glampern upward.

Haplo glanced around. Yes, he knew where he was now. He remembered. He was directly beneath the Factree. A ladder led pward, and, at the top of the ladder, a piece of the tunnel's eiling slid aside, permitting access to the Factree itself. Haplo tudied the ladder, looked back at Limbeck.

"Do you have any idea what's up there now? I don't want to ome out in the middle of an elven dining hall during breakfast."

Limbeck shook his head. "None of our people have been in he Factree since the elves took it over."

"I'll go look," Bane offered, eager for adventure.

"No, Your Highness." Haplo was firm. "You stay down here. Dog, keep an eye on him."

"I'll go." Limbeck gazed around vaguely. "Where's the lader?"

"Put your spectacles on!" Jarre scolded.

Limbeck flushed, reached into a pocket, discovered the specta-les. He pulled them over his ears.

"Everyone stay put. I'll go and take a look," said Haplo, who lready had his foot on the first rung. "When's that diversion of ours supposed to start?"

"Should be anytime now," Limbeck answered, peering near-ightedly up into the shadows.

"Do you . . . do you want the glampern?" Jarre asked hesi-antly. She was obviously impressed with Haplo's blue-glowing kin, a sight she'd never seen.

"No," Haplo answered shortly. His body was giving off light nough. He didn't need to encumber himself with the glampern. Ie began to climb.

He had gone about halfway when he heard a scuffle at the ottom and Bane's voice rise in a yelp. Haplo glanced down. Ap-arently, the boy had been about to follow. The dog had its teeth lamped firmly in the seat of His Highness's pants.

"Shhh!" Haplo hissed, glaring down at them.

He continued his climb, came to the metal plate. As he re-alled from the last time he'd done this, the plate slid aside easily nd—what was more important—quietly. Now, if some elf just adn't set a bed on top of it . . .

Haplo placed his fingers on the plate, gave it a cautious shove.

It moved. A crack of light shone down on him. He halted, vaited, ears straining.

Nothing.

He moved the plate again, about as far as the length of hi first finger. He halted again, keeping perfectly still, perfectly si lent.

Up above, he could hear voices: light, delicate voices of elves But they sounded as if they were coming from a distance, non near, none directly overhead. Haplo glanced down at the sigla on his skin. The blue glow had not intensified, but neither had i gone away. He decided to risk a look.

Haplo slid the plate aside, peeped warily up over the edge. I took his eyes some time to become accustomed to the bright ligh The fact that the elves had light at all was disquieting. Perhap he'd been wrong, perhaps they *had* learned how to operate th Kicksey-winsey and had cut off light and heat to the dwarves.

Further investigation revealed the truth. The elves—know for their magical mechanics—had rigged up their own lightin; system. The glimmerglamps belonging to the Kicksey-winsey which had once lit the Factree, were dark and cold.

And no light at all shone on this end of the Factree. This en was empty, deserted. The elves were bivouacked at the far end near the entrance. Haplo was at eye level with neat rows of cots stacked around the walls. Elves were moving about, sweeping th floor, checking their weapons. Some were asleep. Several sur rounded a cooking pot, from which came a fragrant odor and cloud of steam. One group squatted on the floor, playing at som type of game to judge by their talk of "bets" and exclamations o either triumph or disgust. No one was at all interested in Haplo' part of the Factree. The lighting system didn't even extend thi far.

Directly across from where he stood, he could see the statue o the Manger—the robed and hooded figure of a Sartan holding single, staring eyeball in one hand. Haplo took a moment to ex amine the eyeball, was glad to see it was dark and lifeless as th machine.

The eyeball, once activated, revealed the secret of the Kicksey winsey to any who looked at its moving pictures.[2] Either the elve

---

[2] Limbeck discovered that the eyeball was, in actuality, a magic lantern Bane, watching the moving pictures exhibited in the eyeball, figured ou what the Kicksey-winsey was supposed to do—bring the various floatin

adn't discovered the eyeball's secret, or, if they had, they'd discounted it, as had the dwarves all these years. Perhaps, like the dwarves, the elves used this empty portion of the huge building only for meetings. Or perhaps they didn't use it at all.

Haplo slid the plate back all but a crack, descended the ladder.

"It's all right," he told Limbeck. "The elves are all in the front of the Factree. But either your diversion hasn't started or else they don't give a damn—"

He paused. A trumpet call sounded faintly from above. Then came the sound of shouts, weapons rattling, beds scraping, voices raised in either irritation or satisfaction, depending on whether the soldiers found this a welcome break in their dull routine or a nuisance.

Haplo swiftly climbed back up the ladder again, peered out the opening.

The elves were strapping on swords, grabbing bows and quivers of arrows, and running to the call, their officers shouting curses and urging them to hurry.

The diversion had started. He wasn't certain how much time they had, how long the dwarves could harass the elves. Probably not long.

"Come on!" he said, motioning. "Quickly! It's all right, boy. Let him go."

Bane was the first up, climbing like a squirrel. Limbeck followed more slowly. Jarre came after him. She had forgotten, in the heat of soup-pan tossing, to change her skirt for trousers, and was having difficulty managing the ladder. The dog stood at the bottom, regarding them with interest.

"Now!" said Haplo, keeping watch, waiting until the last elf had left the Factree. "Run for it!"

He shoved the plate aside, pulled himself up onto the floor. Turning, he gave Bane a hand, hauled the boy up beside him. Bane's face was flushed, his eyes shone with excitement.

"I'll go look at the statue—"

"Wait."

Haplo cast a swift glance around, wondering why he hesi-

---

continents of Mid and High Realms into alignment, supply them with water. *Dragon Wing*, vol. 1 of *The Death Gate Cycle*.

tated. The elves had gone. He and the others were alone in th Factree. Unless, of course, the elves had been forewarned of thei coming and were lying in wait. But that was a risk they had t take, and not much of a risk at that. Haplo's magic could dea efficiently with any ambush. But his skin tingled, shone a fain disturbing blue.

"Go ahead," he said, angry at himself. "Dog, go witl him."

Bane dashed off, accompanied by the dog.

Limbeck poked his head up out of the hole. He stared at th animal, gamboling at Bane's side, and the dwarf's eyes widened "I could have sworn . . ."

He stared back down the ladder. "The dog was dowr there . . ."

"Hurry up!" Haplo grunted. The sooner they left this place the happier he'd be. He dragged Limbeck over the top, reachec out a hand to help Jarre.

Hearing a startled shout and an excited bark, Haplo turned swiftly, nearly yanking Jarre's arm out of its socket.

Bane, lying prone across the statue's feet, was pointing down. "I've found it!" The dog, standing spraddle-legged at the top, gazed into the hole with deep suspicion, not liking whatever was down there.

Before Haplo could stop him, Bane slid down into the hole like an eel and disappeared.

The statue of the Manger began to revolve upon its base, sliding shut.

"Go after him!" shouted Haplo.

The dog jumped into the slowly closing gap. The last Haplo saw was the tip of a tail.

"Limbeck, stop it from closing!" Haplo all but dropped Jarre and started for the statue at a run. But Limbeck was ahead of him.

The stout dwarf lumbered across the Factree floor, short, thick legs pumping furiously. Reaching the statue, he hurled himself bodily into the slowly narrowing gap and wedged himself firmly between the base and floor. Giving the statue a push, he shoved it back open, then bent to examine it.

"Ah, so that's how it works," he said, pushing his spectacles back up his nose. He reached out a hand to check his theory by fiddling with a catch he'd discovered.

Haplo planted his foot gently but firmly on the dwarf's fingers.

"Don't do that. It might close again and maybe this time we couldn't stop it."

"Haplo?" Bane's voice floated up out of the hole. "It's awfully dark down here. Could you hand me the glampern?"

"Your Highness might have waited for the rest of us," Haplo remarked grimly.

No answer.

"Keep still. Don't move," Haplo told the boy. "We'll be down in a minute. Where's Jarre?"

"Here," she said in a small voice, coming to stand by the statue. Her face was pale. "Alfred said we couldn't get back out this way."

"Alfred said that?"

"Well, not in so many words. He didn't want me to be afraid. But that had to be the reason why we went into the tunnels. I mean, if we could have escaped by coming up through the statue, we would have, wouldn't we?"

"With Alfred, who knows?" Haplo muttered. "But you're probably right. This must close whenever anyone goes down. Which means we have to find some way to prop this thing open."

"Is that wise?" Limbeck asked anxiously, looking up at them from his position half in and half out of the hole. "What if the elves come back and find it open?"

"If they do, they do," Haplo said, though he didn't consider it likely. The elves seemed to avoid this area. "I don't want to end up trapped down there."

"The blue lights led us out," said Jarre softly, almost to herself. "Blue lights that looked like that." She pointed at Haplo's glowing skin.

Haplo said nothing, stalked off in search of something to use as a wedge. Returning with a length of stout pipe, he motioned Jarre and Limbeck into the hole, followed after them. As soon as he had passed across the base's threshold, the statue began to slide shut, slowly, quietly. Haplo thrust the pipe into the opening.

The statue closed on it, held it fast. He shoved on it experimentally, felt the statue give.

"There. The elves shouldn't notice that. And we can open it
when we return. All right, let's get a look at where we are."

Jarre held up the glampern and light flooded their surroundings.

A narrow stone staircase spiraled down into darkness below.
A darkness that was, as Jarre had said, unbelievably quiet. The
silence lay over the place like thick dust, seemed not to have been
disturbed in centuries.

Jarre gulped, her hand holding the glampern trembled,
caused the light to wobble. Limbeck took out his handkerchief,
but used it to mop his forehead, not to clean his spectacles.
Bane, huddled at the bottom of the stairs, his back pressed flat
against the wall, looked subdued and awed.

Haplo scratched the burning sigla on the back of his hand and
firmly suppressed the urge to leave. He had hoped to evade, by
coming down here, whatever unseen danger threatened them. But
the runes on his body continued to glow blue, neither brighter nor
dimmer than when he'd been standing in the Factree. Which
made no sense, for how could the threat be both above and below?

"There! Those things make the lights," said Jarre, pointing.

Looking down, Haplo saw a row of Sartan runes running
along the base of the wall. He recalled, in Abarrach, seeing the
same series of runes, recalled Alfred using them as guides out of
the tunnels of the Chamber of the Damned.

Bane crouched down to study them. Smiling to himself,
pleased with his cleverness, he put his finger on one and spoke
the rune.

At first, nothing happened. Haplo could understand the
Sartan language, although it jarred through him like the screeching of rats. "You've mispronounced it."

Bane glowered up at him, not liking to be corrected. But the
boy repeated the rune again, taking time to form the unfamiliar
and difficult sounds with care.

The sigil flared into light, shared that light with its neighbor.
One at a time, the sigla each caught fire. The base of the wall,
down the stairs, began to glow blue.

"Follow it," said Haplo unnecessarily, for Bane and Limbeck and the dog were already clambering down the steps.

Only Jarre lingered behind, face pale and solemn, her hands kneading and twisting a tiny fold of her skirt.

"It's so sad," she said.

"I know," Haplo replied quietly.

CHAPTER 14

WOMBE, DREVLIN

LOW REALM

♦

Limbeck came to a halt at the foot of the stairs. "Now what?"

A veritable honeycomb of tunnels branched off from the one in which they were standing, lit by the blue runes on the floor. The sigla advanced no farther, almost as if waiting for instructions.

"Which way do we go?"

The dwarf spoke in a whisper, they all spoke in whispers, though there was no reason why they shouldn't have talked out loud. The silence loomed over them, strict and stern, prohibiting speech. Even whispering made them feel uneasy, guilty.

"The time we were here, the blue lights led us to the mausoleum," said Jarre. "I don't want to go back there again."

Neither did Haplo. "Do you remember where that was?"

Jarre, holding fast to Haplo's hand, as she had once held fast to Alfred's, shut her eyes and thought. "I think it was the third one to the right." She pointed.

At that instant, the sigla flared and branched off in that direction. Jarre gasped and crowded closer to Haplo, hanging on to him with both hands.

"Wow!" Bane whistled softly.

"Thoughts," said Haplo, recalling something Alfred had told him when they were running for their lives through the tunnels in Abarrach. "Thoughts can affect the runes. Think of where we want to go and the magic will lead us there."

"But how can we think of it when we don't know what it is?" Bane argued.

Haplo rubbed his itching, burning hand against his trouser leg, forced himself to remain patient, calm. "You and my lord must have talked about how the machine's central control would work, Your Highness. What do you think it's like?"

Bane paused to consider the matter. "I showed Grandfather the pictures I'd made of the Kicksey-winsey. He noticed how all the machine's parts look like parts of our own bodies or the bodies of animals. The gold hands and arms of the Liftalofts, the whistles made in the shape of mouths, the claws like bird feet that dig up the coralite. And so the controls must be—"

"A brain!" guessed Limbeck eagerly.

"No." Bane was smug. "That's what Grandfather said, but *I* said that if the machine had a brain it would know what to do, which it obviously doesn't, since it's not doing it. Aligning the islands, I mean. If it had a brain, it would do that on its own. It's working, but without purpose. What I think we're looking for is the heart."

"And what did Grandfather say to that?" Haplo was skeptical.

"He agreed with me," Bane replied, loftily superior.

"We're supposed to think about hearts?" Limbeck asked.

"It's worth a shot." Haplo frowned, scratched his hand. "At least it's better than standing around here. We can't afford to waste any more time."

He set his mind to thinking about a heart, a gigantic heart, a heart pumping life to a body that has no mind to direct it. The more he considered it, the more the notion made sense, though he would never admit as much to Bane. And it fit in with the Patryn's own theory, too.

"The lights are going out!" Jarre clutched Haplo's hand, fingers digging into his skin.

"Concentrate!" he snapped.

The sigla that had lit the hallway to the right flickered, dimmed, and died. They all waited, breathlessly, thinking about hearts, all now acutely conscious of the beating of their own hearts, which sounded loud in their ears.

Light glimmered to their left. Haplo held his breath, willing the runes to come to life. The sigla burned stronger, brighter, lighting their way in a direction opposite that of the mausoleum.

Bane shouted in triumph. His shout bounded back to him, but the voice didn't sound human anymore. It sounded hollow, empty, reminded Haplo unpleasantly of the echoing voice of the dead, the lazar on Abarrach. The glowing sigla on Haplo's skin flashed suddenly, their light becoming more intense.

"I wouldn't do that again, if I were you, Your Majesty." The Patryn spoke through gritted teeth. "I don't know what's out there, but I have the feeling someone heard you."

Bane, eyes wide, had shrunk back against the wall.

"I think you're right," he whispered through quivering lips. "I-I'm sorry. What do we do?"

Haplo heaved an exasperated sigh, endeavored to loosen Jarre's pinching fingers, which were cutting off his circulation. "Let's go. But let's be quick about it!"

No one needed any urging to hurry. By now, all of them, including Bane, were anxious to complete their task, then get out of this place.

The glowing sigla led them through the myriad hallways.

"What are you doing?" Bane demanded, pausing to watch Haplo, who had stopped for about the fourth time since they'd started down the tunnel. "I thought you said to hurry."

"This will ensure us finding our way out, Your Highness," Haplo replied coolly. "If you'll notice, the sigla fade after we pass them. They might not light up again or they might take us another way, a way that could bring us out into the arms of the elves."

He stood facing the arched entryway of the tunnel branch they had just entered and, with the point of his dagger, was scratching a sigil of his own on the wall. The rune was not only useful, but he felt a certain amount of satisfaction in leaving a Patryn mark on hallowed Sartan walls.

"The Sartan runes will show us the way out," argued Bane petulantly.

"They haven't shown us much of anything yet," remarked Haplo.

But eventually, after a few more twists and turns, the runes led them to a closed door at the end of a hall.

The glowing sigla that ran across the floor and skipped over other doorways, leaving them in darkness, now arched up and over, outlining this door in light. Recalling the warding runes on Abarrach, Haplo was glad to see the sigla glow blue and not red. The door was formed in the shape of a hexagon. In its center was inscribed a circlet of runes surrounding a blank spot. Unlike most Sartan runes, these were not complete, but appeared to have been only half finished.

Haplo registered the odd shape of the door and the sigla formation as something he had seen or encountered before, but his memory offered no help, and he thought little more of it.[1] It looked to be a simple opening device, the key being sigla drawn in the center.

"I know this one," said Bane, studying it for a moment. "Grandfather taught me. It was in those old books of his." He looked back at Haplo. "But I need to be taller. And I need your dagger."

"Be careful," said Haplo, handing the weapon over. "It's sharp."

Bane took a moment to study the dagger with wistful longing. Haplo lifted the boy, held him up level with the rune-structure on the door.

Brow furrowed, tongue thrust out in concentration, Bane stuck the dagger's tip into the wooden door and began slowly and laboriously to draw a sigil.[2] When the last stroke was completed, the sigil caught fire. Its flame spread to the runes around it. The entire rune-structure flared briefly, then went out. The door opened a tiny crack. Light—bright, white—flared out, the brilliance making them blink after the darkness of the tunnel.

From inside the room came a metallic clanking sound.

Haplo dropped His Highness unceremoniously on the ground, shoved the boy behind him, and made a grab for the

---

[1] Undoubtedly the gates to the Sartan city of Pryan, which Haplo describes in his journal *Pryan, World of Fire*.

[2] Haplo should have recognized this from Pryan as well. The dwarf Drugar wore the very same sigil on an amulet around his neck. A common Sartan key and locking device, the sigla were more ornamental than they were functional, for—as Bane demonstrates—even a mensch could learn to operate the elemental magic. Places the Sartan wanted to truly guard and prohibit entry to were surrounded by runes of warding.

excited Limbeck, who was preparing to march right inside. The dog growled, low in its throat.

"There's something in there!" Haplo hissed beneath his breath. "Move back! All of you!"

More alarmed by the tension in Haplo than by the half-heard sound in the room, Bane and Limbeck obeyed, edged back against the wall. Jarre joined them, looking scared and unhappy.

"What—" Bane began.

Haplo cast him a furious glance, and the boy quickly shut his mouth. The Patryn paused, continuing to listen at the crack of the partially opened door, puzzled by the sounds he heard within. The clanking metallic jingle was sometimes a rhythmic pattern, sometimes a chaotic clashing, and other times completely stilled. Then it would start up again. And it was moving, first near to him, then advancing away.

He could have sworn that what he was hearing were the sounds of a person, clad in full plate armor, walking about a large room. But no Sartan—or Patryn, either—had ever in the history of their powerful races worn such a mensch device as armor. Which meant that whatever was inside that room had to be a mensch, probably an elf.

Limbeck was right. The elves had shut down the Kicksey-winsey.

Haplo listened again, listened to the clanking sounds move this way and that, moving slowly, purposefully, and he shook his head. No, he decided, if the elves had discovered this place, they would be swarming around it. They would be as busy as ants inside this tunnel. And there was, as far as Haplo could determine, only one person making those strange sounds inside that room.

He looked at his skin. The sigla still glowed warning blue, but were still faint.

"Stay here!" Haplo mouthed, glaring at Bane and Limbeck.

The boy and the dwarf both nodded.

Haplo drew his sword, gave the door a violent kick, and rushed inside the room, the dog at his heels. He halted, came near dropping his weapon. He was dumbstruck with amazement.

A man turned to meet him, a man made all of metal.

"What are my instructions?" asked the man in a monotone, speaking human.

"An automaton!" cried Bane, disobeying Haplo and running inside the room.

The automaton stood about Haplo's height, or somewhat taller. His body—the replica of a human's—was made of brass. Hands, arms, fingers, legs, toes were jointed and moved in a life-like, if somewhat stiff, manner. The metal face had been fancifully molded to resemble a human face, with nose and mouth, though the mouth did not move. The brows and lips were outlined in gold, bright jewels gleamed in the eye sockets. Runes, Sartan runes, covered its entire body, much as the Patryn's runes covered his body, and probably for the same purpose—all of which Haplo found rather amusing, if somewhat insulting.

The automaton was alone in a large and empty circular room. Surrounding it, mounted in the room's walls, were eyeballs, hundreds of eyeballs, exactly like the one eyeball held in the hands of the Manger statue far above them. Each unwinking eye portrayed in its vision a different part of the Kicksey-winsey.

Haplo had the eerie impression that these eyes belonged to him. He was looking out through every one of these orbs. Then he understood. The eyes belonged to the automaton. The metallic clanking Haplo had heard must have been the automaton moving from eyeball to eyeball, making his rounds, keeping watch.

"There's someone alive in there!" Jarre gasped. She stood in the doorway, not daring to venture inside. Her own eyes were opened so wide it seemed likely they might roll out of her head. "We have to get him out!"

"No!" Bane scoffed at the notion. "It's a machine, just like the Kicksey-winsey."

"I am the machine," stated the automaton in its lifeless voice.

"That's it!" cried Bane, excited, turning to Haplo. "Don't you see? *He's* the machine! See the runes that cover him? All the parts of the Kicksey-winsey are connected magically to him. He's been running it, all these centuries!"

"Without a brain," murmured Haplo. "Obeying his last instructions, whatever those were."

"This is wonderful!" Limbeck breathed a sigh. His eyes filled with tears, the glass in his spectacles steamed over. He snatched them off his nose.

The dwarf stood staring myopically and with reverent awe at the man-machine, making no move to come near it, content to worship at a distance. "I never imagined anything so marvelous."

"I think it's creepy," said Jarre, shivering. "Now that we've seen it, let's go. I don't like this place. And I don't like that thing."

Haplo could have echoed her sentiments. He didn't like this place, either. The automaton reminded him of the living corpses on Abarrach, dead bodies brought to life by the power of necromancy. He had the feeling that the same sort of dark magic was working here, only in this instance it had given life to what was never meant to be alive. A degree better, he supposed, than bringing to life rotting flesh. Or perhaps not. The dead at least possessed souls. This metal contraption was not only mindless but soulless as well.

The dog sniffed at the automaton's feet, looked up at Haplo, baffled, apparently wondering why this thing that moved like a man and talked like a man didn't smell like a man.

"Go watch the door," Haplo ordered the dog.

Bored with the automaton, the animal was happy to obey.

Limbeck pondered, fell back on his favorite question. "Why? If this metal man's been running the machine all these years, why did the Kicksey-winsey stop?"

Bane pondered, shook his head. "I don't know," he was forced to admit, shrugging.

Haplo scratched his glowing hand, mindful that their danger had not lessened. "Perhaps, Your Highness, it has something to do with the opening of Death's Gate."

Bane scoffed. "A lot you know—" he began.

The automaton turned in Haplo's direction.

"The Gate has opened. What are my instructions?"

"That's it," said Haplo in satisfaction. "I thought as much. *That's* why the Kicksey-winsey stopped."

"What gate?" Limbeck asked, frowning. He'd wiped his spectacles, replaced them on his nose. "What are you talking about?"

"I suppose you could be right," Bane mumbled, glancing at Haplo balefully. "But what if you are? What then?"

"I demand to know what's going on!" Limbeck glared at them.

"I'll explain in a minute," said Haplo. "Look at it this way, Your Highness. The Sartan intended that the four worlds all work together. Let's say that the Kicksey-winsey was not meant to simply draw the floating islands into alignment on Arianus. Suppose the machine has other tasks, as well, tasks that have something to do with all the other worlds."

"My true work begins with the opening of the Gate," said the automaton. "What are my instructions?"

"What is your true work?" Bane parried.

"My true work begins with the opening of the Gate. I have received the signal. The Gate is open. What are my instructions?"

Where are the citadels?

Haplo was reminded, suddenly, of the tytans on Pryan. Other soulless creatures, whose frustration over not having their question answered led them to murder whatever hapless being crossed their path. *Where are the citadels? What are my instructions?*

"Well, give it the instructions. Tell it to turn the machine on and let's go!" Jarre said, shuffling nervously from one foot to the other. "The diversion can't last much longer."

"I'm not leaving until I know exactly what's going on," Limbeck stated testily.

"Jarre's right. Tell it what to do, Your Highness, then we can get out of here."

"I can't," said Bane, glancing at Haplo slyly out of the corner of his eye.

"And why not, Your Highness?"

"I mean I can, but it will take a long time. A long, long time. First I'll have to figure out what each different part of the machine is meant to do. Then I'll have to give each part of the machine its own instructions—"

"Are you certain?" Haplo eyed the boy suspiciously.

"It's the only safe way," Bane replied, all glittering innocence. "You want this to be done safely, don't you? If I made a mistake— or *you* made a mistake—and the machine started running amok . . . maybe sending islands scooting here and there, perhaps dropping them into the Maelstrom." Bane shrugged. "Thousands of people could die."

Jarre was twisting her skirt into knots. "Let's leave this place, right now. We're well enough off, as it is. We'll learn to live without the Kicksey-winsey. When the elves find out it isn't going to work again, they'll go away—"

"No, they won't," said Limbeck. "They can't or they'll die of thirst. They'll search and poke and prod until they discover this metal man and then *they'll* take it over—"

"He's right," agreed Bane. "We must—"

The dog began to growl, then gave its warning bark. Haplo glanced down at his hand and arm, saw the sigla glowing brighter.

"Someone's coming. Probably discovered the hole in the statue."

"But how? There weren't any elves up there!"

"I don't know," Haplo said grimly. "Either your diversion didn't work or they were tipped off. It doesn't matter now. We've got to clear out of here, fast!"

Bane glared at him, defiant. "That's stupid. *You're* being stupid. How can the elves find us? The runes went dark. We'll just hide in this room—"

The kid's right, Haplo thought. I am being stupid. What am I afraid of? We could shut the door, hide in here. The elves could search these tunnels for years, never find us.

He opened his mouth to give the order, but the words wouldn't come. He'd lived this long relying on his instincts. His instincts told him to get away.

"Do as you're told, Your Highness." Haplo took hold of Bane, started dragging the squirming boy toward the door.

"Look at that." The Patryn thrust his brightly glowing hand underneath the child's nose. "I don't know how they know we're down here but, believe me, they know. They're looking for us. And if we stay in this room, this is where they'll find us. Here . . . with the automaton. You want that? Would Grandfather want that?"

Bane glared at Haplo; the hatred in the child's eyes gleamed bare and cold, like a drawn blade. The intensity of his hate and the malevolence accompanying it appalled Haplo, momentarily disrupted his thinking. His hand loosened its grasp.

Bane jerked himself free of Haplo's grip. "You're so stupid," he said softly, lethally. "I'll show you just how stupid you are!" Turning, he shoved Jarre aside, ran out the door and into the hallway.

"After him!" Haplo ordered the dog, who dashed off obediently.

Limbeck took off his spectacles, was gazing wistfully at the automaton. Unmoved, it remained standing in the center of the room.

"I still don't understand . . ." Limbeck began.

"I'll explain later!" Haplo said in exasperation.

Jarre took over. Grabbing hold of the august leader of WUPP, much as she used to do, she hustled Limbeck out of the room and into the hall.

"What are my instructions?" the automaton asked.

"Shut the door," Haplo growled, relieved to be away from the metal corpse.

Out in the hallway, he paused to get his bearings. He could hear Bane's pounding footsteps running up the tunnel, back the way they'd come. The Patryn sigil Haplo had scratched above the arch shone with a flickering bluish green light. At least Bane had had sense enough to run off in the right direction, although that was likely going to take him right into the arms of their pursuers.

He wondered what the fool kid had in mind. Anything to make trouble, Haplo supposed. Not that it mattered. He's a mensch, so are the elves. I can handle them easily. They'll never know what hit them.

Then why are you afraid, so afraid you can barely think for the fear?

"Beats the hell out of me," Haplo answered himself. He turned to Limbeck and Jarre. "I've got to stop His Highness. You two keep up with me as best you can, get as far away from this room as possible. That"—he pointed at the burning Patryn symbol—"won't last long. If the elves catch Bane, keep out of sight. Let me do the fighting. Don't try to be heroes."

With that, he ran down the hallway.

"We'll be right behind you!" Jarre promised, and turned to find Limbeck.

He had removed his spectacles, was staring myopically at the door that had shut behind him.

"Limbeck, come on!" she ordered.

"What if we never find it again?" he said plaintively.

"I hope we don't!" was on the tip of Jarre's tongue, but she swallowed her words. Taking hold of his hand—something she realized she had not done in a long while—she tugged at him urgently. "We have to leave, my dear. Haplo's right. We can't let *them* find it."

Limbeck heaved a great sigh. Putting on his spectacles, he planted himself in front of the door, folded his arms across his broad chest.

"No," he said resolutely. "I'm not leaving."

CHAPTER ◆ 15

WOMBE, DREVLIN

LOW REALM

◆

"As I suspected, the Gegs staged the diversion to cover their tracks," stated the elven captain. He stood near the statue of the Manger, peering down at the crack at the base. "One of you men, remove that pipe."

None of the members of the small squad of elves rushed forward to do the captain's bidding. Shifting their feet, they glanced at each other or looked sidelong at the statue.

The captain turned to see why his order hadn't been obeyed. "Well? What's the matter with you?"

One of the elves saluted, spoke up. "The statue's cursed, Captain Sang-drax. Everyone knows it, who's served here *any length of time.*" A none-too-subtle reminder to the captain that he hadn't been here all that long.

"If the Gegs went down there, that's an end of them, sir," said another.

"Cursed!" Sang-drax sniffed. "You'll be cursed, if you don't obey orders. *My* curse! And you'll find my curse more damning than anything this ugly hunk of rock could do to you!" He glared at them. "Lieutenant Ban'glor, remove that pipe."

Reluctantly, afraid of the curse, but more afraid of his captain, the chosen elf came forward. Reaching down gingerly, he took hold of the pipe. His face was pale, sweat trickled down his skin. The other elves involuntarily backed up a pace, caught the baleful glare of their captain, and froze. Ban'glor yanked on the pipe, nearly tumbled over backward when it slid out easily. The statue's base revolved, opened, revealing the staircase leading down into darkness.

"I heard noise down there." The captain walked over, stared down into the hole. The other elves gazed at it in unhappy silence. They all knew what their next order would be.

"Where did High Command find this enthusiastic bastard?" whispered one soldier to another.

"Came in on the last troop ship," said the other gloomily.

"Just our luck we'd get stuck with him. First Captain Ander'el has to go and get himself killed—"

"Did you ever wonder about that?" asked his companion abruptly.

Captain Sang-drax was staring intently into the hole at the statue's base, apparently listening for a repetition of the sound that had drawn his attention.

"Silence in the ranks." He glanced around irritably.

The two soldiers hushed, stood unmoving, faces expressionless. The officer resumed his reconnaissance, descending about halfway down into the hole in a futile attempt to see into the darkness.

"Wonder about what?" the soldier whispered after the captain had disappeared.

"The way Ander'el died."

The other shrugged. "He got drunk and wandered out in the storm—"

"Yes, and when did you ever see Captain Ander'el when he couldn't hold his liquor?"

The soldier flashed his companion a startled glance. "What are you saying?"

"What a lot of people are saying. That the captain's death was no accident—"

Sang-drax returned. "We're going in." He gestured to the two who had been talking. "You two men, take the lead."

The two exchanged glances. *He couldn't have overheard,* they said to each other silently. *Not from that distance.* Glumly and without haste, they moved to obey. The remainder of the squadron marched down after them, most eyeing the statue nervously, giving it a wide berth. Last to descend, Captain Sang-drax followed his men, a slight smile on his thin, delicate lips.

♦

Haplo ran after Bane and the dog. As he ran, he glanced down at his skin—which was now burning a bright blue tinged with fiery red—and he cursed beneath his breath. He shouldn't have come here, shouldn't have allowed Bane to come, or the dwarves. He should have heeded the warning his body was trying to give him, even though it made no sense. In the Labyrinth, he would have never made this mistake.

"I've grown too damn cocky," he muttered, "too sure of myself, counting myself safe in a world of mensch."

But he *was* safe, that was the inexplicable, maddening part of all this. Yet his runes of defense and protection glowed blue and now red in the darkness.

He listened for the pounding, heavy footfalls of the two dwarves, but couldn't hear them. Perhaps they'd gone in another direction. Bane's steps sounded nearer, yet still some distance away. The kid was running with all the speed and heedless abandon of a frightened child. He was doing the right thing—keeping the elves from finding the automaton's room. But getting himself captured in the process wasn't likely to help.

Haplo rounded a corner, paused a moment, listening. He had heard voices, he was certain—elven voices. How close was beyond his ability to guess. The twisting halls distorted sound and he had no way of knowing how near he was to the statue.

Haplo sent an urgent message to the dog, *Stop Bane! Hold on to him!*, started running again. If he could just reach the kid ahead of the elves—

A cry, sounds of a scuffle, and the dog's urgent, angry snarling and growling brought Haplo up short. Trouble ahead. He cast a swift glance behind him. The dwarves were nowhere in sight.

Well, they were on their own. Haplo couldn't be responsible for them and Bane, too. Besides, Limbeck and Jarre would be most at home within these tunnels, quite capable of finding a hiding place. Putting them from his mind, he crept forward.

Shut up, dog! he ordered the animal. *And listen!*

The dog's barking ceased.

"And what have we here, Lieutenant?"

"A kid! Some human's brat, Captain." The elf sounded considerably astonished. "Ouch! Cut it out, you little bastard!"

"Let go of me! You're hurting me!" Bane shouted.

"Who you? What you do down here, brat?" demanded the officer, speaking the crude form of elven that most elves are convinced is the only form humans can understand.

"Mind your manners, brat." The sound of a slap—hard and cold and impersonal. "The captain ask you question. Answer nice captain."

The dog growled. *No, boy!* Haplo commanded silently. *Let it go.*

Bane gasped from the pain, but he didn't blubber or whimper. "You'll be sorry you did that," he said softly.

The elf laughed, slapped the child again. "Speak up."

Bane gulped, drew in a hissing breath. When he spoke, he spoke elven fluently. "I was looking for you elves when I saw the statue open and I was curious and came down. And I'm not a brat. I'm a prince, Prince Bane, son of King Stephen and Queen Anne of Volkaran and Ulyndia. You better treat me with respect."

Good for you, kid. Haplo awarded the boy grudging praise. That will make them stop and think.

The Patryn slipped silently closer to the hallway in which the elves held the child captive. He could see them, now—six elven soldiers and one officer, standing near the staircase that led back up to the statue.

The soldiers had fanned out down the hallway, stood with weapons drawn, looking nervously this way and that. Obviously, they didn't like it down here. Only the officer appeared cool and unconcerned, although Haplo could see that Bane's answer had taken the elf by surprise. He rubbed a pointed chin, eyed the boy speculatively.

"King Stephen's whelp is dead," said the soldier holding the boy. "We should know. He accused us of the murder."

"Then you should know that you didn't do it," returned Bane cunningly. "I *am* the prince. The very fact that I'm here on Drevlin should prove that to you." The boy spoke scornfully. His hand started to rub his aching jaw, but he changed his mind, stood proudly, too proud to admit he was hurt, glaring at his captors.

"Oh, yes?" said the captain. "How?"

The captain was obviously impressed. Hell, Haplo was impressed. He'd forgotten how smart and manipulative Bane could be. The Patryn relaxed, took time to study the soldiers, tried to

decide what magic he could use that would render the elves helpless and leave Bane unharmed.

"I'm a prisoner, King Stephen's prisoner. I've been looking for
a way to escape and, when the stupid Gegs left to attack your
ship, I had my chance. I ran away and came searching for you,
only I got lost, coming down here. Take me back to Tribus. It will
be well worth your while." Bane smiled ingenuously.

"Take you back to Tribus?" The elven captain was highly
amused. "You'll be lucky if I waste energy enough taking you
back up the stairs! The only reason I haven't killed you yet, you
little worm, is that you are right about one thing: I *am* curious to
know what a human brat is doing down here. And I suggest that
this time you tell me the truth."

"I don't see the need to tell *you* anything. I'm not alone!" Bane
crowed shrilly. Turning, he pointed down the hallway, back the
way he'd come. "There's a man guarding me, one of the mysteriarchs. And some Gegs are with him. Help me escape before he
can stop me!"

Bane ducked beneath the elf captain's arm, headed for the
shelter of the stairs. The dog, after a swift glance back at Haplo,
bolted after the boy.

"You two, catch the brat!" shouted the captain swiftly. "The
rest of you, come with me!"

He drew a dagger from a sheath worn on his belt, headed
down the hallway in the direction Bane had pointed.

Damn the little bastard! Haplo swore. He called upon the
magic, speaking and drawing the sigla that would fill the hallway
with a noxious gas. Within seconds, everyone—including Bane—
would be comatose. Haplo raised his hand. As the first fiery sigil
burned in the air beneath his fingers, he wondered who Bane was
truly trying to escape.

A short, stout figure darted suddenly from around back of
Haplo. "I'm here! Don't hurt me! I'm the only one!" shouted Jarre.
Trundling clumsily down the hall, she was headed straight for the
elves.

Haplo had not heard the dwarf approach and he dared not
stop his magic long enough to grab her, keep her out of the line of
his spell-casting. She'd end up right in the midst of the sleeping
gas. He had no choice but to continue. He'd pick her up when he
picked up Bane. He stepped out from his hiding place.

The elves came to a confused halt. They saw runes flashing in the air, a man with shimmering red and blue skin in front of them. This was no mysteriarch. No human could cast magic like this. They looked to their captain for orders.

Haplo drew the last sigil. The magic was nearly complete. The elven captain was prepared to hurl his dagger, but the Patryn paid it scant attention. No mensch weapon could harm him. He completed the sigil, stepped back, and waited for the spell to work.

Nothing happened.

The first sigil had, inexplicably, flickered and gone out. Haplo stared at it. The second sigil, dependent on the first, began to fade. He couldn't believe it. Had he made a mistake? No, impossible. The spell was a simple one . . .

Pain flared in Haplo's shoulder. Looking down, he saw the hilt of a dagger protruding out of his shirt. A dark splotch of blood flowered beneath it. Anger and confusion and pain robbed him of coherent thought. None of this should be happening! The dagger should not have touched him! The runes on his body should have protected him! The damn spell should be working! Why wasn't it?

He looked into the eyes—the red eyes—of the elven captain and saw the answer.

Haplo clutched at the dagger, but he lacked the strength to pull it out. A sickening, horrible warmth had begun flowing through his body. The warmth made him queasy, twisted him up inside. The terrible sensation weakened his muscles. His hand dropped, limp, lifeless. His knees buckled. He staggered, almost fell, and stumbled over to lean against the wall in an effort to try to keep on his feet.

But now the warmth was spreading up into his brain. He slumped to the floor . . .

And then he wasn't anywhere.

CHAPTER 16

WOMBE, DREVLIN

LOW REALM

✦

ARRE SAT CROSS-LEGGED ON THE FLOOR OF THE FACTREE, NEAR THE STATUE OF the Manger, trying not to look at the opening at the statue's base, the opening that led back down the stairs into the strange tunnels. Yet as often as she determined not to look at it, that was how often she discovered herself looking at it.

She fixed her gaze on some other object: one of the elven guards, Bane, the unhappy dog. The next thing Jarre knew, she was looking back at the opening.

Waiting, watching for Limbeck.

She had planned exactly what she'd do when she saw Limbeck come peering and stumbling his way up out of the hole. She'd create a diversion, just like the diversion she'd created back down there in the tunnels. She'd make it look like she was trying to escape. She'd run toward the front of the Factree, away from the statue. That would give Limbeck time to sneak across the floor and slip back down into the dwarven tunnels, the way they'd come up.

"I just hope he won't do anything stupid and chivalrous," Jarre said to herself, her gaze sliding back to the statue. "Like try to rescue me. That's what the old Limbeck would have done. Fortunately, he has more sense now."

Yes, he has more sense. He's extremely sensible. It was sensible of him to let me sacrifice myself, allow the elves to capture me, let *me* lead them away from the room with the automaton. It was

my plan, after all. Limbeck agreed to it immediately. Very sensible
of him. He didn't argue, didn't try to convince me to stay, didn't
offer to go with me.

"Take care of yourself, my dear," he said, peering at me
through those infernal spectacles, "and don't tell them about this
room."

All very sensible. I admire sensible people.

Which made Jarre wonder why she had a sudden desire to
slug Limbeck in his sensible mouth.

Sighing, she stared at the statue and remembered her plan and
what it had gained them.

Running down the tunnel, she'd been more frightened at the
sight of Haplo, his skin glowing with bright magic, than she had
been of the elves. She almost hadn't been able to go through with
her plan, then Bane had shouted out something in elven about
Gegs and had pointed down the tunnel, in the direction of the
room.

After that, it had been all confusion. Terrified that they'd find
Limbeck, Jarre ran out in the open, shouting that she was alone.
Something whizzed past her ear. She heard Haplo cry out in pain.
Looking around, she saw him writhing on the floor, the magical
glow of his skin fading rapidly. She'd turned to go back to help
him, but two elves caught hold of her, held her fast.

One of the elves bent down near Haplo, examined him
closely. The others kept back. A shout from upstairs, followed by
a whining cry from Bane, indicated that the elves had managed to
catch the boy.

The elf kneeling beside Haplo glanced up at his men, said
something Jarre couldn't understand, and made an imperative
gesture. The two elves hauled her up the stairs, back up here into
the Factree.

She found Bane sitting on the floor, looking smug. The dog
had flopped down beside the boy, who had his hand on the animal's ruff. Every time the dog tried to get up, probably to go
check on its master, Bane coaxed it to stay put.

"Don't move!" the elves ordered Jarre, speaking crude
dwarven.

She obeyed meekly enough, plopping herself down beside
Bane.

"Where's Limbeck?" the boy asked her, speaking dwarven in a loud whisper.

When had he learned to speak her language? The last time he'd been here, he couldn't speak dwarven. She'd only just now thought of it, noticed how irritating it was.

Jarre fixed him with a blank stare, as if he'd been speaking elven and she didn't understand. Glancing surreptitiously at their guards, she saw them engaged in low-voiced conversation, saw them glance more than once at the opening in the statue's base.

Turning back to Bane, Jarre placed two fingers on the boy's arm, pinched him hard.

"I'm alone," she said to him. "And don't you forget it."

Bane opened his mouth to cry out. Taking one look at Jarre's face, however, the boy decided it was best to keep silent. Nursing his bruised arm, he scooted away from her and was now sitting quietly, either sulking or plotting some new mischief.

Jarre couldn't help but think that, somehow, this was all his fault. She decided she didn't like Bane.

Nothing much was happening now. The other elves paced restlessly about the statue, guarding their prisoners and casting nervous glances down the stairs. The elf captain and Haplo did not return. And there was no sign of Limbeck.

Time crawled when you were caught in situations like this. Jarre knew that and made allowances. And even with allowances, it occurred to her that she'd been sitting here a long, long time. She wondered how long those magic symbols Haplo had put above the arches to show the way out would last, didn't think it would be as long as this.

Limbeck wasn't coming. He wasn't coming to rescue her. Or join her. He was going to be . . . sensible.

Booted footsteps rang on the Factree floor. A voice called out, the guards snapped to attention. Jarre, hope in her heart, prepared to run. But no respectable, bespectacled leader of WUPP appeared.

It was only an elf. And he was coming from a different direction, from the front of the Factree. Jarre sighed.

Pointing to Bane and Jarre, the elf said something in elven that Jarre didn't understand. The guards were quick to respond. They appeared relieved, in fact.

Bane, looking more cheerful, jumped to his feet. The dog bounded up with an eager whimper. Jarre stayed where she was.

"Come on, Jarre," the boy said, with a smile that magnanimously forgave all. "They're taking us out of here."

"Where?" she asked suspiciously, standing up slowly.

"To see the lord commander. Don't worry. Everything's going to be all right. I'll take care of you."

Jarre wasn't buying it. "Where's Haplo?"

She glowered at the approaching elves, folded her arms across her chest, braced to stay put, if necessary.

"How should I know?" Bane asked, shrugging. "The last I saw of him, he was down there, about to let loose some of that magic of his. I guess it must not have worked," he added.

Smugly, Jarre thought. "It didn't. He was hurt. The elf threw a knife at him."

"That's too bad," said Bane, blue eyes wide. "Was . . . um . . . was Limbeck with him?"

Jarre stared at the boy blankly. "Limbeck who?"

Bane flushed in anger, but before he could badger her, a guard broke up the conversation.

"Move along, Geg," he ordered in dwarven.

Jarre didn't want to move along. She didn't want to see this lord commander. She didn't want to leave without knowing what had happened to Limbeck and to Haplo. She looked defiant, was about to make a stand that would have probably earned her a blow from the guard, when it suddenly occurred to her that Limbeck might be hiding down there, waiting for exactly this opportunity. Waiting for the guards to leave so that he could make good his escape.

Meekly, she fell into step beside Bane.

Behind them, one of the elves shouted a question. The newly arrived elf answered with what sounded like an order.

Uneasy, Jarre glanced back.

Several elves were gathering around the statue.

"What are they doing?" she asked Bane fearfully.

"Guarding the opening," said Bane, with a sly smile.

"Watch where you're going! And keep moving, maggot," ordered the elf. He gave Jarre a rough shove.

Jarre had no choice but to obey. She walked toward the Factree entrance. Behind her, the elves took up positions near the statue, but not too near the forbidding opening.

"Oh, Limbeck." Jarre sighed. "Be sensible."

CHAPTER ♦ 17

WOMBE, DREVLIN

LOW REALM

♦

HAPLO WOKE IN PAIN, ALTERNATELY SHIVERING AND BURNING. LOOKING UP, HE saw the eyes of the elven captain gleam red through a shadowed dimness.

Red eyes.

The captain squatted on his haunches, long, thin-fingered elven hands hanging between bent knees. He smiled when he saw Haplo conscious, watching him.

"Greetings, master," he said pleasantly, his tone light and bantering. "Feeling sickish, are you? Yes, I suppose so. I've never experienced the nerve poison, but I understand it produces some remarkably uncomfortable sensations. Don't worry. The poison is not deadly, its effects wear off soon."

Haplo gritted his teeth against the chill that made them rattle in his head, closed his eyes. The elf was speaking Patryn, the rune language of Haplo's people, the language that no elf living or dead had ever spoken, could ever speak.

A hand was touching him, sliding beneath his wounded shoulder.

Haplo's eyes flared open, he instinctively lashed out at the elf . . . or that was what he intended. In reality, he flopped his arm around a little. The elf smiled with a mocking compassion, clucked over Haplo like a distracted hen. Strong hands supported the injured Patryn, eased him to an upright, sitting position.

"Come, come, master. It's not that bad," said the captain

heerily, switching to elven. "Yes, if looks could kill, you'd have my head hanging from your trophy belt." Red eyes glinted in musement. "Or should I say, perhaps, a *snake's* head, don't you gree?"

"What . . . what are you?" At least, that's what Haplo tried o say. His brain shaped the words clearly, but they came out nush.

"Talking's difficult just now, I fancy, isn't it?" remarked the lf, speaking Patryn again. "No need. I can understand your houghts. You know what I am. You saw me on Chelestra, though ou probably don't remember. I was only one of many. And in a lifferent body. *Dragon-snakes,* the mensch dubbed us. Here, what vould you say? *Serpent-elf?* Yes, I rather like that."

Shape-changers . . . Haplo thought in a vague kind of hor-or. He shivered, mumbled.

"Shape-changers," agreed the serpent-elf. "But come. I'm tak-ng you to the Royal One. He's asked to speak with you."

Haplo willed his muscles to respond to his command, willed .is hands to strangle, hit, jab, anything. But his body failed him. His muscles twitched and danced in erratic spasms. It was all he ould do to remain standing, and then he was forced to lean on he elf.

Or, he supposed he should start thinking, the serpent.

"Suppose you try standing, Patryn. Oh, I say, that's quite ood. Now walking. We're late as it is. One foot in front of the ther."

The serpent-elf guided the stumbling Patryn's footsteps as if e were a feeble old man. Haplo shuffled forward, feet falling ver each other, hands jerking aimlessly. A cold sweat soaked his hirt. His nerves flamed and tingled. The sigla tattooed on his ody had gone dark, his magic disrupted. He shook and shivered nd burned, leaned on the elf, and kept going.

Limbeck stood in the darkness that was so extraordinarily ark—far darker than any darkness he could ever remember—nd began to think that he'd made a mistake. The sigil Haplo had ft above the arched passageway still glowed, but it cast no light, nd, if anything, its solitary brilliance so far above the dwarf only erved to make his own darkness darker.

And then the light of the sigil began to dim.

"I'm going to be trapped down here in the dark," said Limbeck. Removing his spectacles, he started to chew on the earpiece a habit of his when nervous. "Alone. They're not coming back."

This possibility had not occurred to him. He'd seen Haplo perform marvelous feats of magic. Surely, a handful of elves wouldn't be a problem for a man who had driven away a marauding dragon. Haplo would scare away the elves, then come back, and Limbeck could continue investigating that wondrous metal personage inside the room.

Except Haplo didn't come back. Time passed. The sigil grew dimmer. Something had gone wrong.

Limbeck wavered. The thought of leaving this room, perhaps forever, was agony. He had been so close. Give the metal man its instructions and the metal man would start the heart of the great machine beating again. Limbeck was not quite clear on what the instructions were or how they were to be given or what would happen once the great machine started up, but he had faith that all would be made clear to him in time—just like putting on his spectacles.

But, for now, the door was closed. Limbeck couldn't get back inside. He knew he couldn't get back inside, because he'd given the door a push or two, after Jarre had left him. He supposed he should be encouraged because the metal man had at least followed Haplo's orders, but right at the moment Limbeck could have opted for a more slovenly, undisciplined attitude on the metal man's part.

The dwarf considered beating on the door, shouting, demanding to be let in.

"No," Limbeck muttered, grimacing at an awful taste in his mouth, a taste left behind by the earpiece, "yelling and shouting might alert the elves. They'd come searching and find the Heart Room [as he was now terming it]. If I had a light, I could see the symbol Bane drew on the door, then maybe I could open it. But I don't have a light and no way to get a light without going away and bringing one back. And if I go away to bring one back, how will I get back when I don't know the way?"

Sighing, Limbeck put his spectacles back on. His gaze went to the archway, to the sigil that had once shone brightly but now was hardly more than a pale ghost of itself.

"I could leave a trail, like Haplo did," murmured Limbeck

rowning in deep thought. "But with what? I don't have anything to write with. I don't"—he felt hastily in his pockets—"even have a single wing nut on me." He had been thinking of a story he'd heard as a child, in which two young Gegs, before entering the tunnels of the great machine, had marked their route by leaving behind a trail of nuts and bolts.

A thought came to him, then—a thought whose brilliance nearly took his breath away.

"My socks!"

Limbeck plunked himself down on the floor. One eye on the vigil, whose glow was growing dimmer by the minute, and one on what he was doing, he hauled off his boots, stood them neatly by the door. Pulling off one of his long, thick woolen socks, which he had knit himself,[1] he fumbled about at the top of the sock, searching for the knot that marked the end of the thread. He found it without much trouble, not having bothered to try to incorporate it into the fabric. Giving the knot a good swift wrench with his teeth, he tugged it loose.

His next problem was: how to anchor the end of the thread? The walls were smooth, as was the door. Limbeck groped about in the dark, hoping to find some protrusion, but discovered nothing. At length, he wrapped the thread around the buckle on his boot, then stuffed the top of the heavy boot beneath the door until only the sole could be seen, sticking out.

"Just leave that alone, will you?" he called to the metal man within the room, thinking that perhaps the automaton might take it into its steel head to either shove the boot back out or (if it took a fancy to the boot) pull it the rest of the way inside.

The boot remained in place. Nothing disturbed it.

Hastily, Limbeck took hold of his sock, began to unravel it. He started down the hall, leaving a trail of woolen thread behind.

---

[1] Since the lives of the dwarves on Drevlin revolve solely around the Kicksey-winsey, male and female dwarves divide household chores such as child rearing, cooking, sewing, and cleaning. Thus all dwarves are adept at knitting, crocheting, darning, and, in fact, consider such skills a form of recreation. All dwarves must have something to do with their hands; to sit idle, dreaming (such as Limbeck did as a youth), is considered a terrible sin.

Limbeck knew how to knit, but he evidently wasn't much good at it, as is evidenced by the fact that his socks unravel with such ease.

He had gone under about three sigil-marked archways and unraveled about half his sock when the flaw in his plan occurred to him.

"Bother," said Limbeck, irritated.

For, of course, if *he* could find his way back, following the trail of the sock, then so could the elves. But there was no help for that now. He could only hope he came across Haplo and Bane quickly, then he could take them back to the Heart Room before the elves discovered it.

The sigla over the archways continued to give off their faint glow. Limbeck followed their lead, used up one sock. Taking off the other, he tied the end of its thread to the end of the thread of the first and continued on. He was trying to figure out what he would do when he ran out of socks. He was considering starting on his sweater and even thinking that he must be somewhere near the stairs that led to the statue, when he rounded a corner and almost ran smack into Haplo.

The Patryn was no help to Limbeck, however, for two reasons. Haplo wasn't alone and he didn't look at all well. An elf was half carrying the Patryn.

Startled, Limbeck ducked back into a recessed doorway. Pattering about on his bare feet, the dwarf made hardly a sound. The elf, who had slung Haplo's limp arm across his shoulders, was talking to Haplo and did not hear Limbeck's approach or his retreat. The elf and Haplo continued without pause on down a hallway that branched off from Limbeck's.

Limbeck's heart sank. The elf was moving confidently through the tunnels, which meant that the elves must know all about them. Did they know about the Heart Room and the metal man? Were the elves the ones responsible for shutting down the Kicksey-winsey?

The dwarf had to find out for certain and the one way to find out was to spy on the elves. He would see where they took Haplo and, if possible, what they did to him. And what he did to them.

Wadding what was left of his sock into a ball, Limbeck wedged the sock into a corner and, moving more quietly (without his boots) than any dwarf had ever moved in the history of the race, he crept down the hall after Haplo and the elf.

♦

Haplo had no idea where he was, except that he had been
brought to one of the underground tunnels dug by the Kicksey-
winsey. *Not* a Sartan tunnel . . . No. A quick glance at the wall
confirmed his thinking. No Sartan runes, anywhere. He banished
the thought as swiftly as it came. Of course, the serpents now
knew about the secret Sartan tunnels, if they didn't know about
them before. But best not to let them know anything else, if he
could help it.

Except that Bane . . .

"The boy?" The serpent-elf glanced at Haplo. "Don't concern
yourself. I sent him back with my men. They're real elves, of
course. I'm their captain—Sang-drax is my name in elven. Rather
clever, don't you agree?[2] Yes, I've sent Bane along to the real
elves. He'll be of far more value to us in their hands. Quite a
remarkable mensch, that Bane. We have great hopes for him.

"No, no, I assure you, master." The red eyes flickered. "The
child's not under our control. No need. Ah, but here we are. Feeling better? Good. We want you to be able to concentrate fully on
what the Royal One has to say."

"Before you kill me," Haplo mumbled.

Sang-drax smiled, shook his head, but he made no response.
He cast a casual glance up and down the corridor. Then, keeping
a firm grip on the Patryn, the serpent-elf reached out, knocked on
a door.

A dwarf opened it.

"Give me a hand," said Sang-drax, indicating Haplo. "He's
heavy."

The dwarf nodded. Between them, they manhandled the still-
groggy Patryn into the room. The dwarf kicked at the door to shut
it, but didn't bother to see if he'd succeeded. Apparently, they felt
secure in their hideout.

"I have brought him, Royal One," called Sang-drax.

"Enter and welcome to our guest," was the response, given in
human.

Limbeck, stealing along behind the two, soon became completely lost. He suspected the elf had doubled back on his own

---

[2] "Drax" means "dragon" in elven. "Sang" means "snake."

trail, and he watched anxiously, half afraid that the elf woul
come across the woolen thread. But Limbeck concluded he mus
have been mistaken, for they never did.

They traveled a great distance through the tunnels. Limbec
grew tired of walking. His bare feet were icy cold and bruise
from stubbing his toes on walls in the dark. He hoped that Hapl
would start to feel better; then, with Limbeck's help, they coul
both jump the elf and escape.

Haplo groaned, didn't look particularly energetic, howeve
The elf didn't appear concerned over his prisoner. He woul
pause occasionally, but that was only to shift his burden mor
comfortably on his shoulders. He'd then continue on, an eerie re
glow—coming from some unknown source—lighting his way.

"My goodness, elves are strong," Limbeck remarked to hin
self. "Far stronger than I'd imagined." He noted down this fact t
be taken into account should full-scale war ever be mounte
against the enemy.

They took many twists and turns down winding corridor
Then the elf came to a halt. Easing the injured Haplo back agains
the wall, the elf glanced casually up and down the corridor.

Limbeck shrank back into a convenient passageway locate
directly across from where the elf was standing and flattened hin
self against the wall. Now Limbeck knew the source of the eeri
red glow—it emanated from the elf's eyes.

The strange eyes with their fiery gaze flared in Limbeck's d
rection. The horrible, unnatural light almost blinded him. H
knew he'd been discovered and he crouched, cowering, waiting t
be apprehended. But the eyes' flaming gaze passed right ove
him, flitted on down the corridor, and back again.

Limbeck went limp in relief. He was reminded of the time on
of the 'lectric zingers on the Kicksey-winsey had gone amok, sp
out great bolts of lightning, before the dwarves managed to get
under control. One of those bolts had whizzed right past Lin
beck's ear. Had he been standing six inches to his left, he woul
have been sizzled. Had the dwarf been standing six inches i
front of himself, the elf would have spotted him.

As it was, the elf was satisfied that he was unobserved. Bu
then he hadn't seemed all that worried about it to begin witl
Nodding to himself in satisfaction, the elf turned and knocked o
a door.

It opened. Light streamed out. Limbeck blinked, his eyes adjusting to the sudden brilliance.

"Give me a hand here," said the elf.[3]

Expecting another elf to come to the aid of the first, Limbeck was astonished beyond measure to see a dwarf emerge from the doorway.

A dwarf!

Fortunately for Limbeck, his shock at seeing a dwarf assisting an elf to carry the reviving Haplo into this secret, subterranean room was so great that it paralyzed his tongue and all his other faculties into the bargain. Otherwise, he might have cried out "Hey!" "Hullo!" or "What in the name of Great-aunt Sally's side whiskers do you think you're doing?" and given himself away.

As it was, by the time Limbeck's brain had reestablished communication with the rest of Limbeck, the elf and the dwarf had dragged a groggy Haplo into the room. They closed the door behind them, and Limbeck's heart traveled down to where his boots had once been. Then he noticed a crack of light, and his heart jumped, though it didn't quite manage to make it back up to its proper place, for it still seemed to be beating somewhere around the level of his knees. The door had been left slightly ajar.

It wasn't courage that urged Limbeck forward. It was: What? Why? How?

Curiosity, the driving force in his life, drew him toward that room as the 'lectrical iron-tuggers on the Kicksey-winsey tugged iron. Limbeck was standing at the door, one bespectacled eye to the crack, before he realized what he was doing or gave a thought to his peril.

Dwarves in collusion with the enemy! How could such a thing be? He'd find out who the traitors were and he'd . . . well, he'd . . . or maybe he'd . . .

Limbeck stared, blinked. He drew back, then brought two eyes to the crack, thinking that one had been playing tricks on him. It hadn't. He took off his spectacles, rubbed his eyes, looked again.

Humans were in the room! Humans and elves and dwarves.

Limbeck learned to speak the elven language from Captain Bothar'el.

All standing around as peaceful as can be. All getting along together. All, apparently, united in brotherhood.

With the exception that their eyes glowed red and that they filled Limbeck with a cold, nameless terror, he couldn't remember having seen a more wonderful sight.

Humans, elves, dwarves—one.

Haplo stood in the room, staring around him. The horrible sensation of alternately freezing and burning had ceased, but now he was weak, wrung out. He longed to sleep, recognized this as his body's desire to heal itself, reestablish the circle of his being, his magic.

And I'll be dead long before that can happen.

The room was large and dimly lit by a few flickering lanterns hanging from pegs on the walls. Haplo was at first confused by what he saw. But then, on second thought, it made sense. It was logical, brilliant. He sank into a chair that Sang-drax shoved beneath his limp legs.

Yes, it made perfect sense.

The room was filled with mensch: elves like Sang-drax, humans like Bane, dwarves like Limbeck and Jarre. An elven soldier was tapping the toe of his boot with the point of his sword. An elven nobleman smoothed the feathers of a hawk he held on his wrist. A human female, clad in a tattered skirt and a deliberately provocative blouse, lounged in a bored manner against a wall. Beside her, a human wizard was amusing himself by tossing a coin in the air, making it disappear. A male dwarf, in the dress of the Gegs, grinned through a thick tangle of beard. All mensch, all completely different in looks and appearance except for one thing. Each gazed at Haplo with gleaming red eyes.

Sang-drax, posting himself beside Haplo, indicated a human male, clad as a common laborer, who came forward to stand in the center of the group. "The Royal One," the serpent-elf said, speaking Patryn.

"I thought you were dead," said Haplo, his words slurred and faltering, but coherent.

The serpent king looked confused for a moment, then laughed. "Ah, yes. Chelestra. No, I am not dead. We can never die."

"You looked pretty dead to me, after Alfred was finished with you."

"The Serpent Mage? I admit that he killed a part of me, but for every part of me that dies, two more parts are born. We live, you see, as long as you live. You keep us alive. We are indebted to you." The serpent-human bowed.

Haplo stared, confused. "Then what is your true form? Are you snakes or dragons or mensch or what?"

"We are whatever you want us to be," said the serpent king. "You give us shape, as you give us life."

"Meaning you adapt to the world you're in, whatever suits your purpose." Haplo spoke slowly, his thoughts struggling through a drugged haze. "In the Nexus, you were a Patryn. On Chelestra, it suited your purpose to appear in the guise of terrifying snakes. . . ."

"Here, we can be more subtle," said the serpent king, with a casual wave of his hand. "We have no need to appear as ferocious monsters to throw this world into the turmoil and chaos on which we thrive. We have only to be its citizens."

The others in the room laughed appreciatively.

Shape-changers, Haplo realized. The evil can assume any form, any guise. On Chelestra—dragon-snakes; in this world—mensch; in the Nexus—his own people. No one will recognize them, no one will know they are here. They can go anywhere, do anything, foment wars, keep dwarf fighting elf, elf fighting human . . . Sartan fighting Patryn. Too eager to hate, never realizing our hatred makes us weak, we are open and vulnerable to the evil that will eventually devour us all!

"Why have you brought me here?" Haplo asked, almost too sick and despairing to care.

"To tell you our plans."

Haplo sneered. "A waste of time, since you intend to kill me."

"No, no, *that* would be the waste!"

Walking past rows of elves and dwarves and humans, the serpent king came to stand directly in front of Haplo. "You still haven't grasped it, yet, have you, Patryn?"

The king reached out his hand, stabbed a finger at Haplo's chest, tapped it. "*We* live only so long as *you* live. Fear, hatred, vengeance, terror, pain, suffering—that is the foul and turgid quagmire in which we breed. You live in peace and each of us dies a little bit. You live in fear and your life gives us life."

"I'll fight you!" Haplo mumbled.

"Of course you will!" laughed the serpent-human.

Haplo rubbed his aching head, his bleary eyes. "I get it. That's what you want."

"Now you are beginning to understand. The harder you struggle, the stronger we grow."

What about Xar? Haplo wondered. *You pledged to serve him. I that, too, a trick . . . ?*

"We will serve your lord." The serpent king was sincere, earnest.

Haplo scowled. He had forgotten they could read his thoughts.

"We serve Xar with enthusiasm," the serpent king continued. "We are with him on Abarrach, in the guise of Patryns, of course. We are assisting him to learn the secret of necromancy. We will join his army when he launches his attack, aid him in his war, fight his battles, do willingly whatever he asks of us. And after that . . ."

"You'll destroy him."

"We will be forced to, I'm afraid. Xar wants unity, peace. Achieved through tyranny and fear, of course. We'd gain some sustenance from that, but, all in all, a starvation diet."

"And the Sartan?"

"Oh, we don't play favorites. We're working with them, as well. Samah was inordinately pleased with himself when several 'Sartan' answered his call, came to 'their dear brothers' from out of Death's Gate. He has gone to Abarrach, but, in his absence, the newly arrived 'Sartan' are urging their fellow Sartan to declare war upon the mensch.

"And, soon, even the peaceful mensch of Chelestra will fall to quarreling among themselves. Or should I say . . . *ourselves.*"

Haplo's head sagged, heavy as rock. His arms were stones, his feet boulders. He found himself lying on the table.

Sang-drax grabbed Haplo by the hair, jerked his head up, forced him to look at the serpent, whose form now became hideous. The creature loomed large, its body swelling and expanding. And then the body started to break apart. Arms, legs, hands detached themselves from the torso, floated away. The head dwindled in size until all Haplo could see were two slit, red eyes.

"You will sleep," said a voice in Haplo's mind. "And when you wake, wake to health, fully restored. And you will remember. Remember clearly all I have said, all I have yet to say. We find ourselves in danger, here, on Arianus. There exists an unfortunate trend toward peace. The Tribus empire, weak and corrupt within, is fighting a two-front war, one which we do not think they can win. If Tribus is overthrown, the elves and their human allies will negotiate a treaty with the dwarves. This cannot be allowed.

"Nor would your lord want this to happen, Haplo." The red eyes flamed with laughter. "That will be your dilemma. An agonizing one. Help these mensch and you thwart the will of your lord. Help your lord and you help us. Help us and you destroy your lord. Destroy your lord and you destroy your people."

Darkness, soothing and welcome, blotted out the sight of the red eyes. But he still heard the laughing voice.

"Think about it, Patryn. Meanwhile, we'll grow fat on your fear."

Peering inside the room full of mensch, Limbeck could see Haplo clearly—they'd dropped him on the floor, just inside the door. The Patryn, looking around, appeared to be as astounded as the dwarf, to see this unique gathering.

Haplo didn't seem to be at all pleased, however. In fact, as near as Limbeck could tell, Haplo looked as terrified as Limbeck felt.

A human, dressed as a common laborer, came forward. He and Haplo began to converse in a language that Limbeck didn't understand, but which sounded harsh and angry and chilled him with dark and frightening sensations. At one point, however, everyone in the room laughed and commented and seemed extremely happy, agreeing to something that had been said.

At that point, Limbeck understood some of the conversation, for the dwarves spoke in dwarven and the elves in elven and the humans, presumably, since Limbeck didn't speak their language, spoke human. None of this cheered Haplo, however, who appeared more tense and desperate than before, if that were possible. He looked, to Limbeck, like a man about to meet a terrible end.

An elf took hold of Haplo by the hair, jerked the Patryn's head up, forcing him to look at the human. Limbeck watched wide-eyed, having no idea what was going on, but certain—somehow—that Haplo was going to die.

The Patryn's eyes fluttered, closed. His head sagged, he sank back into the arms of the elf. Limbeck's heart, which had struggled up from his feet, now lodged firmly in his throat. He was certain that Haplo was dead.

The elf stretched the Patryn out on the floor. The human looked down at him, shook his head, and laughed. Haplo's head turned, he sighed. He was, Limbeck saw, asleep.

Limbeck was so relieved that his spectacles steamed up. He took them off and wiped them with a shaking hand.

"Some of you Tribus elves, help me carry him," ordered the elf who had brought Haplo down here. Once again, he was speaking the elven language, not the strange language that Limbeck couldn't understand. "I've got to get him back up to that Factree place, before the others grow suspicious."

Several elves—at least Limbeck supposed they were elves; it was difficult to tell, because they were wearing some type of clothing that made them look more like the walls of the tunnels than elves—gathered around the slumbering Haplo. They lifted him by his legs and shoulders, carried him easily, as though he weighed no more than a child, and started for the door.

Limbeck ducked hastily back down the tunnel, watched as the elves bore Haplo off in the opposite direction.

It occurred to Limbeck that, once again, he was going to be left alone down here, with no idea how to get out. He must either follow them or . . .

"Perhaps I could ask one of the dwarves."

He turned to look into the room and almost dropped his spectacles. Hurriedly, he wrapped the earpieces around his ears, stared hard through the lenses of thick glass, not believing what he was seeing.

The room, which had been filled with light and laughter and humans and elves and dwarves, was empty.

Limbeck sucked in a deep breath, let it out with a shivering sigh. His curiosity overwhelmed him. He was about to slip into the room and investigate when it struck him that the elves—his way out—were rapidly leaving him behind. Shaking his side whiskers over the strange and inexplicable things he'd seen, Limbeck trotted down the hallway, following the strangely dressed elves.

The eerie red glow of their eyes lit the passages brightly, showed their way. How they could tell one tunnel from another, one arched entry from an exit, was beyond Limbeck. They moved at a rapid pace, never pausing, never taking a wrong turn, never forced to back up or start over.

"What are your plans, Sang-drax?" asked one. "Clever name, by the way."

"You like it? I thought it appropriate," said the elf who had brought Haplo down here. "I must see to it that the human child, Bane, and the Patryn, here, are taken to the emperor. The child has a plan in mind that should foment chaos in the human kingdom far more effectively than anything we could do ourselves. You will, I trust, pass the word along to those near the emperor and urge his cooperation?"

"He'll cooperate, if the Unseen[4] advise it."

"I am amazed that you managed to join such an elite and powerful unit so quickly. My congratulations."

One of the oddly dressed elves shrugged. "It was quite simple, really. Nowhere else on Arianus does there exist a group whose means and methods coincide so well with our own. With the exception of an unfortunate tendency to revere elven law and order and to perpetrate their deeds in the name of such, the Unseen Guard are perfect for us."

"A pity we cannot penetrate the ranks of the Kenkari[5] as easily."

"I begin to think that will be impossible, Sang-drax. As I ex-

---

[4] An elite unit of soldiers created by the emperor, ostensibly to search out and destroy rebel elves. The Unseen—so called because of their mysterious ability to make themselves very nearly invisible—have gained enormous power—even before the infiltration by the evil serpents.

[5] One of the seven original clans of elves brought by the Sartan to Arianus after the Sundering. All elven clans had wizards among them, but the Kenkari were more powerful in magic than most and, through strict policies of intermarriage, they were able, over many generations, to enhance their magical powers. Consequently, the Kenkari are much in demand by other elven clans. Though they have no lands of their own, they are greatly revered

plained to the Royal One this evening, prior to your arrival, the Kenkari are spiritual in nature, and therefore extraordinarily sensitive to us. We have concluded that they do not pose a threat, however. Their only interest is in the spirits of the dead, whose power feeds the empire. Their main object in life consists of guarding these captive souls."

More conversation followed, after that, but Limbeck, slogging along behind and beginning to feel very tired from all this unaccustomed exertion, soon lost interest in trying to follow it. Most of what they discussed he hadn't understood anyhow, and the small part he understood confused him. He did think it odd that elves, who, moments ago, had been quite chummy with humans, should now be talking about "fomenting chaos."

"But then nothing either humans or elves do would surprise me," he decided, wishing that he could sit down and rest. Then certain half-heard words of the elves' conversation jolted Limbeck into forgetting about sore feet and aching ankles.

"What will you do with the dwarf female your men captured?" one of the elves was asking.

"Did they?" Sang-drax replied carelessly. "I wasn't aware."

"Yes, they took her while you were occupied with the Patryn. She's in custody now, with the boy."

Jarre! Limbeck realized. They were talking about Jarre!

Sang-drax considered. "Why, I suppose I'll take her along. She might come in handy in future negotiations, don't you think? If those fool elves don't kill her first. The hatred they have for these dwarves is perfectly marvelous."

Kill Jarre! Limbeck's blood ran cold with shock, then burned hot with rage, then drained from his head into his stomach with the sickly feeling of remorse.

"If Jarre dies, it will be because of me," he mumbled to himself, barely watching where he was going. "She sacrificed herself for my sake . . ."

"Did you hear something?" asked one of the elves who was holding on to Haplo's legs.

"Vermin," said Sang-drax. "The place is crawling with them. You'd think the Sartan would have taken more care. Hurry up.

---

in the elven nation, live as "guests" among the various royal families. Their main duties, however, lie with the Keeping of the Souls.

My men will assume I'm lost down here and I don't want any of them deciding to play hero and come searching for me."

"I doubt that," said the oddly dressed elf with a laugh. "From what I've overheard, your men have little love for you."

"True," said Sang-drax implacably. "Two of them suspect me of having murdered their former captain. They're right, of course. Quite clever of them to have figured it out, actually. A pity such cleverness will prove fatal. Ah, here we are, the entrance to the Factree. Quietly, quietly."

The elves fell silent, all intent on listening. Limbeck—outraged, upset, and confused—came to a halt some distance behind. He knew where he was now, having recognized the entrance to the stairway that led back up to the statue of the Manger. He could still see the faint glow of the rune-mark Haplo had left behind.

"Someone's moving about up there," said Sang-drax. "They must have set a guard. Put him down. I'll take it from here. You two return to your duties."

"Yes, sir, Captain, sir." The other elves grinned, saluted mockingly, and then—to the distraught Limbeck's intense astonishment—both vanished.

Limbeck removed his spectacles, cleaned them. He had the vague idea that spots on the lenses might account for the elves' disappearance. Clean lenses weren't any help, however. Two of the elves were still gone. The elf captain was dragging Haplo to his feet.

"Wake up now." Sang-drax slapped the Patryn's face. "That's it. Feeling a bit groggy? It will take you some time to fully recover from the poison's effects. We'll be well on our way to the Imperanon by then. Don't worry. I'll take over the care of the mensch, especially the child."

Haplo could barely stand, and then he was forced to lean heavily on the elf captain. The Patryn looked extremely ill, but even then, sick as he was, he seemed loath to have anything to do with the elf. But he had no choice, apparently. He was too weak to climb the stairs on his own. If he wanted out of the tunnel, he had to accept the assistance of Sang-drax's strong arm.

And Limbeck had no choice. The infuriated dwarf longed to rush out and confront the elf, demand Jarre's immediate and safe return. The old Limbeck would have done so, without any regard for the consequences.

This Limbeck peered through his spectacles and saw an unusually strong elf. He recalled that the captain had mentioned other elves standing guard above, noted that Haplo was in no shape to help. Sensibly, Limbeck remained where he was, hiding in the darkness. Only when he judged by the sound of their footsteps that the two were halfway up the stairs did the dwarf pad barefooted over to crouch at the bottom.

"Captain Sang-drax, sir," came a voice from above. "We were wondering what happened to you."

"The prisoner ran," said Sang-drax. "I had to go after him."

"He ran with a knife in his shoulder?" The elf sounded impressed.

"These damned humans are tough, like wounded animals," said Sang-drax. "He led me a merry chase until the poison brought him down."

"What is he, sir? Some type of wizard? I never saw a human whose skin glowed blue like that."

"Yes. He's one of those so-called mysteriarchs. Probably down here to guard the boy."

"You believe the little bastard's story, sir?" The elf sounded incredulous.

"I think we should let the emperor determine what we believe, don't you, Lieutenant?"

"Yes, sir. I suppose so, sir."

"Where have they taken the boy?"

Blast the boy, Limbeck thought irritably. Where have they taken Jarre?

The elf and Haplo had reached the top of the stairs. The dwarf held his breath, hoping to hear more.

"To the guardhouse, Captain. Awaiting your orders, sir."

"I'll need a ship, ready to fly back to Paxaria—"

"I'll have to clear that with the lord commander, sir."

"Then do so, at once. I'll be taking the boy and this wizard and that other creature we captured—"

"The dwarf, sir?" The elf was astounded. "We had thought to execute her, as an example . . ."

Limbeck didn't hear any more. A roaring sound in his ears made him dizzy and light-headed. He swayed on his feet, was forced to lean against the wall. Jarre—executed! Jarre, who'd saved *him* from being executed! Jarre, who loved him far more than he deserved. No, it wouldn't happen! Not if he could help it and . . . and . . .

The roaring subsided, replaced by a cold emptiness that made him feel hollow and dark inside, as cold and dark and empty as these tunnels. He knew what to do. He had a Plan.

And now he could hear once again.

"What should we do about this opening, sir?"

"Close it," said Sang-drax.

"Are you sure, sir? I don't like the feel of that place. It seems . . . evil. Perhaps we should leave it open, send down teams to explore—"

"Very well, Lieutenant," said Sang-drax casually. "I saw nothing of interest down there, but if you would like to investigate, feel free. You'll be exploring on your own, of course. I can't spare any men to assist you. However—"

"I'll see to it that the opening is closed, sir," the elf said hastily.

"Whatever you decide. The choice is yours. I'll need a litter and some bearers. I can't carry this heavy bastard much farther."

"Let me help you, sir."

"Throw him down on the floor. Then you can close the opening. I'll—"

The elves' voices were receding. Limbeck dared wait no longer. He crept up the stairs, keeping his head low, until he could peep out the top of the hole. The two elves, involved with maneuvering the semiconscious Haplo off the statue's base, had their backs to the opening. Two other elves, standing guard, were eyeing the wounded human—one of the notorious mysteriarchs—with interest. They, too, had their backs turned.

It was now or never.

Planting his spectacles securely on his nose, Limbeck crawled out of the opening and made a mad, desperate dash for the hole in the floor that led back down to the Gegs' underground system of tunnels.

This part of the Factree was only dimly lit. The elven guards, wary of the strange and forbidding statue, were not standing particularly close to it. Limbeck made it to safety without being seen.

In his panicked flight, he nearly plummeted down into the

hole headfirst. Managing to catch himself at the last moment, he threw himself on the floor, grasped hold of the rungs of the ladder, and, executing a clumsy somersault, tumbled down inside. He hung suspended a moment, his hands clinging awkwardly to the top rung of the ladder, his bare feet scrabbling wildly for purchase. It was a long drop down.

Limbeck caught hold of the ladder with his toes, planted his feet more or less securely. Prying his sweating hands loose from their hold, he turned himself around and clung to the ladder thankfully, catching his breath, listening for sounds of pursuit.

"Did you hear something?" one elf was asking.

Limbeck froze against the ladder.

"Nonsense!" The lieutenant's voice was crisp. "It's that damn opening. It's making us all hear things. Captain Sang-drax is right. The sooner we shut it up, the better."

He heard a grinding sound, made by the statue sliding shut on its base. Limbeck climbed down the ladder and headed, grim-faced and coldly angry, back to his headquarters, there to institute the Plan.

His thread trail back to the automaton, the automaton itself, the unlikely peaceful union of humans, elves, dwarves—none of that mattered now.

And it might not ever matter again.

He would have Jarre back . . . or else.

CHAPTER ◆ 18

THE CATHEDRAL

OF THE ALBEDO

ARISTAGON, MID REALM

◆

THE WEESHAM[1] EXPERIENCED AN OVERWHELMING SENSE OF THANKFULNESS AS she approached the Cathedral of the Albedo.[2] It was not the beauty of the structure that touched her, though the cathedral was rightfully considered to be the most beautiful of any structure built by the elves on Arianus. Nor was she overly influenced by the awe and reverence most elves felt on approaching the repository for the souls of the elven royal families. The weesham was too frightened to notice the beauty, too bitter and unhappy to be reverent. She was thankful because she had, at last, reached a safe haven.

Clutching the small lapis and chalcedony box in her hand, she hastened up the coralite steps. Gold-gilt edges gleamed in the sunshine, seemed to shine on her path. She made her way around the octagon-shaped building until she came to the central door.

---

[1] An elven wizard whose function is to capture the soul of a dying member of elven royalty and deliver it to the Cathedral of the Albedo. A weesham is assigned to a royal child at its birth and follows the child continually throughout life, waiting for death and the release of the soul, which is captured in a magical box.

[2] An ancient word taken from old Earth. Originally "albedo" referred to that proportion of solar light shining on a planet that is reflected from that planet. The elves use the word in a highly romanticized form, to denote the light of elven souls reflecting back to their people.

As she walked, the weesham glanced more than once over her shoulder—a reflexive action, born of three days of terror.

She should have realized that it was not possible for even the Unseen to trail her here, into this sacred precinct. But her fear made her incapable of rational thought. Fear had consumed her, like the delirium of a fever, made her see things that were not there, hear words that weren't spoken. She blanched and trembled at the sight of her own shadow and, reaching the door, began beating on it with a clenched fist, rather than tapping softly and reverently as she was supposed to do.

The Keeper of the Door, whose exceptionally tall stature and thin, almost emaciated-looking form marked him as one of the Kenkari elves, jumped at the sound. Hastening to the door, he stared through the crystal panes and frowned. The Kenkari was accustomed to weesham—or geir, as they were less formally but more appropriately known[3]—arriving in various stages of grief. The stages ranged from the resigned, quiet grief of the elderly, who had lived with their charges since they were young, to the stiff-lipped grief of the soldier-weesham, who had seen their charges brought down by the war currently raging on Arianus, to the anguished grief of a weesham who has lost a child. The emotion of grief on the part of the weesham was acceptable, even laudable. But lately the Keeper of the Door had been seeing another emotion connected with grief, an emotion that was unacceptable—fear.

He saw the signs of fear in this geir, as he had seen the same signs in too many other weesham of late. The hasty pounding on the door, the distraught glances over the shoulder, the pale skin marred by gray smudges of sleepless nights. The Keeper solemnly and slowly opened the door, met the geir with grave mien, forced her to go through the ritual proceedings before she was permitted entry. The Kenkari, experienced in these matters, knew that the familiar words of the ritual, though it seemed tedious at the time, brought comfort to the grieving and the fearful.

"Please, let me in!" gasped the woman when the crystal door swung open on silent hinges.

The Keeper barred the way with his own slender body. He

---

[3] Geir is a slang term meaning "vulture."

lifted his arms high. Folds of cloth, embroidered in silken threads of iridescent reds and yellows and oranges, surrounded by velvet black, simulated the wings of a butterfly. The elf seemed, in fact, to become a butterfly—his body the body of the insect that was sacred to the elves, the wings spreading on either side.

The sight was dazzling to eye and mind and reassuring as well. The geir was immediately recalled to her duties; her training and teaching returned to her. Color came to her pallid cheeks, she remembered the proper way to introduce herself and, after a few moments, quit trembling.

She gave her name, her clan name,[4] and that of her charge. This last name she spoke with a choke in her voice and was forced to repeat it before the Keeper understood. He searched swiftly through the repositories of his memory, found the name filed there, among hundreds of others, and ascertained that the soul of this young princess rightly belonged in the cathedral. (Difficult to believe, but, in this degenerate age, there were those elves of common blood who attempted to insinuate their own plebeian ancestors into the cathedral. The Keeper of the Door—through his extensive knowledge of the royal family tree and its numerous offshoots, both legitimate and otherwise—discovered the imposters, made them prisoners, and turned them over to the Unseen Guard.)

Now the Keeper was in no doubt and made his decision immediately. The young princess, a second cousin of the emperor on his father's mother's side, had been renowned for her beauty and intellect and spirit. She should have lived years longer, become a wife, mother, borne more such as herself to grace this world.

The Keeper said as much, when—the ritual ended—he admitted the geir into the cathedral, shut the crystal door behind her. He noticed, as he did so, that the woman almost wept with relief, but still glanced about her in terror.

---

[4] Elves of other clans may become weesham, though only the Kenkari may serve in the cathedral. The weesham, who must be highly skilled in spirit magic, study with the Kenkari from the time they enter adolescence until they become adults (equivalent in human terms to the age of twenty). At this time, the geir are assigned to their charges, usually members of their own clans.

"Yes," replied the geir in a low voice, as if, even in this sanctuary, she was afraid to talk aloud, "my beautiful girl should have lived long. I should have sewed the sheets of her wedding bed, not the hem of her shroud!"

Holding the box in her open palm, the geir—a woman of around forty years—smoothed its intricately carved lid with her hand and murmured some broken words of affection for the poor soul held within.

"What was it struck her down?" asked the Keeper solicitously. "The plague?"

"Would it were!" the geir cried bitterly. "That I could have borne." She covered the box with her hand, as if she could still protect the one inside. "It was murder."

"Humans?" The Keeper was grim. "Or rebels?"

"And what would my lamb, a princess of the blood, be doing with either humans or the rebel scum[5]?" the geir flashed, forgetting in her grief and anger that she was speaking to a superior.

The Keeper reminded her of her place with a look.

The geir lowered her eyes, caressed the box. "No, it was her own that killed her. Her own flesh and blood!"

"Come, woman, you're hysterical," stated the Keeper sternly. "What possible reason—"

"Because she was young and strong, her spirit is young and strong. Such qualities," said the geir, tears trailing unheeded down her cheeks, "are more valuable to some in death than they are in life."

"I cannot believe—"

"Then believe this." The geir did the unthinkable. Reaching out her hand, she grasped hold of the Keeper's wrist, drew him near to hear her low, horror-filled words. "My lamb and I always had a glass of hot negus before retiring.[6] We shared the drink that night. I thought it tasted odd, but I assumed that the wine was bad. Neither of us finished ours, but went to bed early. My lamb

---

[5] Reference to the rebel elves, who were currently attempting to overthrow the Tribus empire.

[6] The geir never leave their charges, but remain at their sides, day and night, in case death should take them.

had been plagued with evil dreams . . .'' The geir had to pause, to regain her composure.

''My lamb fell asleep almost immediately. I was puttering about the room, sorting her dear ribbons and laying out her dress for the morrow, when a strange feeling came over me. My hands and arms felt heavy, my tongue dry and swollen. It was all I could do to stagger to my bed. I fell instantly into a strange state. I was asleep, yet I wasn't. I could see things, hear things, yet I could not respond. And thus, I saw them.''

The geir pressed the Keeper's hand more tightly. He leaned close to hear her, yet was barely able to understand her words spoken fast and tight.

''I saw the night crawl through her window!''

The Keeper frowned, drew back.

''I know what you think,'' the geir said. ''That I was drunk or dreaming. But I swear it is the truth. I saw movement, dark shapes blotted out the window frame, crept over to the wall. Three of them. And for an instant they were holes of blackness against the wall. They stood still. And then they *were* the wall!

''But I could still see them move, though it was as if the wall itself were writhing. They slid to my lamb's bed. I tried to scream, to cry out, but my voice made no sound. I was helpless. Helpless.''

The geir shuddered. ''Then a pillow—one of my lamb's silk embroidered pillows that she'd sewn with her own dear hands—rose up in the air, borne by unseen hands. They laid it over her face and . . . and pressed it down. My lamb struggled. Even in her sleep, she fought to live. The unseen hands held the pillow over her face until . . . until her struggles ceased. She lay back limp.

''Then I sensed one of them come over to me. There was nothing else visible, not even a face. Yet I knew one was near. A hand touched my shoulder and shook me.

'' 'Your charge is dead, geir,' a voice said. 'Quickly, catch her soul.'

''The terrible drugged feeling left me. I screamed and sat up and reached for the evil creature, to hold him until I could summon the guards. But my hands passed through air. They had gone. They were no longer the walls, but the night. They fled.

''I ran to my lamb, but she was dead. Her heartbeat stilled, her life smothered out of her. They had not even given her a chance to free her own soul. I had to cut her.[7] Her smooth, pale skin. I had—''

The geir began to sob uncontrollably. She did not see the look on the Keeper's face, did not see his forehead crease, his large eyes darken.

"You must have dreamed it, my dear," was all he said to the woman.

"No," she replied in hollow tones, her tears wept out. "I did not dream it, though that is what they would have me believe. And I've sensed them, following me. Everywhere I go. But that is nothing. I have no reason to live. I wanted only to tell someone. And they could not very well kill me before I fulfilled my duty, could they?"

She gave the box a last fond, grieving look, then placed it gently and reverently in the Keeper's hand.

"Not when this is what they wanted."

Turning, head bowed, she walked back through the crystal door.

The Keeper held it open for her. He spoke a few comforting words, but they were empty of conviction and both the speaker and the hearer—if she heard them at all—knew it. Holding the lapis and chalcedony box in his hand, he watched the geir wend her way down the gilt-edged stairs and out onto the large and empty courtyard surrounding the cathedral. The sun shone brightly. The geir's body cast a long shadow behind her.

The Keeper felt chilled. He watched closely until the woman had vanished beyond his sight. The box in his hand was still warm from the geir's fast hold on it. Sighing, he turned away, rang a small silver gong that stood on a wall sconce near the door.

Another Kenkari, clad in the multicolored butterfly robes, drifted down the hall on silent, slippered feet.

---

[7] The first words an elven child of royal blood learns are those that will release his soul from the body after death. He repeats these at the time of death and the geir then captures the soul to take it to the cathedral. However, if the elf dies before the words can be spoken, the geir may free the soul by cutting open a vein in the left arm and drawing off heart's blood. This must be done within moments after death.

"Take over my duties for me," the Keeper commanded. "I must deliver this to the Aviary. Summon me if there is need."

The Kenkari, the Keeper's chief assistant, nodded and took up his place at the door, ready to receive the soul of any new arrival. Box in hand, the Keeper, his brow furrowed, left the great door and headed for the Aviary.

The Cathedral of the Albedo is built in the shape of an octagon. Coralite, magically urged and pruned, swoops majestically up from the ground to form a high, steeply pitched dome. Crystal walls fill the space left between the coralite ribs, the crystal planes shine with blinding brilliance in the light of the sun, Solaris.

The crystal walls create an optical illusion, making it appear to the casual observer (who is never allowed very close) that he can see completely through the building from one side to the other. In reality, mirrored walls on the inside of the octagon reflect the interior walls of the outside. One outside cannot see inside, therefore, but those inside can see everything. The courtyard surrounding the cathedral is vast, empty of all objects. A caterpillar cannot cross it without being observed. Thus do the Kenkari keep their ancient mysteries safely guarded.

Within the octagon's center is the Aviary. Located in a circle around the Aviary are rooms for study, rooms for meditation. Beneath the cathedral are the permanent living quarters of the Kenkari, the temporary living quarters for their apprentices, the weesham.

The Keeper turned his steps toward the Aviary.

The largest chamber in the cathedral, the Aviary is a beautiful place, filled with living trees and plants brought from all over the elven kingdom to be grown here. Precious water—in such short supply elsewhere in the land, due to the war with the Gegs—was freely dispensed in the Aviary, lavishly poured to maintain life in what was, ironically, a chamber for the dead.

No singing birds flew in this Aviary. The only wings spread within its crystal walls were unseen, ephemeral—the wings of the souls of royal elves, caught, kept captive, forced to sing eternally their silent music for the good of the empire.

The Keeper paused outside the Aviary, looked within. It was truly beautiful. The trees and flowering plants grew lush here as nowhere else in the Mid Realms. The emperor's garden was not as green as this, for even His Imperial Majesty's water had been rationed.

The Aviary's water flowed through pipes buried deep beneath the soil that had been brought, so legend had it, from the garden island of Hesthea, in the High Realms, now long since abandoned.[8] Other than being watered, the plants were given no further care, unless the dead tended them, which the Keeper sometimes liked to imagine that they did. The living were only rarely permitted to enter the Aviary. And that had not happened in the Keeper's inordinately long lifetime, nor in any lifetime that any Kenkari could remember.

No wind blew in the enclosed chamber. No draft, not even a whisper of air could steal inside. Yet the Keeper saw the leaves of the trees flutter and stir, saw the rose petals tremble, saw flower stalks bend. The souls of the dead flitted among the green and living things. The Keeper watched a moment, then turned away. Once a place of peace and tranquillity and hope, the Aviary had come to take on a sinister sadness for him. He looked down at the box he held in his hand, and the dark lines in his thin face deepened.

Hastening to the chapel that stood adjacent to the Aviary, he spoke the ritual prayer, then gently pushed open the ornately carved wooden door. Within the small room, the Keeper of the Book sat at a desk, writing in a large, leather-bound volume. It was her duty to record the name, lineage, and pertinent life-facts of all those who arrived in the small boxes.

The body to the fire, the life to the book, the soul to the sky. That was how the ritual went. The Keeper of the Book, hearing someone enter, halted her writing. She looked up.

"One to be admitted," said the Door, heavily.

The Book (titles were shortened, for convenience' sake) nodded and rang a small silver gong that sat on her desk. Another Kenkari, the Keeper of the Soul, entered from a side room. The Book rose respectfully to her feet. The Door bowed. Keeper of the Soul was the highest rank attainable among the Kenkari. A wizard of the Seventh House, the Kenkari who held this title was not

---

[8] For a history of the High Realms, see *Dragon Wing*, vol. 1 of *The Death Gate Cycle*.

only the most powerful of his clan, but also one of the most powerful elves in the empire. The Soul's word, in times past, had been enough to bring kings to their knees. But now? The Door wondered.

The Soul held out his hand, reverently accepted the box. Turning, he laid the box upon the altar and knelt to begin his prayers. The Door told the maiden's name and recited all he knew of the young woman's lineage and history to the Book, who jotted down notes. She would record the details more fully, when she had time.

"So young," said the Book, sighing. "What was the cause of death?"

The Door licked dry lips. "Murder."

The Book raised her eyes, stared at him, glanced over at the Soul. The Soul ceased his prayers, turned around.

"You sound certain this time."

"There was a witness. The drug did not take complete hold. Our weesham has a taste for fine wine, it seems," the Door added, with a twisted smile. "She knew bad from good and wouldn't drink it."

"Do they know?"

"The Unseen know everything," said the Book in a low voice.

"She is being followed. They have been following her," said the Door.

"Here?" The Soul's eyes flared. "Not onto the sacred grounds."

"No. *As yet* the emperor does not dare send them here."

The words *as yet* hung ominously in the air.

"He grows careless," said the Soul.

"Or more bold," suggested the Door.

"Or more desperate," said the Book softly.

The Kenkari stared at one another. The Soul shook his head, passed a trembling hand through his white, wispy hair. "And now we know the truth."

"We have long known it," said the Door, but he said it quietly, and the Soul did not hear.

"The emperor is slaying his own kin for their souls, to aid him in his cause. The man fights two wars, three enemies: the rebels, the humans, the Gegs below. Ancient hatred and mistrust keeps these three groups divided, but what if something should happen and they should unite? That is what the emperor fears, that is what drives him to this madness.

"And it is madness," said the Door. "He is decimating the royal line, lopping off its head, cutting out its heart. Who does he have slaughtered but the young, the strong, those whose souls cling most stubbornly to life. He hopes that these souls will add their strong voices to the holy voice of Krenka-Anris, give our wizards more magical power, strengthen the arms and wills of our soldiers."

"Yet for whom does Krenka-Anris speak now?" asked the Soul.

The Door and Book kept silent, neither daring to respond.

"We will ask," said the Keeper of the Soul. He turned back to the altar.

The Keeper of the Door and the Keeper of the Book knelt alongside, one to the Soul's left, the other to his right. Above the altar, a pane of clear crystal permitted them to see within the Aviary. The Keeper of the Soul lifted a small bell from the altar, a bell made of gold, and rang it. The bell had no clapper, made no sound that living ears could hear. Only the dead could hear it, or so the Kenkari believed.

"Krenka-Anris, we call to you," said the Keeper of the Soul, raising his arms in appeal. "Holy Priestess, who first knew the wonder of this magic, hear our prayer and come to give us counsel. Thus we pray:

Krenka-Anris,
Holy Priestess.
Three sons, most beloved, you sent to battle;
around their necks, lockets, boxes of magic,
wrought by your hand.
The dragon Krishach, breathing fire and poison,
slew your three sons, most beloved.
Their souls departed. The lockets opened.
Each soul was captured. Each silent voice called to you.

Krenka-Anris,
Holy Priestess.
You came to the field of battle.
You found your three sons, most beloved,

and wept over them, one day for each.
The dragon Krishach, breathing fire and poison,
heard the grieving mother,
and flew to slay you.

Krenka-Anris,
Holy Priestess.
You cried out to your three sons, most beloved.
Each son's soul sprang from the locket,
was like a shining sword in the belly of the dragon.
Krishach died, fell from the skies.
The Kenkari were saved.

Krenka-Anris,
Holy Priestess.
You blessed your three sons, most beloved.
You kept their spirits with you, always.
Always, their spirits fought for us, the people.
You taught us the holy secret, the capturing of souls.

Krenka-Anris,
Holy Priestess,
Give us counsel in this, our trying hour,
For lives have been taken, their deaths untimely,
To serve blind ambition.
The magic that you brought us, that was once blessed,
Is now a thing perverted, dark and unholy.
Tell us what to do,
Krenka-Anris,
Holy Priestess,
We beseech you.

The three knelt before the altar in profound silence, each waiting for the response. No word was spoken aloud. No flame flared suddenly on the altar. No shimmering vision appeared before them. But each heard the answer clearly in his or her own soul, as each heard the clang of the tongueless bell. Each rose up and stared at the others, faces pale, eyes wide, in confusion and disbelief.

"We have our answer," said the Keeper of the Soul in awed and solemn tones.

"Do we?" whispered Door. "Who can understand it?"

"Other worlds. A gate of death that leads to life. A man who

is dead but who is not dead. What are we to make of this?" aske
Book.

"When the time is propitious, Krenka-Anris will make a
known," said the Soul, firmly, regaining his composure. "Unt
then, our way is clear. Keeper," he said, speaking to the Doo
"you know what to do."

The Keeper bowed in acquiescence to the Soul, knelt a fina
time before the altar, then left upon his duty. The Keeper of th
Soul and the Keeper of the Book waited in the small room, lister
ing with inheld breath and fast-beating hearts for the sound tha
neither had ever thought to hear.

It came—a hollow boom. Grillwork made of gold, fashione
in the form of butterflies, had been lowered into place. Delicate
lovely, fragile-seeming, the grille was imbued with magic tha
made it stronger than any iron portcullis that served the sam
function.

The great central door that led inside the Cathedral of th
Albedo had been closed.

CHAPTER ♦ 19

DEEPSKY

MID REALM

♦

Haplo raged inside a prison cell that was open and airy and wide as the world. He tried helplessly to batter his way through bars that were flimsy as strands of silken spiderweb. He paced a floor compassed round by no walls, he pounded on an open door, guarded by no guards. Yet a man who'd been born in a prison knew no worse prison than that in which he now found himself. By setting him free, by letting him go, by granting him the privilege of doing whatever he desired, the serpents had thrown him into a cage, bolted the door, tossed away the key.

For there was nothing he could do, nowhere he could go, no way to escape.

Feverish thoughts and plans raced through his mind. He had first wakened from his sleep to find himself on one of the elven dragonships, bound—according to Sang-drax—for the elven city of Paxaris, located on the continent of Aristagon. Haplo considered killing Sang-drax, considered taking over the elven ship, considered leaping off the ship himself, to fall to his death through the empty skies. When he reviewed his plans coldly and rationally, the last seemed the only one likely of accomplishing anything constructive.

He could kill Sang-drax, but—as the serpents had told him—their evil would only return, and be twice as strong. Haplo could take over the elven ship; the Patryn's magic was powerful, far too powerful for the puny ship's wizard to counter. But Haplo's magic couldn't fly the dragonship, and where would he go any-

way? Back to Drevlin? The serpents were there. Back to the
Nexus? The serpents were there, too. Back to Abarrach? Most assuredly, the serpents would be there.

He could warn someone, but who? . . . Warn them of what?
Xar? Why should Xar believe him? Haplo wasn't sure he believed
himself.

The fevered dreaming and plotting, the eventual ice-cold de-
liberation and rejection were not the worst of what Haplo suffered
in his prison. He knew that Sang-drax knew every scheme, every
desperate grasp. And Haplo knew that the serpent-elf approved
of all of them, was actually mentally encouraging Haplo to act.

And thus, as his only form of rebellion against the serpent-elf
and his prison, the Patryn did nothing. But he found little satisfaction in that, for Sang-drax thoroughly approved of this, too.

Haplo did nothing during the voyage, and did it with a grim
ferocity that worried the dog, frightened Jarre, and apparently
daunted Bane, for the child took care to keep clear of the Patryn's
path. Bane was up to other devices. Haplo's one source of amusement was to watch the child working hard to ingratiate himself
with Sang-drax.

"Not exactly the person I'd choose to put my trust in," Haplo
warned Bane.

"Who should I choose? You?" Bane sneered. "A lot of good
you were to me! You let the elves capture us. If it hadn't been for
me and my quick thinking we'd all be dead by now."

"What do you see when you look at him?"

"An elf." Bane was sarcastic. "Why, what do you see?"

"You know what I mean. With that clairvoyant talent of yours.
What images come to your mind?"

Bane looked suddenly uncomfortable. "Never mind what I
see. It's my business. And I know what I'm doing. Just leave me
alone."

Yeah, you know what you're doing, kid, Haplo thought
tiredly. And maybe you do, after all. *I* sure as hell don't.

Haplo had one hope. It was a fleeting one, and he wasn't
certain it was hope or what to do about it. He had come to the
conclusion that the serpents didn't know about the automaton
and its connection to the Kicksey-winsey.

He'd discovered this by eavesdropping on a conversation taking place between Sang-drax and Jarre. Haplo found it darkly

ascinating to watch the serpent in action, watch him spread the
contagion of hatred and divisiveness, watch it infect those who
might have once been immune.

Shortly after arriving in the Mid Realm, the dragonship flew
to Tolthom, an elven farming community, to drop off a shipment
of water.[1] They did not stay long, but unloaded their cargo as
swiftly as possible, this isle being a favored target of human water
pirates. Every elf on board stood armed and ready to fend off
possible attack. The human galley slaves, who operated the
dragonship's gigantic wings, were brought up on deck, in plain
view. Guards stood nearby, arrows nocked, prepared to shoot the
prisoners through the heart should any humans attack. Tolthom's
own dragonships circled overhead as the precious water was
pumped from the ship into giant holding tanks on the continent.

Haplo stood on deck, watching the water flow, watching the
sun glisten on its sparkling surface, and imagined his life flowing
like the water, pouring out of him, and knew he was as powerless
to stop it as he was to stop the water. He didn't care. It didn't
matter. Nothing mattered.

Standing near him, the dog whined in anxious concern,
rubbed its head against his knee, trying to get his attention.

Haplo would have reached down to pet the animal, but reaching took too much effort.

"Go away," he told the dog.

Hurt, the animal wandered over to Jarre, curled up unhappily
at her feet.

Haplo leaned over the rail, watched the water.

"I'm sorry, Limbeck. I understand, now."

The words came to Haplo through the dog's ears.

Jarre stood some distance away from him, staring in awe at
the coralite isle floating in the pearl-blue sky. The busy port
town's streets were filled with people. Small, neat houses lined

---

[1] Any dragonship, even one carrying political prisoners, would be required
to take water up into the Mid Realm. The elves stockpiled water on Drevlin
prior to the shutting down of the Kicksey-winsey. They had also developed
various means of collecting the rainwater from the almost continual storms
that sweep Drevlin. This was certainly not enough for the requirements of
the Mid Realm, however.

the coralite cliffs. Wagons trundled down the streets, formed
row, each farmer waiting patiently for his or her share of water
The elves laughed and visited together, their children played an
ran in the sunshine and open air.

Jarre's eyes filled with tears.

"We could live here. Our people would be happy here. I
might take some time—"

"Not as long as you think," said Sang-drax. The elf walked i
casual, leisurely fashion along the deck. The dog sat up, growled

"Listen," Haplo silently instructed it, though he wondered
why he bothered.

"Once colonies of dwarves used to live on these isles. That
was long ago," the serpent-elf added, with a shrug of his slender
shoulders, "but they prospered, at least so legend has it.

"Unfortunately, the Gegs' lack of magical talent proved you
undoing. The elves forced the dwarves to leave the Mid Realm
shipped your people down to Drevlin, to work with the other
already serving the Kicksey-winsey. Once you were gone, th
elves took over your homes and lands."

Sang-drax extended an elegant, shapely hand, pointed. "Se
that cluster of houses, the ones that burrow into the hillside
Dwarven-built. Who knows how old? And still standing. Thos
are the fronts of warrens that run far back into the hills. They ar
snug, dry. Your people found a way of sealing up the coralite,[2] t
keep the rainwater from dripping through. The elves use th
houses now for storage."

Jarre examined the dwellings, barely visible on the distan
hillside. "We could return, move in. This wealth, this paradis
that should have been ours, could be ours again!"

"Why, so it could," Sang-drax agreed, lounging against th
rail. "If and when you Gegs develop an army large enough t

---

[2] Coralite is extremely porous; water runs through it like a sieve. All race
have tried to develop various means of catching and containing the water b
sealing up the coralite, but, because the coralite is essentially a living entity
undergoing constant alteration, these have met with only mediocre succes
Detailed explanations of coralite and the construction of the floating cont
nents of the Mid Realm can be found in *Dragon Wing*, vol. 1 of *The Death Ga*
Cycle.

ush us elves off this isle. That's what it would take, you know.
Do you honestly think we'd let your kind live among us again?"

Jarre's small hands clenched the slats of the rail. She was too
hort to see over the top, was forced to peer out between the bars.
Why torment me like this?" she demanded, her voice cold and
ght. "I hate you enough already."

Haplo stood on the deck, watched the water flow, heard the
words flow around him, and thought that it all amounted to
pretty much the same: nothing. He noticed, as a matter of idle
uriosity, that his magical defenses no longer reacted when Sang-
rax was around. Haplo wasn't reacting to anything. But deep
nside, some part of him fought against his prison, struggled to
reak loose. And he knew that if he could only find the energy,
e'd be able to free that part of him and then he could . . . he
ould . . .

. . . watch the water flow.

Except that now the water had stopped flowing. The holding
anks were only about half full.

"You talk of hate," Sang-drax was saying to Jarre. "Look
own there. Do you know what is going on?"

"No," Jarre said. "And I don't care."

The line of wagons, loaded with barrels, had begun moving
ast the storage tanks. But after the first few had gone by, the
armers pulled to a halt, began to shout angrily. Word spread
apidly, and soon a mob was milling about the holding tanks, fists
aised.

"Our people have just been told that their water is being ra-
oned. From now on, very little water will be coming from Drev-
n. They've been told that you Gegs have shut off the supply."

"But that's not true!" Jarre cried, speaking before she thought.

"It isn't?" Sang-drax said, interested.

Undoubtedly interested.

Haplo was roused from his lethargy. Listening through the
og, the Patryn glanced at the serpent-elf sharply.

Jarre stared at the water in the tanks. Her face hardened. She
cowled, said nothing more.

"I think you're lying," said Sang-drax, after a moment's
ause. "I think you'd better hope you're lying, my dear."

Turning, he strolled off. The elves on board ship, their mission
ompleted, were herding the human slaves back to the galley.

Elven guards arrived to march Patryn, dwarf, and dog back t▶ their quarters. Jarre clung to the bars, taking one last, long look her eyes fixed on the tumbledown buildings on the hillside. Th▶ elves were forced to wrench her hands loose, practically had t▶ drag her below.

Haplo grinned sourly, shook his head. Built by dwarves! Cen turies old. What a crock. She believes it, though. And she hate▶ Yes, Jarre is beginning to hate in earnest. Can't get enough hat▶ can you, Sang-drax?

Haplo drifted along, going docilely where he was led. Wha did it matter where? His cell was always around him. The dog le▶ Jarre, returned to its master's side, growled at any elf who cam▶ too close.

But Haplo had learned something. The serpents didn▶ know the truth about the Kicksey-winsey. They assumed th▶ dwarves had shut it down. And that was good, he suppose▶ although what difference it might make was beyond him to figu▶ out.

Yes, good for him. Good for Bane, who would be able to g▶ the machine up and running. Good for the dwarves and for Lim▶ beck.

But not, probably, good for Jarre.

That was the only incident worthy of note during the enti▶ voyage, except for one last conversation with Sang-drax, shortl before the dragonship arrived in the imperial capital.

Once they left Tolthom (after beating off the angry mob, wh▶ discovered that there was more water on board, bound for th▶ main continent), the trip to Aristagon was completed rapidly. Th▶ human galley slaves were worked to the point of exhaustion, ▶ which point they were flogged and ordered to work some mor▶ The dragonship was alone in Deepsky, an easy target.

Only a year before, lumbering, water-laden dragonships suc▶ as these would have been escorted by a fleet of small warship▶ Built along the same lines as the larger dragonships, the warship▶ were able to maneuver quickly in the air and carried various py▶ rotechnic magicks designed to battle human raiders. But not any▶ more. Now the dragonships were on their own.

The emperor's official public position was that the human

ad become such a weak threat that escorts were no longer neces-
ary.

"The truth of the matter," Sang-drax informed Haplo on the
nal night of their voyage, "is that the armies of the Tribus elves
re spread too thin. The warships are being used to keep Prince
ees'ahn and his rebels bottled up in the Kirikai Outlands. So far,
's working. Rees'ahn hasn't a dragonship to his name. But if he
llies with King Stephen, Rees'ahn will have dragons, enough to
aunch an all-out invasion. So the warships are not only keeping
ees'ahn in, they're busy keeping Stephen out."

"What's stopped them from allying before this?" Haplo asked
hurlishly. He detested talking to the serpent-elf, but he was
orced to do so in order to find out what was going on.

Sang-drax grinned. He knew Haplo's dilemma, and reveled in
. "Old fears, old mistrust, old hatred, old prejudices. Flames that
re easy to kindle, hard to douse."

"And you serpents are busy fanning them."

"Naturally. We have people working for both sides. Or should
say against both sides. But I don't mind telling you that it's been
ifficult and that we are not easy in our minds. One reason we
ppreciate Bane. A remarkably clever child. A credit to his father.
nd I don't mean Stephen."

"Why? What has Bane got to do with it? You must know that
gmarole he told you in the tunnel was a pack of lies." Haplo was
neasy. Had Bane said anything to Sang-drax about the Kicksey-
vinsey?

"Oh, yes, we know he's lying. But others don't. Nor will
ney."

"My lord has taken a fancy to the child," Haplo warned qui-
tly. "He won't like it if anything happens to Bane."

"Implying that we might do something to harm him. I assure
ou, Patryn, that we will guard this human child with as much
are as if he were one of our own hatchlings. It's all been his
dea, you see. And we find that you mortal beings work much
nore efficiently when your own greed and ambition fuel the
ngine."

"What's the plan?"

"Come, come. Life must hold a few surprises, master. I
vouldn't want you to grow bored."

The following morning, the dragonship landed in Paxaria, whose name means Land of Peaceful Souls.

Anciently, the Paxaria (Souls at Peace) were the dominating clan in the elven realms.

The founder of the clan, according to elven legend, was Paxa Kethin, who purportedly "fell from the firmament" when he was a baby and landed in a beautiful valley, from which he took his name. Minutes were to him as years. He grew to manhood on the spot and determined that he would found a great city here, having seen the three riverbeds and the Everwell in a vision while still in his mother's womb.

Each clan on Aristagon has a similar story, differing in almost all points with one exception. All elves believe that they "came from above," which is, essentially, the truth. The Sartan, on first arriving in the World of Sky, settled the mensch in the High Realms while they worked to build the Kicksey-winsey and waited for the signal from the other worlds. This signal was, of course, a long time coming. The Sartan were forced to resettle the mensch—whose populations were growing rapidly—to the Mid and Low realms. In order to bring water to the mensch (until the Kicksey-winsey could be made to work), they built the Everwell.

The Sartan constructed three huge towers at Fendi, Gonster, and Templar. These rune-covered towers, working through Sartan magic, collect rainwater, store it, and parcel it out on a controlled basis. Once every month, the three towers open their floodgates and send three rivers of water cascading down channels cut into the coralite, channels that have been magically sealed to keep the water from seeping away into the porous material.

The rivers converge at a central point, forming the shape of a Y, and plummet in a magnificent fall down into the Everwell—an underground cavern lined with rock brought from the Ancient Earth. A fountain called "Wal'eed" gushes from the center, providing water to all who need it.

This system was designed to be temporary, was intended to provide water to a small populace. But the mensch population grew, and the Sartan population dwindled. The water supply—once so plentiful no one thought of conserving it—was now counted almost drop by drop.

Following the War of the Firmament,[3] the Paxar elves, reinforced by the Kenkari, emerged as strongest of the clans. They claimed the Everwell, set guards over the Wal'eed fountain, and built their king's palace around the site.

The Paxar continued to share water with the other elven clans and even the humans, who had once lived on Aristagon, but who had moved to Volkaran and Ulyndia. The Paxar never cut the water off, never charged for it. Paxar rule was benevolent and well-intentioned, if patronizing. But the threat to disrupt vital water supplies was omnipresent.

The hot-blooded Tribus clan considered it demeaning and humiliating to be forced to beg—as they considered it—for water. They were not pleased at having to share water with humans, either. This dispute eventually resulted in the Brotherblood, a war between the Tribus and the Paxar elves that lasted three years and resulted in the Tribus clan taking over Paxaria.

The final blow came to the Paxar when the Kenkari, self-proclaimed neutrals in the conflict, secretly threw the support of the elven souls, held in the Cathedral of the Albedo, to the Tribus. The Kenkari have always denied that they did this. They insist that they remained neutral, but no one, particularly the Paxar, believes them.)

The Tribus razed the Paxar king's palace and built a larger one on the site of the Everwell. Known as the Imperanon, it is almost a small city within itself. It includes the Palace, the Sanctuary Parks, used exclusively by the royal family, the Cathedral of the Albedo, and, below ground, the Halls of the Unseen.

Once a month, the towers built by the Sartan sent forth life-giving water. But now the Tribus controlled it. Other elven clans were forced to pay a tax, supposedly for upkeep and maintenance costs. The humans were denied water altogether. Tribus coffers were getting rich. Other elven clans, angered at the tax, sought

---

A battle fought when the Paxar attempted to settle what later became known as the Valley of the Dragons. It was during this battle that Krenka-nris discovered how to capture souls and use them to enhance elven magic. The Paxar allied with the Kenkari to defeat the dragons. Those dragons that survived flew to human lands, where they found a welcome. Human magic, which deals with living things and natural properties, can enchant dragons. Elven magic, which deals with mechanics, cannot.

their own supplies of water and found them, down below, in Drevlin.

The other clans, particularly the Tretar, who invented the fa mous dragonships, began to prosper. Tribus might have withered on its own vine, but, fortunately for them, desperate humans be gan to attack the dragonships, steal the water. Faced with this threat, the various elven clans forgot old differences, banded to gether, and formed the Tribus empire, whose heart is the Impera non.

The war against the humans was going well for the elves They were near victory. Then their charismatic and most skilled military general, Prince Rees'ahn, fell under the influence (some say the magic) of a song sung by a black-skinned human known as Ravenlark. This song made the elves remember the ideals of Paxar Kethin and Krenka-Anris. Elves who hear this song see truth, see the corrupt, dark heart of the dictatorial Tribus empire and know that it means the destruction of their world.

Now, the towers of the Sartan continue to send forth water but armed elves stand guard along its route. Rumor has it that large parties of human slaves and captured elven rebels are build ing secret aqueducts that lead from the rivers directly into the Imperanon. Every month, the water flowing from the towers is less than the amount that flowed last month. The elven wizards who have studied the towers at length, report that for some un known reason, their magic is starting to fail.

And none knows how to save it.

CHAPTER ♦ 20

THE IMPERANON

ARISTAGON, MID REALM

♦

"THEY CANNOT DO THIS," AGAH'RAN STATED WITH A SHRUG. HE WAS FEEDING a slice of orange to a pet hargast[1] bird and did not look up as he spoke. "They simply cannot do this."

"Ah, but they can, O Exalted One," replied Count Tretar, head of the Tretar clan,[2] and currently His Imperial Majesty's most trusted and valued adviser. "What is more to the point, they have."

"Closed the Cathedral of the Albedo? Accepting no more souls? I refuse to permit it. Send them word, Tretar, that they have incurred our extreme displeasure and that the cathedral is to be reopened at once."

"That is precisely what Your Imperial Majesty must *not* do."

"*Not* do? Explain yourself, Tretar." Agah'ran lifted painted eyelids slowly, languidly, as if the effort were almost beyond his strength. At the same time, he waggled his hands in helpless fash-

---

[1] A rare species claimed, by legend, to nest in the brittle branches of the hargast tree. Since no one has ever found a hargast-bird nest, this cannot be verified. The birds are difficult to net and are therefore extremely expensive. Their song is quite exquisite.

[2] The seven elven clans are: Paxar, Quintar, Tretar, Savag, Melista, Tribus, and Kenkari. The emperor is a member of the Tribus clan, as is his son, the rebel prince, Rees'ahn. Intermarriage has blurred most clan lines, with the exception of the Kenkari, who are forbidden to marry or bear children outside the clan. None has ever been known to disobey.

ion. His fingers had juice on them, and the stickiness displeased him.

Tretar motioned for the valet de chambre, who summoned a slave, who ran with alacrity to bring the emperor a warm, moist towel. Agah'ran laid his fingers limply on the cloth. The slave reverently cleansed them.

"The Kenkari have never proclaimed allegiance to the empire. Historically, My Liege, they have always been independent, serving all clans, owing loyalty to none."

"They approved of the forming of the empire." It was nearing his nap time and Agah'ran was inclined to be petulant.

"Because they were pleased to see the union of the six clans. And therefore they have served Your Imperial Majesty and have supported Your Majesty's war against your rebel son, Rees'ahn. They even cast him out, as Your Imperial Majesty commanded, ordered his weesham to leave him, essentially damning his soul to live outside the Blessed Realm."

"Yes, yes, we know all this, Tretar. Come to the point. I grow fatigued. And Solaris is very hot. If I am not careful, I shall begin to sweat."

"If Your Radiance will bear with me a moment longer."

Agah'ran's hand twitched, an action that, in another man might have been the clenching of a fist. "We need those souls, Tretar. You were present. You heard the report. Our ungrateful son Rees'ahn—may the ancestors devour him—has been conducting secret negotiations with that barbaric fiend, Stephen of Volkaran. If they ally . . . Ah, see what this upset has done to us. We are trembling. We feel weak. We must retire."

Tretar snapped his fingers. The valet clapped his hands. Slaves brought forth a sedan chair that had been standing nearby. Other slaves lifted His Imperial Majesty gently in their arms, carried him bodily from the cushions on which he'd been seated to the sedan chair, where His Majesty was settled, with much fuss and bother, among the cushions. The slaves hoisted the chair onto their shoulders.

"Gently, gently," ordered the valet. "Don't lift too fast. The motion makes His Majesty giddy."

Slowly, solemnly, the sedan chair started off. The Royal Weesham rose and followed after. Count Tretar came after the weesham. The valet de chambre, watching anxiously, hovered about the sedan chair in case His Majesty felt faint. The procession, led by the sedan chair, moved from the garden to the emperor's sitting room—a fatiguing journey of about ten paces.

Agah'ran—an extraordinarily handsome elf (beneath the paint) in his early two hundreds—was not, as some first supposed on meeting him, crippled. Nothing in the slightest was wrong with His Imperial Majesty's limbs. Agah'ran (in midlife, by elven standards) was quite capable of walking and did so, when required. The unusual effort fatigued him for cycles afterward, however.

Once inside the sumptuously furnished sitting room, Agah'ran made a languid motion with his fingers.

"His Majesty wishes to stop," Tretar instructed.

The valet echoed the count's orders. The slaves complied. The chair was lowered, slowly, so as not to make His Imperial Majesty nauseous, to the floor. The emperor was lifted out of it and placed in a chair, facing out on the garden.

"Turn us a bit to the left. We find the view far less fatiguing from this angle. Pour us some chocolate. Will you partake, Tretar?"

"I am honored that Your Imperial Majesty thinks of me." Count Tretar bowed. He detested chocolate, but would never dream of offending the emperor by refusing.

One of the slaves reached for the samovar. The weesham, looking uneasy (as well he might, considering the discussion was dealing with his true masters, the Kenkari), saw a way to escape and intervened. "I fear the chocolate has grown tepid, O Exalted One. It would give me great pleasure to bring Your Imperial Majesty more. I know precisely the temperature Your Imperial Majesty likes it."

Agah'ran glanced at Tretar. The count nodded.

"Very well, Weesham," the emperor said languidly. "You are dismissed from our royal presence. Six degrees above room temperature and not a degree higher."

"Yes, My Liege." The geir, hands plucking nervously at his black robes, bowed himself out. Tretar waved his hand. The valet de chambre hustled the slaves out of the room. The valet himself faded into the background.

"A spy, do you think?" Agah'ran asked, referring to the departed weesham. "The Kenkari found out through him?"

"No, My Liege. The Kenkari would never dream of anything so crude. They may be very powerful in magic, but they are a simple people, politically naive. The geir is sworn to one duty and that is the safekeeping of Your Imperial Majesty's soul. That is a holy duty, and one with which the Kenkari would not interfere."

Tretar leaned forward, lowered his voice to a whisper. "From what I have been able to learn, My Liege, it was the ineptness of the Unseen that precipitated this crisis."

A corner of the painted eyelid twitched. "The Unseen do not make mistakes, Tretar," said Agah'ran.

"They are men, O Radiant One. They are fallible, as all men are fallible, with the exception of Your Imperial Majesty. And I have heard it said"—Tretar moved still closer—"that the Unseen have taken steps to discipline the elves involved. They are no more. And neither is the geir who carried news of the princess's murder to the Kenkari."

Agah'ran appeared considerably relieved. "The matter is settled, then, and nothing like this will occur again. You will see to that, Tretar. Express our wishes to the Unseen forcibly."

"Of course, My Liege," said Tretar, who had absolutely no intention of doing any such thing. Let those cold-blooded demons mind their own affairs! He wanted no part of them.

"That does not help us with our current problem, however, Tretar," pursued Agah'ran mildly. "The eggs have been broken, so to speak. We see no way of putting the yolks back into their shells."

"No, O Radiant One," Tretar agreed, glad to return to a subject less dangerous and of far more importance. "And, therefore, I propose to His Imperial Majesty that he make an omelet."

"Quite clever, Tretar." The emperor's painted lips creased slightly. "Do we partake of this omelet ourselves or feed it to the Kenkari?"

"Neither, Majesty. We feed it to our enemy."

"A poisoned omelet, then."

Tretar bowed in homage. "Your Majesty is, I see, far ahead of me."

"You are referring to that human child . . . What's his name? The one who was brought to the Imperanon yesterday."

"Bane, Your Majesty."

"Yes. Charming child, or so we hear. Passable looks, for a human, we are told. What are we to make of him, Tretar? Is this wild tale of his to be believed?"

"I have done some investigating, Your Imperial Majesty. If you would be interested to hear what I have discovered?"

"Amused, at least," said the emperor, with a languid lift of a plucked eyebrow.

"Your Majesty has, among his slaves, a human who once served in the royal household of King Stephen. A minor footman, he was pressed into service in the Volkaran army. I took the liberty of bringing this man and the child, Bane, together. The footman recognized the child immediately. In fact, the wretched man nearly passed out, thinking he'd seen a ghost."

"Appallingly superstitious—humans," Agah'ran commented.

"Yes, My Liege. Not only did this man recognize the boy, the boy knew the footman. He spoke to him by name—"

"By name? A footman? Bah! This Bane cannot have been a prince!"

"Humans tend to be democratic-minded, Sire. I am told that King Stephen admits any human, even those of the lowest, most common rank, into his presence, if they have a suit or a grievance."

"Gad! How dreadful! I feel quite faint," said Agah'ran. "Hand me those smelling salts, Tretar."

The count lifted a small bottle, decorated with silver, and motioned to the valet de chambre, who motioned to a slave, who took the bottle and held it at the proper distance beneath the imperial nose. Several sniffs of the aromatic salts restored Agah'ran to clear-minded attentiveness, alleviated the shock of hearing about the barbaric practices of humans.

"If you are feeling quite well, My Liege, I will continue."

"Where is all this leading, Tretar? What has the child to do with the Kenkari? You cannot fool us, Count. We are sharp. We see a connection developing here."

The count bowed in homage. "Your Imperial Majesty's brain is a veritable dragon-trap. If I might presume upon Your Radiance's patience, I beg Your Majesty to permit me to introduce the child into the Royal Presence. I believe Your Imperial Majesty will find the story the boy has to tell quite interesting."

"A human? Into *our* presence? Suppose . . . suppose"—Agah'ran appeared distraught, fluttered his hand—"suppose we catch something?"

"The boy has been quite thoroughly scrubbed, Your Majesty," said the count with becoming gravity.

Agah'ran motioned to the valet, who motioned to the slave, who handed the emperor a scented pomander. Holding it up in front of his nose, Agah'ran indicated with a slight nod that Tretar was to proceed. The count snapped his fingers. Two of the royal guard marched in, conveying the child between them.

"Stop! Stop there!" Agah'ran commanded, though the boy had not taken four steps into the large room.

"Guards, leave us," Tretar ordered. "Your Imperial Majesty, I present His Highness, Bane, Prince of Volkaran."

"*And* Ulyndia *and* the High Realms," added the child. "Now that my real father's dead."

He stepped forward with an imperious air, bowed gracefully from the waist. The prince indicated respect for the emperor, but made it clear he was offering it to an equal, as an equal.

Agah'ran, accustomed to seeing his own people prostrate themselves flat on the floor before their emperor, was considerably taken aback by such arrogance and bravado. It would have cost an elf his soul. Tretar held his breath, thinking perhaps he'd made a serious mistake.

Bane raised his head, straightened his small body, and smiled. He had been bathed and dressed in whatever finery Tretar could find to fit him (human children being considerably rounder than elven children). The golden curls had been combed into ringlets that glistened in the light. Bane's skin was like fine porcelain, his eyes were bluer than the lapis on the box held by the emperor's geir. Agah'ran was impressed with the child's beauty, or so Tretar judged, noting the emperor lift his eyebrow and slightly lower the scented pomander.

"Come nearer, boy—"

Tretar coughed delicately.

Agah'ran took the hint. "Come nearer, *Your Highness*, that we may look at you."

The count breathed again. The emperor was charmed. Not literally, of course. Agah'ran wore strong talismans that protected him against magic. Tretar, in his first interview with Bane, had been amused to see the human boy attempt to work some type of crude magic upon himself, some sort of enchantment spell. The magic had no effect, but its use was one of the first indications Tretar had that the boy might be telling at least part—if not all—the truth.

"Not too close," said Agah'ran. Not all the perfume in Aristagon could mask the human smell. "There, that's near enough. So you claim to be the son of King Stephen of Volkaran."

"No, I do not, O Exalted Being," said Bane, frowning slightly.

Agah'ran cast a stern glance at Tretar, who inclined his head. "Patience, My Liege," he said softly. "Tell His Imperial Majesty your father's name, Your Highness."

"Sinistrad, Your Imperial Majesty," said Bane proudly. "A mysteriarch of the High Realm."

"A term the humans use for a wizard of the Seventh House, My Liege," explained Tretar.

"Seventh House. And your mother's name?"

"Anne of Ulyndia, Queen of Volkaran and Ulyndia."

"Dear, dear," murmured Agah'ran, shocked, though he had himself fathered more illegitimate children than he could count. "I fear you've made a mistake, Count. If this bastard is not the king's son, then he is not the prince."

"Yes, I am, My Liege!" Bane cried in childish impetuosity that was quite becoming and, moreover, quite convincing. "Stephen claimed me as his legitimate son. He made me his heir. My mother forced him to sign papers. I've seen them. Stephen has to do what my mother says. She's head of her own army. He needs her support if he wants to remain king."

Agah'ran glanced at Tretar.

The count rolled his eyes as much as to say, "What do you expect of humans?"

The emperor almost smiled, refrained. A smile might muss his paint. "Such an arrangement sounds quite satisfactory to all concerned, Your Highness. We sense something happened to upset it, since you were found on that Geg place. What's its name . . ."

"Drevlin, My Liege," Tretar murmured.

"Yes, Drevlin. What were you doing down there, child?"

"I was a prisoner, Your Radiance." Bane's eyes glittered with sudden tears. "Stephen hired an assassin, a man called Hugh the Hand—"

"Surely not!" Agah'ran's painted eyelids fluttered.

"My Liege, please, do not interrupt," Tretar admonished gently.

"Hugh the Hand traveled to the High Realms. He murdered my father, Your Imperial Majesty, and was going to murder me, but, before he died, my father managed to fatally wound the assassin first. But then I was captured by an elven captain named Bothar'el. He's in league with the rebels, I think."

Agah'ran glanced again at Tretar, who confirmed this with a nod.

"Bothar'el took me back to Volkaran. He figured that Stephen would pay to have me back safely." Bane's lip curled. "Stephen paid to have me out of the way. Bothar'el sent me to the Gegs, paid them to keep me prisoner."

"Your Radiance will recall," Tretar struck in, "that around this time, Stephen let it be known among the humans that the prince had been taken prisoner and murdered by elves. The story stirred up the humans against us."

"But tell me, Count, why didn't Stephen simply do away with the child?" Agah'ran asked, regarding Bane as if he were some sort of exotic animal, let loose from its cage.

"Because the mysteriarchs had, by this time, been forced to flee the High Realm, which, our spies tell us, has become untenable for their kind. They moved onto Volkaran and told Stephen it would be as much as his life was worth to harm the son of Sinistrad, who had been a powerful leader among them."

"Yet the queen permits her child to remain a prisoner. Why would your mother allow such a thing?" Agah'ran asked Bane.

"Because if the people found out she'd been whoring with one of the mysteriarchs, they would have burned her for a witch," said Bane, with an air of innocence that made his use of the crude, if descriptive, verb quite charming.

The count gave a deprecating cough. "I believe there is more to it than that, Your Imperial Majesty. Our spies report that Queen Anne wants to gain the throne herself. She intended to do so, in league with this mysteriarch, Sinistrad—the boy's father. But he died, and now neither she nor the surviving wizards are powerful enough to overthrow Stephen and take control of Volkaran themselves."

"But I am, My Liege," Bane said, ingenuously.

Agah'ran appeared highly diverted. He actually removed the pomander in order to get a better look. "*You* are, boy?"

"Yes, O Radiant One," said Bane. "I've been thinking this all out. What if I turned up suddenly, safe and sound, on Volkaran? I'd say publicly that you elves kidnapped me, but I had managed to escape. The people love me. I'd be a hero. Stephen and Anne would have no choice but to claim me, take me back."

"But Stephen would only get rid of you again," said Agah'ran, yawning and passing a fatigued hand over his brow. It was past nap time. "And, though it might gain *you* something, we fail to see what this would gain *us*."

"A lot, My Liege," said Bane coolly. "If the king and queen were to both suddenly die, I'd be heir to the throne."

"My, my," murmured Agah'ran, eyes opening so wide that the paint on the lids cracked.

"Valet, summon the guards," ordered Tretar, reading the signs. "Remove the boy."

Bane flared. "You, sir, are speaking to a prince of Volkaran!"

Tretar glanced at the emperor, saw the painted eyelids flicker in amusement. The count bowed to the prince.

"I beg your pardon, Your Highness. His Imperial Majesty has greatly enjoyed this interview, but he now grows weary."

"We suffer from the headache," said Agah'ran, pressing polished fingernails to his temple.

"I am sorry His Majesty is indisposed," said Bane, with dignity. "I will withdraw."

"Thank you, Your Highness," said Tretar, making a gallant effort to keep from laughing. "Guards, please escort His Royal Highness back to his quarters."

The guards marched in, marched Bane out. Bane cast a secret, inquiring glance at Tretar. The count smiled, indicated that all was well. Bane appeared pleased, walked away between his guards with a grace and elegance not seen in many elven children.

"Remarkable," Agah'ran said, having recourse, once again, to the smelling salts.

"I trust I have no need to remind Your Majesty that we are dealing with humans and must not allow ourselves to be shocked by their barbaric ways."

"All very well for you to say so, Count, but we are convinced that this nauseating tale of assassins and whores has quite destroyed our inclination for lunch. We have an extremely delicate digestive system, Tretar."

"I am sadly aware of the fact, Your Majesty, and for that I do deeply apologize."

"Still," the emperor mused, "if the boy *were* to succeed to the throne of Volkaran, he would have reason to be extremely grateful to us."

"Indeed, O Exalted One," said Tretar. "At the very least he would refuse to ally with Prince Rees'ahn, leave the rebels to shift for themselves, might even be persuaded to declare war on them. I further suggest that Your Imperial Majesty offer to serve in the capacity of protectorate to the young king Bane. We could send in an occupation force to keep peace among the warring factions of humans. For their own good, of course."

Agah'ran's lid-painted eyes glittered. "You mean, Tretar, that this boy would simply hand us Volkaran."

"I do, indeed, My Liege. In return for rich reward, naturally."

"And what of these wizards, these 'mysteriarchs'?" The emperor grimaced at being forced to speak the human word.

The count shrugged. "They are dying out, Your Imperial Majesty. They're arrogant, willful, disliked and distrusted even by those of their own race. I doubt if they will trouble us. If they do, the boy will keep them in line."

"And the Kenkari? What of *our* wizards?"

"Let them do what they will, My Liege. Once the humans are conquered and subdued, you will be able to concentrate your forces on destroying the rebels. That accomplished, you wipe out the Gegs in Drevlin and take over the Kicksey-winsey. You will then have no more need for the souls of the dead, O Exalted One. Not when you have at your command the souls of all the living in Arianus."

"Most ingenious, Count Tretar. We commend you."

"Thank you, My Liege." The count bowed deeply.

"But this will take time."

"Yes, Your Imperial Majesty."

"And what are we to do about these wretched Gegs? Shutting the machine down, cutting off our water!"

"Captain Sang-drax—an excellent officer, by the way, I draw Your Imperial Majesty's attention to him—has brought us a Geg prisoner."

"So we heard." The emperor held the pomander to his nose, as though the stench had somehow managed to seep into his half of the palace. "We fail to see why. We have a pair for the royal zoo, don't we?"

"Your Imperial Majesty is in good humor this day," Tretar said, adding the laugh he knew was expected.

"We aren't," Agah'ran stated petulantly. "Nothing is going right. But we assume that this Geg is of some importance to you?"

"As a hostage, My Liege. I suggest that we offer the Gegs an ultimatum: they either start the Kicksey-winsey or what is left of this Geg female will be returned to them in several small boxes."

"And what is one Geg more or less, Tretar? They breed like rats. I fail to see—"

"Begging Your Radiance's pardon, but the Gegs are quite a close-knit race. They have a rather quaint belief that what happens to one Geg happens to all. I think this threat should be sufficient inducement for them to do our bidding."

"If you think so, Count, then such will be our command."

"Thank you, My Liege. And now, as Your Radiance appears fatigued—"

"We are, Tretar. We admit it. The pressures of state, dear count, the pressures of state . . . However, one thought occurs to us."

"Yes, O Exalted One?"

"How do we return the boy to Volkaran without rousing the humans' suspicions? And what's to keep King Stephen from simply doing away with him quietly if we do send him back?" Agah'ran shook his head, wearied himself greatly with the effort. "We see too many difficulties—"

"Rest assured, O Exalted One, I have taken all this into consideration."

"Truly?"

"Yes, My Liege."

"And what is your intent, Count?"

The count glanced at the slaves and the valet. He leaned down, whispered into His Radiant Majesty's perfumed ear.

Agah'ran stared, confounded, at his minister, for a moment. Then a slow smile spread over the lips that were touched with ground coral. The emperor was aware of his minister's intelligence, just as his minister was aware that his emperor—despite appearances—was no fool.

"We approve, Count. You will make the arrangements?"

"Consider them made, Your Imperial Majesty."

"What will you tell the boy? He will be eager to leave."

The count smiled. "I must admit, My Liege, it was the boy who suggested the plan."

"The cunning little devil. Are all human children like this, Tretar?"

"I should not think so, O Exalted One, or the humans would have long ago defeated us."

"Yes, well, this one bears watching. Keep your eye on him, Tretar. We should love to hear further details, but some other time." Agah'ran passed his hand weakly over his brow. "The headache grows severe."

"Your Radiance suffers much for his people," said Tretar, with a low bow.

"We know, Tretar. We know." Agah'ran heaved a pain-filled sigh. "And they do not appreciate it."

"On the contrary, they adore you, My Liege. Attend to His Majesty," Tretar ordered, snapping his fingers.

The valet de chambre leapt to action. Slaves came running from all directions, bearing cold compresses, hot towels, warm wine, chilled water.

"Carry us to our bedchamber," said Agah'ran faintly.

The valet took over, marshaling the complicated procedure.

Count Tretar waited until he had seen the emperor lifted from the couch, placed among silken pillows on a gilded litter, and carried in a procession, moving at a coral grub's pace (so as not to disturb the royal equilibrium) toward the bedchamber. Near the door, Agah'ran made a feeble gesture.

Tretar, who had been watching closely, was instantly attentive.

"Yes, My Liege?"

"The boy has someone with him. A human freak, whose skin has turned blue."

"Yes, Your Imperial Majesty," answered Tretar, not thinking it necessary to explain. "So we have been informed."

"What of him?"

"You have nothing to worry about, My Liege. I did hear it

rumored that this man was one of the mysteriarchs. I questioned Captain Sang-drax about him, and according to the captain, this blue-skinned fellow is only the boy's manservant."

Agah'ran nodded, lay back among the pillows, and closed the painted eyelids. The slaves bore him off. Tretar waited until certain he was no longer needed, then—smiling to himself in satisfaction—he went off to put the first steps of his plan into action.

CHAPTER 21

ROYAL PALACE

VOLKARAN ISLES

MID REALM

♦

Kɪɴɢ sᴛᴇᴘʜᴇɴ's ᴄᴀsᴛʟᴇ ᴏɴ ᴛʜᴇ ɪsʟᴇ ᴏꜰ ᴘʀᴏᴠɪᴅᴇɴᴄᴇ ᴡᴀs ꜰᴀʀ ᴅɪꜰꜰᴇʀᴇɴᴛ ɪɴ appearance from his elven counterpart's on Aristagon. The Imperanon was a vast collection of gracefully designed and elegant buildings, with spiraling towers and minarets decorated with tile mosaics, painted furbelows, and carved curlicues. King Stephen's fortress was solid, massive, constructed on square lines; its grim, tooth-edged towers rose dark and unlovely into the smoke-colored sky. The difference in the stone could be seen in the flesh, so the saying went.

Night on the Imperanon was ablaze with flambeaux and candelabra. On Volkaran, lambent light from the Firmament glittered on the scaled skin of guard-dragons, perched atop the towers. Watch fires shone red in the twilight, lighting the way for returning dragon marauders and providing warmth for the human watchers, whose eyes ceaselessly scanned the skies for elven dragonships.

The fact that no elven dragonship had dared fly Volkaran's skies for a long while did not make the watchers less vigilant. There were some, living in the town of Firstfall, which crowded close to the castle walls, who whispered that Stephen did not watch for elven dragonships. No, he watched for enemies closer to home, flying the kiratrack,[1] not the kanatrack.

---

[1] Directional reference system. Defined in detail in *Dragon Wing*, vol. 1, *The Death Gate Cycle*. For general purposes, kiratrack corresponds to west, kana-

Alfred, who lived among the humans for a time, wrote the following discourse on the race. The title is *A Baffling History*.[2]

The elves in Arianus would not have grown strong and powerful if the humans had been able to unite. United as a race, the humans could have formed a wall through which the elves could not have penetrated. The humans could have easily taken advantage of the various elven clan wars to have established strong footholds on Aristagon (or, at the very least, keep from being pushed off!).

But the humans, who consider elves foppish and weak, made the mistake of discounting them. The various human factions, with their long history of blood feuds, were far more interested in battling each other than in fending off elven attacks. The humans, in essence, defeated themselves, leaving themselves so weak that all the powerful Paxar had to do was stamp their feet and shout, "Boo!" and the humans fled in terror.

The humans were driven off Aristagon. They flew to the Volkaran Isles and the larger continent of Ulyndia, and here they might have regrouped, united. During the Brotherblood War that raged among the elves, the humans could have easily recaptured all the territory they had lost. It is altogether possible that they might have taken the Imperanon, for the humans had among them then the mysteriarchs, whose skills in magic are far greater than those attained by the elves, with the exception of the Kenkari. And the Kenkari were, in this war, supposedly neutral.

But their own race's internecine wars offended and sickened the powerful mysteriarchs. Finding that their efforts to bring peace to the warring factions were in vain, the mysteriarchs left the Mid Realm, traveled up to the High Realm, to the cities built by the Sartan, where the mysteriarchs hoped to live in peace. Their departure left the humans vulnerable to attack by the

---

track is east, trackward is north, and backtrack is south. This statement implies that Stephen is more worried about dragons flying from Ulyndia than from the elven kingdoms.

[2] Found in the library of Castle Volkaran. Alfred wrote the history in the human language, undoubtedly with the intent of using it to instruct the humans in their own folly. True to his vacillating nature, the Sartan could never bring himself to show the book to the king, but placed it in the library, apparently in the forlorn hope that Stephen or Anne might stumble across it.

Tribus elves, who, having defeated and forcibly united the elven clans, turned their attention to the human raiders, who had been attacking and pirating elven water shipments from Drevlin.

The Tribus elves conquered many human realms on Volkaran, using bribes and betrayal as well as the sword to divide and conquer. The humans saw their sons and daughters taken into slavery; they saw most of their food going into elven mouths; they saw elf lords slaughter dragons for sport. Eventually, the humans came to the conclusion that they hated elves more than they hated each other.

The two most powerful human clans, working in secret, formed an alliance, sealed by the marriage of Stephen of Volkaran with Anne of Ulyndia. The humans began to push the occupying forces off Volkaran, culminating in the famous Battle of Seven Fields, a battle remarkable for the fact that the loser ended up the victor.[3]

The subsequent rebellion among the elves, led by Prince Rees'ahn, forced the withdrawal of elven occupying forces.

Alfred's history concludes on a sad note:

Ulyndia and Volkaran are once again under human control. But now, once the elven threat is removed, the humans have decided it is safe to start hating each other again. Factions howl war and snap at each other's throats. Powerful barons on both sides mutter darkly that the alliance of Stephen and Anne has outlived its usefulness. The king and queen are forced to play a dangerous game.

These two, in truth, love each other dearly. A marriage of convenience, planted in the muck of years of hatred, has blos-

---

[3] Defeated in battle, King Stephen was forced to surrender his army to Prince Rees'ahn. The elves took the humans prisoner and were marching them to slavery when a human minstrel named Ravenlark began to sing a song of defiance. The song turned out to have a powerful, almost magical effect on the elves. It transports all elves who hear it back to a time when they lived in peace, when their society gloried in all things beautiful. The elves threw down their weapons; many began to weep for what was lost. The king and his army retreated into a nearby castle. The elves left the field of battle, returned to their ships. Thus began the elven revolution. *Dragon Wing*, vol. 1, *The Death Gate Cycle*.

somed into mutual respect and affection. But each knows that the flower will wither and die untimely, unless they can keep control of their followers.

Thus each pretends to hate what each most dearly values— the other. They quarrel loudly in public, cling to each other most fondly in private. Thinking the marriage and therefore the alliance is crumbling, the members of each opposing faction whisper their intrigues to king and queen openly, not realizing that these two are—in reality—one. Thus Stephen and Anne have been able to control and put out blazes that might have consumed their kingdom.

But now there is a new problem—Bane. And what we are to do about him is beyond me to figure out. I am afraid for the mensch, though. Afraid for them all.

The problem had been solved.[4] Bane had disappeared, purportedly carried off to a faraway realm by a man with blue skin— at least such had been the vague report given King Stephen by Bane's real mother, Iridal of the High Realms.

The farther away they took Bane, the better, was Stephen's view of the matter. Bane had vanished over a year ago, and a curse seemed to have been lifted from the entire kingdom with the boy's removal.

Queen Anne became pregnant again, and was safely delivered of a baby girl. The child was princess of Ulyndia and, though the crown of Volkaran could not now, by law, be given into female hands, laws had a way of changing over the years, especially if Stephen did not father any sons. King and queen both adored their daughter. Magi of the Third House were hired to stand guard day and night to make certain that this time no strange, fey changeling appeared in the cradle.

Also, during this momentous year, the rebellion of the Gegs of the Lower Realms further weakened the elves, depleted their forces. Stephen's armies had managed to push the elves from their last toehold on the outlying islands of Volkaran.

An elven dragonship loaded with water had just fallen into human hands. The water harvest had been good this year. Stephen had been able to call off water rationing, which pleased the

---

[4] Bane's story is told in full in *Dragon Wing*, vol. 1, *The Death Gate Cycle*.

people. The quarreling factions—for the most part—thought well of each other, and the fights that broke out among them now were of the good-natured variety, resulting in bloody noses, not bloody knives.

"I am even beginning to think seriously, my dear, of telling the world that I love you," said Stephen, leaning over his wife's shoulder to make faces at the baby.

"Don't go too far," said Anne. "I've rather come to enjoy our public bickering. I think it's good for us. Whenever I do get truly mad at you, I put all my anger into the next mock battle, and I feel much better. Oh, Stephen, what a dreadful face! You'll frighten her."

The baby, however, laughed in delight and reached out a hand to try to grab the king's graying beard.

"So, all these years, you've actually meant those terrible things you said to me!" Stephen teased.

"I hope your face freezes like that. It would serve you right! Isn't he an ugly papa?" Anne said to the baby. "Why don't you fly up and attack such an ugly papa. There, my little dragon. Fly to Papa."

Lifting the baby, Anne "flew" the child at Stephen, who caught hold of his daughter and tossed her lightly in the air. The baby laughed and crowed and tried again to grasp hold of the man's beard.

The three were in the nursery, enjoying a brief and precious time together. Such moments were all too rare for the royal family, and the man who stood in the doorway stopped to watch, a sad and regretful smile on his lips. The moment would end. He, himself, would end it. But he paused to enjoy the extra few seconds of unclouded happiness that he must snatch away.

Perhaps Stephen felt the shadow of the cloud pass over him. The visitor had made no sound, but the king was aware of his presence. Trian—king's magus—and Trian alone had permission to open doors without knocking, without being announced. Stephen looked up, saw the wizard standing in the doorway.

The king smiled at the sight and started to make some jest, but the expression on Trian's face was more frightening than those Stephen had been making to entertain his tiny daughter. The king's smile faded and grew cold. Anne, who had been fondly watching her husband and child play together, saw his brow larken, glanced over her shoulder in alarm. At the sight of Trian, he queen rose to her feet.

"What is it? What's wrong?"

Trian cast a swift glance from beneath lowered lashes back nto the hallway, made a slight gesture with his hand to indicate hat people were in earshot.

"A messenger has arrived from Baron Fitzwarren, Your Majesty," the magus said loudly. "A minor skirmish with the elves at Kurinandistai, I believe. I am truly sorry to draw Your Majesties away from more pleasant pursuits, but you both know the baron."

They both did indeed know the baron, having received a report from him only that morning stating that he hadn't seen an elf or weeks, complaining bitterly about the inaction—which was bad for discipline—and asking for permission to go chasing elven dragonships.

"Fitzwarren is a hothead," said Stephen, taking his cue. He handed his daughter to the nursemaid, who had entered at a summons from Trian. "One of *your* cousins, my Queen. A Ulyndian." This said with a sneer.

"He's a man who won't run away from a fight, which is more than I can say for the men of Volkaran," answered Anne with spirit, though her face was pale.

Trian gave the gentle and long-suffering sigh of one who would like to administer a good caning to spoiled children, but who is not permitted to do so. "If Your Majesties would both be so good as to hear the messenger's report. He is in my study. Fitzwarren has asked for a charm to protect against frostbite. I will prepare it, while Your Majesties interview the messenger. That will save time."

A meeting in Trian's study. The king and queen exchanged unhappy glances. Anne pressed her lips together tightly, placed chill fingers in her husband's hand. Stephen frowned, escorted his wife down the hallway.

Trian's study was the only room in the castle where the three could meet in private, be certain that their conversation would not be overheard. The castle was a breeding ground for intrigue and gossip. Half the servants were in the pay of one baron or another. The other half passed on their information for free.

Located in a light and airy turret room, the wizard's study

was far removed from the noise and rowdiness of the boisterou
castle life. Trian was fond of revels himself. His youthful good
looks and charming manner ensured that, though unmarried, h
rarely spent a night in bed alone, unless he wanted. No one in th
kingdom could dance with such grace, and many a noble would
have given untold sums to know the magus's secret for imbibing
large quantities of wine and never showing the slightest ill effect

But though Trian might revel through the night, he was seri
ous and intent on the business of assisting to run the kingdom
during the day. He was completely, totally, devotedly loyal to hi
king and queen, loved them both as friends, respected them as hi
rulers. He knew their every secret and could have made his for
tune ten times over by selling out one or the other. He would
have as soon jumped into the Maelstrom. And though he wa
twenty years younger than Stephen, Trian was councillor, adviser
minister, and mentor to the older man.

Entering the wizard's study, king and queen discovered two
people waiting for them there. One—a man—they did not know
though he seemed vaguely familiar. The other—a woman—they
knew by sight, and, at the sight of her, the cloud that had covered
them grew thicker and darker.

The woman rose and made respectful reverence to Their Maj
esties. Stephen and Anne returned the bow with respect on thei
side, for though the woman and her followers had acknowledged
the two as king and queen, the bond forged was an uneasy one. I
is difficult ruling those who are far more powerful than onesel
and who could, with a whispered word, bring one's castle tum
bling down about one's ears.

"You know the Lady Iridal, I believe, Your Majesty," said
Trian unnecessarily, gently endeavoring to set everyone at ease
before he let loose the blast that would shatter their lives.

Polite pleasantries were exchanged, everyone mouthing
words learned by rote, none of them thinking about what they
said. Thus "How nice to see you again" and "It's been far too
long" and "Thank you for the sweet baby gift" died away swiftly
Especially when the baby was mentioned. Anne turned deathly
white and sank down in a chair. Iridal clasped her hands together
tightly, looked down, unseeing, at her fingers. Stephen coughed
cleared his throat, and frowned at the stranger in the room, trying
to recall where he'd seen the man.

"Well, what is it, Trian?" the king demanded. "Why have you ummoned us here? I assume it has nothing to do with Fitzwar-en," he added with heavy irony, his gaze shifting to the Lady ridal, for though she lived near the palace, she rarely ventured to visit, well aware that she brought back unwelcome and painful memories to this couple, as they revived such memories in her.

"Will it please Your Majesty to take a seat?" asked Trian. No one in the room could sit down unless the king sat first.

Stephen frowned, then threw himself into a chair. "Get on with it."

"Half a moment, if you please, Your Majesty," said Trian. He raised his hands, fluttered his fingers in the air, and imitated the sound of a piping of birds. "There. Now we may speak safely."

Anyone listening outside the door, outside the circle of the spell, would overhear only what sounded like twittering bird calls. Those within the compass of the spell itself could hear and understand each other perfectly.

Trian cast a deprecating glance at the Lady Iridal. A mysteriarch, she ranked Seventh House, while Trian could attain no higher than Three. Iridal could have changed them all to singing birds, if she'd desired.

Iridal smiled reassuringly. "Very well done, Magicka," she said.

Trian flushed in pleasure, not immune to praise for his art. He had serious business at hand, though, and moved to it swiftly.

He laid a hand on the arm of the stranger, who had risen when his king entered, then resumed his seat near the wizard's desk. Stephen had been staring at the stranger as if he knew him, but could not place from where.

"I see Your Majesty recognizes this man. He has changed much in appearance. Slavery does that. He is Peter Hamish of Pitrin's Exile, once royal footman."

"By the ancestors! You're right!" stated Stephen, banging his hand on the arm of the chair. "You went for a squire to my lord Gwenned, didn't you, Peter?"

"That I did, sire," said the man, smiling broadly, his face red with pleasure at the king's remembrance. "I was with him at the Battle of Tom's Peak. The elves had us surrounded. My lord was struck down, and I was made prisoner. It wasn't my lord's fault, sire. The elves come upon us unexpected—"

"Yes, Peter, His Majesty is fully aware of the truth of the mat ter," interposed Trian smoothly. "If you could proceed on to the rest of your story. Don't be nervous. Tell it to Their Majesties and the Lady Iridal as you told it to me."

Trian saw the man cast a longing glance at the empty glass near his hand. The wizard immediately filled it with wine. Peter made a thankful grab for it, then, realizing he was drinking in the presence of his king, paused with the glass halfway to his mouth.

"Please, go ahead," said Stephen kindly. "You've obviously been through a terrible ordeal."

"Wine is good for strengthening the blood," added Anne, out wardly composed, inwardly quaking.

Peter swallowed a grateful gulp, sending the sweet wine to join another glassful, given him by the wizard, already strength ening the blood.

"I was took prisoner, sire. The elves made most of the others oarsmen in those devil dragonships of theirs. But somehow or other they found out I'd once served in the royal household. They hauls me off and asks me all sorts of questions about you, sire. They beat me till the whites of my ribs showed, Your Majesty, but I never told them fiends nothin'."

"I commend your bravery," said Stephen gravely, knowing full well that Peter had probably poured out his soul at the first touch of the lash, just as he'd told the elves he was a member of the royal household to save himself from the galleys.

"When it was clear to them fiends that they couldn't get nothin' from me, Your Majesty, they set me up in their own royal castle, what they calls the 'Imp-er-non.'" Peter was obviously proud of his ability to speak elven. "I figured they wanted me to show 'em how things should be done in a royal household, but they only set me to scrubbin' floors and talkin' to other prison ers."

"What other—" Stephen began, but Trian shook his head, and the king fell silent.

"Please tell His Majesty about the latest prisoner you saw in the elven palace."

"He warn't no prisoner," Peter objected, on his fourth glass of wine. "More like an honored guest, he was. The elves are treating him real good, sire. You needn't be worried."

"Tell us who it was you saw," urged Trian gently.

"Your son, sire," said Peter, growing a bit maudlin. "Prince Bane. I'm happy to bring you news that he is alive. He spoke to me. I woulda brought him along, when me and the others was plannin' to escape, but he said he was too well guarded. He'd only hinder us. A true little hero, your son, sire.

"He gave that there to me." The footman pointed to an object lying on Trian's desk. "Said I was to bring it to his mother. She'd know, then, that it was him as sent it. He made it for her."

Peter raised the glass in an unsteady hand. Tears came to his eyes. "A toast to His Highness and to Your Majesties."

Peter's bleary attention was focused on the wine in his hand, as much as his attention could focus on anything by now. Thus he missed the fact that the joyful news of Bane's return caused Stephen to go rigid, as if struck by a poleax. Anne stared at the man in horror, sagged in her chair, her face ashen. Lady Iridal's eyes flamed with sudden hope.

"Thank you, Peter, that will be all for now," said Trian. He took hold of Peter's arm, hoisted the man from his chair, led him —bowing and staggering—past king and queen and mysteriarch.

"I'll see to it that he has no memory of this, Your Majesty," Trian promised in a low voice. "Oh, may I suggest that Your Majesties do *not* drink the wine." He left the room with Peter, shutting the door behind them.

The wizard was gone a long time. His Majesty's guards did not accompany the king to the wizard's study, but took up positions at a discreet distance, about thirty paces away, at the far end of the hall. Trian accompanied Peter down the hall, relinquished the inebriated footman to the guards, with orders that the man be taken somewhere to sleep off his intoxication. Such was the effect of the wizard's sweet wine that when the befuddled Peter awoke, he would have no memory of having ever been in the Imp-er-non.

By the time Trian returned to his study, he found that the shock of the news had worn off somewhat, though the alarm was, if anything, more intense.

"Can this be true?" Stephen demanded. The king had risen to his feet and was pacing the study. "How can we trust this great idiot?"

"Simply because he is a great idiot, sire," said Trian, standing, his hands folded before him, his manner deliberately calm and tranquil. "This is one reason I wanted you to hear his story from the man himself. He is certainly not clever enough to have made up such a tale. I have questioned him most extensively and am satisfied that he is not lying. And then there is this."

Trian lifted the object from his desk, the object that Peter had brought—a present from Bane to his mother. Trian held it out, not to Anne, but to Iridal.

She stared at it, blood mounting her cheeks, then draining, to leave her more pale than before. The object was a hawk feather, decorated with beads, suspended from a leather thong. Innocent in appearance, the gift was such as a child might make under the instructions of his nursemaid, to please any mother's fond heart. But this feather necklace had been made by a child of magic, son of mysteriarchs. The feather was an amulet and through it, the child could communicate with the mother. His true mother. Iridal reached out a trembling hand, took the feather, and held it tight.

"It *is* from my son," she said, though she spoke without a voice.

Trian nodded. "Let me assure you all, Your Majesties, Lady Iridal, that I would not have put you through this ordeal if I weren't absolutely certain that what Peter says is the truth. The child he saw was Bane."

Stephen flushed at the implied rebuke, muttered something beneath his breath that might have been an apology. With a heavy sigh, he slumped into his seat. The king and queen moved nearer each other, leaving Lady Iridal sitting alone, slightly apart.

Trian came to stand before the three. The wizard stated firmly and calmly what they all knew, but perhaps had not, even now, accepted.

"Bane is alive, and he is in elven hands."

"How is this possible?" Anne demanded in a choked voice, her hand at her throat, as though she were suffocating. She turned to Lady Iridal. "You said they took him away! To another land! You said Alfred took him away!"

"Not Alfred," Iridal corrected. The initial shock was receding; the mysteriarch was beginning to realize that her dearest wish was coming true. "The other man. Haplo."

"The man you described to me, the one with the blue skin," said Trian.

"Yes." Iridal's eyes shone with the brilliance of her hope. "Yes, he was the one. He took my son away . . ."

"Then he has apparently brought him back," said Trian dryly. "For he is also in the elven castle. The footman saw a man with blue skin in company with the prince. It was this detail, perhaps more than any other, that convinced me the man's story was true. Aside from the Lady Iridal, myself, and Your Majesties, none here knows about the man with blue skin or his connection with Bane. Add to this the fact that Peter not only saw Bane, but spoke to him. Bane recognized the footman and called him by name. No, sire. I repeat. There can be no doubt."

"So the child is held hostage," said Stephen grimly. "The elves plan, no doubt, to use this threat to force us to stop our attacks on their shipping, perhaps even try to disrupt the negotiations with Rees'ahn. Well, it won't work. They can do what they like with him. I wouldn't trade one drop of water—"

"My dear, please!" said Anne quietly, laying her hand on her husband's arm. She glanced beneath her eyelids at the Lady Iridal, who was sitting, pale and cold, hands clenched in her lap, staring at nothing, pretending not to hear. "She is his mother!"

"I am well aware that this lady is the child's mother. May I remind you, my dear, that Bane had a father—a father whose evil very nearly destroyed us all. Forgive me for speaking plainly, Lady Iridal," said Stephen, undeterred by his wife's pleading gaze, "but we must face the truth. You have said yourself that your husband wielded a powerful, dark influence over the child."

A faint flush came to Iridal's ivory cheeks, a shudder shook her slender frame. She did not reply, however, and Stephen looked over at Trian.

"I wonder, even, how much of this is Bane's doing," stated the king. "But, be that as it may, I am adamant. The elves will find they have made a bad bargain—"

Iridal's faint flush of shame had deepened to anger. She seemed about to speak. Trian raised his hand to forestall her.

"Lady Iridal, if I may," he said quietly. "Matters are not this simple, sire. The elves are clever. The wretched Peter did not escape. He was permitted to escape, intentionally. The elves knew he would bring you this information, probably subtly encouraged him to do so. The elves made his 'escape' look very real and convincing. Just as they did all the others."

"Others?" Stephen looked up vaguely, frowning.

Trian sighed. He had been putting off bad news. "I am afraid sire, that Peter was not the only one to return bearing news that His Highness, Prince Bane, is alive. More than twenty other slaves 'escaped' that night. All have returned to their various home lands, all carrying the same tale. I've erased Peter's memory, but might just as well have left him alone. Within a very few cycles the news that Bane is alive and in elven hands will be the talk of every tavern from Pitrin's Exile to Winsher."

"Blessed ancestors protect us," murmured Anne.

"I am certain you are aware of the vicious rumors that have been spread concerning Bane's illegitimacy, sire," continued Trian gently. "If you cast the boy to the wolves, so to speak, people will believe these rumors to be the truth. They will say that you rid yourself of a bastard. Our queen's reputation will be irreparably damaged. The barons of Volkaran will demand that you divorce her, marry one of their own. The barons of Ulyndia will take Queen Anne's part and rise against you. The alliance we've worked hard and long to build will crumble into dust. It could lead to civil war."

Stephen huddled in his chair, his face gray and haggard. Ordinarily he did not look his fifty years. His body was firm and muscular. He could hold his own with any of the younger knights in tourney competition, frequently beat the best. Yet now his shoulders sagged, his frame had collapsed. His head bowed, he was suddenly an old man.

"We could tell the people the truth," said Lady Iridal.

Trian turned to her, smiled. "A magnanimous offer, my lady. I know how painful that would be for you. But it would only make matters worse. Your people have wisely kept out of public view since their return from the High Realms. The mysteriarchs have lived quietly, aiding us in secret. Would you want Sinistrad's evil designs upon us made known? People would suspect and turn against you all. Who knows what terrible persecution might follow?"

"We are doomed," said Stephen heavily. "We must give in."

"No," responded Iridal, voice and demeanor cool. "There is another alternative. Bane is my responsibility. He is my son. I want him back. I will rescue my child from the elves."

"Go into the elven kingdom alone and snatch away your son?" Stephen lifted his hand from his brow, looked up at his wizard.

The king needed the mysteriarchs' powerful magic. No use offending the magus. He made a slight motion with his head, asking Trian to urge Iridal to depart. They had serious business to discuss, alone. "The woman's gone mad," he mouthed, though, of course, he did not say this aloud.

Trian shook his own head slightly. "Listen to what she has to offer," he advised the king silently. Aloud, he said, "Yes, my lady? Please continue."

"Once I've recovered him, I will take my son to the High Realms. Our dwelling is livable, for a short time, at least.[5] Alone with me, without anyone else to influence him, Bane will draw back from the dark path he walks, the path his father taught him to walk." She turned to Stephen. "You must let me try, Your Majesty. You must!"

"Faith, Lady, you don't need my sanction," said Stephen bluntly. "You may fly off the top parapet of this castle, if you're so minded. What could I do to stop you? But you're talking about traveling into elven lands, a human woman, alone! Walking into an elven dungeon and back out again. Perhaps you mysteriarchs have discovered some means of turning yourselves invisible—"

Both Anne and Trian endeavored to stem the king's tirade, but it was Iridal who brought Stephen up short.

"You are right, Your Majesty," she said, with a faint, apologetic smile, "I will go, whether you grant me permission or not. I ask only out of courtesy, for the sake of maintaining good relations between all parties. I am well aware of the danger and the difficulty. I have never been in elven lands. I have no means of journeying there—yet. But I will. I do not intend to go alone, Your Majesty."

Anne reached out her hand impulsively, took hold of Iridal's and clasped it fast. "I would go any distance, face any danger to

---

[5] The Sartan constructed a magical shell around the High Realm to make its rarefied atmosphere suitable for mensch habitation. This shell is beginning to break down and no one now knows the secret of its reconstruction.

find my child, if she were lost to me! I know how you feel. I understand. But, dear lady, you must listen to reason—"

"Indeed, Lady Iridal," said Stephen gruffly. "Forgive me if I spoke harshly at first. It is the weight of this burden, bearing down on me—when it seemed that at last all burdens had been lifted from my shoulders—that caused me to lose my temper. You say that you will not go alone." The king shrugged. "Lady, a legion would not benefit you—"

"I do not want a legion. I want one man, one man who is worth a legion. He is the best. You said so yourself. If I am not mistaken, you scoured the kingdom in search of him. You saved him from the executioner's block. You know his mettle better than anyone else, for you hired him to do a job dangerous and delicate."

Stephen was staring at the woman in horror, Trian in troubled perplexity. Anne let loose Iridal's hand. Stricken with guilt, the queen shrank back in her chair.

Iridal rose to her feet, tall and majestic, proud and imperious. "You hired this man to kill my son."

"Gracious ancestors forfend!" cried Stephen hoarsely. "Have you mysteriarchs discovered the power to raise the dead?"

"Not us," said Iridal softly. "Not us. For which I am grateful. It is a terrible gift."

For long moments, she was silent, then, sighing, she lifted her head, brisk and business-minded. "Do I have Your Majesty's permission to try? You have nothing to lose. If I fail, none will be the wiser. I will tell my people I am traveling back to the High Realms. You may tell them that I died there. No blame will come to you. Grant me a fortnight, Your Majesty."

Stephen stood up, clasped his hands behind his back, began to pace the room. He paused, glanced at Trian. "Well, what say you, Magicka? Is there no other way?"

"None that has half the chance of succeeding, slim though this chance might be. The Lady Iridal speaks truly, sire. We have nothing to lose and much to gain. If she is willing to take the risk? . . ."

"I am, Your Majesty," said Iridal.

"Then I say, yes, sire," said Trian.

"My queen?" Stephen looked to his wife. "What do you say?"

"We have no choice," said Anne, her head bowed. "We have no choice. And after what we did . . ." She covered her eyes with her hand.

"If you refer to hiring an assassin to kill the boy, we did *that* because we had no choice," said Stephen, grim and stern. "Very well, Lady Iridal. I grant you a fortnight. At the end of that time, we meet with Prince Rees'ahn at Seven Fields, there to make final plans for the alliance of our three armies and the eventual overthrow of the Tribus empire. If Bane is still in elven hands by that time . . ."

He sighed, shook his head.

"Do not worry, Your Majesty!" said Iridal. "I will not fail you. This time, I will not fail my son." She made a low reverence, to both king and queen.

"I will escort you out, my lady," offered Trian. "It would be best if you left the way you entered. The fewer who know you were here, the better. If Your Majesties—"

"Yes, yes. Dismissed." Stephen waved his hand abruptly.

He cast a meaningful glance at the magus as Trian left. Trian lowered his eyes, indicating he understood.

Magus and mysteriarch left the room. Stephen sat down to wait his wizard's return.

The Lords of Night spread their cloaks over the sky. The glitter of the Firmament faded. The room in which king and queen waited together, silent and unmoving, grew dark. Neither moved to strike a light. Their dark thoughts were suited to night's shadows.

A door opened softly—not the door by which the magus and Lady Iridal had left but another door, a secret door, located in the back of the study and concealed by a wall painting. Trian emerged, carrying an iron glowlamp to light his way.

Stephen blinked in the light, lifted his hand to shield his eyes. "Douse that thing," he ordered.

Trian did as he was told.

"She told us herself Hugh the Hand was dead. She described his death to us."

"Obviously, she lied, sire. Either that, or she is insane. And I do not believe she is insane. I think rather she foresaw the day when this knowledge would be of use to her."

Stephen grunted, was silent again. Then he said, slowly, heavily, "You know what must be done. I presume that was why you brought her here."

"Yes, sire. Although I must confess I had not dreamed she would offer to go fetch the child herself. I had hoped only that she might establish contact with him. This makes matters much simpler, of course."

Queen Anne rose to her feet. "Is that necessary, Stephen? Couldn't we let her try? . . ."

"So long as that boy lives—whether in High Realm, Low Realm, this realm, any realm—he is a danger to us . . . *and* to our daughter."

Anne lowered her head, said nothing more. Stephen looked at Trian, nodded. The magus bowed, glided out of the room, leaving by the secret door.

King and queen waited a moment longer in the darkness to compose themselves, to put on the false smiles, to summon carefree laughter, to play at plotting and at intrigue, while, beneath the supper table, where no one could see, their cold hands would join, clasp together tightly.

CHAPTER ◆ 22

KIR MONASTERY

VOLKARAN ISLES

MID REALM

◆

THE SHARP LINES OF GRANITE WALLS THAT FORMED THE KIR MONASTERY STOOD out, stark and black, against the shimmering, lambent light given off by the coralite of the hills surrounding it. The monastery itself was dark and silent; no light shone within, no sound came from within. A single, solitary glowlamp burning feebly over the entrance—a signal to those in need—was the only evidence that anyone lived here.

Iridal dismounted from her dragon, stroked its neck, spent a few moments calming it. The creature was nervous, restive, and would not respond immediately to the sleep spell she tried to cast upon it. Riders always caused their dragons to sleep after flight. Not only did the spell provide the dragon needed rest, but also the enforced slumber rendered the creature harmless, so that it would not take it into its head to raid the countryside during the mysteriarch's absence.

But this dragon refused to be enchanted. It jerked its head away, tugged at its harness, lashed its tail this way and that. Had Iridal been an experienced dragon-rider, she would have recognized these signs as indicative of another dragon somewhere near.

Dragons are very companionable creatures, fond of their own kind, and this dragon of Iridal's was much more inclined for a friendly chat than sleep.[1] The dragon was too well trained to call

---

A note on dragons. The creatures who live permanently on Arianus are true dragons, an advanced species of reptile, who possess varying degrees of

out (they are taught to keep silent, lest a cry give away their position to an enemy). But the creature had no need to vocalize; it could sense a companion in many other ways: smell and hearing, among other, more subtle means.

If the other dragon in the area had responded, Iridal would have been forced to resort to firm measures in order to subdue her mount. As it was, the other dragon refused to acknowledge in any way its fellow's presence. Iridal's borrowed dragon—a mild creature, not exceptionally quick-witted—was hurt, but was too stupid to be deeply offended. Tired from the long journey, the dragon finally relaxed and listened to Iridal's soothing words.

Seeing its eyelids droop and noting the tail begin to curl about the feet, the claws to dig more firmly in the ground to gain steady purchase, Iridal quickly intoned the spell. Her dragon soon slept deeply. Never thinking to wonder why it had been restive, her mind preoccupied with thoughts of this coming meeting that she knew would not be at all a pleasant one, Iridal forgot about the odd behavior of the dragon and set out to walk the short distance between herself and the monastery.

No outer walls surrounded the monastery. No gate barred entrance. The death monks needed no such protection. When the elves occupied human lands and entire villages were razed and destroyed, the Kir monasteries remained untouched. The most drunken, blood-mad elf sobered instantly on finding himself anywhere near the black, chill walls.[2]

Repressing a shiver, Iridal focused her mind on what was important—the recovery of her lost child—and, drawing her cloak more closely about her, proceeded with firm step to the baked clay door illuminated by the glowlamp. An iron bell hung over the door. Iridal took hold of the bellpull and jerked it. The iron tones of the bell were muffled and almost immediately swallowed

---

magical power, depending on each creature's own intelligence and a variety of other factors. The dragons on Arianus are not to be confused with those who occasionally appear in the guise of dragons—such as the serpent-elf Sang-drax or the dragon-serpents of Chelestra.

[2] It is rumored that the Kenkari elves feel a kinship to the Kir monks, whose death-worship religion derived from a failed attempt to emulate the Kenkari in the capture of souls. Many believe that the powerful Kenkari stretched protective hand over the human monks, forbidding elven soldiers to persecute the Kir.

p, absorbed by the building's thick walls. Accepted as a neces-
ity for contact with the outside world, the bell was permitted to
peak, but not to sing.

There came a grating sound. An opening appeared in the
oor. An eye appeared in the opening.

"Where is the corpse?" the voice asked in a disinterested
onotone.

Iridal, her thoughts on her son, was chilled by the question,
larmed and startled. It seemed a terrible portent, and she very
early turned around and ran off. But logic prevailed. She re-
inded herself of what she knew of the Kir monks, told herself
at this question—so frightful to her—was perfectly natural for
em.

The Kir monks worship death. They view life as a kind of
rison-house existence, to be endured until the soul can escape
nd find true peace and happiness elsewhere. The Kir monks will
ot, therefore, come to the aid of the living. They will not nurse
e sick, they will not feed the hungry or bind the wounds of the
jured. They will, however, tend to the dead, celebrating the fact
at the soul has moved on. The Kir are not disturbed by death in
ven its more horrible forms. They claim the victim when the
urderer has done. They walk the fields of battle when the battle
ended. They enter the plague town when all others have fled.

The one service the Kir offer the living is to take in unwanted
ale children: orphans, bastards, inconvenient sons. These chil-
ren are raised in the Order, raised to worship death, and so the
rder continues.

The question the monk asked Iridal was a common question,
ne he asked of all who come to the monastery at this hour of
ight. For there would be no other reason to approach these for-
idding walls.

"I do not come about the dead," said Iridal, recovering her
omposure. "I come about the living."

"About a child?" demanded the monk.

"Yes, Brother," answered Iridal. "Though not in the way *you*
ean," she added silently.

The eye disappeared. The small panel in the clay door
ammed shut. The door opened. The monk stood to one side, his
ce hidden by the black cowl he wore low over his head. He did
ot bow, did not offer her welcome, showed her no respect, re-

garded her with very little interest. She was alive, and the living did not count for much with the Kir.

The monk proceeded down a corridor without glancing back at Iridal, assuming she would follow or not as she chose. He led her to a large room not far from the entrance, certainly not far enough for her to catch more than a glimpse inside the monastery walls. It was darker within than without, for outside the walls, the coralite gave off its faint silvery glow. Inside, no lamps lit the hallways. Here and there, she caught a glimpse of a candle, its pinprick of wavering light providing safe walking for the one who held it. The monk showed Iridal into the room, told her to wait, the Abbot would be with her shortly. The monk left and shut the door behind him, locked her inside, in the dark.

Iridal smiled even as she shivered and huddled deeper within her cloak. The door was baked clay, as were all the doors in the monastery. She could, with her magic, shiver it like ice. But she sat and waited in patience, knowing that now was not the time to resort to threats. That would come later.

The door opened; a man entered, carrying a candle. He was old and large-framed, lean and spare, his flesh seeming insufficient to cover his bones. He did not wear his cowl over his head but let it fall on his thin shoulders. His head was bald, perhaps shaved. He barely spared Iridal a glance as he crossed in front of her without courtesy, came to sit behind a desk. Lifting a pen, he reached out, drew forth a sheet of parchment, and—still not looking at Iridal—prepared to write.

"We do not offer money, you know," said the man, who must have been the Abbot, though he did not bother to introduce himself. "We will take the child off your hands. That is all. Are you the boy's mother?"

Again, the question struck painfully near the mark of her thoughts. Iridal knew well the Abbot assumed she had come to rid herself of an unwanted burden; she had decided to use this ruse to obtain entry. But she found herself answering nonetheless.

Yes, I am Bane's mother. I gave him up. I let my husband take my child and give him to another. What could I do to stop him? I was frightened. Sinistrad held my father's life in bondage. And when my child returned to me, I tried to win him back. I did try. But, again, what could I do? Sinistrad threatened to kill then those who came with Bane. The Geg, the man with the blue skin, and . . . and . . .

"Really, madam," said the Abbot coldly, raising his head, regarding her for the first time since he'd come into the room. "You should have made up your mind to this before you disturbed us. Do you want us to take this boy or don't you?"

"I didn't come about a child," said Iridal, banishing the past. "I came to talk to someone who resides in this house."

"Impossible!" stated the Abbot. His face was pinched and gaunt, the eyes sunken. They glared at her from dark shadows, reflected the candlelight that was two flickering points of flame in the glistening orbs. "Once man or boy enters that door, he leaves the world behind. He has no father or mother, sister or brother, lover or friend. Respect his vows. Be gone, and do not disturb him."

The Abbot rose. So did Iridal. He expected her to leave, was somewhat surprised and considerably displeased—to judge by his baleful expression—to see her take a step forward, confront him.

"I do respect your ways, Lord Abbot. My business is not with any of the brothers, but one who has never taken vows. He is the one who is permitted to reside here, against—I may add—all rules, in defiance of tradition. He is called Hugh the Hand."

The Abbot did not flicker an eyelid. "You are mistaken," he said, speaking with such conviction that Iridal must have believed him had she not known positively the monk was lying. "One who called himself by that name used to live with us, but that was as a child. He left, long ago. We have no knowledge of him."

"The first is true," Iridal answered. "The second is a lie. He came back to you, about a year ago. He told a strange tale and begged admittance. You either believed his story or thought him mad and took pity on him. No," she interrupted herself. "You pity no one. You believed his story, then. I wonder why?"

An eyebrow moved, lifted. "If you saw him, you would have no need to ask why." The Abbot folded his hands across his lank body. "I will not bandy words with you, Lady. It is obviously a waste of time. Yes, one who calls himself Hugh the Hand does reside here. No, he has not taken vows that shut him off from the world. Yet, he is shut off. He has done so himself. He will not see a living soul from the outside. Only us. And then only when we bring him food and drink."

Iridal shuddered, but she stood firm. "Nonetheless, I will see him." Drawing aside her cloak, she revealed a silvery gray dress, trimmed in cabalistic symbols on the hem, the neck, the cuffs of the sleeves and the belt she wore around her waist. "I am one you term a mysteriarch. I am of the High Realm. My magic could crack that clay door, crack these walls, crack your head if I choose. You *will* take me to see Hugh the Hand."

The Abbot shrugged. It was nothing to him. He would have allowed her to tear the Abbey down stone by stone before he permitted her to see one who had taken the vows. But the man Hugh was different. He was here by sufferance. Let him look out for himself.

"This way," said the Abbot, ungraciously, walking past her to the door. "You will speak to no one, nor lift your eyes to look at anyone. On pain of expulsion." He was not, it seemed, particularly impressed by her threats. After all, a mysteriarch was just another corpse, as far as the Kir were concerned.

"I said I respected your vows and I will do what is required of me," responded Iridal crisply. "I care nothing for what goes on in here. My *business*"—she emphasized the word—"is with Hugh the Hand."

The Abbot stalked out carrying the candle, the only light, and he blocked out most of it with his robed body. Iridal, coming behind, found it difficult to see her footing. She was forced, therefore, to keep her eyes fixed on the ground, for the floors of the ancient building were cracked and uneven. The halls were deserted, quiet. She had a vague impression of shut doors on either side of her. Once she thought she heard a baby cry, and her heart ached for the poor child, alone and abandoned in such a dismal place.

They reached a stairway, and here the Abbot actually stopped and obtained a candle for her before proceeding downward. Iridal concluded that he was not so much concerned for her safety as trying to avoid the nuisance of dealing with her should she fall and break anything. At the bottom of the stairs, they came to water cellars. Doors stood barred and locked to protect the precious liquid that was not only used for drinking and cooking but was also part of the Abbey's wealth.

Apparently, however, not all doors guarded water. The Abbot stalked over to one, reached down and rattled the handle.

"You have a visitor, Hugh."

No answer. Just a scraping sound, as of a chair, lurching across the floor.

The Abbot rattled the handle more loudly.

"He is locked in? You've made him a prisoner?" asked Iridal in a low voice.

"He makes himself a prisoner, Lady," retorted the Abbot. "He has the key inside with him. We may not enter—*you* may not enter—unless he hands the key to us."

Iridal's resolve wavered. She very nearly left again. She doubted now if Hugh could help her, and she was afraid to face what he had become. Yet, if he didn't help her, who would? Not Stephen, that much had been made clear. Not the other mysteriarchs. Powerful wizards, most of them, but with no love for her dead husband, no reason to want progeny of Sinistrad's returned to them.

As for other mundane humans, Iridal knew very few, was not impressed by those she'd met. Hugh alone filled all her needs. He knew how to pilot an elven dragonship, he had traveled in elven lands, he spoke the elven language fluently, was familiar with elven customs. He was bold and daring; he'd earned his livelihood as a professional assassin, and he'd been the best in the business. As Iridal had reminded Stephen, he—a king who could afford the best—had once hired Hugh the Hand.

The Abbot repeated, "Hugh, you have a visitor."

"Go to hell," said a voice from within.

Iridal sighed. The voice was slurred and harsh from smoking stregno—Iridal could smell the reek of his pipe out in the hall—from strong drink and disuse. But she recognized it.

The key. That was her hope. He kept the key himself, obviously afraid that if he gave it to others, he might be tempted to tell them to let him out. There must be part of him, then, that wanted out.

"Hugh the Hand, it is Iridal of the High Realm. I am in desperate need. I must speak with you. I . . . I want to hire you."

She had little doubt that he'd refuse and she knew, from the slight, disdainful smile on the Abbot's thin lips, that he thought the same.

"Iridal," repeated Hugh, in puzzled tones, as if the name was wandering around the liquor-soaked dregs of his mind. "Iridal!"

The last was a harsh whisper, an expelled breath, as of something long wished for and finally achieved. But there was neither love nor longing in that voice. Rather, a rage that might have melted granite.

A heavy body thudded against the clay door, followed by a fumbling and scraping. A panel slid aside. A red eye, partially hidden beneath a mat of filthy hair, stared out, found her, fixed on her, unblinking.

"Iridal . . ."

The panel slid shut abruptly.

The Abbot glanced at her, curious to see her response, probably expecting her to turn and flee. Iridal stood firm, the fingers of one hand, hidden beneath her cloak, digging into her flesh. The other hand, which held the candle, was steady.

Frantic activity sounded inside: furniture being overturned, casks upset, as if Hugh was searching for something. A snarl of triumph. A metal object struck the lower half of the door. Another snarl, this one of frustration, then a key shot out from beneath the crack.

The Abbot leaned down, picked the key up, held it in his hand a moment, eyeing it speculatively. He looked at Iridal, silently asking her if she wanted him to proceed.

Lips pressed together, she indicated with a cold nod that he was to open the door. Shrugging, the Abbot did so.

The moment the lock clicked, the clay door was flung open from the inside. An apparition appeared in the doorway, silhouetted against dimly lit, smoke-filled shadows behind, illuminated by the candlelight before him.

The apparition sprang at Iridal. Strong hands grabbed hold of her arms, dragged her inside the cell, and flung her back against a wall. She dropped the candle; it fell to the floor, the light drowning in a pool of spilled wax.

Hugh the Hand, blocking the door with his body, faced the Abbot.

"The key," the Hand commanded.

The Abbot gave it over.

"Leave us!"

Catching hold of the door, Hugh slammed it shut. Turning, he aced Iridal. She heard the Abbot's soft footfalls pad disinterest-dly away.

The cell was small. The furniture consisted of a crude bed, a able, a chair—overturned—and a bucket in a corner, used—by he stench—to hold the body's wastes. A thick wax candle stood n the table. Hugh's pipe lay beside it. A mug stood near that, long with a plate of half-eaten food and a bottle of some liquor hat smelled almost as bad as the stregno.

Iridal took in all these objects with a swift glance that was also searching for weapons. Her fear was not for herself; she was ar-mored with her powerful magic that could subdue the man more swiftly and easily than she subdued her dragon. She feared for Hugh, that he might do some harm to himself before she could stop him, for she assumed that he was drunk beyond the point of sanity.

He stood before her, staring at her, his face—with its hawk nose, strong forehead, deep-set, narrow eyes—was hideous, half-hidden by wandering shadows and a haze of yellow-tinged smoke. He breathed heavily, from the frenzied exertion, the li-quor, and an avid excitement that made his body tremble. He lurched unsteadily toward her, hands outstretched. The light fell full upon his face and then Iridal was afraid for herself, for the liquor had inflamed his skin but did not touch his eyes.

Some part of him, deep within, was sober; some part that could not be touched by the wine, no matter how much he drank; some part that could not be drowned. His face was almost un-recognizable, ravaged by bitter grief and inner torment. His black hair was streaked with gray; his beard, once rakishly braided, was uncombed, and had grown long and scraggly. He wore a torn shirt and a leather vest and breeches—stained and stiff with dirt. His hard-muscled body had gone soft, yet he had a strength born of the wine, for Iridal could still feel the bite of his fingers on her bruised arms.

He staggered closer. She marked the key in his shaking hand. The words of a spell were on her lips, but she didn't say them. She could see his face clearly now, and she could have wept for him. Pity, compassion, the memory that he had given his life, died horribly to save her child, moved her to reach out her hands to him.

He caught hold of her wrists, his grasp crushing and painfu
and fell to his knees before her.

"End this curse!" he pleaded, his voice choked. "I beg yo
Lady! End this curse you have put upon me! Free me! Let me go

He bowed his head. Harsh, dry sobs tore his body. He shoo
and shivered, his nerveless hands let slip their hold. Iridal bea
over him, her tears falling on the graying hair that she smoothe
with chill fingers.

"I'm sorry," she whispered brokenly. "So sorry."

He raised his head. "I don't want your damn pity! Free me
he repeated again, harsh, urgent. His hands clutched at hers. "Yo
don't know what you've done! End it . . . now!"

She regarded him for long moments, unable to speak.

"I can't, Hugh. It was not me."

"Yes!" he cried fiercely. "I *saw* you! When I woke—"

She shook her head. "Such a spell is far beyond my powe
thank the ancestors. You know," she said to him, looking into th
pleading, hopeless eyes. "You must know. It was Alfred."

"Alfred!" He gasped the word. "Where is he? Did h
come . . . ?"

He saw the answer in her eyes and threw his head back as
the agony was more than he could endure. Two great tears welle
from beneath squinched-shut eyelids, rolled down his cheeks in
the thick and matted beard. He drew a deep and shivering breat
and suddenly went berserk, began to scream in terrible ange
claw at his face and hair with his hands. And, as suddenly, h
pitched forward on his face and lay still and unmoving as th
dead.

Which he had once been.

CHAPTER ◆ 23

KIR MONASTERY

VOLKARAN ISLES

MID REALM

◆

HUGH WOKE WITH A BUZZING IN HIS HEAD—A DULL, THROBBING ACHE THAT ʋent up his neck and stabbed through to the back of his eyeballs –and a tongue thick and swollen. He knew what was wrong with ɪim and he knew how to fix it. He sat up on the bed, his hand ᴦoping for the wine bottle that was never far from reach. It was ɪen he saw her and memory hit him a blow that was cruel and ꭒrt worse than the pain in his head. He stared at her wordlessly.

She sat in a chair—the only chair—and had, by her attitude, ꬓeen sitting there for some time. She was pale and cold, colorless –with her white hair and silver robes—as the ice of the Firma-ɪent. Except for her eyes, which were the myriad colors of sun-ᴣht on a crystal prism.

''The bottle's here, if you want it,'' she said.

Hugh managed to get his feet beneath him, heaved himself up ɴd out of bed, paused a moment to wait until the light bursting ꭓ his vision had faded enough for him to see beyond it, and ᴍade his way to the table. He noted the arrival of another chair, ꬑoted at the same time that his cell had been cleaned.

And so had he.

His hair and beard were filled with a fine powder, his skin ᴡas raw and it itched. The pungent smell of grise[1] clung to him.

Those who can't afford water for bathing use grise to cleanse the body or ɴy other surface. A pumicelike substance made from ground coralite, grise

The smell brought back vivid memories of his childhood, of th
Kir monks scrubbing the squirming bodies of young boys—abar
doned bastards, like himself.

Hugh grimaced, scratched his bearded chin, and poured him
self a mug of the cheap, raw wine. He was starting to drink
when he remembered that he had a guest. There was only on
mug. He held it out to her, grimly pleased to note that his han
did not tremble.

Iridal shook her head. "No, thank you," she said, not alou
her lips forming the words.

Hugh grunted, tossed down the wine in one swift gulp tha
kept him from tasting it. The buzzing in his head receded, th
pain dulled. He lifted the bottle without thinking, hesitated. H
could let the questions go unanswered. What did it matter any
way? Or he could find out what was going on, why she'd com

"You gave me a bath?" he said, eyeing her.

A faint flush stained the pale cheeks. She did not look at him
"The monks did," she said. "I made them. And they scrubbed th
floor, brought fresh linen, a clean shirt."

"I'm impressed," said Hugh. "Amazing enough they let yo
in. Then do your bidding. What'd you threaten 'em with? How
ing winds, quakes; maybe dry up their water . . . ?"

She did not respond. Hugh was talking for the sake of fillin
up the silence, and both knew it.

"How long was I out?"

"Many hours. I don't know."

"And you stayed and did all this." He glanced around hi
cell. "Must be important, what you came for."

"It is," she said, and turned her eyes upon him.

He had forgotten their beauty, her beauty. He had forgotte
that he loved her, pitied her, forgotten that he'd died for her, fc
her son. All lost in the dreams that tormented him at night, th
dreams that not even the wine could drown. And he came
realize, as he sat and looked into her eyes, that last night, for th
first time in a long time, he had not dreamed at all.

"I want to hire you," she said, her voice cool and busines
like. "I want you to do a job for me—"

---

is often mixed with headroot, an herb with a strong, but not offensive odo
used to kill lice, fleas, ticks, and other vermin.

"No!" he cried, springing to his feet, oblivious to the flash of pain in his head. "I will not go back out there!"

Fist clenched, he smashed it on the table, toppled the wine bottle, sent it crashing to the floor. The thick glass did not break, but the liquid spilled out, seeping into the cracks in the stone.

She stared at him, shocked. "Sit down, please. You are not well."

He winced at the pain, clutched his head, swayed on his feet. Leaning heavily on the table, he stumbled back to his chair, sank down.

"Not well." He tried to laugh. "This is a hangover, Lady, in case you've never seen one." He stared into the shadows. "I tried it, you know," he said abruptly. "Tried going back to my old calling. When they brought me down from that place. Death is my trade. The only thing I know. But no one would hire me. No one can stand to be around me, except them." He jerked his head in the direction of the door, indicating the monks.

"What do you mean, no one would hire you?"

"They sit down to talk to me. They start to tell me their grievances, start to name the mark they want assassinated, start to tell me where to find him . . . and, little by little, they dry up. Not just once. It happened five times, ten. I don't know. I lost count."

"What happens?" Iridal urged gently.

"They go on and on about the mark and how much they hate him and how they want him to die and how he should suffer like he made their daughter suffer or their father or whoever. But the more they tell me this, the more nervous they get. They look at me and then look away, then sneak a look back, and look away again. And their voices drop, they get mixed up in what they've said. They stammer and cough and then usually, without a word, they get up and run. You'd think," he added grimly, "they'd stabbed their mark themselves and were caught with the bloody knife in their hands."

"But they did, in their hearts," said Iridal.

"So? Guilt never plagued any of my patrons before. Why now? What's changed?"

"You've changed, Hugh. Before, you were like the coralite, soaking up their evil, absorbing it, taking it into yourself, freeing them of the responsibility. But now, you've become like the crystals of the Firmament. They look at you, and they see their own evil reflected back to them. You have become our conscience."

"Hell of a note for an assassin," he said, sneering. "Makes it damn hard to find work!" He stared unseeing at the wine bottle, nudged it with his foot, sent it rolling around in circles on the floor. His blurred gaze shifted to her. "I don't do that to you."

"Yes, you do. That's how I know." Iridal sighed. "I look at you, and I see my folly, my blindness, my stupidity, my weakness. I married a man I knew to be heartless and evil out of some romantic notion that I could change him. By the time I understood the truth, I was hopelessly entangled in Sinistrad's snares. Worse, I'd given birth to an innocent child, allowed him to become tangled in the same web.

"I could have stopped my husband, but I was frightened. And it was easy to tell myself that he would change, that it would all get better. And then you came, and brought my son to me, and, at last, I saw the bitter fruit of my folly. I saw what I had done to Bane, what I'd made him through my weakness. I saw it then. I see it now, looking at you."

"I thought it was them," said Hugh, as if he hadn't heard her. "I thought the world had gone mad. Then I began to realize it was me. The dreams . . ." He shuddered, shook his head. "No, I won't talk about the dreams."

"Why did you come here?"

He shrugged, voice bitter. "I was desperate, out of money. Where else could I go? The monks said I would return, you know. They always said I'd be back." He glanced around with a haunted look, then shook himself, shook off the memories.

"Anyway, the Abbot told me what was wrong. He took one look at me and told me what had happened. I had died. I'd left this life . . . and been dragged back. Resurrected." Hugh gave the bottle a sudden, vicious kick, sent it spinning across the floor.

"You . . . don't remember?" Iridal faltered.

He regarded her in silence, dark, glowering. "The dreams remember. The dreams remember a place beautiful beyond words, beyond . . . dreams. Understanding, compassion . . ." He fell silent, swallowed, coughed, and cleared his throat. "But the journey to reach that place is terrible. The pain. The guilt. The knowledge of my crimes. My soul wrenched from my body. And now I can't go back. I tried."

Iridal stared at him, horrified. "Suicide . . . ?"

He smiled, a terrible smile. "I failed. Both times. Too damn scared."

"It takes courage to live, not to die," said Iridal.

"How the hell would you know, Lady?" Hugh sneered.

Iridal looked away, stared at her hands twisting in her lap.

"Tell me what happened," said Hugh.

"You . . . you and Sinistrad fought. You stabbed him, but the wound was not mortal. He had the power to turn himself into a snake, attacked you. His magic . . . poison in your blood. He died, but not before he had . . ."

"Killed me," said Hugh dryly.

Iridal licked her lips, did not look at him. "The dragon attacked us. Sinistrad's dragon, the quicksilver. With my husband dead, the dragon was free from his control and went berserk. Then, it all becomes confused in my mind. Haplo—the man with the blue skin—took Bane away. I knew I was going to die . . . and I didn't care. You're right." She looked up, smiled at him wanly. "Death did seem easier than living. But Alfred enchanted the dragon, put it in thrall. And then . . ."

The memory came back. . . .

Iridal gazed in awe at the dragon, whose giant head was swaying back and forth, as if it heard a soothing, lulling voice.

"You've imprisoned it in its mind," she said.

"Yes," Alfred agreed. "The strongest cage ever built."

"And I am free," she said in wonder. "And it isn't too late. There is hope! Bane, my son! Bane!"

Iridal ran toward the door where she'd last seen him. The door was gone. The walls of her prison had collapsed, but the rubble blocked her path.

"Bane!" she cried, trying vainly to drag aside one of the heavy stones that the dragon had knocked down in its fury. Her magic would help her, but she couldn't think of the words. She was too tired, too empty. But she had to reach him. If only she could move this rock!

"Don't, my dear," said a kind voice. Gentle hands took hold of her. "It won't do any good. He has gone far away by now, back to the elven ship. Haplo has taken him."

"Haplo taken . . . my son?" Iridal couldn't make any sense of it. "Why? What does he want with him?"

"I don't know," Alfred replied. "I'm not sure. But don't worry. We'll get him back. I know where they're going."

"Then we should go after them," said Iridal.

But she gazed helplessly about. Doors had disappeared, blocked by debris. Holes gaped in the walls revealing more destruction beyond. The room was changed so completely that it was suddenly unfamiliar to her, as if she had walked into the house of a stranger. She had no idea where to go, how to leave, how to find her way out.

And then she saw Hugh.

She'd known he'd died. She'd tried to make him hear before he died, that he'd helped her, that now she understood. But he'd left her too soon, too quickly. She sank down beside the body, took the chill hand in her own, pressed it to her cheek. His face, in death, was calm and reflected a peace the man had never known in life, a peace Iridal envied.

"You gave your life for me, for my son," she told him. "I wish you could have lived, to see that I will make use of this gift. You taught me so much. You could teach me still. You could help me. And I could have helped you. I could have filled the emptiness inside you. Why didn't I, when I had the chance?"

"What would have happened to him, do you suppose, if he had not died?" Alfred asked.

"I think he would have tried to make up for the evil he did in his life. He was a prisoner, like me," Iridal answered. "But he managed to escape. Now he is free."

"You, too, are free," said Alfred.

"Yes, but I am alone," said Iridal.

She sat by Hugh, holding his lifeless hand, her mind empty as her heart. She liked the emptiness. She didn't feel anything and she was afraid of feeling. The pain would come, more awful than dragon claws tearing at her flesh. The pain of regret, tearing her soul.

She was vaguely aware of Alfred chanting, of him dancing his slow and graceful dance that looked so incongruous—the elderly man, with his bald head and flapping coattails, his too-big feet and clumsy hands—whirling and dipping and bobbing about the rubble-filled room. She had no idea what he was doing. She didn't care.

She sat, holding Hugh's hand . . . and felt his fingers twitch.

Iridal didn't believe it. "My mind is playing tricks. When we want something very badly, we convince ourselves—"

The fingers moved in hers, spasmodic motion, death throes.

Except Hugh had been dead a long time, long enough for the flesh to chill, the blood to drain from lips and face, the eyes to have fixed in the head.

"I'm going mad," said Iridal, and dropped the hand back on the unmoving breast. She leaned forward to close the staring eyes. They shifted, looked at her. His lids blinked. His hand stirred. His breast rose and fell.

He gave an anguished, agonized scream. . . .

When Iridal regained her senses, she was lying in another room, another house—a friend's house, belonging to one of the other mysteriarchs of the High Realm.

Alfred stood beside her, gazing down on her with an anxious expression.

"Hugh!" cried Iridal, sitting up. "Where is Hugh?"

"He's being cared for, my dear," said Alfred solicitously and —so it seemed to Iridal—somewhat confusedly. "He's going to be all right. Don't worry yourself over him. Some of your friends took him away."

"I want to see him!"

"I don't think that would be wise," said Alfred. "Please, lay back down."

He fussed with the blanket, covered her, wrapped it tenderly around her feet, smoothed out imaginary wrinkles.

"You should rest, Lady Iridal. You've been through a terrible ordeal. The shock, the strain. Hugh was grievously wounded, but he is being treated—"

"He was dead," said Iridal.

Alfred wouldn't look at her. He kept fiddling with the blankets.

Iridal tried to catch hold of his hand, but Alfred was too quick for her. He backed away several steps. When he spoke, he spoke to his shoes.

"Hugh wasn't dead. He was terribly wounded. I can see how

you would have been mistaken. The poison has that effect, sometimes. Of . . . of making the living appear to be dead."

Iridal threw back the blanket, rose to her feet, advanced on Alfred, who attempted to sidle away, perhaps even flee the room. But he fell over his feet and stumbled, caught himself on a chair.

"He was dead. You brought him back to life!"

"No, no. Don't be ridiculous." Alfred gave a feeble laugh. "You . . . you've suffered a great shock. You're imagining things. I couldn't possibly. Why, no one could!"

"A Sartan could," said Iridal. "I know about the Sartan. Sinistrad studied them. He was obsessed with them, with their magic. Their library is here, in the High Realms. He could never find the key that unlocked their mysteries. But he knew about them, from the writings they left in human and elven. And they had the power to resurrect the dead. Necromancy—"

"No!" Alfred protested, shuddering. "I mean yes, they . . . we have the power. But it must never be used. Never used. For every life that is brought back untimely, another dies untimely. We may help the grievously injured, do all we can to draw them back from the threshold, but once they cross beyond . . . never!

"Never. . . ."

"Alfred was insistent, calm, and firm in his denial," said Iridal, returning from the past with a gentle sigh. "He answered all my questions freely, if not fully. I began to think that I *had* been mistaken. That you were only wounded.

"I know," she said, seeing Hugh's bitter smile. "I know the truth now. I knew it then, I think, but I didn't want to believe it, for Alfred's sake. He was so kind to me, helping me search for my child, when he could have easily abandoned me, for he has troubles of his own."

Hugh grunted. He had little use for another man's troubles. "He lied. He was the one who brought me back! The bastard lied."

"I'm not so sure," said Iridal, sighing. "It's odd, but I believe that he believes he is telling the truth. He has no memory of what truly happened."

"When I get hold of him, he'll remember. Sartan or not."

Iridal glanced at him, somewhat astonished. "You believe me?"

"About Alfred?" Hugh eyed her grimly, reached for his pipe. "Yes, I believe you. I think I knew all along, though I didn't want to admit it. That wasn't the first time he performed this resurrection trick of his."

"Then why did you think I did it?" she asked, puzzled.

"I don't know," Hugh muttered, fumbling with the pipe. "Maybe I wanted to believe it was you who brought me back."

Iridal flushed, averted her head. "In a way, it was. He saved you out of pity for my grief, and out of compassion for your sacrifice."

The two sat long moments in silence, Iridal staring at her hands, Hugh sucking on the cold and empty pipe. To light it would mean standing up and walking over to the fire grate and he wasn't certain he could navigate even that short distance without falling. He eyed the empty wine bottle with regret. He could have called for another, but decided against it. He had a clear purpose now, and he had the means to obtain it.

"How did you find me?" he asked. "And why did you wait so long?"

Her flush deepened. She raised her head, answered the last question first. "How could I come? To see you again . . . the pain would have been more than I could bear. I went to the other mysteriarchs, the ones who took you from the castle and brought you down here. They told me . . ." Iridal hesitated, not certain where her words might lead her.

"That I'd gone back to my old profession, as if nothing had happened. Well, I tried to pretend it hadn't," Hugh said grimly. "I didn't think you'd appreciate having me show up on your doorstep."

"It wasn't like that. Believe me, Hugh, if I had known—" She couldn't quite see where that was going either and fell silent.

"Known that I'd turned into a drunken sot, you would have been glad to give me a few barls and a bowl of soup, and a place to sleep in your stable? Well, thanks, Lady, but I don't need your pity!"

He stood up, ignored the pain that shot through his head, and glared down at her.

"What do you want of me?" he snarled, teeth clenched over the pipe stem. "What can I do for Your Ladyship?"

She was angry in her turn. No one—especially drunken,

washed-up assassins—spoke to a mysteriarch like that. The rainbow eyes glittered like the sun through a prism. She rose to her feet, drew herself up in offended dignity.

"Well?" he demanded.

Looking at him, seeing his anguish, she faltered, "I suppose I deserved that. Forgive me—"

"Damn it!" Hugh cried, nearly biting the pipe stem in two. His jaws ached with the strain. He slammed his fist on the table. "What the devil do you want with me?"

She was pale. "To . . . to hire you."

He regarded her silently, grimly. Turning away from her, he walked over to the door, stared at the closed panel.

"Who's the mark? And keep your voice down."

"There is no mark!" Iridal replied. "I have not come to hire you to kill. My son has been found. He is being held hostage by the elves. I intend to try to free him. And I need your help."

Hugh grunted. "So that's it. Where've the elves got the kid?"

"In the Imperanon."

Incredulous, Hugh turned, stared at Iridal. "The Imperanon? Lady, you need help, all right." Taking his pipe from his mouth, he pointed it at her. "Maybe someone should lock *you* up in a cell . . ."

"I can pay you. Pay you well. The royal treasury—"

"—doesn't hold enough," said Hugh. "There's not enough barls in the world that could pay me to march into the heart of the enemy empire and fetch back that little—"

The flare of her rainbow eyes warned him not to proceed.

"Obviously I have made a mistake," she said coldly. "I will trouble you no further."

She walked toward the door. Hugh remained standing in front of it, blocking it, did not move.

"Step aside," she ordered.

Hugh put the pipe back in his mouth, sucked on it a moment, regarded her with grim amusement. "You need me, Lady. I'm the only chance you've got. You'll pay me what I ask."

"What *do* you ask?" she demanded.

"Help me find Alfred."

She stared at him, shocked into silence. Then she shook her head. "No . . . that's not possible! He's gone. I have no way of finding him."

"Maybe he's with Bane."

"The other is with my son. Haplo, the man with the blue skin. And if Haplo is with Bane, Alfred is not. They're bitter enemies. I can't explain, Hugh. You wouldn't understand."

Hugh flung his pipe to the floor. Reaching out, he caught hold of her, gripped her arms hard.

"You're hurting me," she protested.

"I know. I don't give a damn. *You* try to understand, Lady," said Hugh. "Imagine you've been blind from birth. You're content in a world of darkness, because you know nothing different. Then, suddenly, you're given the gift of sight. You see all the wonders you've never even been able to imagine—the sky and trees, clouds and the Firmament. And then, suddenly, the gift is ripped away. You're blind again. You're plunged back into darkness. But this time, you *know* what you've lost."

"I'm sorry," whispered Iridal. She started to lift her hand, to touch his face.

Hugh flung her back. Angry, ashamed, he turned away.

"I agree to the bargain," she said softly. "If you do this for me, I'll do what I can to help you find Alfred."

Neither spoke for a moment, neither was able.

"How much time do we have?" he asked gruffly.

"A fortnight. Stephen meets then with Prince Rees'ahn. Though I don't think the Tribus elves know about . . ."

"The hell they don't, Lady. The Tribus don't dare let that meeting come off. I wonder what they had in mind before that kid of yours fell into their hands? Rees'ahn's smart. He's survived three assassination attempts by their special guard, the ones they call the Unseen. Some say the prince is being warned by the Kenkari . . ."

Hugh paused, pondered. "Now that gives me an idea."

He fell silent, felt about his clothing for his pipe, forgetting he'd thrown it from him.

Iridal reached down, picked it up, handed it to him.

He took it from her almost absentmindedly, fished some stregno out of a greasy leather pouch, and stuffed it into the bowl. Walking to the fire grate, he lifted a glowing coal with a pair of tongs, touched the coal to the bowl. A thin trail of smoke rose, bringing with it the acrid odor of the stregno.

"What—" Iridal began.

"Shut up," Hugh snapped. "Look, from now on, Lady, you do what I say, when I say it. No questions. I'll explain, if I have time, but if I don't, then you have to trust me. I'll rescue that kid of yours. And you help me find Alfred. Do we have a deal?"

"Yes," Iridal answered steadily.

"Good." He lowered his voice, his glance going again to the door. "I need two monks in here, no one watching. Can you manage that?"

Iridal walked over to the door, slid aside the panel. A monk stood in the hallway, probably ordered to wait for her.

She nodded. "Are you capable of walking?" she asked loudly, in disgust.

Hugh took the hint. He placed his pipe carefully near the grate, then, catching up the wine bottle, he smashed it on the floor. He kicked over the table, tumbled down into the puddle of spilled wine and broken glass, and rolled about in the mess.

"Oh, yeah," he mumbled, trying to stand and falling back down. "I can walk. Sure. Let's go."

Iridal stepped to the door, rapped on it briskly. "Go fetch the Abbot," she ordered.

The monk left. The Abbot returned. Iridal unlocked the door, opened it.

"Hugh the Hand has agreed to accompany me," she said, "but you see the state he's in. He can't walk without assistance. If two of your monks could carry him, I would be extremely grateful."

The Abbot frowned, looked dubious. Iridal removed a purse from beneath her cloak. "My gratitude is of a material nature," she said, smiling. "A donation to the Abbey is always welcome, I believe."

The Abbot accepted the purse. "Two of the brethren will be sent. But you may neither see nor speak to them."

"I understand, Lord. I am ready to leave now." She did not look back at Hugh, but she could hear the crunch of broken glass, heavy breathing, and muttered curses.

The Abbot appeared highly pleased and gratified at her departure. The mysteriarch had disturbed his Abbey with her imperious demands, caused a stir among the brethren, brought too much of the world of the living into one devoted to the dead. He himself escorted Iridal up the stairs, through the Abbey, and out the front entrance. He promised that Hugh would be sent out to meet her, if he could walk, carried if he could not. Perhaps the Abbot was not sorry to rid himself of this troublesome guest as well.

Iridal bowed, expressed her thanks. She hesitated, wanting to remain nearby, in case Hugh needed her help.

But the Abbot, clutching the purse, did not go back inside the Abbey. He waited beneath the glowlamp, intending to make certain that the woman was truly leaving.

Iridal had no recourse, therefore, but to turn and depart the Abbey grounds, make her way back to her slumbering dragon. Only then, when the Abbot saw her with the dragon, did he turn and stalk into the Abbey, slam shut the door.

Looking back, Iridal wondered what to do, wished she knew what Hugh had planned. She decided that the best thing she could do was awaken the dragon, have it ready to carry them speedily away from this place.

Waking a slumbering dragon is always a tricky maneuver, for dragons are independent by nature, and if the beast woke up free of the spell that enthralled it, it might decide to fly away, attack her, attack the Abbey, or a combination of all three.

Fortunately, the dragon remained under enchantment. It emerged from sleep only slightly irritated at being awakened. Iridal soothed and praised it, promised it a treat when they returned home.

The dragon stretched its wings, lashed its tail, and proceeded to inspect its scaly hide for signs of the tiny and insidious dragonwyrm, a parasite fond of burrowing beneath the scales and sucking the dragon's blood.

Iridal left it to its task, turned to watch the Abbey entrance, which she could see from her vantage point. She was just beginning to be anxious, more than half-afraid that Hugh might have changed his mind. She was wondering how to cope if he had, for the Abbot would most certainly not let her return, no matter what dire magics she threatened.

Then Hugh burst out the front door, almost as if he had been shoved from behind. He carried a bundle in one arm—a cloak and clothes for the journey, no doubt—and a bottle of wine in the other. He fell, caught himself, glanced backward, said something it was probably just as well Iridal couldn't hear. Then he straightened, stared around, obviously wondering where she was.

Iridal lifted her arm, waved to draw his attention, called out to him.

Perhaps it was the sound of her voice—startlingly loud in the clear, frosty night—or her sudden movement. She never knew. Something jolted the dragon out of its enchantment.

A shrill shriek rose behind her, wings flapped, and, before she could stop it, the dragon had taken to the air. The dragon's disenchantment was nothing more than a minor annoyance for a mysteriarch. Iridal had only to recast a very simple spell, but, to do so, she was forced to turn her attention away from Hugh for a few moments.

Unfamiliar with the intrigues and machinations of the royal court, it never occurred to Iridal that the distraction was deliberate.

CHAPTER ♦ 24

KIR MONASTERY

VOLKARAN ISLES

MID REALM

♦

HUGH SAW THE DRAGON TAKE TO THE AIR, KNEW IMMEDIATELY THAT IT HAD slipped the reins of its enchantment. He was no magus. There was nothing he could do to help Iridal recapture it or cast a spell on it. Shrugging, he pulled the cork of the wine bottle out with his teeth and was about to take a drink when he heard a man's voice, speaking to him from the shadows.

"Make no sudden movement. Give no indication you hear me. Walk over this direction."

Hugh knew the man, searched to give the voice a name and a face, but failed. The wine-soaked months of self-imposed captivity had drowned the memory. He could see nothing in the darkness. For all he knew, an arrow was nocked and aimed at his heart. And though he sought death, he sought it on his own terms, not on someone else's. He wondered briefly if Iridal had led him into this ambush, decided not. Her anxiety over that kid of hers had been too real.

The man seemed to know Hugh was only pretending to be drunk, but the Hand figured it couldn't hurt to keep up the pretense. He acted as if he hadn't heard, lurched in the general direction of the voice by accident. His hands fumbled with his bundle and wine bottle—which had now become shield and weapon. Using his cloak to conceal his motions, he shifted the heavy bundle in his left hand, ready to lift it to protect himself, readjusted his right hand's grip on the neck of the wine bottle. With one quick motion, he could smash the glass against a head, across a face.

Muttering beneath his breath about the inability of women to control dragons, Hugh staggered out of the small pool of light that illuminated the Abbey grounds, found himself among a few scraggly bushes and a grove of twisted trees.

"Stop there. That's near enough. You only need to hear me. Do you know me, Hugh the Hand?"

And then he did know. He gripped the bottle tighter. "Trian, isn't it? House magus to King Stephen."

"We haven't much time. The Lady Iridal mustn't know we've had this conversation. His Majesty wishes to remind you that you have not fulfilled the agreement."

"What?" Hugh shifted his eyes, stared into the shadows without seeming to stare.

"You did not do what you were paid to do. The child is still alive."

"So?" said Hugh harshly. "I'll give you your money back. You only paid me half of it anyway."

"We don't want the money back. We want the child dead."

"I can't do it," said Hugh to the night.

"Why?" the voice asked, sounding displeased. "Surely you of all men haven't found a conscience. Are you suddenly squeamish? Don't you like killing anymore?"

Hugh dropped the wine bottle, made a sudden lunge. His hand caught hold of the wizard's robes. He dragged the man forth.

"No," said Hugh, holding the wizard's handsome, fine-boned face close to his own grizzled jowl. "I might like it *too much!*"

He shoved Trian backward, had the satisfaction of watching him crash into the bushes. "I might not be able to stop myself. Tell that to your king."

He couldn't see Trian's face; the wizard was a robed hump of blackness, silhouetted against the luminescent coralite. Hugh didn't want to see him. He kicked aside the shards of the wine bottle, cursed the waste, and started to walk away. Iridal had managed to coax the dragon out of the sky. She was petting it, whispering the words of the spell.

"We offered you a job," said Trian, picking himself up, calm, nonplussed. "You accepted it. You were paid for it. And you failed to complete it."

Hugh kept walking.

"You had only one thing that raised you above the level of common cutthroat, Hugh the Hand," Trian told him, the words a whisper, carried by the wind. "Honor."

Hugh made no response, did not look back. He strode rapidly up the hill toward Iridal, found her disheveled, irritated.

"I'm sorry for the delay. I can't understand how the enchantment could have slipped like that . . ."

I can, Hugh told her silently. Trian did it. He followed you. He foiled your spell, freed the dragon, in order to distract you while he talked to me. King Stephen's not sending you to rescue your son, Lady. He's using you to lead me to the child. Don't trust him, Iridal. Don't trust Trian, don't trust Stephen. Don't trust me.

Hugh could have said that to her, the words were on his lips . . and they stayed there, unspoken.

"Never mind that now," he told her, voice harsh and sharp. "Will the spell hold?"

"Yes, but—"

"Then fly the beast out of here. Before the Abbot finds two of his brethren stripped to their skins, bound hand and foot in my cell."

He glowered at her, expecting questions, prepared to remind her that she had agreed to ask none.

She cast him one wondering glance, then nodded and swiftly mounted the dragon. Hugh tied the bundle securely on the back of the ornate, two-person saddle that bore the Winged Eye—King Stephen's device.

"No wonder the damn wizard was able to disrupt the spell," Hugh muttered beneath his breath. "Riding a friggin' royal dragon!"

He pulled himself up on the creature's back, settled himself behind Iridal. She gave the command and the dragon sprang into the air, wings lifted and flapped, bearing them upward. Hugh did not waste time searching to see if he could find the magus. That was futile. Trian was too good. The question was: would he follow them? or simply wait for his dragon to return and report?

Hugh smiled grimly, leaned forward. "Where are we bound?"

"To my dwelling. To pick up provisions."

"No, we're not." Hugh spoke loudly, to be heard over the rush of the wind, the beating of the dragon's wings. "You have money? Barls? With the king's stamp?"

"Yes," Iridal replied. The dragon's flight was erratic, wild. The wind tore at Iridal's cloak, her white hair blew free, was like a cloud around her face.

"We'll buy what we need," Hugh told her. "From this moment, Lady Iridal, you and I disappear. A pity the night is so clear," he added, glancing about. "A rainstorm would be a useful thing about now."

"A storm can be conjured," said Iridal, "as you well know. I may not have much skill over dragons, but wind and rain are a different matter. How shall we find *our* way, then?"

"By the feel of the wind on my cheek," said Hugh, grinning at her. He slid forward, put out his arms—one on either side of Iridal—and reached for the reins. "Summon your storm, Lady."

"Is this necessary?" she asked, stirring uneasily at the Hand's overwhelming nearness, his body pressed against hers, his strong arms encircling her. "I can manage the dragon. You give me the directions."

"Wouldn't work," said Hugh. "I fly by feel; don't even think about it, most of the time. Lean back against me. You'll stay dryer. Relax, Lady. We've a long journey ahead of us this night. Sleep, if you can. Where we're going, there won't be many nights ahead of us when you'll be able to afford the luxury."

Iridal sat stiff and rigid a moment longer, then, with a sigh, she sank back against Hugh's breast. He shifted himself to better accommodate her, tightened his arms around her more securely.

He grasped the reins with a firm, experienced grip. The dragon, sensing skilled hands, calmed down and flew evenly. Iridal spoke the words of magic beneath her breath, words that snatched high drifting clouds from the sky far above them, brought fog down to wrap around them, a damp and misty blanket. Rain began to fall.

"I can't keep this up long," she said, feeling herself growing drowsy. The rain pelted softly on her face. She burrowed deeper into Hugh's arms.

"Doesn't need to be long."

Trian likes his comforts, Hugh thought. He won't chase us

through a rainstorm, especially when he figures out where we're headed.

"You're afraid of being followed, aren't you?" Iridal said.

"Let's just say I don't like to take chances," Hugh responded.

They flew through the storm and the night in silence so warm and comfortable that both were loath to disturb it. Iridal could have asked more questions—she knew well enough that the monks would not be likely to follow them. Who else did he fear? But she didn't say anything.

She had promised not to and she meant to keep that promise. She was glad he'd put such restrictions on her, in fact. She didn't want to ask, didn't want to know.

She rested her hand over her bosom, over the feather amulet that she wore hidden beneath her gown, the amulet that put her in mental contact with her child. She had not told him about that, nor would she. He would disapprove, would probably be angry. But she would not break this link with her child—lost to her once, now blessedly found.

Hugh has his secrets, she said to herself. I will keep mine.

Resting in his arms, glad of his strength and sheltering presence, Iridal let go of the past with its bitter sorrows and even more bitter self-recriminations, let go of the future with its certain peril. She let go of both as easily as she had let go the reins, allowing someone else to steer, to guide. There would come a time when she would need to grasp hold of them again, perhaps even fight for control. But until then, she could do what Hugh suggested—relax, sleep.

Hugh sensed more than saw that Iridal slept. The rain-soaked darkness was thick, blotted out the faint glow of the coralite below, making it seem as if ground and sky were one and the same. He shifted the reins to one hand, drew his cloak over the woman with the other, forming a tent to keep her warm and dry.

In his mind, he heard the same words, over and over and over.

You had only one thing that raised you above the level of common cutthroat, Hugh the Hand.

Honor . . . Honor . . . Honor . . .

♦

"You spoke to him, Trian? You recognized him?"

"Yes, Your Majesty."

Stephen scratched his bearded chin. "Hugh the Hand lives and has been alive, all this time. She lied to us."

"One can hardly blame her, sire," said Trian.

"We were fools to believe her! A man with blue skin! The bumbling Alfred gone looking for her son. Alfred couldn't find himself in the dark. She lied about it all!"

"I'm not so certain, Your Majesty," said Trian thoughtfully. "There was always more—much more—to Alfred than he let on. And the man with the blue skin. I have myself come across certain interesting references in those books the mysteriarchs brought with them—"

"Does any of this have anything to do with Hugh the Hand or Bane?" Stephen demanded, irritated.

"No, sire," said Trian. "But it might be of importance later on."

"Then we will discuss it later on. Will the Hand do as you told him?"

"I cannot say, sire. I wish I could," Trian added, seeing Stephen look highly displeased. "We had little time for speech. And his face, Your Majesty! I caught a glimpse of it, by the ground light. I could not look at it long. I saw there evil, cunning, desperation—"

"What of it? The man is, after all, an assassin."

"The evil was my own, sire," said Trian.

He lowered his gaze, stared down at several of the books, lying on the desk in his study.

"And mine, too, by implication."

"I didn't say that, sire—"

"You don't need to, damn it!" Stephen snapped, then he sighed heavily. "The ancestors be my witness, Magicka, I don't like this any more than you do. No one was happier than I was to think that Bane had survived, that I *wasn't* responsible for the murder of a ten-year-old child. I believed Lady Iridal because I wanted to believe her. And look where we are now. In far worse danger than before.

"But what choice do I have, Trian?" Stephen slammed his fist on the desk. "What choice?"

"None, sire," said Trian.

Stephen nodded. "So," he said abruptly, back to business. "Will he do it?"

"I don't know, sire. And we have reason to be afraid if he does. 'I might like the killing too much,' was what he said. 'I might not be able to stop myself.' "

Stephen looked gray, haggard. He lifted his hands, stared at them, rubbed them. "That need not be a worry. Once this deed is done, we will eliminate the man. At least in his case, we can feel justified. He has long cheated the executioner's ax. I assumed you followed the two when they left the monastery? Where did they go?"

"Hugh the Hand is skilled in shaking pursuit, sire. A rainstorm blew up, out of a cloudless sky. My dragon lost their scent, and I was soaked to the skin. I deemed it best to return to the Abbey and question the Kir monks who sheltered the Hand."

"With what result? Perhaps they knew what he intended."

"If so, sire, they did not tell me." Trian smiled ruefully. "The Abbot was in an uproar over something. He informed me that he'd had his fill of magi, then he slammed the door in my face."

"You did nothing?"

"I am merely Third House, sire," said Trian humbly. "The Kir's own magi are of a level equal to mine. A contest was neither appropriate nor called for. It would not do to offend the Kir, sire."

Stephen glowered. "I suppose you're right. But now we've lost track of the Hand and the Lady Iridal."

"I warned you to expect as much, Your Majesty. And we must have done so in any case. I surmised, you see, where they were headed—a place I, for one, dare not follow. Nor would you find many here willing or able to do so."

"What place is that? The Seven Mysteries[1]?"

---

[1] Seven islands in the Griphith Cluster, rumored, among humans, to be haunted by the ghosts of ancestors who had done some misdeed during their lives and who died unrepentant, cast off by their families. The elves have a similar belief; a common threat in elven is "You'll be sent to the Seven Mysteries for that!" Several expeditions, both human and elven, have been sent to explore the islands. None ever returned.

Alfred wrote that he intended to explore the islands himself, but he never did so. He appeared to have a vague theory that Sartan magic was involved, but how it worked or for what purpose, he was unable to say.

"No, sire. A place better known and, if anything, more dreaded, for the dangers in this place are real. Hugh the Hand is on the heading for Skurvash, Your Majesty."

CHAPTER ♦ 25

SKURVASH

VOLKARAN ISLES

MID REALM

♦

Hugh roused Iridal from her slumber while they were still in the skies, the weary dragon searching eagerly for a place to land. The Lords of Night had removed their dark cloaks, the Firmament was beginning to sparkle with the first rays of Solaris. Iridal started to wakefulness, wondering that she had slept so deeply and heavily.

"Where are we?" she asked, watching with half-drowsy pleasure the island emerge from the shadows of night, the dawn touching villages that were like toy blocks from this height. Smoke began to drift up from chimneys. On a cliff—the highest point on the island—a fortress made of the rare granite much prized on Arianus cast the shadow of its massive towers over the land, now that the Lords of Night had departed.

"Skurvash," said Hugh the Hand. He steered the dragon away from what was obviously a busy port, headed for the forested side of town, where landings could be kept private, if not necessarily secret.

Iridal was wide awake now, as if cold water had been thrown into her face. She was silent, thoughtful, then said in a low voice, "I suppose this is necessary."

"You've heard of the place."

"Nothing good."

"And that probably overrates it. You want to go to Aristagon, Lady Iridal. How did you plan to get there? Ask the elves to pretty please let you drop by for tea?"

"Of course not," she said coolly, offended. "But—"

"No 'buts.' No questions. You do what I say, remember?"

Every muscle in Hugh's body ached from the unaccustomed rigors of the flight. He wanted his pipe, and a glass—several glasses—of wine.

"Our lives will be in danger every minute we're on this island, Lady. Keep quiet. Let me do the talking. Follow my lead and, for both our sakes, don't do any magic. Not so much as a disappearing barl trick. They find out you're a mysteriarch and we're finished."

The dragon had spotted a likely landing site, a cleared patch near the shoreline. Hugh gave the beast its head and allowed it to spiral downward.

"You could call me Iridal," she said softly.

"Are you always on a first-name basis with your hired help?"

She sighed. "May I ask one question, Hugh?"

"I don't promise to answer."

"You spoke of 'they.' 'They' mustn't know I'm a mysteriarch. Who are 'they'?"

"The rulers of Skurvash."

"King Stephen is the ruler."

Hugh gave a sharp, barking laugh. "Not of Skurvash. Oh, the king's promised to come in, clean it up, but he knows he can't. He couldn't raise a force large enough. There's not a baron in Volkaran or Ulyndia who hasn't a tie to this place, though you won't find one who'd dare admit it. Even the elves, when they ruled most of the rest of the Mid Realms, never conquered Skurvash."

Iridal stared down at the island. Outside of its formidable-looking fortress, it had little else to recommend it, being mostly covered with the scraggly brush known as dwarf-shrub, so named because it looked somewhat like a dwarf's thick, russet beard and because once it dug its way into the coralite, it was almost impossible to uproot. A small and scraggly-looking town perched on the edge of the shoreline, holding on as tenaciously as the shrubs. A single road led from the town through groves of hargast trees, climbed the side of the mountain to the fortress.

"Did the elves lay siege to it? I can believe such a fortress could hold out long—"

"Bah!" Hugh grimaced, flexed his arms, tried to ease the muscles in his stiff neck and shoulders. "The elves didn't attack. War's a wonderful thing, Your Ladyship, until it begins to cut into your profits."

"You mean these humans trade with the elves?" Iridal was shocked.

Hugh shrugged. "The rulers of Skurvash don't care about the slant of a man's eyes, only the glint of his money."

"And who is this ruler?" She was interested and curious now.

"Not one person," Hugh responded. "A group. They're known as the Brotherhood."

The dragon settled down for a landing in a broad, cleared space that had obviously been used for this purpose many times before, to judge by the broken tree limbs (snapped off by the wings), the tracks of claws left in the coralite, and the droppings scattered around the field. Hugh dismounted, stretched his aching back, flexed his cramped legs.

"Or perhaps I should say 'we,' " he amended, coming to assist Iridal down from the dragon's back. "*We* are known as the Brotherhood."

She had been about to place her hand in his. Now she hesitated, stared at him, her face pale, her eyes wide. Their rainbow hue was muddied, darkened by the shadows of the hargast trees surrounding them.

"I don't understand."

"Go back, Iridal," he said to her, grimly earnest. "Leave, right now. The dragon's tired, but the beast'll make it, take you at least as far as Providence."

The dragon, hearing itself mentioned, shifted irritably from foot to foot and rustled its wings. It wanted to be rid of its riders, wanted to skulk off into the trees, go to sleep.

"First you were eager to join me. Now you're trying to drive me away." Iridal regarded him coldly. "What happened? Why the change?"

"I said no questions," Hugh growled, staring moodily out over the rim of the island, into the fathomless blue depths of deepsky. He flicked a glance at her. "Unless you'd care to answer a few I could ask."

Iridal flushed, drew back her hand. She dismounted from the

dragon without assistance, used the opportunity to keep her head lowered, her face concealed in the recesses of the hood of her cloak. When she was standing on the ground, and certain of maintaining her composure, she turned to Hugh.

"You need me. You need me to help find Alfred. I know something of him, quite a lot, in fact. I know who he is and what he is and, believe me, you won't discover him without my assistance. Will you give that up? Will you send me away?"

Hugh refused to look at her. "Yes," he said in a low voice. "Yes, damn it. Go!" His hands clenched on the dragon's saddle, he laid his aching head on them.

"Damn Trian!" he swore softly to himself. "Damn Stephen! Damn this woman and damn her child. I should have set my head on the block when I had the chance. I knew it then. Something warned me. I would have wrapped death around me like a blanket and slipped into slumber . . ."

"What are you saying?"

He felt Iridal's hand, her touch, soft and warm, on his shoulder. He shuddered, cringed away.

"What terrible grief you bear!" she said gently. "Let me share it."

Hugh rounded on her, savage, sudden. "Leave me. Buy someone else to help you. I can give you names—ten men—better than me. As for you, I don't need you. I can find Alfred. I can find any man—"

"—so long as he's hiding in the bottom of a wine bottle," Iridal retorted.

Hugh caught hold of her, his grip tight and painful. He shook her, forced her head back, forced her to look at him.

"Know me for what I am—a hired killer. My hands are stained with blood, blood bought and paid for. I took money to kill a child!"

"And gave your life for the child . . ."

"A fluke!" Hugh shoved her away, flung her back from him. "That damned charm he cast over me. Or maybe a spell *you* put on me."

Turning his back on her, he began to untie the bundle, using swift, violent tugs.

"Go," he said again, not looking at her. "Go now."

"I will not. We made a bargain," said Iridal. "The one good

thing I've heard said about you is that you never broke a contract."

He stopped what he was doing, turned to stare at her, his deep-set eyes dark beneath frowning, overhanging brows. He was suddenly cold, calm.

"You're right, my lady. I never broke a contract. Remember that, when the time comes." Freeing the bundle, he tucked it under his arm, nodded his head at the dragon. "Take off the enchantment."

"But . . . that will mean it will fly loose. We might never catch it."

"Precisely. And neither will anyone else. Nor is it likely to return to the king's stables any time in the near future. That will be long enough for us to disappear."

"But it could attack us!"

"It wants sleep more than food." Hugh glared at her, his eyes red from sleeplessness and hangover. "Free it or fly it, Lady Iridal. I'm not going to argue."

Iridal looked at the dragon, her last link with her home, her people. The journey had all been a dream, up until now. A dream such as she had dreamed asleep in Hugh's arms. A glorious rescue, of magic and flashing steel, of snatching her child up in her arms and defying his enemies to seize him, of watching the elves fall back, daunted by a mother's love and Hugh's prowess. Skurvash had not been a part of that dream. Nor had Hugh's blunt and shadowed words.

I'm not very practical, Iridal told herself bleakly. Or very realistic. None of us are, who lived in the High Realms. We didn't need to be. Only Sinistrad. And that was why we let him proceed with his evil plans, that was why we made no move to stop him. We are weak, helpless. I swore I would change. I swore I would be strong, for my child's sake.

She pressed her hand over the feather amulet, tucked beneath the bodice of her gown. When she felt stronger, she lifted the spell from the dragon, broke the last link in the chain.

The creature, once freed, shook its spiky mane, glared at them ferociously, seemed to consider whether or not it should make a meal of them, decided against it. The dragon snarled at them, took to the air. It would seek a safe place to rest, somewhere high and hidden. Eventually it would tire of being alone and go back to its stables, for dragons are social creatures, and it would soon feel the longing for its mate and companions left behind.

Hugh watched it well away, then turned and began to walk up a small path that led to the main road they had seen from the air. Iridal hastened to keep up with him.

As he walked, he was rummaging through the bundle, extracted an object from it—a pouch. Its contents gave off a harsh, metallic jingle. He looped its ties over the belt he wore at his waist.

"Give me your money," he ordered. "All of it."

Silently, Iridal handed over her purse.

Hugh opened it, gave it a swift eye-count, then thrust the purse inside his shirt, to rest snugly and firmly against his skin. "The lightfingers[1] of Skurvash live up to their reputation," he said dryly. "We'll need to keep what money we have safe, to buy our passage."

"*Buy* our passage! To Aristagon?" repeated Iridal, dazed. "But we're at war! Is flying to elven lands . . . is it that simple?"

"No," said Hugh, "but anything can be had for a price."

Iridal waited for him to continue, but he was obviously not going to tell her more. Solaris was bright and the coralite glistened. The air was warming rapidly after night's chill. In the distance, perched high on the side of a mountain, the fortress loomed strong and imposing, as large as Stephen's palace. Iridal could not see any houses or buildings, but she guessed they were heading for the small village she'd seen from the air. Spirals of smoke from morning cooking fires and forges rose above the brush.

"You have friends here," she said, recalling his words, the "they" that had been altered to "we."

"In a manner of speaking. Keep your face covered."

"Why? No one here will know me. And they can't tell I'm a mysteriarch just by looking at me."

He stopped walking, eyed her grimly.

"I'm sorry," Iridal said, sighing. "I know I promised not to question anything you did and that's all I've done. I don't mean to, but I don't understand and . . . and I'm frightened."

"I guess you've a right to be," he said, after a moment spent

---

[1] Pickpockets.

tugging thoughtfully on the long thin strands of braided beard. "And I suppose the more you know, the better off we'll both be. Look at you. With those eyes, those clothes, that voice—a child can see you're noble born. That makes you fair game, a prize. I want them to know you're *my* prize."

"I will not be anyone's prize!" Iridal bristled. "Why don't you tell them the truth—that I'm your employer."

He stared at her, then he grinned, then threw back his head and laughed. His laughter was deep, hearty; it released something inside him. He actually smiled at her, and the smile was reflected in his eyes.

"A good answer, Lady Iridal. Perhaps I will. But, in the meanwhile, keep close to me, don't wander off. You're a stranger here. And they have rather a special welcome for strangers in Skurvash."

The port town of Klervashna was located close to the shoreline. It was built out in the open, no walls surrounded it, no gates barred entry, no guards asked them their business. One road led from the shore into town, one road—the same road—led out of town and up into the mountains.

"They're certainly not worried about being attacked," said Iridal, accustomed to the walled cities of Volkaran and Ulyndia, whose citizens, continually on the alert for elven raiders, lived in an almost constant state of fear.

"If anything did threaten them, the residents would pack up and head for the fortress. But no, they're not worried."

A group of boys, playing at pirate in an alley, were the first ones to take note of them. The children dropped their hargast-limb swords and ran up to stare at them with ingenuous frankness and open curiosity.

The boys were about Bane's age, and Iridal smiled at them. A little girl, clad in rags, ran up, held out her hand.

"Will you give me money, beautiful lady?" begged the child, with a winsome, pretty smile. "My mother is sick. My father is dead. And there is me and my baby sister and brother to feed. Only one coin, beautiful lady—"

Iridal started to reach for her purse, remembered she didn't have it with her.

"Off with you," Hugh said harshly. He held up his right hand, palm out.

The little girl looked at him shrewdly, shrugged, and skipped off, returning to the game. The boys trailed after her, whooping and shouting, except for one, who dashed up the road into town.

"You didn't need to be so rough with the child," Iridal said reprovingly. "She was so sweet. We could have spared a coin—"

"—and lost your purse. That 'sweet' child's job is to find out where you keep your money. Then she passes the word to her light-fingered father, who is undoubtedly very much alive, and who would have relieved you of your wealth once you were in town."

"I don't believe it! A child like that . . ."

Hugh shrugged, kept walking.

Iridal drew her cloak more closely about her. "Must we stay long in this dreadful place?" she asked in a low voice, moving nearer Hugh.

"We don't even stop here. We go on. To the fortress."

"Isn't there another route?"

Hugh shook his head. "The only way is through Klervashna. It allows them to get a look at us. Those boys play here for a reason, to watch for strangers. But I've given them the sign. One's gone now, to report our arrival to the Brotherhood. Don't worry. No one'll bother us, from now on. But you best keep quiet."

Iridal was almost grateful for the order. Child thieves. Child spies. She might have been shocked to think parents could abuse and destroy the innocence of childhood. But she recalled a father who had used his son to spy on a king.

"Klervashna," said Hugh, gesturing with his hand.

Iridal looked about in surprise. From his introduction, she had been expecting a raucous, brawling city of sin—thieves lurking in the shadows, murder done openly in the streets. She was considerably startled therefore to see nothing more frightening than young girls driving geese to market, women carrying baskets laden with eggs, men hard at apparently legitimate work.

The town was bustling, thriving. Its streets were crowded, and the only difference she could see between it and any respectable city of Ulyndia was that the population appeared to be of a widely varied nature, encompassing every type of human, from the dark-skinned inhabitants of Humbisash to the fair-haired wanderers of Malakal. But even this did not prepare her for the astonishing sight of two elves, who emerged from a cheese shop, almost ran into them, elbowed past with a muttered oath.

Iridal was startled, glanced at Hugh in alarm, thinking perhaps that the town had been conquered, after all. He did not appear concerned, barely glanced at the elves. The human inhabitants paid the enemy scant attention, except for a young woman who followed after them, trying to sell them a bag of pua fruit.

The rulers of Skurvash don't care about the slant of a man's eyes, only the glint of his money.

Equally astounding was the sight of well-bred servants, belonging to wealthy estates of other islands, strolling through the streets, packages in their arms. Some wore their liveries outright, not caring who knew the names of their masters. Iridal recognized the coat of arms of more than one baron of Volkaran, more than one duke of Ulyndia.

"Smuggled goods," Hugh explained. "Elven fabric, elven weapons, elven wine, elven jewels. The elves are here for the same reason, to buy human goods they can't get in Aristagon. Herbs and potions, dragon's teeth and claws,[2] dragon skin and scales to use on their ships."

The war for these people is profit, Iridal realized. Peace would mean economic disaster. Or perhaps not. The winds of changing fortune must have blown through Klervashna often. It would survive, just as legend held it the rat had survived the Sundering.

They walked through the town at a leisurely pace. Hugh stopped once, to buy stregno for his pipe, a bottle of wine, and a cup of water, which he gave to Iridal. Then they moved on, Hugh shoving his way through the crowds, keeping firm hold of "his prize," his hand over Iridal's upper arm. A few passersby gave them sharp, inquisitive glances that flicked over Hugh's stern, impassive face, noted Iridal's rich clothing. An eyebrow or two raised, a knowing smile quirked a lip. No one said a word, no one stopped them. What one did in Klervashna was one's own business.

And that of the Brotherhood.

"Are we going to the fortress now?" asked Iridal.

The rows of neat, gable-roofed houses had come to an end.

---

[2] Believed to cure impotence.

They were heading back into the wilderness. A few children had seen them on their way, but even they had disappeared.

Hugh pulled the cork out of the wine bottle with his teeth, spit it on the ground. "Yeah. Tired?"

Iridal raised her head, looked up at the fortress that seemed a great distance away. "I'm not used to walking, I'm afraid. Could we stop and rest?"

Hugh gave this thoughtful consideration, then nodded abruptly. "Not long," he said, assisting her to sit on a large out-growth of coralite. "They know we've left town. They'll be expecting us."

Hugh finished off the wine, tossed the bottle into the bushes at the side of the road. He took another moment to fill his pipe— shaking the dried fungus out of the bag—then lit it, using tinder and flint. Puffing on the pipe, drawing the smoke into his lungs, he repacked the bundle, tucked it beneath his arm, and stood up.

"We best be going. You'll be able to rest when we get there. I've got some business to transact."

"Who are 'they'?" Iridal asked, rising wearily to her feet. "What is this Brotherhood?"

"I belong to it," he said, teeth clenched on the pipe stem. "Can't you guess?"

"No, I'm afraid I can't."

"The Brotherhood of the Hand," he said. "The Assassins' Guild."

CHAPTER ✦ 26

SKURVASH

VOLKARAN ISLES

MID REALM

✦

THE FORTRESS OF THE BROTHERHOOD REIGNED, SOLID AND IMPREGNABLE, OVER the island of Skurvash. A series of structures, built over time, as the Brotherhood grew and its needs changed, the fortress commanded a view of deepsky and its flight tracks, as well as the land all around it and the one meandering road that led up to it.

An approaching single-rider dragon could be spotted at a thousand menkas, a large troop-laden dragonship at two thousand. The road—the only road through the rough land, covered with the brittle-limbed and occasionally deadly hargast trees[1]— wandered through deep ravines and over numerous swinging bridges. Hugh showed Iridal, as they crossed, how a single stroke of a sword could send the bridge and everyone on it plunging into the sharp rocks far below. And if by chance an army made it to the top of the mountain, it would have to take the fortress itself —a sprawling complex, guarded by desperate men and women who had nothing to lose.

Small wonder both King Stephen and Emperor Agah'ran had given up all thoughts—except wishful ones—of attacking it.

The Brotherhood knew itself to be safe, secure. Its vast network of spies warned it instantly of any threat, long before that threat was seen. Vigilance was, therefore, easy and relaxed. The

---

[1] Bane was nearly killed when the limb from a hargast broke during a windstorm and fell down on him. See *Dragon Wing*, vol. 1 of *The Death Gate Cycle*.

gates stood open wide. The guards played at rune-bone and didn't even bother to glance up from their game as Hugh and Iridal walked through the gates to a cobblestone courtyard beyond. Most of the outbuildings were empty, though they would have been filled rapidly enough with the citizens of Klervashna had attack threatened. Hugh and Iridal saw no one in their walk along the winding avenues, leading up a gentle slope to the main building.

Older than the rest, this structure was central headquarters for the Brotherhood, which had the temerity to fly its own flag—a blood-red banner bearing a single upheld hand, palm flat, fingers together. The entrance door—a rarity on Arianus, for it was made of wood, decorated with intricate carvings—was closed fast and barred.

"Wait here," Hugh ordered, pointing. "Don't move from this spot."

Iridal, numb and dazed with exhaustion, looked down. She stood on a flat piece of flagstone that was, she noticed (now that she examined it more closely) a different shape and color from the flagstone walkway leading to the door. The stone was cut to resemble vaguely the shape of a hand.

"Don't move off that rock," Hugh warned again. He indicated a narrow slit in the stonework, positioned above the door. "There's an arrow pointed at your heart. Step to either the right or the left and you're dead."

Iridal froze, stared at the dark slit, through which she could see nothing—no sign of life, no movement. Yet she had no doubt, from Hugh's tone, that what he said was true. She remained standing on the hand-shaped rock. Hugh left her, walked up to the door.

He paused, studied the carvings on the door, carvings that were done in the shape of hands—open, palm flat, resembling the symbol on the flag. There were twelve in all, ranged round in the shape of a circle, fingers out. Choosing one, Hugh pressed his own hand into the carving.[2] The door swung open.

---

[2] Haplo made a study of the Brotherhood and was able to penetrate many of their secrets. He surmises, in his writings, that the carvings on the door correspond to some sort of ritual cycle in the Brotherhood's calendar. A

"Come," he said to Iridal, motioning for her to join him. "It's safe now."

Glancing askance at the window above, Iridal hastened to Hugh's side. The fortress was oppressive, filled her with a sense of terrible loneliness, gloom, and dark foreboding. She caught hold of Hugh's outstretched hand, held on to it fast.

Hugh looked concerned at her chill touch, her unnatural pallor. He squeezed her hand reassuringly, a grim look warned her to remain calm, in control. Iridal lowered her head, pulled her hood down to hide her face, and accompanied him inside a small room.

The door shut immediately behind them, bars thundered into place with a boom that stopped the heart. After the bright light outside, Iridal was half blind. Hugh stood blinking, motionless, until he could see.

"This way," said a dry voice that sounded like the crackle of very old parchment. Movement sounded to their right.

Hugh followed, knowing well where he was and where he was going. He kept fast hold of Iridal, who was grateful for his guidance. The darkness was daunting, unnerving. It was intended to be. She reminded herself that she had asked for this. She had better get used to being in dark and unnerving places.

"Hugh the Hand," said the dry voice. "How very good to see you, sir. It's been a long time."

They entered a windowless chamber, lit by the soft light of a glowstone in a lantern. A stooped and wizened old man stood regarding Hugh with a gentle, benign expression, made remarkable by a pair of wonderfully clear and penetrating eyes.

"It has that, Ancient," said Hugh, his stern expression relaxing into a smile. "I'm surprised to find you still at work. I thought you'd be taking your ease by a good fire."

"Ah, this is all the duties I undertake now, sir," said the old

---

member chooses the correct hand based on this cycle and presses his hand against it. A small hole carved in the door admits sunlight into the watch room. The sunlight is cut off by the hand covering the hole, and thus the watcher knows the member is one who has a right to enter. At night, or on cloudy days, a candle flame or some other source of light is held up to the correct hand, is seen through the hole.

Those who fail to perform this ritual are killed instantly by the archer stationed at all times in the window above.

man. "I've put the other away long since, except for a bit of instruction, now and then, to those like yourself, who ask for it. A skilled pupil you were, too, sir. You had the proper touch—delicate, sensitive. Not like some of these ham-fisted louts you see today."

The Ancient shook his head, the bright eyes shifted unhurriedly from Hugh to Iridal, taking in every detail to the extent that she had the feeling he could see through her clothes, perhaps even through flesh.

He shifted the penetrating gaze back to Hugh. "You'll forgive me, sir, but I must ask. Wouldn't do to break the rules, not even for you."

"Of course," said Hugh, and held up his right hand, palm out, fingers together.

The Ancient took Hugh's hand in his own, peered at it intently by the light of the glowstone.

"Thank you, sir," said the Ancient gravely. "What is your business?"

"Is Ciang seeing anyone today?"

"Yes, sir. One's come to be admitted. They'll be performing the ceremony at the stroke of the hour. I'm sure your presence would be welcome. And what is your wish concerning your guest?"

"She's to be escorted to a room with a fire. My business with Ciang may take a while. See to it that the lady's made comfortable, given food and drink, a bed if she desires."

"A room?" asked the old man mildly. "Or a cell?"

"A room," said Hugh. "Make her comfortable. I may be a long time."

The Ancient eyed Iridal speculatively. "She's a magus, I'll wager. It's your call, Hand, but are you sure you want her left unguarded?"

"She won't use her magic. Another's life, more precious to her than her own, hangs in the balance. Besides," he added dryly, "she's my employer."

"Ah, I see." The Ancient nodded and bowed to Iridal with a rusty grace that would have become one of Stephen's royal courtiers.

"I will escort the lady to her chamber myself," said the old man in courteous tones. "It is not often I have such pleasant duty allotted me. You, Hugh the Hand, may go on up. Ciang has been informed of your coming."

Hugh grunted, not surprised. He knocked the ashes out of his pipe, refilled it. Placing his pipe in his mouth, he cast Iridal one look that was empty and dark, without comfort, hint, or meaning. Then he turned and walked into the shadows beyond.

"We go through this door, my lady," said the Ancient, gesturing in a direction opposite from that which Hugh had taken.

Lifting the lantern in his wrinkled hand, the old man apologized for preceding her, saying that the way was dark and the stairs in ill repair and occasionally treacherous. Iridal begged him, in a low voice, not to think of it.

"You've known Hugh the Hand long?" she asked, feeling herself blush to ask the question, trying hard to make it sound like casual conversation.

"Over twenty years," said the Ancient. "Since he first came to us, little more than a gangling youth."

Iridal wondered at that, wondered about this Brotherhood, who ruled an island. And Hugh was one of them and seemingly respected at that. Amazing, for a man who went out of his way to isolate himself.

"You mentioned teaching him a skill," she said. "What was it?" It might have been music lessons, to judge by the Ancient's benign and gentle appearance.

"The knife, my lady. Ah, there has never been one as skilled with a blade as Hugh the Hand. I was good, but he bettered me. He once stabbed a man he was sitting next to in an inn. Made such a neat job of it that the man never moved, never let out a cry. No one knew he was dead until the next morning, when they found him sitting in the same place, stiff as the wall. The trick is knowing the right spot, slipping the blade between the ribs in order to pierce the heart before the mark knows what hit him.

"Here we are, my lady. A room nice and cozy, with a fire well laid and a bed, if you'd care to take a nap. And will you have white wine or red with your meal?"

Hugh walked slowly through the halls of the fortress, taking time to feel pleasure in this return to familiar surroundings. Nothing had changed, nothing except him. That's why he had not come back, when he knew he would have been welcome. They wouldn't understand and he couldn't explain. The Kir didn't understand either. But they didn't ask questions.

More than a few of the Brotherhood had come here to die. Some of the elders, like the Ancient, returned to spend fading years among those who had been their only family—a family more loyal and closely bound than most. Others, younger, came to either recover from wounds—a hazard of the business—or to die from them. More often than not, the patient recovered. The Brotherhood, from long association with death, had amassed considerable knowledge on the treatment of knife, sword, and arrow wounds, dragon bites and claw attacks, had devised antidotes for certain poisons.

The Brotherhood's own magi were skilled in reversing the spells cast by other Magicka, at lifting the enchantments from cursed rings, that sort of work. Hugh the Hand had shared some of his own knowledge, gleaned from the Kir monks, whose works took them always among the dead and whose magi had developed magics that protected against contagion, contamination.[3]

"I could have come here," Hugh reflected, puffing on his pipe, eyeing the dark and shadowed hallways with nostalgic interest. "But what would I have told them? I'm not sickening from a mortal wound, but one that's immortal."

He shook his head, quickened his steps. Ciang would still ask questions, but now Hugh had a few answers, and since he was here on business, she wouldn't press him. Not as she would have if he'd come here first.

He climbed a spiraling staircase, arrived in a shadowed and empty hall. A series of doors stood shut on either side. One, at the end, was open. Light streamed out into the hallway. Hugh advanced toward the light, paused on the door's threshold to give his eyes time to adjust from the fortress's dark interior to the brightness of the room.

Three people were inside. Two were strangers—a man and a youngster of perhaps about nineteen. The other Hugh knew well. She turned to greet him, not rising from the desk behind which

---

[3] For though the Kir monks worship death, consider death the final triumph over life, they were forced to face the realization that, unless they took sensible precautions, they might not have any worshipers left.

she sat, but tilting her head to gaze at him with the slanted, shrewd eyes that took in all, gave back nothing.

"Enter," she said. "And welcome."

Hugh knocked the pipe's ashes out in the hallway, tucked his pipe into a pocket of his leather vest.

"Ciang,"[4] he said, walking into the room. Coming to stand before her, he bowed low.

"Hugh the Hand." She extended her hand to him.

He brought it to his lips—an action that appeared to amuse her.

"You kiss that old wrinkled claw?"

"With honor, Ciang," Hugh said warmly, and meant it.

The woman smiled at him. She was old, one of the oldest living beings on Arianus, for she was an elf and long-lived, even for her kind.

Her face was a mass of lines, the skin drawn taut over high cheekbones, the fine-boned, beaked nose white as ivory. She followed the elven custom of painting her lips, and the red flowed among the wrinkles like tiny rivulets of blood. Her head was bald, her hair having fallen out long ago. She scorned to wear a wig and one was truly not necessary, for her skull was smooth and well shaped. And she was aware of the startling effect she had on people, the power of the look of the bright dark eyes set in the bone-white skull.

"Once princes fought to the death for the privilege of kissing that hand, when it was smooth and delicate," she said.

"They would still, Ciang," said Hugh. "They'd be only too happy, some of them."

"Yes, old friend, but not for the sake of beauty. Still, what I have now is better. I would not go back. Sit beside me, Hugh, at my right. You will be witness to this young man's admittance."

Ciang motioned for him to draw up a chair. Hugh was about to do so when the youngster leapt to do it for him.

"Allow m-me, sir," said the boy, stuttering, his face flushed red.

---

[4] Not her real name. Elven meaning of the word "ciang" is "merciless" or "without pity." She is one of the great mysteries of Arianus. No one knows her past; the oldest elf living is young to Ciang.

He lifted a heavy chair made of the precious wood that is in short supply in Arianus and set it down where Ciang indicated, at her right hand.

"And . . . and you're truly Hugh the Hand?" the boy blurted, when he had set the chair down and stepped back to stare.

"He is," answered Ciang. "Few are granted the honor of the Hand. Someday it may be you, boy, but, for now, meet the master."

"I . . . I can't believe it," stammered the boy, overcome. "To think Hugh the Hand should be here, at my investiture! I . . . I . . ." Words failed him.

His older companion, whom Hugh did not recognize, reached out, plucked the boy's sleeve, tugged him back to his place at the end of Ciang's desk. The young man retreated, moving with the awkwardness of youth, at one point stumbling over his feet.

Hugh said nothing, glanced at Ciang. A corner of the woman's mouth twitched, but she spared the boy's feelings, refrained from laughing.

"Right and proper respect," she said gravely. "From younger to elder. His name is John Darby. His sponsor is Ernst Twist. I do not think you two know each other?"

Hugh shook his head. Ernst did likewise, darting a glance sideways, bobbing and reaching up to tug at his hair, a foolish, country-bumpkin gesture of respect. The man looked like a bumpkin, dressed in baggy patched clothes, a greasy hat, broken shoes. This was no bumpkin, however; those who took him for such probably never lived long enough to regret their mistake. The hands were slender and long-fingered and had certainly never done manual labor. And the cold eyes, that never met Hugh straight on, had a peculiar cast to them, a red glint that Hugh found disconcerting.

"Twist's scars are still fresh," said Ciang. "But he has already advanced from sheath to tip. He'll make blade, before the year is out."

High praise, from Ciang.[5] Hugh regarded the man with loathing. Here was an assassin who would "kill for a plate of stew" as

[5] See Appendix I, *The Brotherhood of the Hand.*

the saying went. Hugh guessed, from a certain stiffness and coolness in her tone, that Ciang shared his feelings of disgust. But the
Brotherhood needed all kinds, and this one's money was as good
as the next. So long as Ernst Twist followed the laws of the Brotherhood, how he thwarted the laws of man and nature was his
business, vile though it might be.

"Twist needs a partner," continued Ciang. "He has brought
forth the young man, John Darby, and, after review, I have
agreed to admit him to the Brotherhood under the standard
terms."

Ciang rose to her feet, as did Hugh. The elven woman was tall
and stood straight, a slight stoop in the shoulders her only concession to old age. Her long robes were of the very finest silk, woven
in the shimmering color and fantastic designs favored by elves.
She was a regal presence, daunting, awful in her majesty.

The youth, undoubtedly a cold-blooded killer, for he could
not have obtained entry without some proof of his skill, was
abashed, blushing and flustered, looked as if he was about to be
sick.

His companion poked the young man roughly in the back.
"Stand up tall. Be a man," Ernst muttered.

The boy gulped, straightened, drew a deep breath, then said,
through white lips, "I'm ready."

Ciang cast a sidelong glance at Hugh, rolled her eyes, as much
as to say, "Well, we were all young once." She pointed a long
finger at a wooden box, encrusted with sparkling gems, that stood
in the center of the desk.

Hugh leaned over, respectfully took hold of the box and
moved it within the woman's reach. He lifted the lid. A sharp-
bladed dagger, whose golden hilt was fashioned in the shape of a
hand—palm flat, fingers pressed together. The extended thumb
formed the crosspiece. Ciang drew forth the dagger, handling it
carefully. The firelight gleamed in the razor-sharp blade, made it
burn.

"Are you right-handed or left?" Ciang asked.

"Right," said John Darby. Droplets of sweat ran down his
temples, trickled down his cheeks.

"Give me your right hand," Ciang ordered.

The young man presented his hand, palm open, out.

"Sponsor, you may offer support—"

"No!" the boy gasped. Licking dry lips, he thrust Twist's proffered arm away. "I can stand it on my own."

Ciang expressed approval with a raised eyebrow. "Hold your right hand in the proper position," she said. "Hugh, show him."

Hugh lifted a candle from the mantelpiece, brought it over to the desk, set it down. The candle's flame shone in the wooden finish—a finish spotted and stained with dark splotches. The young man looked at the splotches. The color fled his face.

Ciang waited.

John Darby pressed his lips tightly together, held his hand closer. "I'm ready," he repeated.

Ciang nodded. She raised the dagger by the hilt, its blade pointing downward.

"Grasp the blade," said Ciang, "as you would the hilt."

John Darby did so, wrapping his hand gingerly around the blade. The hilt, in the shape of the hand, rested on his hand, the thumb-shaped crosspiece running parallel to his own thumb. The young man began to breathe heavily.

"Squeeze," said Ciang, cool, impassive.

John Darby's breath halted an instant. He almost shut his eyes, caught himself in time. With a glance of shame at Hugh, the youngster forced himself to keep his eyes open. He swallowed, squeezed his hand over the dagger's blade.

He caught his breath with a gasp, but made no other sound. Drops of blood fell down on the desk, a thin stream trickled down the young man's arm.

"Hugh, the thong," said Ciang.

Hugh reached into the box, drew out a soft strip of leather, about as wide as a man's two fingers. The symbol of the Brotherhood made a pattern up and down the long strip of leather. It, too, was stained dark in places.

"Give it to the sponsor," said Ciang.

Hugh gave the thong to Ernst Twist, who took it in those long-fingered hands of his, hands that were undoubtedly splotched with the same dark stains that marred the thong.

"Bind him," said Ciang.

All this time, John Darby had been standing, his hand squeezing the dagger's blade, the blood dripping from it. Ernst wrapped the thong around the young man's hand, bound it tight, leaving the ends of the thong free. Ernst grasped one free end, held onto it. Hugh took hold of the other. He looked to Ciang, who nodded.

The two of them yanked the bond tight, forcing the dagger's blade deeper into the flesh, into bone. The blood flowed faster. John Darby could not hold back his anguish. He cried out in pain, a shuddering "ah!" wrenched from him in agony. He closed his eyes, staggered, leaned against the table. Then, gulping, drawing short, quick breaths, he stood straight, looked at Ciang. The blood dripped onto the desk.

Ciang smiled as though she had sipped that blood, found it to her liking. "You will now repeat the oath of the Brotherhood."

John Darby did so, bringing back through a haze of pain the words he'd laboriously memorized. From now on, they would be etched on his mind, as surely as the scars of his investiture would be etched on his hand.

The oath completed, John stood upright, refusing, with a shake of his head, any help from his sponsor. Ciang smiled at the young man, a smile that for a single instant brought to the aged face a hint of what must have been remarkable beauty. She laid her hand upon the youth's tortured one.

"He is acceptable. Remove the binding."

Hugh did so, unwrapping the leather thong from John Darby's bloody hand. The young man opened his palm, slowly, with an effort, for the fingers were gummed and sticky. Ciang plucked the dagger from the trembling grip.

It was now, when all was ended, the unnatural excitement drained, that the weakness came. John Darby stared at his hand, at the cut flesh, the pulsing of the red blood welling out of the wounds, and was suddenly aware of the pain as if he'd never felt it. He turned a sickly gray color, swayed unsteadily on his feet. Now he was grateful for Ernst Twist's arm, which kept the young man upright.

"He may be seated," said Ciang.

Turning, she handed the gory dagger to Hugh, who took the blade and washed it in a bowl of water, brought specifically for the purpose. This done, the Hand wiped the dagger carefully on a clean, white cloth until it was completely dry, then brought it back to Ciang. She shut it and the leather thong back in the box, replaced the box in its proper place on her desk. The blood spattered on the desk would be allowed to soak into the wood, mingling young Darby's blood with that of countless others who had undergone the same rite.

One more small ceremony remained to be completed.

"Sponsor," said Ciang, her gaze going to Ernst Twist.

The man had just settled the pale and shivering young Darby into a chair. Smiling that deceptively foolish smile, Twist shuffled forward and held out his right hand, palm up, to Ciang. The woman dipped the tips of her fingers in Darby's blood, traced two long red lines along scars on Twist's palm, scars that corresponded to the fresh wounds on Darby's.

"Your life is pledged to his life," Ciang recited, "as his is pledged to yours. The punishment for oath-breaking is visited upon both."

Hugh, watching absently, his thoughts going to what would be a difficult conversation with Ciang, thought he saw, again, the man's eyes glisten with that strange red light, like the eyes of a cat by torchlight. When the Hand looked more closely, curious about this phenomenon, Twist had lowered his eyelids in homage to Ciang and was shuffling backward to resume his place near his new partner.

Ciang shifted her gaze to young Darby. "The Ancient will give you herbs to prevent infection. The hand may be bandaged until the wounds are healed. But you must be prepared to remove the bandage should any require it. You may remain here until you feel you are well enough to travel. The ceremony takes its toll, young man. Rest this day, renew your blood with meat and drink. From this day on, you have only to open your palm in this fashion"—Ciang lifted her hand to demonstrate—"and those in the Brotherhood will know you for one of our own."

Hugh looked at his own hand, at the scars that were now barely visible on a calloused palm. The scar taken in the meaty part of the thumb was clearest, largest, for that had been the last to heal. It ran in a thin white strip, cutting across what the palm readers know as the life line. The other scar ran almost parallel to the head and heart lines. Innocent-looking scars; no one ever noticed them, not unless they were meant to.

Darby and Twist were leaving. Hugh rose, said what was appropriate. His words brought a faint flush of pleasure and pride to the young man's gray cheeks. Darby was already walking more steadily. A few draughts of ale, some boasting of his prowess, and he'd be thinking quite well of himself. Tonight, when the throbbing pain awakened him from feverish dreams, he would have second thoughts.

The Ancient stood in the hallway as if on command, though Ciang had made no summons. The old man had been through many of these rites, knew to the second how long they lasted.

"Show our brothers to their rooms," Ciang ordered.

The Ancient bowed, looked at her inquiringly. "May I bring madam and her guest anything?"

"No, thank you, my friend," said Ciang graciously. "I will take care of our needs."

The Ancient bowed again and escorted the two off down the hallway.

Hugh tensed, shifted in his chair, preparing himself to meet those wise and penetrating eyes.

He was not prepared for her remark.

"And so, Hugh the Hand," said Ciang pleasantly, "you have come back to us from the dead."

CHAPTER ♦ 27

SKURVASH

VOLKARAN ISLES

MID REALM

♦

Stunned by the comment, Hugh stared at Ciang in wordless amazement. His look was so wild and dark that it was now Ciang's turn to regard him with astonishment.

"Why, what is the matter, Hugh? One would think I spoke the truth. But I am not talking to a ghost, am I? You are flesh and blood." She reached out her hand, closed it over his.

Hugh released his breath, realized the woman had made the remark in jest, referring to his long absence from Skurvash. He held his hand steady beneath her touch, managed a laugh, and made some muttered explanation that his last job had taken him too close to death to make it a laughing matter.

"Yes, that is what I heard," said Ciang, studying him intently, new thoughts awakened.

Hugh saw, from the expression on her face, that he'd given himself away. The woman was too shrewd, too sensitive to have missed his unusual reaction. He waited nervously for the question, was relieved, yet somewhat disappointed, when it did not come.

"That is what comes of traveling to the High Realm," said Ciang. "Of dealing with mysteriarchs . . . and other powerful people." She rose to her feet. "I will pour the wine. And then we will talk."

And other powerful people. What did she mean? Hugh wondered, watching her move slowly toward the sideboard on which stood a lovely crystal bottle and two goblets. Could she know about the Sartan? Or the man with the blue, tattooed skin? And if she did know about them, what was it she knew?

Probably more than I do, Hugh thought.

Ciang walked slowly, a concession to her age, but her dignity and carriage made it appear that it was she who chose to walk with measured tread, the years had not chosen for her. Hugh knew better than to assist her. She would have taken his offer for an insult. Ciang always served her guests with her own hands, a custom that dated back to early elven nobility when kings had served wine to their nobles. It was a custom long since abandoned by modern elven royalty, yet said to have been revived in this age by the rebel, Prince Rees'ahn.

Ciang poured the wine into the goblets, placed them upon a silver salver, and carried it across the room to Hugh.

Not a drop spilled.

She lowered the tray to Hugh, who took a goblet, thanked her, and held it until the woman had returned to her chair. When she had lifted the goblet in her hand, Hugh rose to his feet, pledged Ciang's health, and drank deeply.

Ciang bowed graciously, pledged his health, and brought the cup to her lips. When the ceremony was complete, both resumed their seats. Hugh would now be free to pour himself more wine, or to assist her, if she required.

"You were grievously wounded," said Ciang.

"Yes," Hugh replied, not meeting her eyes, staring into the wine that was the same color as the blood of young Darby, drying on the table.

"You did not come here." Ciang set her cup down. "It was your right."

"I know. I couldn't face anyone." He lifted his gaze, dark and grim. "I failed. I hadn't carried out the contract."

"We might have understood. It has happened to others before—"

"Not to me!" said Hugh with a sudden, fierce gesture that almost knocked over the wine goblet. He steadied it, glanced at Ciang, muttered an apology.

The woman gazed at him intently. "And now," she said, after a moment's pause, "you have been called to account."

"I've been called on to fulfill the contract."

"And this conflicts with your desire. The woman you brought with you, the mysteriarch."

Hugh flushed, took another drink of wine, not because he wanted it, but because it gave him an excuse to avoid Ciang's eyes. He heard—or thought he did—a note of rebuke.

"I never sought to hide her identity from you, Ciang," Hugh responded. "Just those fools in town. I didn't want trouble. The woman is my employer."

He heard the rustle of fine silk, guessed that Ciang was smiling, lifting her shoulders in a shrug. He could hear her unspoken words. *Lie to yourself, if you must. You do not lie to me.*

"Quite wise," was all she said aloud. "What is the difficulty?"

"The former contract conflicts with another job."

"And what will you do to reconcile the situation, Hugh the Hand?"

"I don't know," said Hugh, rotating the empty goblet by the stem, watching the light reflect off the jewels at its base.

Ciang sighed softly, her fingernail tapped lightly on the table. "Since you do not ask for advice, I offer none. I remind you, however, to think over the words you heard that young man speak. A contract is sacred. If you break it, we will have no choice but to consider that you have broken faith with us, as well. The penalty will be exacted,[1] even upon you, Hugh the Hand."

"I know," he said, and now he could look at her.

"Very well." She was brisk, clasped her hands, unpleasantness out of the way. "You have come here on business. What may we do to assist you?"

Hugh stood up, walked over to the sideboard, poured another glass of wine, tossed it down in a gulp that took no notice of the fine flavor. If he failed to kill Bane, not only his honor was forfeit, but his life as well. Yet to kill the child was to kill the mother, at least as far as Hugh was concerned.

He thought back to those moments Iridal had slept in his arms, confiding, trusting. She had accompanied him here, to this terrible place, believing in him, believing in something within

---

[1] See Appendix I, *The Brotherhood of the Hand.*

him. Believing in his honor, in his love for her. He had given both to her, as his gift, when he'd given up his life. And, in death, he'd found both returned to him a hundred times over.

And then, he'd been snatched back, and honor and love had died, though he lived. A strange and terrible paradox. In death, perhaps he could find them again, but not if he did this terrible deed. And he knew that if he didn't, if he broke his oath to the Brotherhood, they would come after him and he would fight them instinctively. And he would never find what he'd lost. He'd commit one foul crime after another, until darkness overwhelmed him, utterly, eternally.

It would be better for us all if I told Ciang to take that dagger from its box and stab me to the heart.

"I need passage," he said abruptly, turning to face her. "Passage to the elven lands. And information, whatever you can tell me."

"The passage is not a problem, as you well know," answered Ciang. If she had been disturbed by his long silence, she did not show it. "What about disguise? You have your own means of concealment in enemy lands, for you have traveled Aristagon before and never been found out. But will the same disguise work for your companion?"

"Yes," Hugh replied briefly.

Ciang asked no questions. A brother's methods were a brother's business. Most likely she knew anyway.

"Where is it you need to go?" Ciang lifted a quill pen, drew forth a sheet of paper.

"Paxaria."

Ciang dipped the pen in ink, waited for Hugh to be more specific.

"The Imperanon," Hugh said.

Ciang pursed her lips, replaced the pen in the inkwell. She gazed at him steadily.

"Your business takes you there? Into the castle of the emperor?"

"It does, Ciang." Hugh drew out his pipe, thrust it in his mouth, sucked on it moodily.

"You may smoke," said Ciang, with a gracious nod at the fire. "If you open the window."

Hugh lifted the small, lead-paned window a crack. He filled

the pipe with stregno, lit it from a glowing coal at the fire, drew the biting smoke gratefully into his lungs.

"That will not be easy," Ciang continued. "I can provide you with a detailed map of the palace and its environs. And we have someone within who will help you for a price. But to get inside the elven stronghold . . ." Ciang shrugged, shook her head.

"I can get in," Hugh said grimly. "It's getting out again . . . alive."

He turned, strode back to seat himself at the chair by her desk. Now that they were discussing business, now that the pipe was in his hands, the stregno mixing pleasantly with the wine in his blood, he could for a time banish the horrors that hounded him.

"You have a plan, of course," Ciang said. "Else you would not have come this far."

"Only a partial one," he told her. "That's why I need information. Anything at all, no matter how small or seemingly irrelevant might help. What is the emperor's political situation?"

"Desperate," said Ciang, leaning back in her chair. "Oh, life is not changed within the Imperanon itself. Parties, gaiety, merriment every night. But they laugh from wine, not from the heart, as the saying goes. Agah'ran dares not let this alliance between Rees'ahn and Stephen come about. If it does, the Tribus empire is finished, and Agah'ran knows it."

Hugh grunted, puffed on his pipe.

Ciang regarded him through languid eyes, lids half closed. "This has to do with Stephen's son, who is not, they say, Stephen's son. Yes, I heard the boy was in the emperor's clutches. Be easy, my friend. I ask nothing. I begin to see the tangle you are in all too clearly."

"Whose side is the Brotherhood on in this?"

"Our own, of course." Ciang shrugged. "War has been profitable for us, for Skurvash. Peace would mean an end to smuggling. But I've no doubt new business opportunities would arise. Yes, so long as greed, hatred, lust, ambition remain in this world—in other words, so long as mankind remains in this world—we will thrive."

"I'm surprised no one's hired us to murder Rees'ahn."

"Ah, but they have. He's remarkable, that one." Ciang sighed, gazed far away. "I don't mind admitting to you, Hugh the Hand, that the prince is one man I would have liked to have known when I was young and attractive. Even now . . . But that is not to be."

The elven woman sighed again, came back to business, to the present. "We lost two good men and my best woman on that one job. Reports say he was warned by the magus who is always with him, the human female known as Ravenslark. You wouldn't be interested in taking on this assignment yourself, my friend? His head would fetch a fine price."

"Ancestors forbid," Hugh said shortly. "There isn't enough money in the world could pay me for that."

"Yes, you are wise. We would have said, when we were younger, that Krenka-Anris guards him."

Ciang sat silent, her eyes again half closed, one finger making an absentminded circle in the blood on the polished wood. Hugh, thinking she was tired, was ready to take his leave when she opened her eyes, stared full at him.

"There is one piece of information I have that may help you. It is strange, only rumor. But if so, it has great portent."

"And that is?"

"The Kenkari, they say, have stopped accepting souls."

Hugh took the pipe from his mouth, his own eyes narrowed. "Why?"

Ciang smiled, made a slight gesture. "They discovered that the souls being brought to the Temple of the Albedo were not yet ready to come. Sent there by royal decree."

It took Hugh a moment to assimilate her meaning. "Murder?" He stared at her, shaking his head. "Is Agah'ran insane?"

"Not insane. Desperate. And, if this is true, he is also a fool. Murdered souls will not aid his cause. All their energy is expended, crying out for justice. The magic of the Albedo is withering. Another reason Rees'ahn's power grows."

"But the Kenkari are on the emperor's side."

"For now. They have been known to switch allegiances before this, however. They could do it again."

Hugh sat silent, thoughtful.

Ciang said nothing further, left Hugh to his thoughts. She took up the pen again, wrote several lines upon the paper in a firm, bold hand that looked more human than elven. She waited for the ink to dry, then rolled the paper up in a complex twist that was as much her signature as that writing upon it.

"Is this information helpful to you?" she asked.

"Maybe," Hugh muttered, not being evasive, just attempting to see his way. "At least it gives me the beginnings of an idea. Whether or not it comes to anything . . ."

He rose to his feet, preparatory to taking his leave. Ciang stood to escort him out. Courteously, he offered her his arm. Gravely, she accepted it, but took care not to lean on him. He matched his pace to her slow one. At the door, she handed him the twist of paper.

"Go to the main docks. Give this to the captain of a ship called the *Seven-eyed Dragon*. You and your passenger will be admitted on board without question."

"Elven?"

"Yes." Ciang smiled. "The captain won't like it, but he'll do what I ask. He owes us. But it would be politic to wear your disguise."

"What's his destination?"

"Paxaua. I trust that will suit?"

Hugh nodded. "The central city. Ideal."

They reached the door. The Ancient had returned from his previous task and now waited patiently for Hugh.

"I thank you, Ciang," said Hugh, taking the woman's hand and lifting it to his lips. "Your help has been inestimable."

"As is your danger, Hugh the Hand," said Ciang, looking up at him, eyes dark and cold. "Remember the policy. The Brotherhood can help you get into the Imperanon. . . . perhaps. We cannot help you get out. No matter what."

"I know." He smiled, then looked at her quizzically. "Tell me, Ciang. Did you ever have a weesham, waiting around to catch your soul in one of those Kenkari boxes?"

The woman was startled. "Yes, I had one, once. As do all of royal birth. Why do you ask?"

"What happened, if the question's not too personal?"

"It *is* personal, but I don't mind answering. One day I decided that my soul was my own. As I have never been a slave in life, so I would not be one in death."

"And the weesham? What happened to her?"

"She would not leave, when I told her to. I had no choice."

Ciang shrugged. "I killed her. A very gentle poison, swift acting. She had been at my side since birth and was fond of me. For that crime alone my life is forfeit in elven lands."

Hugh stood silent, withdrawn into himself, perhaps not even listening to the answer, though he was the one who had asked the question.

Ciang, who was usually able to read men's faces as easily as she read the scars upon their palms, could make nothing of Hugh. She could almost have believed, at that moment, that the absurd tales she had heard about him were true.

Or that he has lost his nerve, she said to herself, eyeing him.

Ciang withdrew her hand from his arm, a subtle indication that it was time he left. Hugh stirred, came back to himself and to business.

"You said there was someone in the Imperanon who might aid me?"

"A captain in the elven army. I know nothing of him, except by report. That very man who was previously here—Twist—recommended him. The captain's name is Sang-drax."

"Sang-drax," repeated Hugh, committing it to memory. He raised his right hand, palm outward. "Farewell, Ciang. Thank you for the wine . . . and the help."

Ciang bowed her head slightly, lowered her eyelids. "Farewell, Hugh the Hand. You may go on ahead alone. I have need to speak with the Ancient. You know the way. The Ancient will meet you in the central hall."

Hugh nodded, turned, and walked off.

Ciang watched him through narrowed eyes until he was out of hearing. Even then, she kept her voice low.

"If he comes here again, he is to be killed."

The Ancient looked stricken, but gave silent agreement. He, too, had seen the signs.

"Do I send round the knife?"[2] he asked unhappily.

"No," answered Ciang. "That will not be necessary. He carries his own doom within him."

---

[2] See Appendix I, *The Brotherhood of the Hand.*

CHAPTER 28

THE IMPERANON

ARISTAGON, MID REALM

♦

Most elves did not believe in the existence of the dread dungeons of the Unseen, the emperor's own personal guard. Most elves considered the dungeons little more than dark rumor, a threat held over small children when they misbehaved.

"If you don't stop hitting your little sister, Rohana'ie," scolds the long-suffering parent, "the Unseen will come in the night and carry you off to their prison! And then where will you be?"

Few elves ever saw the Unseen; thus their name. The elite guard did not walk the streets, or roam the alleyways. They did not come knocking on the door in the hours when the Lords of Night had spread their cloak. And though the elves might not believe in the dungeons, almost all elves believed that the Unseen themselves existed.

For law-abiding citizens, the belief was a comforting one. Miscreants—thieves, murderers, and other social misfits—had a convenient way of simply disappearing. No fuss. No bother. None of that spectacle elves associated with the strange human habit of granting criminals a public trial that might result in their being set free (why arrest them in the first place?) or execution in the middle of the village square (barbaric!).

Rebel elves claimed that the dungeons existed. They claimed that the Unseen were not bodyguards but the emperor's own personal assassination squad, that the dungeons held more political prisoners than robbers and murderers.

There were those among the royal families who were begin-

ning to think, in their hearts, that Prince Rees'ahn and his rebels
were right. The husband who woke after a strangely heavy sleep
to find his wife gone from their bed. The parents whose eldest son
vanished without a trace on his way home from university. Those
who dared make open inquiries were advised, by the head of
their clan, to keep their mouths shut.

Most elves, however, dismissed the rebel claims or would reply with a shrug and the popular proverb that if the Unseen
smelled a dragon they had probably found a dragon.

But in one matter, the rebels were right. The dungeons of the
Unseen did truly exist. Haplo knew. He was in them.

Located far below the Imperanon, the dungeons were not particularly terrible, being little more than holding cells. Long-term
imprisonment was unknown among the Unseen. Those elves permitted to live long enough to see the dungeons were here for a
reason—the main one being that they had some sort of information the Unseen needed. When that information was extracted, as
it invariably was, the prisoner disappeared. The cell was cleaned
and readied for the next.

Haplo was a special case, however, and most members of the
Unseen weren't sure quite why. A captain—an elf with the peculiar name of Sang-drax—took a proprietary interest in the human
with the blue skin, and word went around that he was to be left in
the captain's hands.

Cycle after cycle, Haplo sat in an elven prison, whose iron
bars he could have melted with a sigil. He sat in his prison cell
and wondered if he were going mad.

Sang-drax had cast no spell over him. The shackles that bound
Haplo were those of his own choosing. Imprisonment was another ploy of the serpent-elf to torment him, to tempt him, to force
him into taking some type of rash action. And because he believed that Sang-drax wanted Haplo to do something, the Patryn
decided to thwart Sang-drax by doing nothing.

At least, that's what he told himself he was doing. It was
then he would ask himself bitterly if he might not be going
insane.

"We're doing the right thing," he assured the dog.

The animal lay on the floor, nose on paws, gazed up at its
master dubiously, seemed to think that it wasn't so certain.

"Bane's up to something. And I doubt if the little bastard has his 'grandfather's' interests in mind. But I'll have to catch him in the act in order to prove it."

To prove what? the dog's sad eyes asked. Prove to Xar that his trust in the boy was misplaced, that he should have trusted you alone? Are you that jealous of Bane?

Haplo glared at the animal. "I'm not—"

"Visitor!" rang out a cheery voice.

Haplo tensed. Sang-drax appeared out of nowhere, as usual stood just outside the cell door. The door was made of iron, with a square grate in the upper portion, a grate covered by bars. Sang-drax peered through the grate. He never asked, on his daily visits, that the cell door be opened, never entered the cell.

Come and get me, Patryn! His presence—just out of reach—taunted Haplo silently.

"Why should I?" Haplo wanted to shout, frustrated, unable to cope with the feeling of panicked fear that was building inside him, rendering him increasingly helpless. "What is it you want me to do?"

But he controlled himself, to outward appearances, at least, and remained seated on his cot. Ignoring the serpent-elf, he stared at the dog.

The animal growled and bared its teeth, its hackles raised, lip curling back over sharp fangs, as it did whenever the serpent-elf was either within sight or smell.

Haplo was tempted to give the dog the order to attack. A series of sigla could change the animal into a gigantic monster. Its bulk would burst open the cells, its teeth could rip off a man's—or a snake's—head. The powerful and fearful aberration Haplo could create would not have an easy battle. The serpent-elf possessed his own magic, stronger than Haplo's. But the dog might distract Sang-drax long enough to give Haplo a chance to arm himself.

The Patryn had left his cell one night, the first night of arrival, to acquire weapons. He picked up two—a dagger and a short-bladed sword—from a cache the Unseen kept in their guardroom. Returning to his cell, he spent the remainder of the night etching runes of death upon each blade, runes that would work quite well against mensch, less well against the serpents. Both weapons were hidden in a hole beneath a stone he'd magically removed, magically replaced. Both weapons would come quickly to hand.

Haplo moistened his mouth. The sigla on his skin burned. The dog's growl grew louder; it understood matters were becoming serious.

"Haplo, for shame," said Sang-drax softly. "You might well destroy me, but what would you gain? Nothing. And what would you lose? Everything. You need me, Haplo. I am as much a part of you"—his gaze shifted—"as that animal is a part of you."

The dog sensed Haplo's resolve waver. It whined, begging to be allowed to sink its teeth into the serpent-elf's shins, if nothing better offered itself.

"Leave your weapons where they are," said Sang-drax, with a glance at the very rock under which they were hidden. "You'll have use for them later on, as you will see. I've come this very moment to bring you information."

Haplo, with a muttered curse, ordered the dog into a corner.

The animal obeyed reluctantly, first venting its feelings by rearing up on its hind legs, lunging, barking and snarling, at the door. Its head came to the level of the barred grate. Teeth flashed. Then it dropped down, slunk off.

"Keeping that animal is a weakness," the serpent-elf remarked. "I'm surprised your lord permits it. A weakness in him, no doubt."

Haplo turned his back on the serpent-elf, went over and threw himself down on his cot. He stared grimly at the ceiling. He saw no reason to discuss either the dog or his lord with Sang-drax, or to discuss anything at all for that matter.

The serpent-elf lounged against the door, began to make what he termed his "daily report."

"I've spent the morning with Prince Bane. The child is well and in high spirits. He appears to have taken a fancy to me. He is permitted to come and go about the palace as he chooses, with the exception of the imperial suites, of course, so long as I escort him. In case you were wondering, I've requested and been granted reassignment to this duty. An elven count named Tretar—who has the ear of the emperor, as the saying goes—has also taken a fancy to me.

"As for the dwarf's health, I'm afraid I cannot say the same. She is extremely wretched."

"They haven't hurt her, have they?" Haplo demanded, forgetting he wasn't going to talk to the serpent-elf.

"Oh, dear, no," Sang-drax assured him. "She is far too valuable for the elves to mistreat her. She has a room next to Bane's, though she is not permitted to leave it. In fact, the dwarf's value grows, as you will hear shortly. But she is desperately homesick. She can't sleep. Her appetite dwindles. I'm afraid she may die of sorrow."

Haplo grunted, put his hands under his head, settled himself more firmly on the cot. He didn't believe half of what the serpent-elf told him. Jarre was sensible, levelheaded. She was probably fretting over Limbeck more than anything else. Still, it would be beneficial to get her out of here, leave with her, return to Drevlin . . .

"Why *don't* you escape?" asked Sang-drax, with his infuriating habit of intruding on Haplo's thoughts. "I'd be delighted to assist you. I can't think why you don't."

"Maybe because you serpents seem so damn eager to get rid of me."

"That's not the reason. It's the boy. Bane won't leave. You don't dare leave him. You don't dare leave without him."

"Your doing, no doubt."

Sang-drax laughed. "I'm flattered, but I'm afraid I can't take the credit. This scheme is all his own. Quite a remarkable child, that Bane."

Haplo yawned, closed his eyes, grit his teeth. Even through the closed lids, he could see Sang-drax grinning.

"The Gegs have threatened to destroy the Kicksey-winsey," the serpent-elf said.

Haplo flinched involuntarily, cursed himself for doing so, and forced himself to lie still, every muscle in his body rigid.

Sang-drax continued talking in a low voice, meant for Haplo's ear alone. "The elves, laboring under the delusion that the dwarves have shut down the machine, have delivered an ultimatum to that dwarf leader—what's his name?"

Haplo remained silent.

"Limbeck." Sang-drax answered his own question. "Odd name for a dwarf. It never sticks in my mind. The elves told this Limbeck that he either starts operating the Kicksey-winsey again or they will send his female dwarf friend back to him in various assorted pieces.

"The dwarves, laboring under a similar delusion that it is the elves who have caused the machine to cease operations, were understandably confused by this ultimatum, but eventually came to decide, by reason of a few hints, passed on by us, that the ultimatum was a trick, some sort of subtle elven plot against them.

"Limbeck's reply—which, by the way, I've just heard from Count Tretar—is this: If the elves harm one whisker on Jarre's chin, the Gegs will destroy the Kicksey-winsey. Destroy the Kicksey-winsey," Sang-drax repeated. "I fancy they could do it, too. Don't you?"

Yes, Haplo was damn well sure they could do it. They had worked on the machine for generations, kept it running even after the Sartan had abandoned it. The dwarves kept the body alive. They could make it die.

"Yes, so they could," agreed Sang-drax conversationally. "I can picture it now. The Gegs let the steam build up in the boilers, they send the electricity running amok. Parts of the machine would explode, unleashing such a terrible destructive force that the dwarves might unwittingly destroy the entire continent of Drevlin, to say nothing of the machine itself. And there go Lord Xar's plans for conquering the four worlds."

He began to laugh. "I find it all so amusing. The true irony in all this is that neither dwarves nor elves could start the fool machine if they wanted to! Yes, I did some investigating, based on what Jarre told me on board the ship. Up until then, I believed—as do the elves—that the dwarves had shut off the Kicksey-winsey. But they didn't. You discovered the reason. The opening of Death's Gate. That's the key, isn't it? We don't know how, yet, or why. But, to be honest, we serpents really don't care.

"You see, Patryn, it occurred to us that the destruction of the Kicksey-winsey would plunge not only this world into chaos but the others, as well.

" 'Why don't you destroy it yourselves, then?' you ask.

"We could. Perhaps we will. But we much prefer to leave the destruction to the dwarves, to feed off their rage, their fury, their terror. As it is, Patryn, their frustration and anger, their feelings of helplessness and fear have been strong enough to sustain us for a cycle, at least."

Haplo lay unmoving. His jaw muscles were beginning to ache from the strain of keeping them clenched shut.

"The emperor hasn't made up his mind what to do yet," Sang-drax informed him. "Limbeck gave the elves two cycles to decide. I'll let you know what the decision is. Well, sorry to leave, but duty calls. I've promised to teach Bane to play rune-bone."

Haplo heard the serpent-elf's light footfalls walking away. They stopped, came back.

"I grow fat off your fear, Patryn."

CHAPTER 29

PAXAUA

ARISTAGON, MID REALM

♦

THE ELVEN SHIP, THE *SEVEN-EYED DRAGON,* NAMED AFTER A LEGENDARY monster of elven folklore,[1] made a safe, if somewhat ponderous landing, in Paxaua. The ship was heavily loaded. Flying weather had not been good, with rain, wind, and fog the entire distance. They were a cycle late getting into port. The crew was edgy and ill-tempered, the passengers—muffled to the eyes against the cold —looked slightly green. The human galley slaves, whose muscles provided the energy that propelled the gigantic wings, slumped in their bonds, too exhausted to make the march to the prison house, where they were kept until the next voyage.

A customs official, looking bored, left his warm office on shore, strolled up the gangplank. Tripping on his heels in haste to get aboard ship was an overwrought Paxar merchant. He had invested a considerable fortune in a load of pua fruit, to be delivered fresh, and was positive that delay and damp had caused it to rot.

The ship's captain strolled over to meet the customs official.

"Any contraband, Captain?" inquired the official languidly.

"Certainly not, Excellency," answered the captain, with a

---

[1] A monster sent by Krenka-Anris to test the courage and skill of the mythical elven warrior Mnarash'ai. In each of the dragon's eyes, Mnarash'ai beheld seven deaths. She had to overcome her fear of each before she could, at last, slay the dragon.

smile and a bow. "Will you examine the ship's log?" He gestured to his cabin.

"Thank you, yes," said the customs official stiffly.

The two left the deck, entered the cabin. The door shut behind them.

"My fruit! I want my fruit!" gabbled the merchant, dashing excitedly about the deck, tangling himself in the ropes, and nearly tumbling headfirst down an open hatch.

A crew member took the merchant in tow, steered him to the lieutenant, who was accustomed to dealing with such matters.

"I want my fruit!" the merchant gasped.

"Sorry, sir," answered the lieutenant, with a polite salute, "but we cannot off-load any cargo until we receive approval from customs."

"How long will that take?" demanded the merchant, in agony.

The lieutenant glanced at the captain's cabin. About three glasses of wine, he could have said. "I can assure you, sir—" he began.

The merchant sniffed. "I can smell it! The pua fruit. It's gone bad!"

"That would be the galley slaves, sir," said the lieutenant, keeping a straight face.

"Let me see it, at least," begged the merchant, taking out a handkerchief and mopping his face.

The lieutenant, after some thought, agreed that this would be possible and led the way across the deck toward the stairs leading down to the hold. They walked past the passengers, who stood lining the rail, waving to friends and relatives who'd come to meet them. The passengers, too, would not be allowed to leave the ship until they had been questioned, their luggage inspected.

"The market price on pua fruit is the highest I've seen it," said the merchant, floundering along in the lieutenant's wake, tripping and stumbling over coils of rope, careening off casks of wine. "It's due to the raiding, of course. This will be the first shipment of pua to reach Paxar safely in twelve cycles. I'll make a killing. If it's just not rotted—Holy Mother!"

The alarmed merchant made a grab for the lieutenant, nearly sent the officer overboard.

"H-humans!" the merchant quavered.

The lieutenant, seeing the merchant's white face and popping eyes, reached for his sword and searched the skies for dragons, assuming that there must be an army of them, at the very least. Finding nothing more ominous than the dismal overcast, he regarded the merchant with a grim stare. The merchant continued to tremble and point.

He *had* discovered humans—two of them. Two passengers, standing apart from all the others. The humans were clad in long black robes. They kept their hoods up over their heads; one in particular, the shorter of the two, had his pulled low over his face. Though the merchant could not see their features, he knew them for humans. No elf had such broad and well-muscled shoulders as the taller of the two robed men, and no one except a human would wear clothing made of such coarse cloth, in such an ill-omened and unlucky color as black. Everyone on board ship, including the human slaves, gave these two a wide berth.

The lieutenant, looking extremely annoyed, sheathed his sword.

"This way, sir," he said to the merchant, urging the gaping elf along.

"But they . . . they're wandering around loose!"

"Yes, sir," said the lieutenant.

The elf, staring at the humans in horrible fascination, stumbled over the open hatch.

"Here we are, sir. Mind your step. We wouldn't want you to fall and break your neck," the lieutenant said, gazing heavenward, perhaps asking to be kept from temptation.

"Shouldn't they be in irons? Chains or something?" the merchant demanded, as he began to gingerly descend the ladder.

"Probably, sir," said the lieutenant, preparing to follow after. "But we're not permitted."

"Not permitted!" The merchant halted, looked indignant. "I never heard of such a thing. Who doesn't permit it?"

"The Kenkari, sir," said the lieutenant imperturbably, and had the satisfaction of seeing the merchant turn pale.

"Holy Mother," the elf said again, but this time with more reverence. "What's the reason?" he asked in a whisper. "If it's not secret, of course."

"No, no. These two are what the humans call 'death monks.' They come to the cathedral on holy pilgrimage and have safe passage granted here and back, so long as they don't speak to anyone."

"Death monks. Well, I never," said the merchant, descending into the hold, where he found his fruit perfectly sound and only slightly bruised after its rough passage.

The customs official emerged from the captain's cabin, wiping his lips, his cheeks a brighter shade of pink than when he'd entered. There was a noticeable bulge in the vicinity of his breast pocket that had not been there earlier, a look of satisfaction had replaced the look of boredom with which he had boarded. The customs official turned his attention to the passengers, who were eagerly awaiting permission to go ashore.

His expression darkened. "Kir monks, eh?"

"Yes, Excellency," replied the captain. "Came aboard at Sunthas."

"Caused any trouble?"

"No, Excellency. They had a cabin to themselves. This is the first time they've left it. The Kenkari have decreed that we should give the monks safe passage," the captain reminded the official, who was still frowning. "Their personages are sacred."

"Yes, and so is your profit," added the official dryly. "You undoubtedly charged them six times the price of the run."

The captain shrugged. "A man has to earn a living, Excellency," he said vaguely.

The official shrugged. After all, he had his share.

"I suppose I'll have to ask them a few questions." The official grimaced in disgust at the thought, removed a handkerchief from his pocket. "I *am* permitted to question them?" he added dubiously. "The Kenkari won't take offense?"

"Quite all right, Excellency. And it would look well to the other passengers."

The official, relieved to know that he wasn't about to commit some terrible breach of etiquette, decided to get the unpleasant task behind him as quickly as possible. He walked over to the two monks, who remained standing apart. They bowed in silence to him as he approached. He halted at arm's length from them, the handkerchief held over his nose and mouth.

"Where you from?" the official demanded, speaking pidgin elven.

The monk bowed again, but did not reply. The official frowned at this, but the captain, hastening forward, whispered, "They're forbidden to speak."

"Ah, yes." The official thought a moment. "You talk me," he said, slapping himself on the chest. "Me chief."

"We are from Pitrin's Exile, Excellency," the taller of the two monks answered, with another bow.

"Where you go?" the official asked, pretending not to notice that the human had spoken excellent elven.

"We are making a holy pilgrimage to the Cathedral of the Albedo, Excellency," answered the same monk.

"What in sack?" The official cast a scathing glance at the crude scripts each monk carried.

"Items our brethren requested we bring them, herbs and potions and suchlike. Would you like to inspect them?" the monk asked humbly and opened his sack.

A foul odor of decay wafted from it. The official could only imagine what was in there. He gagged, clamped the handkerchief more firmly over his mouth, and shook his head.

"Shut the damn thing! You'll poison us all. Your friend, there, why doesn't he say something?"

"He has no lips, Excellency, and has lost a portion of his tongue. A terrible accident. Would you like to see—"

The official recoiled in horror. He noticed now that the other monk's hands were covered by black gloves and that the fingers appeared to be crooked and deformed. "Certainly not. You humans are ugly enough," he muttered, but he said the last beneath his breath. It would not do to offend the Kenkari, who—for some strange reason—had formed a bond with these ghouls.

"Be off with you then. You have five cycles to make your pilgrimage. Pick up your papers at the port authority, in that house, to your left."

"Yes, Excellency. Thank you, Excellency," said the monk, with still another bow.

The Kir lifted both scripts, slung them over his shoulder, then assisted the other monk to walk. His steps were slow and shuffling, his back bent. Together, the two made their way down the gangplank, passengers, crew, and human slaves all taking care to keep as far from the Kir as possible.

The official shivered. "They make my skin crawl," he said to the captain. "I'll bet you're glad to be rid of them."

"I am, indeed, Excellency," said the captain.

Hugh and Iridal had no difficulty obtaining the papers that would permit them to stay in the realm of Paxaria[2] for a period of five cycles, at which time they must leave or face arrest. Even the Kenkari could not protect their brother monks if they overstayed their allotted time.

The bond between the two religious sects, whose races have been enemies almost since the beginning of Aristagon, can be traced back to Krenka-Anris, the Kenkari elf who discovered the secret magic of trapping the souls of the dead. At that time, shortly after the mensch were removed from the High Realm, humans still lived on Aristagon, and though the relationship between the races was rapidly worsening, a few maintained friendships and contact.

Among these was a human magus who had been known to Krenka-Anris for many years. The humans had heard about the new elven magic that was capable of saving the souls of their dead, but were unable to discover the secret. The Kenkari kept it as a sacred trust. One day this magus, who was a kind and scholarly man, came to Krenka-Anris, begging her help. His wife was dying, he said. He could not bear to lose her. Would the Kenkari please save her soul, if they could not save the body.

Krenka-Anris took pity on her friend. She returned with him and attempted to catch the soul of the dying woman. But Kenkari magic would not work with humans. The woman died, her soul escaped. Her husband, despondent with grief, became obsessed with attempting to catch human souls. He traveled the isles of Aristagon and eventually all the inhabited portion of the Mid

---

[2] A realm on the continent of Aristagon, Paxaria is the land of the Paxar clan of elves. Paxaria's largest city is Paxaua, a port town. Currently united with the Tribus elves, the Paxar are ostensibly permitted to rule their own realm. The Paxar king is nothing but a figurehead, however, and is married to one of Agah'ran's many daughters.

Realm, visiting every deathbed, going among the plague-ridden, standing on the sidelines of every battle, trying various magics to catch the souls of the dying, all without success.

He acquired followers during his travels, and these humans carried on his work after the magus himself died and his own soul had slipped away, despite his followers' best efforts to keep hold of it. The followers, who called themselves "Kir,"[3] wanted to continue their search for the magic, but, due to their habit of arriving at households side by side with death, they were becoming increasingly unpopular among the populace. It was whispered that they brought death with them and they were often physically attacked, driven away from their homes and villages.

The Kir banded together for their own protection, dwelt in isolated parts of the Mid Realm. Their search for the means to capture souls took a darker path. Having had no luck with the living, the Kir began to study the dead, hoping to find out what happened to the soul after it left the body. Now they searched for corpses, particularly corpses abandoned by the living.

The Kir continued to keep to themselves, avoiding contact with outsiders as much as possible, taking far more interest in the dead than in the living. Though still viewed with loathing, they were no longer viewed with fear. They became accepted and even welcome members of society. They eventually gave up the search for the soul-trapping magic, began instead—perhaps naturally enough—to worship death.

And though, over the centuries, their views on death and life had grown divergent and were now far apart, the Kir monks and the Kenkari elves never forgot that the two trees had sprung from the same seed. The Kenkari were among the few outsiders ever permitted to enter a Kir monastery and the Kir were the only humans able to obtain safe passage in elven lands.

Hugh, having been raised by the Kir monks, knew about this bond, knew that this disguise would provide the only safe means of entering elven lands. He'd used it before, with success, and he'd taken the precaution of procuring two black robes before he'd left the monastery, one robe for himself and one for Iridal.

No women being allowed in the order, it was necessary for

---

[3] Probably a corruption of the word "Kenkari."

Iridal to keep her hands and face covered and to refrain from speaking. This was not a great difficulty, since elven law prohibited the Kir from talking to any elf. Nor was any elf likely to break the prohibition. The elves viewed the Kir with loathing and superstitious dread that would make it quite easy for Hugh and Iridal to travel without interference.

The official at the port authority rushed them through with insulting haste, threw their papers at them from a safe distance.

"How do we find the Cathedral of the Albedo?" Hugh asked in fluent elven.

"No understand." The elf shook his head.

Hugh persisted. "What's the best route into the mountains, then?"

"No speak human," the elf said, turned his back, and walked off.

Hugh glowered, but said nothing, made no further argument. He took their papers, thrust them into the rope belt girdling his waist, and walked back out into the streets of the bustling port town of Paxaua.

From the depths of her cowl, Iridal gazed in awe and despair at the row after row of buildings, the winding streets, the crowds of people. The largest city in Volkaran could have fit easily into Paxaua's market district.

"I never imagined anyplace so vast or one filled with so many people!" she whispered to Hugh, taking hold of his arm and crowding close. "Have you ever been here before?"

"My business has never brought me this deep into elven territory," Hugh answered, with a grim smile.

Iridal looked at the numerous, converging, winding, twisting city streets in dismay. "How will we ever find our way? Don't you have a map?"

"Only of the Imperanon itself. All I know is that the cathedral's located somewhere in those mountains," said Hugh, indicating a range of mountains on the distant horizon. "The streets of this rat's warren have never been mapped, to my knowledge. Most of them don't have names, or if they do, only the inhabitants know them. We'll ask directions. Keep moving."

They followed the flow of the crowd, began walking up what appeared to be a main street.

"Asking directions is going to be rather difficult," Iridal remarked in a low voice, after a few moments' walking. "No one comes near us! They just . . . stare . . ."

"There are ways. Don't be afraid. They don't dare harm us."

They continued along the street, their black robes standing out like two dark holes torn from the gaily colored, living tapestry formed by the throngs of elves going about their daily lives. Everywhere the dark figures walked, daily life came to a halt.

The elves stopped talking, stopped bartering, stopped laughing or arguing. They stopped running, stopped walking, seemed to stop living, except for their eyes, which followed the black-robed pair until they had moved on to the next street, where it happened all over again. Iridal began to think that she carried silence in her hand, was draping its heavy folds over every person, every object they passed.

Iridal looked into the eyes, saw hatred—not for what she was, which surprised her, but for what she brought—death. A reminder of mortality. Long-lived though the elves are, they can't live forever.

She and Hugh kept walking, aimlessly, it seemed to Iridal, though they traveled in the same direction, presumably moving toward the mountains, though she could no longer see them, hidden by the tall buildings.

At length, she came to realize that Hugh was searching for something. She saw his hooded head turn from one side of the narrow street to the other, looking at the shops and the signs over the shops. He would leave a street, for no apparent reason, draw her into a street running along parallel. He would pause, study diverging streets, choose one, and head that direction.

Iridal knew better than to ask him, certain she would receive no reply. But she began to use her eyes, studied the shops and the signs as he was studying them. Paxaua's marketplace was divided into districts. Cloth sellers had their street next to the weavers. Swordsmiths were up a block or two from the tinker, the fruit vendors seemed to stretch for a mile. Hugh led her into a street lined with perfumers; the fumes from their aromatic shops left Iridal breathless. A left-angle turn brought them to the herbalists.

Hugh appeared to be nearing his goal, for he moved faster, casting only the briefest glances at the signs hanging above the shops. They soon left the larger herb shops behind, continued on down the street, heading into the central part of Paxaua. Here the shops were smaller and dirtier. The crowds were smaller, as well, for which Iridal was thankful, and appeared to be of a poorer class.

Hugh glanced to his right, leaned near Iridal.

"You're feeling faint," he whispered.

Iridal stumbled, clutched at him obligingly, swayed on her feet. Hugh grasped hold of her, looked around.

"Water!" he called sternly. "I ask for water for my companion. He is not well."

The few elves who had been in the street vanished. Iridal let her body go heavy, sagged in Hugh's arms. He half carried, half dragged her over to a stoop, under a shabby, swinging sign that marked yet another herb shop.

"Rest here," he told her in a loud voice. "I will go inside and ask for water. Keep a watch out," he muttered beneath his breath before he left her.

Iridal nodded silently, drew her hood well over her face, though she still made certain she could see. She sat limply where Hugh left her, darting alarmed glances up and down the street. It had not occurred to her until now that they were being followed. Such a thing seemed ludicrous, when every elf in Paxaua must know by now of their presence and probably where they were bound, for they had certainly made no secret of it.

Hugh entered the shop door, left it open behind him. Out of the corner of her eye, Iridal watched him walk over to a counter. Behind it, long rows of shelving were lined with bottles of every shape, color, and size, containing an astonishing variety of plants, powders, and potions.

Elven magic tends to be mechanical in nature (dealing with machines) or spiritual (the Kenkari). Elves don't believe in mixing a pinch of this herb with a scoop of that powder, except for use in healing. And healing potions weren't considered magical, merely practical. The elf behind the counter was an herbalist. He could dispense ointments to treat boils and blisters and diaper rash, provide liquids to cure coughs and insomnia and fainting spells. And perhaps a love charm or two, delivered under the counter.

Iridal couldn't imagine what Hugh was after. She was reasonably certain it wasn't water.

The elf behind the counter didn't seem at all pleased to see him.

"No like your kind. You go way," said the elf, waving his hand.

Hugh raised his right hand, palm out, as if in greeting. "My companion is feeling faint. I want a cup of water. And we are lost, we need directions. In the name of the Kenkari, you cannot refuse."

The elf regarded him in silence, cast a sharp and furtive glance at the door. "You, monk. You no sit there. Bad for business," he called to Iridal, loudly and irritably. "Come in. Come in."

Hugh returned to assist Iridal to her feet, led her into the shop.

The elf slammed shut the door. Turning to the Hand, he said in a low voice, "What do you need, Brother? Be quick. We don't have much time."

"Directions on the fastest route to the Cathedral of the Albedo."

"Where?" the elf asked, astonished.

Hugh repeated himself.

"Very well." The elf was perplexed, but cooperative. "Go back to Swordsmith Street, turn onto Silversmith Row and follow it to the end. It will merge with a large highway known as King's Way. It winds about some, but it will take you into the mountains. The mountain pass is heavily guarded, but you shouldn't have any trouble. Those disguises—a clever idea. They won't get you inside the Imperanon, though. I presume that's your real destination."

"We're going to the cathedral. Where is it?"

The elf shook his head. "Take my advice, Brother. You don't want to go there. The Kenkari will know you're imposters. You don't want to cross the Kenkari."

Hugh made no reply, waited patiently.

The elf shrugged. "It's your soul, Brother. The Imperanon is built on the mountain side. The cathedral is in front, on a large, level plateau. The structure is a huge crystal dome standing in the center of a large round courtyard. You can see it for menka. Believe me, you won't have any trouble finding it, though why you'd want to go there is beyond me. Still, that's your business. Anything else I can do for you?"

"We heard a rumor that the Kenkari have stopped accepting souls. Is it true?"

The elf raised his eyebrows. This question was certainly not one he'd expected. He glanced out the window, to the empty street, then at the door, to make sure it was shut, and still took the precaution of lowering his voice.

"It is true, Brother. The word is all over town. When you reach the cathedral, you'll find the doors closed."

"Thank you for the help, Brother," said Hugh. "We'll take our leave. We don't want to cause you any trouble. The walls moved."[4]

Iridal looked at Hugh, wondering what he meant. The elf seemed to know, however.

He nodded. "Of course. Don't fret. The Unseen are not watching you so much as they are watching us, their own people. Who you talk to, where you stop."

"I trust we haven't brought trouble on you."

"Who am I?" The elf shrugged. "Nobody. I take care to be nobody. If I were somebody—rich, powerful—yes, then you could bring trouble to me."

Hugh and Iridal prepared to go.

"Here, drink this." The elf handed Iridal a cup of water. She accepted it thankfully. "You look as if you could use it. You're certain I can't do anything else for you, Brother? Poisons? I have some excellent snake venom in stock. Perfect for adding a little bite to your dagger's tooth—"

"Thank you, no," said Hugh.

"So be it," the elf said cheerfully. He threw open the door. His expression altered to a scowl. "And stay out, you dog of a human! And you tell the Kenkari, they owe me a blessing!"

He shoved Hugh and Iridal roughly over the stoop, slammed the door shut after them. The two stood in the street, looking— Iridal trusted—as forlorn and weary and dispirited as she felt.

"We've come the wrong way apparently," said Hugh, speaking human, for the benefit, Iridal presumed, of the Unseen.

So it was the elite elven guard who were following them. She stared around, saw nothing, nobody. She didn't even see the walls move, wondered how Hugh knew.

"We must retrace our steps," he told her.

Iridal accepted the arm Hugh offered for her support, leaned

---

[4] Translation: The Unseen are following us.

on him, thinking wearily of the long distance they had still to travel. "I had no idea your work was so strenuous," she whispered.

He looked down at her with a smile, a rare thing for him. "It's quite a distance into the mountains, I'm afraid. And we don't dare stop again."

"Yes, I understand."

"You must be missing your magic, about now," he said to her, patting her hand, still smiling at her.

"And you must be missing your pipe." Her hand tightened over his. They walked for long moments in companionable silence.

"You were looking for that shop, weren't you?"

"Not that one in particular," Hugh responded. "One with a certain sign in the window."

Iridal couldn't at first recall a sign; the shop had been so poor and shabby. Nothing hung over the door. Then she remembered that there *had* been a sign propped up inside the window. Crudely painted, now that she thought of it—the image was of a hand.

The Brotherhood advertised openly in the streets, it seemed. Elf and human—strangers, mortal enemies—yet they risked their lives to help each other, bound by a bond of blood, of death. Evil, to be sure, but might this not offer a hope of good to come? Wasn't this an indication that the two races were not natural enemies, as some on both sides claimed?

The chance for peace rests with us, Iridal thought. We *must* succeed. Yet, now that she was in this alien land, this alien culture, her hopes for finding her son and freeing him were growing dim.

"Hugh," she said, "I know I'm not supposed to ask questions, but what the elf said is true. The Kenkari *will* know we are imposters. Still you talk as if you truly plan to go to them. I don't understand. What will you say to them? How can you hope—"

"You're right, Lady," said Hugh, cutting her short. His smile had vanished. His tone was grim. "You're not supposed to ask questions. Here, this is the right road."

They entered onto a broad avenue, marked with the royal crest of the King of Paxaria. The two were once again surrounded by crowds, once again surrounded by silence.

In silence, they continued on.

CHAPTER 30

THE CATHEDRAL

OF THE ALBEDO

ARISTAGON, MID REALM

♦

THE KEEPER OF THE DOOR OF THE CATHEDRAL OF THE ALBEDO HAD A NEW responsibility. Once he had waited for the weesham, bearing the souls of their charges for release in the Aviary. Now, he was forced to turn them away.

Word spread rapidly among a shocked populace that the cathedral was closed, though just why the Kenkari had closed it was not revealed. The Kenkari were powerful, but even they did not dare openly accuse their emperor of murdering his own subjects. The Kenkari had been more than half expecting to be attacked or at least persecuted by the emperor's troops, were considerably surprised (and relieved) when they were not.

But, to the Keeper's dismay, the weesham continued to cross the courtyard. Some had not heard the news. Others, though informed that the cathedral was closed, still tried to get in.

"But surely the law doesn't apply to me," the weesham would argue. "To all the others, perhaps, but the soul I bear is the soul of a prince . . ." Or a duchess or a marquis or an earl.

It didn't matter. All were turned away.

The weesham left, bewildered, completely at a loss, clutching the small boxes in trembling hands.

"I feel so terribly sorry for them," said the Door to the Book. They stood conferring together in the chapel. "The weesham look lost. 'Where do I go?' they ask me. 'What am I to do?' It's been their whole life. What can I say except 'Return to your home. Wait.' Wait for what?"

"The sign," said the Book confidently. "It will come. You will see. You must have faith."

"Easy for you to talk," said the Door in bitter tones. "You don't have to turn them away. You don't see their faces."

"I know. I'm sorry," said the Book, laying her hand on the thin hand of her fellow Kenkari. "But things will be easier now the word is out. The weesham have stopped coming. There hasn't been one in the last two cycles. You will no longer be troubled."

"Not by them." His tone was ominous.

"You still fear we might be attacked?"

"I almost begin to wish we would be. Then, at least we would know the emperor's mind. He hasn't publicly denounced us. He hasn't tried to order us to alter our stand. He hasn't sent troops."

"Troops wouldn't come. Not against us," said the Book.

"They wouldn't have come in the old days. But so much is changing now. I wonder . . ."

The sound of the gong rang throughout the cathedral's precincts. Both glanced upward, the notes seeming to shiver on the still air. The Door's chief assistant, left to guard in the Door's absence, was summoning his master.

The Door sighed. "Ah, I spoke too soon. Another."

The Book gazed at him in mute sympathy. The Keeper of the Door rose to his feet, left the Aviary, and hastened back to his post. As he walked—not moving very fast—he glanced unhappily out the crystal walls, expecting to see yet another weesham, expecting yet another argument. What he saw, however, made the Door come to a halt. He stared in astonishment, and, when he started moving again, his haste caused his slippered feet to slip precariously on the polished floors.

His chief assistant was extremely grateful to see him.

"I'm thankful you could come, Keeper. I feared you might be at prayer."

"No, no." The Keeper of the Door stared through the crystal wall, through the golden grille that barred entrance.

He had been hoping that his vision had been blurred, that a trick of light had deceived him, that he wasn't seeing two black-robed humans crossing the vast and empty courtyard. But they were so near now that there could not be much doubt.

His brow furrowed. "Kir monks of all things. At a time like this."

"I know," murmured his assistant. "What do we do?"

"We must admit them," said the Door, sighing. "Tradition demands it. They've come all this way. At grave peril, perhaps, for they cannot know how bad things are. The sacred law that protects them holds, but who knows for how long? Raise the grille. I will speak with them."

The assistant hurried to obey. The Keeper of the Door waited until the Kir, who were moving slowly, had reached the stairs. They both kept their hoods pulled low over their heads.

The grille rose silently, effortlessly. The Keeper of the Door pushed on the crystal door, which moved noiselessly to open. The Kir had halted when the grille went up. They remained standing unmoving, their heads lowered, as the Door walked forth.

He raised his arms; the shimmering robes with their butterfly wings and myriad colors were dazzling in the sunlight.

"I welcome you, brethren, in the name of Krenka-Anris," said the Door, speaking human.

"All praise to Krenka-Anris," said the taller of the two Kir monks in elven. "And to her sons."

The Door nodded. The response was the correct one.

"Enter and be at peace after your long journey," said the Door, lowering his arms, standing to one side.

"Thank you, Brother," said the monk harshly, assisting his companion, who appeared footsore and exhausted.

The two crossed the threshold. The Keeper shut the door. His assistant lowered the grille. The Door turned to his visitors and, though they had said nothing, done nothing to arouse suspicion, the Door knew he'd made a mistake.

The taller of the monks saw, by the Door's altered expression, that their disguises had been penetrated. He drew off his hood. Keen eyes glittered from beneath overhanging brows. His beard was braided into two twists on a strong and jutting jaw. His nose was like the beak of a hawk. The Keeper thought he had never seen a more daunting human.

"You are right, Keeper," said this man. "We are not Kir monks. We made use of these disguises because it is the only way we could travel here in safety."

"Sacrilege!" cried the Door, his voice shaking, not with fear, but with fury. "You have dared enter sacred precincts under false pretenses! I don't know what you hoped to accomplish, but you have made a terrible mistake. You will not leave here alive. Krenka-Anris, I call upon you! Cast down your holy fire. Burn their flesh! Cleanse your temple of their profane presence!"

Nothing happened. The Keeper of the Door was staggered. Then, he began to think he understood how his magic had been thwarted. The other Kir monk had removed her hood, and he saw the rainbow-colored eyes, the wisdom in them.

"A mysteriarch!" said the Door, recovering from the shock. "You may have disrupted my first spell, but you are one and we are many . . ."

"I did not disrupt your spell," said the woman quietly. "Nor will I use my magic against you, not even in my own defense. We mean no harm, intend no sacrilege. Our cause is one of peace between our peoples."

"We are your prisoners," said the man. "Bind us, blindfold us. We won't fight you. We ask only that you take us to see the Keeper of the Souls. We must speak to him. When he has heard us, he may pass judgment on us. If he deems we must die, then so be it."

The Door eyed the two narrowly. His assistant had sounded the alarm, ringing the gong wildly. Other Kenkari came at a run, formed a ring around the false monks. The Keeper, with their assistance, could cast his spell again.

But why hadn't it worked in the first place?

"You know a great deal about us," said the Door, trying to decide what to do. "You knew the correct response—something only a true Kir monk would know; you know about the Keeper of the Souls."

"I was raised by Kir monks," said the man. "And I've lived among them since."

"Bring them to me." A voice sparkled on the air, like frost or the notes of the tongueless bell.

The Keeper of the Door, recognizing the command of his superior, bowed in silent acquiescence. But first, he laid his hand upon each human's eyes, casting a spell that would blind them. Neither attempted to stop him, though the man flinched and stiffened, as if it took enormous will to submit himself to this handicap.

"Profane eyes may not see the sacred miracle," said the Keeper of the Door.

"We understand," replied the mysteriarch calmly.

"We will guide you safely. Have no fear of falling," said the Door, extending his own hand to the woman.

Her hand met his, her touch was light, cool.

"Thank you, Magicka," she said and even managed a smile, though by the weariness on her face, she must be exhausted almost to the point of dropping. Limping on bruised and swollen feet, she grimaced when she walked.

The Door glanced back. His chief assistant had taken hold of the arm of the man, was leading him along. The Door found it difficult to take his eyes from the man's face. It was ugly, its features hard and brutal-looking. But then most human faces appear brutish to the delicate-boned elves. There was something different about this man's face. The Door wondered that he wasn't repulsed, that he kept staring at the man with a sense of awe, a prickling of the skin.

The woman stumbled over the Kenkari's long butterfly robes. The Door had drifted over into her path.

"I beg your pardon, Magicka," he said. He would have liked to ask her name, but it was for his superior to handle the formalities. "I wasn't watching where I was going."

"I'm sorry we've upset you," the woman said, with another wan smile.

The Door was coming to feel pity for her. Her features were not nearly as coarse as those of most humans, she was almost pleasant to look upon. And she seemed so tired and so . . . sad. "It isn't much farther. You've traveled a long distance, I suppose."

"From Paxaua, on foot. I dared not use my magic," said the woman.

"No, I suppose not. No one gave you any trouble, hindered you?"

"The only place we were stopped was in the mountains. The guards at the pass questioned us, but did not detain us long, once we reminded them that we are under your protection."

The Door was pleased to hear this. The troops, at least, have respect for us, haven't turned against us. The emperor is a different matter. Agah'ran is up to something. He would never have allowed our prohibition to stand if he were not. After all, we let him know that we know he's a murderer. He must realize we won't tolerate his rule for long.

And for what do we wait? For a sign. Other worlds. A gate of death that leads to life. A man who is dead and who is not dead. Blessed Krenka-Anris! When would it all be explained?

The Keeper of the Book and the Keeper of the Soul were waiting for them in the chapel. The humans were led inside. The Door's chief assistant, who had brought the human male, bowed and left them. He shut the door. At the sound, the human male turned, frowned.

"Iridal?"

"I'm here, Hugh," she said softly.

"Have no fear," said the Keeper of the Soul. "You are in the chapel of the Aviary. I am here, the one with whom you asked to speak. With me also are the Keepers of the Book and of the Door. I regret that I must leave the blindness upon you, but it is forbidden by law that the eyes of our enemies should look upon the miracle."

"We understand," said Iridal. "Perhaps the day will come when there will be no need for such laws."

"We pray for that day, Magicka," said the Keeper. "What is it you are called?"

"I am Iridal, formerly of the High Realms, now of Volkaran."

"And your companion?" the Keeper prompted, after waiting a moment for the man to answer.

"He is Hugh the Hand," said Iridal, when it became clear Hugh wasn't going to speak. She appeared worried, turned her sightless eyes in what she sensed was his direction, reached out a groping hand.

"A man raised by Kir monks. A man with a most remarkable face," said the Keeper, studying Hugh intently. "I've seen many humans, and there is something different about you, Hugh the Hand. Something awful, something fey. I do not understand. You came to speak to me. Why? What is you want of the Kenkari?"

Hugh opened his lips, seemed about to respond, then said nothing.

Iridal, her hand finding his arm, was alarmed to feel the muscles rigid, shivering.

"Hugh, is everything all right? What's wrong?"

He drew away from her touch. His mouth opened, closed again. The cords in his neck stood out, his throat constricted. At last, apparently angered with himself, he brought the words out with an effort, as if he'd dragged them up from dark depths.

"I came to sell you my soul."

♦

CHAPTER 31

THE CATHEDRAL

OF THE ALBEDO

ARISTAGON, MID REALM

♦

"HE'S INSANE," SAID THE BOOK, THE FIRST TO RECOVER HER POWER OF SPEECH.

"I don't believe so," said the Keeper of the Soul, regarding Hugh with intense, if perplexed, interest. "You are not insane, are you, Hugh." The human word came awkwardly to elven lips.

"No," Hugh answered shortly. Now that the worst was over —and he had not imagined it would be so difficult—he was relaxed, could even view the elves' astonishment with sardonic amusement. The only person he could not face yet was Iridal and, because of this, he was grateful for his blindness.

She said nothing, confused, not understanding, thinking, perhaps, that this was another of his tricks.

No trick. He was in earnest—deadly earnest.

"You were raised by Kir monks. You know something, then, of our ways."

"I know a lot, Keeper. I make it my business to know things," Hugh said.

"Yes," the Soul murmured. "I do not doubt it. You know, then, that we do not accept human souls, that we never *buy* souls at all. The souls we take in are given to us freely . . ."

The Keeper's voice faltered somewhat on the last statement.

Hugh smiled grimly, shook his head.

The Keeper was silent long moments, then said, "You are well informed, sir." Silent again, then, "You have made a long journey, fraught with danger, to offer that which you knew we must reject—"

"You won't reject it," said Hugh. "I'm different."

"I can sense that," said the Keeper softly. "But I don't understand. Why are you different, Hugh? What is there about your soul that would make it valuable to us? That would even permit us to take it?"

"Because my soul, such as it is"—Hugh's mouth twisted—"has passed beyond . . . and has returned."

"Hugh," Iridal gasped, suddenly realizing that this was no trick, "you can't be serious. Hugh, don't do this!"

Hugh paid no attention to her.

"Do you mean," said the Keeper in a stifled tone that sounded as if he were suffocating, "that you have died and been . . . and been . . ."

"Resurrected," Hugh said.

He had expected astonishment, disbelief. But it seemed he had cast a lightning bolt into the elves. He could feel the electricity arc in the air, almost hear it crackle around him.

"That is what I see in your face," said Soul.

" 'The man who is dead and is not dead,' " said Door.

"The sign," said Book.

A moment ago, Hugh had been in control of the situation. Now, somehow, he'd lost it, felt helpless, as when his dragonship had been sucked into the Maelstrom.

"What is it? Tell me!" he demanded harshly, reaching out. He stumbled over a chair.

"Hugh, don't! What do you mean?" Iridal cried, blindly clutching at him. She turned frantically to the elves. "Explain to me. I don't understand."

"I think we may restore their sight," said the Keeper of the Soul.

"Such a thing is unprecedented!" Book protested.

"All is unprecedented," replied Soul gravely.

He took hold of Hugh's hands, held them fast, with a strength startling in one so thin, and laid his other hand on the man's eyes.

Hugh blinked, looked swiftly around him. The Keeper of the Door lifted Iridal's blindness in the same fashion. Neither had ever seen Kenkari elves before, and were amazed by their appearance.

The Kenkari, all three, stood head and shoulders taller than

Hugh the Hand, who was considered a tall man among humans. But the elves were so excessively thin that the three of them might have stood side by side and barely equaled Hugh's breadth. The Kenkari's hair was long, for it is never cut, and is white from birth.

Male and female Kenkari are similar in appearance, particularly when wearing the shapeless butterfly robes that easily hide the female's curves. The most noticeable difference between the sexes is in the way the hair is worn. Males plait it in one long braid, down the back. Females wrap the braid around the head in a crown. Their eyes are large, overlarge in their small, delicate faces; the pupils are extraordinarily dark. Some elves remark disparagingly (but never publicly) that the Kenkari have come to resemble the winged insect they worship and emulate.

Iridal sank weakly into a chair one of the Kenkari provided for her. Once her initial shock at the sight of the strange-looking elves had worn off, she turned her gaze to Hugh.

"What are you doing? Tell me. I don't understand."

"Trust me, Iridal," Hugh said quietly. "You promised you would trust me."

Iridal shook her head, and, as she did so, her eyes were drawn to the Aviary. They softened at the sight of the lush, green beauty, but then she seemed to realize what it was she looked upon. Her gaze shifted back to Hugh with a kind of horror.

"Now, please explain yourself, sir," said the Keeper of the Soul.

"First you explain yourself," Hugh demanded, glaring from one to the other. "You don't seem all that surprised to see me. I get the feeling you were expecting me."

The dark-eyed gazes of the three Keepers slid from one to the other, exchanging thoughts from beneath lowered lids.

"Please, sit down, Hugh. I think we should all sit down. Thank you. You see, sir, we weren't expecting *you* precisely. We didn't know quite what to expect. You've obviously heard that we have closed the Cathedral of the Albedo. Due to . . . shall we say . . . very unhappy circumstances."

"The emperor murdering his own kin for their souls," Hugh stated. Reaching into a pocket of his robes, he drew forth his pipe, stuck it—cold—between his teeth.

Angered by Hugh's bluntness and apparent disdain, the Soul's expression turned hard and brittle. "What right have you humans to judge us? Your hands, too, are wet with blood!"

"It is a terrible war," said Iridal softly. "A war neither side can win."

The Soul grew calmer. Sighing, he nodded in sad agreement. "Yes, Magicka. That is what we have come to understand. We prayed to Krenka-Anris for the answer. And we received it, though we do not understand it. 'Other worlds. A gate of death that leads to life. A man who is dead and who is not dead.' The message was more complicated, of course, but those are the signs we are to look for, to know that the end of this terrible destruction is near."

" 'A gate of death . . .' " Iridal repeated, staring at them in wonder. "You mean: Death's Gate."

"Do you know of such a thing?" the Keeper asked, taken aback.

"Yes. And . . . it leads to other worlds! The Sartan created them, created Death's Gate. A Sartan I knew passed through it, not long ago. The same Sartan . . ." Iridal's voice faded to a whisper. "The same Sartan who restored this man's life to him."

No one spoke. Each one, elf and human, sat in the awed and fearful silence that comes when mortals feel the touch of an Immortal hand, when they hear the whisper of an Immortal voice.

"Why have you come to us, Hugh the Hand?" the Soul demanded. "What bargain did you hope to strike? For," he added, with a wry—if tremulous—smile, "one does not sell one's soul for so paltry a thing as money."

"You're right." Hugh shifted uncomfortably, his glowering gaze upon his pipe, avoiding all eyes, especially Iridal's. "You know, of course, of the human child being held in the castle—"

"King Stephen's son, yes."

"He's not King Stephen's son. He's her son." Hugh pointed the pipe at Iridal. "Her son and her late husband's, also a mysteriarch. How the kid came to be thought of as Stephen's is a long story and one that has nothing to do with why we are here. Suffice it to say, the elves plan to hold the boy hostage, in return for Stephen's surrender."

"Within only a few days' time, King Stephen plans to meet with Prince Rees'ahn, form an alliance between our peoples,

launch a war that will surely bring an end to the cruel Tribus rule.
The emperor plots to use my son to force Stephen into refusing
such an alliance," Iridal explained. "All hope for peace, for unity
among the races, would be shattered. But if I can free my son, the
emperor will have no hold over Stephen. The alliance can proceed."

"But we can't get into the Imperanon to free the kid," said
Hugh. "Not without help."

"You seek our help in obtaining entry into the palace."

"In exchange for my soul," said Hugh, placing the pipe back
in his mouth.

"In exchange for nothing!" Iridal struck in angrily. "Nothing
except the knowledge that you elves have done what is right!"

"You ask us, Magicka, to betray our people," said the Soul.

"I ask you to save your people!" Iridal cried passionately.
"Look at the depths to which your emperor has sunk. He murders
his own! What will happen if this tyrant rules the world unchal-
lenged?"

The Keepers again exchanged glances.

"We will pray for guidance," said Soul, rising to his feet.
"Come, brethren. If you will excuse us?"

The other Keepers stood and left the room, passing through a
small door into an adjoining room, presumably another chapel.
They shut the door carefully behind them.

The two left alone sat in cold, unhappy silence. There was
much Iridal wanted to say, but the grim and dour expression on
Hugh's face let her know that her words and arguments would
not be welcome, might do more harm than good. Iridal could not
think, however, that the elves would accept Hugh's offer. Surely
the Kenkari would aid them without exacting such a terrible
price.

She convinced herself of this, relaxed, and, in her weariness,
must have drifted into sleep, for she was not aware of the
Kenkari's return until Hugh's touch upon her hand brought her to
startled wakefulness.

"You are tired," said Soul, looking at her with a gentle benefi-
cence that strengthened her hope. "And we have kept you
overlong. You shall have food and rest, but first, our answer." He
turned to Hugh, clasped his thin hands before him. "We accept
your offer."

Hugh made no reply, merely nodded once, abruptly.

"You will accept the ritual death at our hands?"

"I welcome it," Hugh said, his teeth clenched over the pipe stem.

"You can't mean this!" Iridal cried, rising to her feet. "You can't demand such a sacrifice—"

"You are very young, Magicka," said Soul, dark eyes turning upon Iridal. "You will come to learn, as we have in our long lives, that what is given freely is often despised. It is only when we pay for something that we treasure it. We will aid your safe entry into the palace. When the boy is removed, you, Hugh the Hand, will return to us. Your soul will be of inestimable value.

"Our charges"—Soul glanced toward the Aviary, to the leaves fluttering and stirring with the breath of the dead—"are beginning to grow restless. Some want to leave us. You will placate them, tell them that they are better off where they are."

"They're not, but fair enough," said Hugh. Removing his pipe, he rose to his feet, stretched tired and aching muscles.

"No!" Iridal protested brokenly. "No, Hugh, don't do this! You can't do this!"

Hugh tried to harden himself against her. Then, suddenly, he sighed, drew her close, held her fast. She began to weep. Hugh swallowed. A single tear crept from beneath his eyes, slid down his cheek, and fell into her hair.

"It's the only way," he said to her softly, speaking human. "Our only chance. And we're getting the best of the deal. An old used-up, misspent life like mine in exchange for a young life, like your son's.

"I want death to come this way, Iridal," he added, his voice deepening. "I can't do it myself. I'm afraid. I've been there, you see, and the journey is . . . is . . ." He shuddered. "But they'll do it for me. And it will be easy this time. If they send me."

She could not speak. Hugh lifted her in his arms. She clung to him, weeping.

"She's tired, Keeper," he said. "We both are. Where may we rest?"

The Keeper of the Soul smiled sadly. "I understand. The Keeper of the Door will guide you. We have rooms prepared for you and food, though I fear it is not what you are accustomed to eating. I cannot permit you to smoke, however."

Hugh grunted, grimaced, said nothing.

"When you are rested, we will discuss arrangements with you. You must not wait long. You are probably not aware of this, but you were most assuredly followed here."

"The Unseen? I'm aware of it. I saw them. Or as much of them as anyone ever sees."

The Keeper's eyes widened. "Truly," he said, "you are a dangerous man."

"I'm aware of that, too," Hugh responded grimly. "This world will be a better place without me in it."

He left, carrying Iridal in his arms, following the Keeper of the Door, on whose face was an expression of hope, mingled with dazed perplexity.

"Will he truly come back to die?" asked Book, when the three were gone.

"Yes," said the Keeper of the Soul. "He will come back."

CHAPTER 32

THE CATHEDRAL

OF THE ALBEDO

ARISTAGON, MID REALM

♦

GUIDED BY THE KEEPER OF THE DOOR, HUGH CARRIED IRIDAL THROUGH THE halls of the cathedral, down to the lower levels, where the rooms allocated to the weesham were located. The Door opened two of the rooms, located side by side. Food, consisting of bread and fruit, and a small pitcher of water had been placed on a table in each.

"The doors seal themselves once they are closed," the elf said apologetically. "Please do not be offended. We do this with our own people, not out of lack of trust, but in order that the quiet and peace of the cathedral may be maintained. No one is permitted to walk the halls except myself or my assistants, the Keeper of the Book, and the Keeper of the Soul."

"We understand. Thanks," said Hugh.

He carried Iridal inside, placed her upon the bed. She caught hold of his hand as he was about to withdraw.

"Please don't go yet, Hugh. Please stay and talk to me. Just a moment."

Hugh's expression was dark. He glanced at the Kenkari, who lowered his eyes, nodded gently.

"I will leave you to enjoy your repast in private. When you are ready to go to your own room, you have but to ring the small silver bell there, by the bed, and I will return to escort you."

The Keeper, bowing, withdrew.

"Sit down," Iridal urged, holding fast to Hugh's hand.

"I'm very tired, Lady," he said, avoiding looking at her. "We'll talk in the morning—"

"We must talk now." Iridal rose to her feet, stood in front of him. Reaching up, she touched his face with her fingers. "Don't do this, Hugh. Don't make this terrible bargain."

"I have to," he said gruffly, jaw clenched against her soft touch, eyes anywhere but on her. "There's no other way."

"Yes, there is. There has to be. The Kenkari want peace as much as we do. Maybe more. You saw them, heard them. They're afraid, Hugh, afraid of the emperor. We'll talk to them, make some other arrangement. Then we'll rescue Bane and I'll help you find Alfred, as I promised—"

"No," said Hugh. Catching hold of her wrist, he forced her hand away from him. And now he looked at her. "No, it's better this way."

"Hugh!" Iridal faltered, cheeks stained crimson, wet with her tears. "Hugh, I love you!"

"Do you?" Hugh regarded her with a grim, sardonic smile. He held up his right hand, held it palm out. "Look, look at the scar. No, don't turn your head. Look at it, Iridal. Imagine my hand caressing your soft flesh. What would you feel? My loving touch? Or this scar?"

Iridal lowered her eyes, lowered her head.

"You don't love me, Iridal," Hugh said, sighing. "You love a part of me."

She raised her head, answered him fiercely. "I love the best part!"

"Then let that part go."

Iridal shook her head, but she said nothing more, made no further argument.

"Your son. He's the one that matters to you, Lady. You have a chance to save him. Not me. My soul was lost a long time ago."

Turning away from him, Iridal sank down on the bed, stared at her hands, clasped in her lap.

She knows I'm right, but she doesn't want to accept it, Hugh decided. She's still fighting against it, but her resistance is weakening. She's a rational woman, not a lovesick girl. By morning, when she's thought about it, she'll go along with it.

"Good night, Lady."

Hugh reached down, rang the small silver bell.

♦

Hugh had judged Iridal correctly, or at least so he supposed. By morning, her tears were dry. She was calm, met Hugh with a quiet smile of reassurance and the whispered words, "You may count on me. I won't fail you."

"You won't fail your son," he corrected her.

She smiled for him again, let him think that was what was important to her. And it was, certainly. Bane would be her redemption, hers and Sinistrad's. All the evil both parents had done —his by commission, hers by omission—would be expurgated by their child. But this was only one factor in her decision to appear to go along with Hugh.

Last night, before she slept, Iridal remembered again the silent counsel of that Immortal voice. What or whose, she couldn't understand, for she had never believed in any Almighty power.

The man who was dead and who is not dead.

Hugh was meant to be here, she realized. I will take this as a hopeful sign and trust that all will be for the best.

And so Iridal no longer argued against the sacrifice. She had convinced herself that the sacrifice would never take place.

She and Hugh met later in the day with the three Keepers, Book, Door, and Soul, in the small chapel room of the Aviary.

"We do not know if you have yet devised a plan for entering the Imperanon," the Keeper of the Soul began, with a deprecating glance at Hugh. "If not, we have some ideas."

The Hand shook his head, indicated that he would be interested to hear what the Keeper had in mind.

"Will you go, Magicka?" the Soul asked Iridal. "The risk is very great. Should the emperor capture a human of your talent—"

"I will go," Iridal interrupted. "The boy is my son."

"We assumed that such would be the case. If all goes according to plan, the danger should be minimal. You will enter the palace very late, when most will be sleeping heavily.

"His Imperial Majesty is giving a party this night, as he does every night, but this one is to celebrate the anniversary of elven unification. Everyone living in the Imperanon will be expected to attend and many are coming from far parts of the kingdom. The celebration will last a considerable length of time and there will be much coming and going and confusion in the castle.

"You will make your way to your son's room, remove the child, bring him back here. He will be quite safe in the cathedral, I assure you, madam," the Soul added. "Even if the emperor should discover the boy were here, Agah'ran would not dare order an attack on the sacred precinct. His own soldiers would rebel against such a command."

"I understand," Iridal replied.

Hugh, sucking on the cold pipe, nodded his approval.

The Keeper appeared pleased. "We will provide you, Magicka, and your son, with safe transportation to your own lands. You, sir"—he bowed slightly in Hugh's direction—"will remain here with us."

Iridal pressed her lips firmly shut at this, made no comment.

"It all sounds easy enough," said Hugh, removing the pipe, "but how do we get into the palace and back out again? The guards won't be sleeping off 'gaiety and merriment.' "

The Keeper of the Soul shifted his gaze to the Keeper of the Door, turning over the remainder of the discussion to his subordinate.

The Door looked to Iridal. "We have heard it said, Magicka, that those humans of your arcane skill, Seventh House, have the gift of creating . . . shall we say . . . false impressions in the minds of others."

"You mean illusion," Iridal answered. "Yes, but there are certain restrictions. The one observing the illusion must want to believe it is true or expect it to be true. For example, I could create an illusion, right now, that would allow me to look just like this woman." Iridal pointed to the Keeper of the Book. "But such an illusion would fail, simply because you would not believe it. Your mind would tell you that, logically, there could not be two of this woman in this room at the same time."

"But if," pursued Door, "you cast the illusion and I met you walking down the hall by yourself. I would be deluded into thinking you were my fellow Kenkari, would I not?"

"Yes. Then you would have little reason to doubt."

"And I could stop and speak to you, touch you? You would seem real to me?"

"That would be dangerous. Even though I speak elven, the timbre and tone of my voice is necessarily human and might give me away. My gestures would be my own, not those of your friend. The longer you were around me, the greater the chances that I could no longer deceive you. However, I begin to see what you have in mind. And you are right. It might work. But only for me. *I* could appear to be an elf, and thus walk safely into the castle. But I cannot cast such a spell on Hugh.''

''No, we had not supposed you could. We have made other arrangements for him. You, sir, are familiar, you said, with those known as the Unseen.''

''Only by reputation.''

''Yes, quite.'' Door smiled faintly. ''Do you know of the magical clothing they wear?''

''No.'' Hugh lowered the pipe, looked interested. ''No, tell me about it.''

''The fabric is woven of a wondrous thread that changes color and texture to match whatever it is around. One of their uniforms lies on the floor there, next to the desk. Do you see it?''

Hugh stared, frowned, raised his eyebrows. ''I'll be damned.''

''Now you see it, of course, since your attention has been drawn to it. Much like Lady Iridal's spell. You see the folds, the shape, the bulkiness. Yet, you were in this room for a considerable length of time, and the clothing passed unobserved, even by you —a man usually quite observant.

''Dressed in this guise, the Unseen can go anywhere, at any time, day or night, and—to the ordinary eye—would be practically invisible. Anyone watching for them would be able to detect them by their movement and . . . substance . . . for lack of a better word. In addition, it takes a certain amount of time for the fabric to alter color and appearance. Thus the Unseen learn to move slowly, silently, with fluid grace, in order to blend in with their surroundings.

''All this you must learn to do, Hugh the Hand. Before you enter the palace this night.''

Hugh walked over, fingered the cloth. Lifting it, he held it against the background of the wooden desk, watched, marveling, to see the fabric shift from the soft green of the carpet on the floor to the dark brown of the wood. As the Kenkari said, the very appearance of the cloth altered as well, taking on the grain and texture of the wood until it seemed to almost disappear in his hand.

" 'The walls move.' What I wouldn't have given for this in the old days," he murmured.

The Brotherhood had long wondered how the Unseen managed to operate so effectively and efficiently, wondered how it was that no one ever saw them or knew what they looked like. But the secrets of the Unseen were kept as closely and carefully as the secrets of the Brotherhood.

It was agreed upon that elven magic must have something to do with this remarkable ability, though what or how was open to debate. The elves did not possess the ability to conjure up illusions, as did the higher ranking human wizards. But they could spin magical thread, it seemed.

This guise that he held in his hand could make his fortune. Add to its obvious advantages his own skill and knowledge and experience . . .

Hugh laughed bitterly at himself, tossed the uniform back to the floor, where it immediately began to change its color to the green of the carpet.

"Will it fit me? I'm bigger than any elf."

"The garments are designed to fit loosely, to flow with the wearer's movements. Then, too, they must adapt to all sizes and shapes of our people. As you might imagine, such uniforms are tremendously rare and prized. It takes a hundred cycles to produce thread enough for the tunic alone, and another hundred cycles after that to do the weaving. The weaving and sewing may only be done by skilled magi, who have spent years learning the secret art. The trousers have a drawstring, to fit around the waist. There are slippers for your feet, a mask for your head, gloves for your hands."

"Let's see what I look like," Hugh said, gathering up the clothing in a bundle. "Or what I *don't* look like."

The uniform fit, though it was tight through the shoulders, and he was forced to let the drawstring on the waist out as far as it would go. Fortunately, he'd lost weight during his self-imposed incarceration. The slippers were meant to slip over boots and did so with ease. Only the gloves didn't fit.

The Kenkari were extremely upset over this. Hugh shrugged. He could always keep his hands out of sight, hide them behind his back or in the folds of the belted tunic.

Hugh looked in the crystal mirror at himself. His body was rapidly blending into the wall. His hands were the only part of him clearly visible, the only part that was flesh and blood, real.

"How appropriate," he remarked.

Hugh spread out his map of the Imperanon. The Keepers examined it, pronounced it accurate.

"In fact," said Soul in wry tones, "I am amazed at its accuracy. No one but another elf—and then one who has spent considerable time in the palace—would have been able to draw this map."

Hugh shrugged his shoulders, made no comment.

"You and the Lady Iridal enter here, through the main gate that leads into the palace proper," said the Keeper, turning back to the map, tracing the route with his thin finger. "The Lady Iridal will tell the guards that she has been summoned to the palace at such a late hour to 'attend a sick relative.' Such excuses are common. Many members of the royal families maintain their own private homes in the hills surrounding the palace and many return under the cover of darkness to keep private appointments. The gatekeepers are accustomed to such trysts and will most assuredly let the lady in without difficulty."

"Wouldn't her weesham be with her?" asked the Book worriedly.

"By rights," the Soul admitted, "but members of the royal family have been known to sneak away from their weesham, especially when looking forward to a night of stolen pleasure.

"While the guards are talking to Lady Iridal, you, sir, will remain hidden in the shadows. You may slip past the guards when the gate is opened. Getting inside will be the easy part, I am afraid. As you can see, the palace is enormous. It contains hundreds of rooms, on numerous levels. The child could be held anywhere. But one of the weesham, who was in the palace a short time ago, told me that a human child had been given a room just off the Imperial Garden. That could be in any one of these suites located here—"

"I know where he is," said Iridal, in a low voice.

The Keepers were silent. Hugh straightened from bending over the map, regarded her with a dark frown.

"How?" he asked in a tone that implied he already knew—and wasn't going to like—her answer.

"My son told me," she said, lifting her head, meeting his eyes. She reached into the bodice of her elven dress, withdrew a hawk feather attached to a leather thong and held it in her hand. "He sent me this. I've been in contact with him."

"Damn!" Hugh growled. "I suppose he knows we're coming?"

"Of course. How else could he be ready?" Iridal was defensive. "I know what you're thinking, that we don't dare trust him—"

"I can't imagine what would give you that idea!" Hugh sneered.

Iridal flushed in anger. "But you're wrong. He's frightened. He wants to get away. That man Haplo was the one who turned him over to the elves. This has all been Haplo's idea. He and this lord of his—a terrible old man called Xar—want the war to continue. They don't want peace."

"Xar, Haplo. Strange names. Who are these people?"

"They are Patryns, Keeper," said Iridal, turning to the Kenkari.

"Patryns!" The Kenkari stared at her, stared at each other. "The ancient enemy of the Sartan?"

"Yes," said Iridal, growing calmer.

"How is that possible? According to their records left behind, the Sartan removed their enemy before bringing us to Arianus."

"I don't know how it's possible. I only know that the Patryns weren't destroyed. Alfred told me about it, but I'm afraid I didn't understand very much of what he said. The Patryns have been in prison, or something like that. Now they're back and they want to conquer the world, take it for themselves."

She turned to Hugh. "We must rescue Bane, but without Haplo's knowledge. That shouldn't be difficult. My son tells me that Haplo is being held by the Unseen, in some sort of dungeon. I looked, but I can't find them located on the map—"

"No," said the Keeper, "they wouldn't be. Not even the very clever person who drew this map could know where the dungeons of the Unseen are located. But does this present a problem, sir?"

"I hope not. For all our sakes," Hugh said coldly. He bent over the map. "Now, let's say we've got the kid, no trouble. What's the best way out?"

"Patryns," murmured the Soul in awe. "What are we coming to? The end of the world . . ."

"Keeper," Hugh urged patiently.

"Forgive me. What was your question? The way out? That would be here. A private exit, used by those who leave with the dawn and want to depart quietly, without bother. If the child was cloaked and wore a woman's bonnet, he might pass for Lady Iridal's handmaid, should anyone see."

"Not good, but the best we can do under the circumstances," Hugh muttered, in an ill humor. "Have you ever heard of an elf named Sang-drax?"

The Kenkari looked at each other, shook their heads.

"But that is not unusual," said the Soul. "Many people come and go. Why do you ask?"

"I was told that if we got into trouble, this elf could be trusted."

"Pray such trust will not be needed," said the Soul solemnly.

"Amen," said Hugh.

He and the Kenkari continued to plan, to discuss, to bring up difficulties, dangers, try to address them, solve them, work around them. Iridal ceased paying attention. She knew what she was to do, what part she was to play. She wasn't frightened. She was elated, wished only that time would move more swiftly. Before now, she had not let herself dwell too much on recovering Bane, afraid that something would go wrong. Afraid she would be disappointed again, as she had been in the past.

But now she was so close. She couldn't imagine anything going wrong. She let herself believe the dream was at last coming true. She yearned for her son, for the little boy she had not seen in a year, the little boy lost to her, now found.

Clasping the feather in her hand, she closed her eyes, pictured him in her mind. "My son, I am coming for you. Tonight we will be together, you and I. And no one will ever take you from me again. We will never be separated again."

CHAPTER ♦ 33

THE IMPERANON

ARISTAGON, MID REALM

♦

"MY MOTHER'S COMING FOR ME TONIGHT," SAID BANE, TWIDDLING THE feather he held in his hand. "It's all arranged. I just spoke to her."

"That is excellent news, Your Highness," said Sang-drax. "Do you know the details?"

"She's coming in the front gate, disguised as an elf woman. An illusion spell. Not all that difficult. I could do it, if I wanted."

"I'm certain you could, Your Highness." Sang-drax bowed. "Is the assassin accompanying her?"

"Yes. Hugh the Hand. I thought he was dead," Bane added. He frowned, shivered. "He certainly *looked* dead. But Mother said no, he was only hurt real bad."

"Appearances can be deceiving, Your Highness, especially when Sartan are involved."

Bane didn't understand this, didn't care. His head was filled with his own concerns, plots, and schemes. "You'll tell Count Tretar? Tell him to be ready?"

"I leave this moment on just such an errand, Your Highness."

"You'll tell everyone who needs to know?" Bane persisted.

"*Everyone*, Highness," Sang-drax said, with a bow and a smile.

"Good," said Bane, making the feather spin and twist in his hands.

"Still here?" Sang-drax said, peering in the cell's grate.

"Easy, boy," Haplo said to the dog, who was barking with

such ferocity it had nearly barked itself hoarse. "Don't waste your breath." The Patryn lay on the bed, his hands beneath his head.

"I am truly amazed. Perhaps we misjudged you. We thought you reckless, full of fire and spirit, eager to advance the cause of your people. Have we"—Sang-drax lounged against the cell door —"frightened you into a stupor?"

Patience, Haplo counseled, clenching the hands concealed beneath his head. He's goading you.

"I should have thought," Sang-drax continued, "that by now you would have engineered the female dwarf's escape."

"And Jarre's unfortunately killed while attempting to break out of prison. And the emperor's extremely sorry, but it can't be helped. And the dwarves are extremely sorry, but they'll have to destroy the machine anyway." Haplo settled himself more comfortably. "Go play rune-bone with Bane, Sang-drax. You could probably beat a child at your games."

"The game is going to get interesting tonight, Haplo," said Sang-drax softly. "And you, I think, will be one of the major players."

Haplo didn't move, stared at the ceiling. The dog, standing near its master, had lost its bark but kept up a constant rumbling growl in its chest.

"Bane's going to have a visitor. His mother."

Haplo lay still, kept his eyes focused above him. He was getting to know that ceiling very well by now.

"Iridal is a strong-willed woman. She's not coming to bring her baby cookies and weep over him. No, she's coming with the intent of taking him with her when she leaves. Of spiriting him away, hiding him from you, you bad man. And she'll succeed, I have no doubt. And where will you go to look for dear little Bane? Mid Realm? High Realm? Low? How long will your search take, master? And what will Bane be doing all this time? He has his own plans, as you well know, and they don't include either you or 'Grandfather.' "

Haplo reached out his hand, petted the dog.

"Well, well." Sang-drax shrugged. "Just thought you might be interested in the information. No, don't thank me. I hate to see you bored, that's all. Shall we expect you tonight?"

Haplo made an appropriate remark.

Sang-drax laughed. "Ah, my dear friend. *We* are the ones who invented *that*!" He produced a sheet of parchment, slid it under the cell door. "Just in case you don't know where the boy's room is, I've drawn you a map. The dwarf's room is right down the hall. Oh, by the way, the emperor is refusing to give in to Limbeck's demands. He's going to execute Jarre and send down an army to finish off her people. Such an entertaining man, that emperor. We've really grown quite fond of him."

The serpent-elf made a graceful bow. "Until tonight, master. We do so look forward to the pleasure of your company. The party just wouldn't be the same without you."

Still laughing, Sang-drax sauntered off.

Haplo, fists clenched, lay on the bed and stared at the ceiling.

The Lords of Night drew their cloaks over the world of Arianus. In the Imperanon, artificial suns banished the darkness, flambeaux lit the hallways, chandeliers were lowered from the ceiling of the ballrooms, candelabra flamed in the drawing rooms. The elves ate, drank, danced, and were as merry as possible with the dark shadows of their watching weesham, carrying their little boxes, in attendance. What the geir were doing with the souls they collected now was a subject of whispered speculation, though not at the dinner table. The gaiety was brighter than usual this night. Since the Kenkari had proclaimed their edict refusing to accept any more souls, the mortality rate among young elven royalty had markedly declined.

The parties lasted far into the night, but eventually even the young must sleep . . . or least retire to more private pleasures. The flambeaux were put out, the chandeliers doused and raised back up into the ceilings, the candelabra were dispersed among the guests to aid them in finding their way either home or back to their chambers.

An hour had passed since the last few elves had left the palace, staggering homeward, arm in arm, trilling an obscene song, ignoring the patient and sober weesham who trotted sleepily behind. The main gate was never closed; it was extraordinarily heavy, mechanically operated, and made a terrible screeching sound that could be heard as far away as Paxaua. The emperor, out of bored curiosity, had ordered it shut once. The experience was a dreadful one, it had taken him a cycle to fully recover his loss of hearing.

The gate was not shut, but the guards who patrolled the main entrance were alert and careful, far more interested in the skies than the ground. All knew that the human invasion force, when it came, would come from the air. Lookouts stood on the towers, keeping watch for raiders whose dragons might succeed in breaking through the elven fleet.

Wearing rich and colorful elven clothing—a high-waisted dress, decorated in jewels and ribbons, with puffed sleeves that came to her wrists, and long, flowing skirts of several layers of filmy silk, covered by a cloak of royal blue satin—Iridal slipped out of the shadows of the Imperanon's walls and walked rapidly to the guardhouse that stood just inside the main gate.

Guards making their rounds on the walls above gave her a swift, cursory glance and dismissed her from their thoughts. Those standing inside the main gate eyed her, but made no move to accost her, leaving that to the porter.

He opened the door, in response to the knock.

"How may I assist you, my lady?"

Iridal could barely hear him above the blood surging in her ears. Her heart beat rapidly. She was almost faint from it, yet it didn't seem to be working properly—didn't seem to be pumping blood to her limbs. Her hands were ice cold and her feet almost too numb to walk.

The guard's casual response and uninterested gaze gave her confidence, however. The illusion was working. He did not see a human woman clad in elven clothes that were too small, fit too tight. He saw an elf maiden with delicate features, almond eyes, porcelain skin.

"I wish to enter the palace," said Iridal faintly, in elven, hoping her fear would be mistaken for maidenly confusion.

"Your business?" the porter asked crisply.

"I . . . that is . . . my aunt is very sick. I've been summoned to her bedside."

Several of the guards, standing nearby, looked at each other with sly grins; one made a whispered comment having to do with surprises that lurked between the sheets belonging to "sick aunts." Iridal, hearing the whispers if not the words, thought it in character to draw herself up, favor the offender with an imperious stare from the confines of her satin-lined hood. And, in doing so, she flashed a quick, searching glance around the gate area.

She saw nothing, and the heart that had beat too rapidly before now seemed to stop altogether. She wished desperately she knew where Hugh was, what he was doing. Perhaps he was—even now—stealing inside the gate, underneath the long noses of the elven guards. It took all Iridal's willpower to keep from looking for him, hoping to catch even the slightest glimpse of movement in the torchlight, hear the tiniest sound. But Hugh was a master of stealthy movement, had adapted himself swiftly and completely to the chameleonlike costume of the Unseen. The Kenkari had been impressed.

The whispering behind Iridal hushed. She was forced to turn her attention back to the porter.

"Have you a pass, my lady?"

She had, written out by the Kenkari. She presented it. All was in order. He handed it back.

"Your aunt's name?"

Iridal supplied it. The Kenkari had supplied her.

The porter disappeared into his guardhouse, wrote the name down in a book kept for the purpose. Iridal might have been worried by this, fearing he would check on her, but the Kenkari had assured her that this was a formality. The porter would have been hard pressed checking up on the whereabouts of the hundreds who came and went during a single nighttime.

"You may enter, my lady. I trust your aunt's health improves," said the porter politely.

"Thank you," Iridal replied and swept past him, beneath the massive gate and the towering walls.

The footsteps of the guards echoed on ramparts above her. She was daunted by the immensity of the Imperanon, which was enormous beyond anything she could have imagined. The main building towered above her, blotting the mountaintops from sight. Innumerable wings branched off from it, wrapped around the base of the mountain.

Iridal thought of the vast numbers of guards patrolling the palace, imagined them all to be standing outside her son's room, and suddenly her task appeared hopeless. How could she have ever dreamed they would succeed?

We will, she told herself. We have to.

Firmly suppressing her doubts, she kept walking. Hugh had warned her not to hesitate. She had to appear as if she knew where she was going. Her steps did not falter, not even when a passing elven soldier, catching a glimpse of her face by torchlight, informed her that he was off duty in an hour, if she cared to wait.

Keeping the map well in mind, Iridal veered to her right, bypassing the main building. Her path took her into the part of the royal dwellings set farther back into the mountains. She walked underneath archways, past barracks and various other outbuildings. Turning a corner, she ascended a tree-lined avenue, continued past what had once been splashing fountains of water (a blatant display of the emperor's wealth) but which were now shut off "for repairs." She was growing worried. She couldn't remember any of this from the map. She didn't think she should have come this far, was tempted to turn around and retrace her steps, when she finally saw something she recognized from the map.

She was on the outskirts of the Imperial garden. The garden, whose terraces ran up the mountainside, was beautiful, though not as lush as in past days, before the water had been rationed. It looked exquisite to Iridal, however, and she paused a moment to relax in relief. Apartments for the imperial guests surrounded the garden, a series of eight buildings. Each building had a central door, that provided admittance. Iridal counted six buildings over; Bane was in the seventh. She could almost look to his window. Pressing the feather amulet tightly in her hand, Iridal hastened forward.

A footman opened a door to her knock, asked to see her pass.

Iridal, standing in the open doorway, fumbled for the pass in the folds of her skirt, dropped it.

The footman bent to pick it up.

Iridal felt, or thought she did, the hem of her gown stir, as though someone had crept by her, slipping through the narrow confines of the open door. She took back the pass—which the footman did not bother to examine—hoped he had not noticed how her hand shook. Thanking him, she entered the building. He offered the use of a candle boy, to escort her through the halls. Iridal declined, stating that she knew the way, but she did accept a lighted flambeau.

She continued down the long hall, certain that the footman was staring at her the entire distance, though in reality he had gone back to exchanging the latest court gossip with the candle boy. Leaving the main corridor, Iridal ascended a flight of carpeted stairs, entered another corridor that was empty, illuminated here and there by light shining from flambeaux mounted in wall sconces. Bane's room was at the very end.

"Hugh?" she whispered, pausing, staring into the shadows.

"I'm here. Hush. Keep going."

Iridal sighed in relief. But the sigh changed to an inaudible gasp when a figure detached itself from the wall and advanced on her.

It was an elf, a male elf, clad in the uniform of a soldier. She reminded herself that she had every right to be here, guessed that this man must be on an errand similar to the one she'd made up. With a coolness that she would have never believed herself capable of, she drew her hood over her face and was about to sweep past the elf, when he reached out a hand, detained her.

Iridal drew back with a show of indignation. "Really, sir, I—"

"Lady Iridal?" he said to her softly.

Astonished, frightened, Iridal retained her composure. Hugh was nearby, though she trembled to think what he might do. And then she knew. His hands materialized in the air behind the elf. A dagger flashed.

Iridal couldn't speak. Her magical powers failed her.

"It *is* you," said the elf, smiling. "I see through the illusion now. Don't be afraid. Your son sent me." He held up a feather, twin to the one Iridal wore. "I am Captain Sang-drax . . ."

The dagger blade held still, but did not reverse. Hugh's hand raised, made a sign to Iridal that she should find out what the elf wanted.

Sang-drax. She vaguely remembered the name, mentioned as someone they could trust if they were in trouble. Were they in trouble?

"I've frightened you. I'm sorry, but I didn't know of any other way to stop you. I came to warn you that you are in danger. The man with the blue skin—"

"Haplo!" Iridal gasped, forgetting caution.

"Yes, Haplo. He was the one who brought your son to the elves. Did you know that? For his own evil purposes, you may be certain. He has discovered your plan to rescue Bane and he means to stop you. He may be here at any moment. We haven't a second to lose!"

Sang-drax took hold of Iridal's hand, urged her down the hall.

"Quickly, my lady, we must reach your son before Haplo does."

"Wait!" Iridal cried, pulled back.

The dagger's blade still gleamed in the torchlight, behind the elf. Hugh's hand was raised, admonishing caution.

"How could he find out?" Iridal swallowed. "No one knew, except my son—"

Sang-drax's expression was grave. "Haplo suspected something was up. Your son is brave, madam, but brave men have been known to break down under torture—"

"Torture! A child!" Iridal was aghast.

"This Haplo is a monster. He will stop at nothing. Fortunately, I managed to intervene. The boy was more frightened than hurt. But he will be very glad to see you. Come. I will carry the light." Sang-drax took the flambeau from her, drew her forward, and this time Iridal went with him.

The hand and the dagger had both vanished.

"It is a pity," Sang-drax added, "that we have no one to stand guard while we make your son ready for his journey. Haplo might arrive at any moment. But I dared not trust any of my men—"

"You need not concern yourself," Iridal said coolly. "I have a companion."

Sang-drax appeared astonished, impressed. "One as gifted in magic as yourself, apparently. No, don't tell me. The less I know the better. There is the room. I will take you to your son, but then I must leave you two for a moment. The boy has a friend, a dwarf-maid named Jarre. She's due to be executed and, brave child that he is, he will not escape without taking her with him. You remain with your son, I will bring the dwarf."

Iridal agreed. They reached the room at the end of the hall. Sang-drax tapped on the door in a peculiar manner.

"A friend," he said in a low voice. "Sang-drax."

The door opened. The room was dark, an odd circumstance if Iridal had thought about it. But at that moment, she heard a choked cry.

"Mother! Mother, I knew you'd come for me!"

Iridal sank to her knees, held out her arms. Bane flung himself into her embrace.

Golden curls and a tear-wet cheek pressed against hers.

"I'll be back," Sang-drax promised.

Iridal heard him only vaguely, paid little attention as the door shut gently behind herself and her son.

It was night in the dungeons of the Unseen. No lights burned here, except for a single glowlamp provided for the benefit of the soldier on duty. And the light was far from Haplo, at the opposite end of the long row of prison cells. Peering through the grate, he could barely see it—a flicker of brightness that seemed, from this distance, no larger than a candle flame.

No sound broke the stillness, except the occasional hacking cough of some wretch in another part of the prison and a moan from another whose political views had come into question. Haplo was so accustomed to these sounds he no longer heard them.

He stared at the cell door.

The dog stood near, ears up, eyes bright, tail wagging slowly. It sensed something was happening and whined softly, urging its master to action.

Haplo reached out his hand, touched the door that he could barely see in the darkness, felt the iron cold and rough from rust beneath his fingers. He traced a sigil on the door, spoke a word, watched it flare blue, then red. The iron melted in the heat of his magic. Haplo stared at the hole he'd created, visible until the magic's glow faded. Two, three more sigla. The hole expanded, and he could walk out, free.

"Free . . ." Haplo muttered.

The serpents had forced him into taking this action, maneuvered him into it, impelled him, driven him.

"I've lost control," he said. "I've got to get it back. That means beating them at their own game. Which is going to be interesting, considering I don't know the damn rules!"

He glared at the hole he'd made.

Now was the time to make his move.

"A move they're expecting me to make," he said bitterly.

He was alone down here at the end of the cell block. No guards, not even the Unseen in their magical fool-the-eye getup. Haplo had spotted them the first day, been mildly impressed by mensch ingenuity. But they weren't around. They had no need to follow him. Everyone knew where he must go. Hell, they'd given him a map!

"I'm surprised the bastards didn't leave the key in the lock," he muttered.

The dog whined, pawed at the door.

Haplo drew two more sigla, spoke the words. The iron melted away. He stepped through the hole. The dog trotted excitedly after.

Haplo glanced at the runes tattooed on his skin. They were dark, dark as the night that cloaked him. Sang-drax wasn't around, and, for Haplo, no other danger existed in this palace. He walked from the cell, the dog at his heels, walked past the soldier on duty, who didn't notice him.[1]

Haplo walked out of the dungeons of the Unseen.

Hugh the Hand took up his position across the hallway opposite Bane's room. The hall was a T-shape, with the boy's room at the cross-point, the stairs they had come up forming the base at the far end, and another hallway running perpendicular. By posting himself at the cross-point, Hugh could see the stairs and all three sections of hall.

Sang-drax had let Iridal into her son's room, had crept back out, shutting the door. Hugh was careful to remain quiet and unmoving, blending into the shadows and the wall behind him. It was impossible that the captain should see him, but Hugh was disconcerted to note the eyes of the elf shift almost right to him. He was also puzzled to note the eyes had a red cast to them, and he was reminded of Ernst Twist, reminded that Ciang had said something about Twist—a human—recommending this Sang-drax.

And Ernst Twist had just happened to be with Ciang. And Sang-drax had just happened to befriend Bane. Coincidence? Hugh didn't believe in coincidence, any more than he believed in luck. Something was wrong here. . . .

"I'm going to get the dwarf," said Sang-drax, and if it hadn't

---

[1] Haplo's magic wouldn't render him invisible, but it does affect the possibility that people not looking for him wouldn't see him.

been impossible, Hugh might have supposed the elf was talking to him. Sang-drax pointed down the hallway to Hugh's left. "Wait here. Keep an eye out for Haplo. He's coming." The elf turned and ran lightly and swiftly down the hall.

Hugh flicked a glance back down the corridor. He'd just looked that direction, seen no one. The hall was empty.

Except it wasn't empty now.

Hugh blinked, stared. A man was walking down the hall that had been empty seconds before, almost as if the elf's words had magicked him into being.

And the man was Haplo.

Hugh had no difficulty recognizing the Patryn—the deceptive, unassuming, self-effacing air; the calm, confident walk; the quiet watchfulness. When Hugh had last seen Haplo, however, the man's hands had been bandaged.

Now Hugh knew why. Iridal had said something about blue skin, but she had said nothing about the blue skin glowing faintly in the dark. Some type of magic, Hugh supposed, but he couldn't worry about magic now. His main concern was the dog. He'd forgotten about the dog.

The animal was looking straight at him. It wasn't threatening. It appeared to have found a friend. Its ears went up, its tail wagged, it opened its mouth in a wide grin.

"What's the matter with you?" Haplo demanded. "Get back here."

The dog fell back obediently, though it continued to eye Hugh, its head cocked to one side, as if it couldn't quite figure out what this new game was but would go along since they were all old comrades.

Haplo continued to walk up the hall. Though he flicked a glance sideways in Hugh's direction, the Patryn appeared to be looking for something . . . or someone . . . else.

Hugh drew the dagger, lunged forward, moving swiftly, silently, with lethal skill.

Haplo made a slight motion with his hand. "Take him, dog."

The dog leapt, mouth open, teeth flashing. Strong jaws closed over Hugh's right arm, the weight of the animal's body crashing into his knocked him to the floor.

Haplo kicked the dagger out of Hugh's hand, stood over him.

The dog began licking Hugh's hand, wagging its tail.

Hugh made a move to stand.

"I wouldn't, elf," said Haplo calmly. "He'll rip your throat out."

But the beast that was supposed to rip out Hugh's throat was sniffing and pawing at him in friendly fashion.

"Get back," Haplo ordered, dragging the dog away. "I said get back." He stared at Hugh, whose face was hidden by the hood of the Unseen. "You know, elf, if it wasn't impossible, I'd say he knows you. Just who the hell are you, anyway?"

Leaning down, the Patryn took hold of Hugh's mask, ripped it from the man's head.

Haplo staggered backward, the shock a paralyzing one.

"Hugh the Hand!" he breathed, awed. "But you're . . . dead!"

"No, you are!" Hugh grunted.

Taking advantage of his enemy's startlement, Hugh lashed out with his foot, aimed a blow at Haplo's groin.

Blue fire crackled around Hugh. He might have driven his foot into one of the 'lectric zingers on the Kicksey-winsey. The jolt knocked him backward, almost head over heels. Hugh lay stunned, nerves twitching, head buzzing.

Haplo bent over him. "Where's Iridal? Bane knew she was coming. Did the kid know about you? Damn it, of course he did." He answered himself. "That's the plan. I—"

A muffled explosion came from the end of the hall, from behind the closed door of Bane's room.

"Hugh! Help—" Iridal screamed. Her voice was cut off in a strangled choke.

Hugh twisted to his feet.

"It's a trap," warned Haplo quietly.

"Of your making!" Hugh snarled, tensing to fight, though every nerve in his body jumped and burned.

"Not mine." Haplo rose slowly, faced the man calmly. "Bane's."

Hugh stared intently at the Patryn.

Haplo met his gaze. "You know I'm right. You've suspected all along."

Hugh lowered his eyes, turned, moved at a groggy, staggering run for the door.

CHAPTER 34

THE IMPERANON

ARISTAGON, MID REALM

♦

Haplo watched Hugh go, intended to follow him, but first looked around warily. Sang-drax was here somewhere; the runes on the Patryn's skin were reacting to the presence of the serpent. Undoubtedly Sang-drax was waiting in that very room. Which meant that—

"Haplo!" A voice shrieked. "Haplo, come with us!"

Haplo turned. "Jarre?"

Sang-drax had the dwarf maid by the hand, was urging her along down the corridor toward the stairs.

Behind Haplo, wood splintered. Hugh had broken down the door. The Patryn heard the assassin crash into the room with a roar. He was met with shouts, orders in elven, a clash of steel against steel.

"Come with me, Haplo!" Jarre reached out to him. "We're escaping!"

"We dare not stop, my dear," warned Sang-drax, dragging the dwarf along. "We must flee before the confusion ends. I've promised Limbeck I'd see you reached home safely."

Sang-drax wasn't looking at Jarre. He was looking at Haplo. The serpent's eyes gleamed red.

Jarre would never reach Drevlin alive.

Sang-drax and the dwarf ran down the stairs; the dwarf stumbling in her haste, her heavy boots clumping and clattering.

"Haplo!" he heard her howl.

He stood in the hall, swearing in bitter frustration. If he could have, he would have split himself in two, but that was impossible, even for a demigod. He did the next best thing.

"Dog, go to Bane! Stay with Bane!" he commanded.

Waiting only to see the dog take off, dashing for Bane's room —over which an ominous silence had now settled—Haplo started down the corridor in pursuit of Sang-drax.

A trap!

Haplo's warning echoed inside Hugh.

You've suspected all along.

Too damn right. Hugh reached Bane's room, found the door locked. He kicked it. The flimsy tik wood splintered, tore at Hugh's flesh as he dashed through it. He had no plan of attack, there wasn't time to form one. But experience had taught him that reckless, unexpected action could often overwhelm an enemy— especially one complacent with success. Hugh abandoned stealth and disguise, made as much noise, wrought as much havoc as possible.

The elven guards who had been hiding inside the room knew Iridal had an accomplice; her call for help had proclaimed as much. Once they had subdued the mysteriarch, they lay in wait for the man, jumped him when he came smashing through the door. But after a few seconds, the elves began wondering if they were grappling with one man or a legion of demons.

The room had been dark, but, now that the door was shattered, light from the flambeaux in the hallway partially illuminated the scene. The flickering light only added to the confusion, however. Hugh's mask was torn off. His head and hands were visible, his body was still camouflaged by the elven magic. It seemed to the startled elves that a disembodied human head loomed over them. Hands carrying death flashed out of nowhere.

Hugh's slashing dagger caught one elf across the face, stabbed another in the throat. He groin-kicked an elf guard, who crumpled with a groan. A battering fist felled another.

The elves, caught flat-footed by the ferocity of the attack, and not exactly certain if they fought a living man or a specter, the elves fell back in confusion.

Hugh ignored them. Bane—his face pale, eyes wide, curls disheveled—crouched beside his mother, who lay unconscious on the floor. The Hand swept aside furniture and bodies. He had very nearly scooped up both mother and child, seemed likely to walk out with them, when a cold voice spoke.

"This is ridiculous. He's one man. Stop him."

Shamed, shaken from their terror, the elven soldiers returned to the attack. Three jumped Hugh from behind, grasped his flailing arms and pinned them to his side. Another struck him a blow across the face with the flat of his sword, two more carried his feet out from underneath him. The fight was over.

The elves bound Hugh's arms and wrists and ankles with bowstrings. He lay on his side, his knees hunched to his chest. He was groggy and helpless. Blood ran down the side of his head, dripped from a cut mouth. Two elves stood watchful guard over him, while the others went to fetch light and assist fallen comrades.

Candles and flaring flambeaux illuminated a scene of destruction. Hugh had no idea what sort of spell Iridal had cast before she'd been struck down, but black scorch marks were burned into the walls, several ornate tapestries were still smoldering, and two elves with severe burns were being carried from the room.

Iridal lay on the floor, eyes closed, her body limp. But she was breathing. She was alive. Hugh could see no sign of a wound, wondered what had felled her. His gaze shifted to Bane, who knelt beside his mother's unmoving form. Hugh recalled Haplo's words, and, though he didn't trust the Patryn, he didn't trust Bane either. Had the child betrayed them?

Hugh stared at Bane hard. Bane stared back, his face impassive, revealing nothing, neither innocence nor guilt. But the longer the child looked at Hugh, the more nervous Bane grew. His gaze shifted from Hugh's face to a point just above Hugh's shoulder. Suddenly Bane's eyes grew wide, he gave a strangled cry.

"Alfred!"

Hugh almost glanced around behind him, then realized that the boy must be trying to trick him, draw his attention away from Iridal.

But if Bane was putting on an act, he was giving a marvelous performance. He shrank back, held up a warding small hand.

"Alfred! What are you doing here? Alfred, go away. I don't

want you here. I don't need you . . ." The child was babbling, almost incoherent.

"Calm down, Your Highness," said the cold voice. "There is no one there."

Bane swelled in anger. "Alfred's there! Standing right at Hugh's shoulder! I can see him, I tell you—"

Suddenly, the boy blinked, stared, narrow-eyed, at Hugh. Bane gulped, managed a sickly, cunning smile.

"I was laying a trap, trying to find out if this man has an accomplice. You spoiled it. You've gone and ruined it all, Count." Bane tried to look indignant, but he kept his gaze fixed on Hugh, and there was a certain uneasiness in the child's eyes.

Hugh had no idea what Bane was up to, cared less. Some sort of trick. The Hand remembered a time when Bane had claimed to see a Kir monk, standing at Hugh's shoulder.[1] The assassin licked blood from his cut lip, glanced around the room, trying to get a look at the man in charge.

A tall, well-formed elf came into view. Dressed in resplendent clothing, the elf had, by some miracle, emerged unscathed, undamaged from the whirlwind of destruction that had leveled much of the room. The count walked forward, studied Hugh with detached interest, as he might have studied some new form of bug life.

"I am Count Tretar, lord of the Tretar elves. You, I believe, are known as Hugh the Hand."

"Me no speak elf," Hugh grunted.

"No?" Tretar smiled. "But you wear our clothes quite well. Come, come, my dear sir." The count continued to speak elven. "The game is ended. Accept your loss with grace. I know a great deal about you—that you speak elven fluently; that you are responsible for the deaths of several of our people; that you stole

---

[1] *Dragon Wing*, vol. 1 of *The Death Gate Cycle*. Bane, as a clairvoyant, possessed the ability to see images of anything or anyone currently exerting a strong influence on a person. In general, with most people, the images would be symbolic and Bane would likely take them for granted, or use them to increase his hold on people, and thus he would not mention them. This one apparently startled the boy into speaking.

one of our dragonships. I have a warrant for your apprehension—
dead or alive."

Hugh glanced again at Bane, who was now regarding the
Hand with the unblinking, guileless innocence children practice
as their best defense against adults.

Hugh grimaced, shifted his body, ostensibly to ease his dis-
comfort, but in reality to test the strength of his bonds. The bowstrings were tied tight. If he attempted to work them loose, he
would only succeed in causing them to dig deeper into his flesh.

This Tretar was no fool. Dissembling would no longer serve
the assassin. Perhaps he could strike a bargain.

"What's happened to the boy's mother?" Hugh demanded.
"What did you do to her?"

The count glanced at Iridal, quirked an eyebrow.

"Poisoned. Oh, nothing fatal, I assure you. A mild form, delivered by a dart, that will render her unconscious and incapacitated
for as long a period as we deem necessary. It is the only way to
deal with those humans known as 'mysteriarchs.' Other than killing them outright, of—"

The count stopped talking. His gaze had shifted to a dog that
had come wandering into the room.

Haplo's dog. Hugh wondered where the Patryn was, what *his*
role was in all this. But the Hand couldn't guess and he certainly
wasn't going to ask, in case the elves had, by some chance, left the
Patryn out of their calculations.

Tretar frowned, glanced round at his soldiers. "That's the dog
that belongs to His Highness's manservant. What's it doing here?
Take the beast out."

"No!" Bane cried. "He's mine!" The child leapt up and threw
his arms around the dog's neck.

The dog responded by licking Bane's cheek, giving every evidence that it had just discovered a long-lost friend.

"He likes me better than Haplo," Bane announced. "I'm going
to keep him."

The count regarded the pair thoughtfully. "Very well, the animal can stay. Go find out how it got loose," he said, in an undertone to a subordinate. "And what's happened to its owner."

Bane pulled the dog down beside him on the floor. The animal lay there panting, looking around with bright eyes.

The count returned to his perusal of Hugh.

"You've captured me," said the Hand. "I'm your prisoner. Lock me up, kill me. What happens to me doesn't matter. Let the lady and the boy go."

Tretar appeared highly amused. "Really, my dear sir, do you think we are that stupid? A renowned assassin and a powerful wizardess fall into our hands and you expect us to literally throw both of you away. What waste! What folly."

"What do you want, then?" Hugh growled.

"To hire you," said Tretar coolly.

"I'm not for sale."

"Every man has his price."

Hugh grunted, shifted his position again. "There's not enough barls in this slimy kingdom of yours to buy me."

"Not money," said Tretar, carefully dusting the soot off the seat of a chair with a silken handkerchief. He sat down, crossed shapely legs, covered by silken hose, leaned back. "A life. *Her* life."

"So that's it."

Rolling over to lie on his back, Hugh bunched his muscles, tried to burst his bindings. Blood—warm and sticky—ran down his hands.

"My dear sir, relax. You're only damaging yourself." Tretar heaved an affected sigh. "I admit that my men are not particularly impressive fighters, but they do know how to tie knots. Escape is impossible, and we would not be foolish enough to kill you in the attempt, as perhaps you hope. After all, we are not asking you to do anything you haven't done countless times before. We want to hire you to kill. As simple as that."

"Who's the mark?" Hugh asked, thinking he knew.

"King Stephen and Queen Anne."

Hugh glanced up at Tretar, surprised.

The count nodded in understanding. "You expected me to say Prince Rees'ahn, didn't you? We considered it, when we knew you were coming. But the prince has survived several such attempts. It is said that he has supernatural powers guarding him. While I don't necessarily believe in that rubbish, I do think you— a human—would have an easier time killing the human rulers. And their deaths will serve much the same purpose. With Stephen and Anne dead and their eldest child on the throne, the alliance with Rees'ahn will crumble."

Hugh looked grimly at Bane. "So this *was* your idea."

"I want to be king," Bane said, petting the dog.

"And you trust this little bastard?" Hugh said to the count. "Hell, he'd betray his own mother."

"That's meant to be some sort of jest, isn't it? Sorry, but I never could understand human attempts at humor. His Highness, Prince Bane, knows where his best interests lie."

Hugh's gaze went to Iridal. He was thankful she was unconscious. He might almost, for her sake, have wished her dead.

"If I agree to kill the king and queen, you let her go. That's the deal?"

"Yes."

"How do I know you'll keep your end?"

"You don't. But then you haven't much choice except to trust us, do you? However, I will make this concession. The boy will accompany you. He will be in contact with his mother. Through him, you will know she is alive."

"And through him you'll know if I've done what you want."

Tretar shrugged. "Naturally. And we will keep the mother informed as to the condition of her son. She would, I imagine, be devastated if anything happened to the child. She would suffer most cruelly . . ."

"You're not to hurt her," Bane ordered. "She's going to convince all the mysteriarchs to be on my side. She loves me," the child added with an impish smile. "She'll do whatever I want her to do."

Yes, and she wouldn't believe me if I told her the truth. Not that I'll be around long enough, Hugh thought. Bane will see to that. He can't let me live. Once I've served my purpose, I'll be "captured" and executed. But how does Haplo figure in all this? Where is he?

"Well, sir, may we have your answer?" Tretar nudged Hugh with the toe of his polished shoe.

"You don't need an answer," Hugh said. "You've got me and you know it."

"Excellent," Tretar stated briskly. Rising to his feet, he beckoned to several of his men. "Remove the lady to the dungeons. Keep her drugged. Otherwise, she is to be well treated."

The elves lifted Iridal to her feet. She opened her eyes, stared around drunkenly, saw her son and smiled. Then her eyelids fluttered, her head lolled, she slumped in the arms of her captors. Tretar drew her hood up over her head, hiding her features.

"There, if anyone sees you, they will think that the lady is merely suffering from a surfeit of wine. Go on."

The elves half carried, half dragged the stumbling Iridal out the door and down the corridor. Bane, his arm around the dog, watched without interest. Then, face brightening, he turned to Hugh.

"When do we leave?"

"It must be soon," Tretar advised. "Rees'ahn is already at Seven Fields. Stephen and Anne are on their way. We will provide you with whatever you need . . ."

"I can't very well travel like this," Hugh remarked from his place on the floor.

Tretar regarded him attentively, then gave a single, brief nod. "Release him. He knows that even if he did manage to escape us and find his way to the dungeons, the lady would be dead by the time he reached her."

The elves cut Hugh's bindings, assisted him to his feet.

"I'll want a short sword," he said, rubbing his arms, trying to restore the circulation. "And my daggers back. And poison for the blades. There's a certain type. Have you an alchemist? Good. I'll speak to him myself. And money. A lot. In case we have to bribe our way through the lines. And a dragon."

Tretar pursed his lips. "The last will be difficult, but not impossible."

"I'll need traveling clothes," Hugh continued. "And so will the boy. Human. Something peddlers might wear. And some elven jewels. Nothing good. Cheap and gaudy."

"That will not be a problem. But where are your own clothes?" Tretar asked, with a sharp look.

"I burned 'em," Hugh responded calmly.

Tretar said nothing more. The count was longing to find out how, from where, and from whom Hugh had obtained the magical uniform of the Unseen. But he must have guessed that on this point Hugh would keep silent. And perhaps the count had a fair idea anyway. Surely, by now, Tretar's spies would have connected Hugh and Iridal with the two Kir monks who entered Paxaua.

Where would Kir monks go but to their spiritual brothers, the Kenkari?

"I'm taking the dog," Bane announced, jumping excitedly to his feet.

"Only if you can teach it to fly dragonback," Hugh told him.

Bane appeared crestfallen for an instant, then ran off to his bed, commanding the animal to follow.

"Now, this is a dragon," Bane said, pointing at the bed. He patted the mattress. "You get up here . . . That's it. And now sit. No, sit. Hind end *down*."

The dog, tongue out, ears up, tail wagging, entered into the spirit of the game, but appeared uncertain what was required of it and offered a front paw to shake.

"No, no, no!" Bane pressed on the dog's rear portion. "Sit!"

"Charming child," observed Tretar. "One would think he was going on holiday . . ."

Hugh said nothing, eyed the dog. The beast was magical, as he recalled. At least he supposed it must be. He'd seen it do some strange things. It wasn't often separated from Haplo and, if it was, there must be a reason. But Hugh was damned if he could figure out what. Not that it much mattered anyway. There was only one way out of this, as far as Hugh could see.

An elf entered the room, glided over to Tretar, spoke in an undertone. Hugh had sharp hearing.

"Sang-drax . . . all going according to plan. He has the dwarf . . . she will arrive in Drevlin safely, story of escape. Emperor's pride saved . . . Kicksey-winsey saved. Boy can keep the dog . . ."

At first, Haplo had no difficulty following Sang-drax and the dwarf. With her heavy boots, her short legs, which couldn't quite keep up with her supposed rescuer, and her huffing and puffing from the unaccustomed exertion, Jarre was moving slowly and making enough noise for the Kicksey-winsey itself.

Which made it all the more inexplicable when Haplo lost them.

He had followed them down the hall outside Bane's room, down the stairs. But when he reached the bottom of the staircase that opened into another hallway (the same hall through which he'd entered) the two were nowhere in sight.

Haplo, cursing in frustration, ran down the hallway, gaze sweeping the floor, the walls, the closed doors on either side. He was near the end of the hall, almost to the front door, when it occurred to him that something about this was wrong.

Lights were burning, where before it had been dark. No footmen yawned and gossiped in the entryway. He saw, in sudden perplexity, that there wasn't an entryway. Reaching the end of the corridor and what should have been a door, Haplo discovered a blank wall and two more corridors, each of which branched off in opposite directions. These halls were far longer than normal, far longer than would have been possible, considering the size of the building. And he had no doubt now that if he ran down either one, he would find both led to other corridors.

He was in a maze, a maze of the serpent-elf's magical creation, a frustrating, nightmarelike concoction that would have Haplo running endlessly, going nowhere except insane.

The Patryn came to a halt. He reached out groping hands, hoping to touch something solid and real, hoping to dispel the magic. He was in danger, for though it appeared to him as if he were standing in an empty corridor, in reality he might be standing in the center of an open courtyard, surrounded by a hundred armed elves.

This was worse, far worse, than being struck suddenly blind. Deprived of his sight, he could have relied on, trusted his other senses. But now his brain was forced to argue with his senses; the dreamlike quality of the illusion was unnerving. He took a step, and the corridor swayed and slanted. The floor he could feel beneath his feet wasn't the floor he saw with his eyes. Walls slid through his fingers. Yet his fingers touched something solid. He was growing dizzy, disoriented.

He shut his eyes, tried to concentrate on sounds, but that proved unreliable. The only sounds he heard were coming through the dog's ears. He might have been standing in the room with Hugh and Bane.

Haplo's skin prickled, the runes activating. Something, someone was coming up on him. And here he stood, with his eyes shut, flailing about helplessly. Now he heard footsteps, but were they near him or near the dog? Haplo fought down a panicked urge to lash out wildly.

A breath of wind touched his cheek. Haplo turned.

The corridor was still empty, but, damn it, Haplo knew someone was there, someone right behind him. He worked his magic, caused the sigla to shine blue, envelop him in a protective shield.

It would work against mensch. But not against . . .

Pain burst in his head. He was falling, falling into the dream. He hit the ground, the shock jolted him back to conscious awareness. Blood rolled into his eyes, gummed the lids. He struggled to open them, but gave up. It hurt to look into the dazzling light. His magic was unraveling.

Another blow . . .

Gigantic birds—horrible creatures with leather wings, razor-sharp beaks and tearing teeth—attacked Haplo. He tried to escape, but they dove at him, repeatedly. Their wings beat around him. He fought, but he couldn't see them. They had pecked out his eyes.

He tried to run from them, stumbled blindly over the rough and uneven terrain of the Labyrinth. They swooped down on him, talons raked across his naked back. He fell, and when he did, they were on him. He turned bleeding eye sockets toward the sound they made, the raucous cries of glee and chortles of sated hunger.

He struck at them with his fists, kicked at them with his feet. They flew just near enough to tease him, let him wear himself out. And when he collapsed, weak, they perched on his body, dug talons into his skin, tore out great gobs of flesh, and feasted on it and on his pain and his terror.

They meant to kill him. But they would devour him slowly. Pick his bones, eat the still-living flesh. Gorged, they would flap away, leave him to agony and darkness. And when he had regained his strength, healed himself, tried to run, he would hear once more the horrible flapping of their leather wings. And each time they attacked, he lost a little more of his power to fight them.

Lost it, never to regain it.

CHAPTER 35

THE CATHEDRAL

OF THE ALBEDO

ARISTAGON, MID REALM

♦

"Keeper," said the kenkari, the door's assistant. "One of the weesham to see you. Count Tretar's weesham, to be precise."

"Tell him that we are not accepting—"

"Begging your pardon, Keeper, but I have told him just that. He is being very stubborn. He insists on speaking to you personally."

Door sighed, took a sip of wine, dabbed his lips with a cloth and left his repast to go to deal with this most irritating weesham.

He was a long time in speech with him, and, when the conversation ended, Door pondered a moment, summoned his assistant, informed him that he would be in the chapel.

The Keepers of the Soul and of the Book were on their knees before the altar in the small chapel. The Door, seeing them in prayer, entered the room silently, shut the door behind him, and himself went down on his knees, clasped his hands, bowed his head.

The Keeper turned. "You have news?"

"Yes, but I feared—"

"No, you do quite right to interrupt us. Look."

Door lifted his head, stared aghast at the Aviary. It was as if a storm were sweeping through the lush greenery; trees shook and shivered and moaned in a wind that was the clamorous breath of thousands of trapped souls. Leaves trembled in violent agitation, branches cracked and broke.

"What is happening?" Door whispered, forgetting in his fright that he was not supposed to speak unless the Keeper of the Soul had spoken first. Recalling this, he cringed, was about to ask forgiveness.

"Perhaps you can tell us."

Door shook his head, perplexed. "A weesham was just here, the one who told us about the human child, Bane. He received our warning and sends us this news. His charge, Count Tretar, has captured the Lady Iridal and Hugh the Hand. The mysteriarch has been imprisoned in the dungeons of the Unseen. The weesham is not certain what has become of Hugh, but thinks that he and the child, Bane, are being taken away somewhere."

The Keeper of the Soul rose to his feet.

"We must act and act swiftly."

"But why do the dead clamor so?" Door faltered. "What has disturbed them?"

"I do not understand." The Keeper of the Soul looked sorrowful, perplexed. "I have the feeling that we may never, in this life, understand. But they do." He stared into the Aviary, his expression changing to one of awe and wistful longing. "They understand. And we must act. We must go forth."

"Go forth!" The Door blanched. He had never, in the countless years he had opened his door to others, passed through it himself. "Go where?"

"Perhaps," said the Keeper with a pale smile, listening to the silent cries of the dead inside the Aviary, "to join them."

In the chill, dark hour before dawn, the Keeper of the Soul shut the door that led to the Aviary, placed a spell of sealing upon it—a thing that had never happened in all the history of the cathedral. Never once, in that time, had the Keeper of the Soul left his sacred post.

The Keeper of the Door and the Keeper of the Book exchanged solemn glances as the door swung shut, the words of the spell were pronounced. Awed and overwhelmed, they were more frightened by this sudden change in their lives than by the vague danger they felt threatening them. For they read in this small change a portent of far greater change that would affect, for good or evil, the lives of all the peoples of all the races of Arianus.

The Keeper of the Soul left the Aviary, proceeded down the

corridor. He was followed two paces behind—as was proper—by the Keeper of the Door on his left, the Keeper of the Book on his right. None of the three spoke, though Door nearly exclaimed aloud as they passed by the hallway that led to the outer doors, continued moving farther into the heart of the cathedral. He had assumed they must leave the cathedral to reach the Imperanon. But then, he had assumed that was their destination. Apparently, he'd assumed wrong.

He dared not question, since the Keeper of the Soul did not speak. Door could only exchange glances of mute astonishment with Book as they accompanied their master down the stairs to the chambers of the weesham, past study rooms and storage rooms, and entered the great library of the Kenkari.

The Keeper spoke a word. Glowlamps burst into light, illuminated the room with a soft radiance. Door guessed now that perhaps they had come in search of some volume of reference, some text that would provide explanation or instruction.

Inside the library of the Kenkari was the entire history of the elves of Arianus and, to a lesser extent, the history of the other two races, as well. The material on the humans was largest; that on the dwarves extremely slim, for the elves considered the dwarves a mere footnote. Here, to this library, Book brought her work when it was complete, carried down each huge volume as it filled with names, and placed it in its correct order on the ever-expanding shelves that housed the Record of Souls. Here, too, were volumes left behind by the Sartan, though not quite as large a collection as could be found in the High Realm.

The elves could not read most of the works of the Sartan. Few could even be opened, for the mysteries of the rune-magic used by the Sartan, whom the elves had considered to be gods, could not be penetrated. The books were kept as sacred relics, however, and no Kenkari ever entered the library without performing a bow of reverence and remembrance in honor of those who had vanished long ago.

Door was not surprised, therefore, to see the Keeper of the Soul pause before the crystal case that held the various Sartan scrolls and leather-bound volumes. Neither was Book. She and Door emulated their master, made their obeisance to the Sartan, but then stared in astonishment to see the Keeper reach out his hand, rest his thin fingers on the crystal, and speak several words of magic. The crystal melted at his touch. He passed his hand through the crystal, took hold of a slim, rather nondescript-looking volume. It was covered with dust, having been relegated to the bottom of the case.

The Keeper withdrew the book. The crystal re-formed, sealed shut. The Soul regarded the book with an air of wistful sadness and fear.

"I begin to think we have made a terrible mistake. But"—he lifted his head to heaven—"we were afraid." He lowered his head, sighed. "The humans and dwarves are different from us. So very different. Who knows? Perhaps this will help us all understand."

Thrusting the book into the voluminous sleeves of his many-colored robes, the Keeper of the Soul led his mystified followers deeper into the library until they came to stand before a blank wall.

The Soul halted. The expression on his face altered, became grim and angry. He turned and, for the first time since they had started on their expedition, looked directly at the other two.

"Do you know why I have brought you here?"

"No, Keeper," each murmured, quite truthfully, for neither of them had a clue as to why they should be standing staring at a blank wall when great and portentous events moved around them.

"This is the reason," the Soul said, his usually gentle voice stern. He put forth his hand, placed it against a portion of the wall, and shoved.

A section of the wall swung out, pivoting silently and smoothly on a central axis, opened on a crudely fashioned staircase, leading down into darkness.

Both Book and Door spoke at once.

"How long has this been here . . . ?"

"Who could have done . . ."

"The Unseen," answered the Soul grimly. "These stairs go to a tunnel that leads directly to their dungeons. I know, because I followed it."

The other two Kenkari stared at the Keeper in unhappy astonishment, unnerved by the discovery and fearful of its portent.

"As to how long this has been here, I have no idea. I found it myself only a few cycles ago. I could not sleep one night, and sought to compose my mind with study. I came here at a late hour when no one would normally be about. At that, I did not catch them quite by surprise. I saw a flutter of movement out of the corner of my eye. I might have passed it off as nothing more than my eyes adjusting from dimness to bright light, except that it was accompanied by an odd sound that drew my attention to this wall. I saw the outline of the door just disappearing.

"For three nights I hid in the darkness, waited for them to return. They did not. Then, on the fourth, they came back. I saw them enter, watched them leave. I could feel the anger of Krenka-Anris at this sacrilege. Cloaked in her anger, I slipped after them, tracked them to their lair. The dungeons of the Unseen."

"But why?" Book demanded. "Have they dared to spy on us?"

"Yes, I believe so," the Keeper of the Soul responded, his expression grave. "Spying and worse, perhaps. The two who entered the night I watched were searching among the books, appeared particularly interested in those of the Sartan. They sought to break into the crystal case, but our magic thwarted them. And there was something very strange about them."

The Keeper lowered his voice, glanced at the open wall. "They spoke a language I had never heard before in this world. I could not understand what they were saying."

"Perhaps the Unseen have developed a secret language of their own," offered Door. "Similar to thieves' cant among the humans . . ."

"Perhaps." The Soul appeared unconvinced. "It was terrible, whatever it was. I was almost paralyzed with fear, just listening to them talk. The souls of the dead trembled and cried out in horror."

"And yet you followed them," said Door, regarding the Keeper with admiration.

"It was my duty," the Keeper replied simply. "Krenka-Anris commanded it. And now we are commanded to enter once again. And we are to walk their path and use their own dark secrets against them."

The Keeper stood in the doorway, raised his arms. The chill, dank wind that flowed from the cavernous tunnel fluttered the silken folds of multicolored fabric, spread them, lifted them, lifted the slender body of the elf. He dwindled in size until he was no larger than the insect he emulated.

With a graceful sweep of his wings, the Kenkari flew through the door and into the dark tunnel. His two companions took to the air, worked their magic, soared after him. Their robes glowed with a luminous brilliance that lit their way, a brilliance that died, changed to the softest black velvet when they reached their destination.

Unheard, the three entered the dungeons of the Unseen.

Once the Kenkari were inside, the elves resumed their normal shape and appearance, with the exception that their robes remained a velvet black, softer than the darkness that surrounded them.

The Keeper of the Soul paused, looked back at his companions, wondering if they felt what he felt.

By their expressions, they did.

"There is great evil at work here," said the Keeper in a low voice. "I've never experienced the like on Arianus before."

"And yet," said the Book, timidly, "it seems ancient, as if it had always been here."

"Older than we are," agreed the Door. "Older than our people."

"How can we fight it?" the Book asked helplessly.

"How can we not?" responded the Soul.

He advanced down the dark cell block, moving toward a pool of light. One of the Unseen, on night duty, had just departed. The day command was taking over the watch. The guard lifted a ring of keys, prepared to make his rounds to check on the prisoners, see who had died in the night.

A figure stepped out of the shadowy darkness, blocked his path.

The Unseen came up short, put his hand to his sword.

"What the—" He stared, fell back a pace before the advancing black-robed elf. "Kenkari?"

The Unseen removed his hand from the sword hilt. He had recovered from his shock and surprise by now, remembered his duty.

"You Kenkari have no jurisdiction here," he said gruffly, albeit with the respect he considered it expedient to show such powerful magi. "You agreed not to interfere. You should honor that agreement. In the name of the emperor, I ask you to leave."

"The agreement we made with His Imperial Majesty has been broken, and not by us. We will leave when we have what we came for," said the Keeper calmly. "Let us pass."

The Unseen drew his sword, opened his mouth to shout for reinforcements. The Keeper of the Soul raised his hand in the air, and, with his motion, the Unseen's motion was arrested. He stood immobile, silenced.

"Your body is a shell," said the Kenkari, "which you will leave someday. I speak to your soul that lives eternally and that must answer to the ancestors for what it did in life. If you are not completely lost to hatred and dark ambition, aid us in our task."

The Unseen began to shake violently, in the throes of some inner struggle. He dropped his sword, reached for the ring of keys. Wordlessly, he handed the keys to the Keeper.

"Which is the cell of the human wizardess?"

The Unseen's living eyes shifted to a corridor that was dark and appeared unused and abandoned. "You mustn't go down there," he said in a hollow voice that was like an echo in a cavern. "*They* are coming down there. They are bringing in a prisoner."

"Who are they?"

"I don't know, Keeper. They came to us not long ago—they pretend to be elves, like us. But they are not. We all know, but we dare say nothing. Whatever they are, they are terrible."

"Which cell?"

The Unseen trembled, whimpered. "I . . . I can't . . ."

"A powerful fear, to work on the soul," murmured the Keeper. "No matter. We will find her. Whatever happens, your body will neither see nor hear anything until we are gone."

The Keeper of the Soul lowered his hand. The Unseen blinked a little as if he'd just woken from a nap, sat down at the desk, picked up the night log, and began to study it with intense interest.

Taking the keys, the Keeper—his expression grave and stern—advanced down the dark corridor. His companions came after. Footsteps faltered, hearts beat rapidly, chill fear shook the body, its cold penetrating to the bone.

The cell block had been ominously silent, but now, suddenly, the elves heard footsteps and a shuffling sound, as of a heavy weight being dragged across the floor.

Four figures stepped out of a wall at the opposite end of the corridor, appeared to take shape and form from the darkness. They dragged a fifth person, limp and lifeless, between them.

The four looked to all others to be elven soldiers. The Kenkari looked beyond what they could see with the mortal eye. Ignoring the outward facade of flesh, the Keepers searched for souls. They did not find any. And though they could not see the serpents in their true form, what the Kenkari did see they knew as Evil—hideous, nameless, old as time's beginning, terrible as time's end.

The serpent-elves sensed the Kenkari's presence—a radiant presence—and turned their attention from their prisoner. The serpent-elves appeared amused.

"What do you want, old twig?" said one. "Come to watch us kill this man?"

"Perhaps you've come for his soul," said another.

"Don't bother," said a third, with a laugh. "He's like us. He doesn't have one."

The Kenkari could not reply, terror had stolen their voices. They had lived long in the world, longer than almost any other elves, and they had never encountered such evil.

Or had they?

The Keeper of the Soul looked around him, looked at the dungeons. Sighing, he looked into his own heart. And he was no longer afraid. Only ashamed.

"Release the Patryn," he said. "Then leave."

"You know what he is." The serpent-elves seemed surprised. "But perhaps you don't realize how powerful he is? We alone can deal with his magic. It is you who should leave—while you are still able to do so."

The Keeper of the Soul clasped his thin hands together, took a step forward.

"Release him," the Keeper repeated calmly. "And leave."

The four serpent-elves dropped Haplo to the ground, but they did not depart. Abandoning their elven forms, they melted into shapeless shadows. Only their eyes were visible, glowing red. They advanced on the Kenkari.

"Long have you worked for us." The darkness hissed like a thousand snakes. "You have served us well. This is a matter that does not concern you. The woman is human, your bitter enemy. The Patryn plans to subjugate you and all your people. Turn away. Go back and live in peace."

"I hear you now and see you for the first time," said the Keeper of the Soul, his voice trembling, "and my shame is very great. Yes, I served you—out of fear, misunderstanding, hate. Having seen you for what you are, having seen myself, I denounce you. I serve you no longer."

The black velvet of his robes began to shimmer, the multicolors flashed to radiant light. The Keeper lifted his arms and the silken material floated around his thin body. He advanced, summoning his magic, summoning the magic of the dead, calling on the name of Krenka-Anris to come to his aid.

The darkness loomed over him, hideous, threatening.

The Kenkari stood his ground, faced it, unafraid.

The darkness hissed, writhed about him, and slid away.

Book and Door stared, gasped.

"You drove it off!"

"Because I was no longer afraid," said the Soul.

He looked down at the unconscious, seemingly lifeless Patryn. "But I believe we are too late."

CHAPTER 36

THE IMPERANON

ARISTAGON, MID REALM

♦

Hugh the hand was awakened in the dawn by the impression that someone stood over him. He roused himself, found Count Tretar.

"Remarkable," said the count. "What they tell of you is not exaggerated. A true professional, a cold and callous killer, if ever there was one. I fancy there are not many men who could sleep soundly the night before they intend to murder a king."

Hugh sat up, stretched. "More than you might imagine. How well did *you* sleep?"

Tretar smiled. "Rather poorly. But I trust that tomorrow I will rest easier. The dragon has been obtained. Sang-drax has a human friend who is quite helpful in such matters—"

"Name wouldn't happen to be Ernst Twist, would it?"

"Yes, as a matter of fact it is," said the count.

Hugh nodded. He still had no idea what was going on, but the knowledge that Twist was involved didn't surprise him.

"The dragon is tethered on the grounds outside the Imperanon's walls. Couldn't permit the beast inside. The emperor would be in a state of nervous prostration for a week. I'll take you and the boy there myself. His Highness is anxious to get started."

Tretar glanced over at Bane, who was dressed and fidgeting with impatience. The dog lay at the boy's side.

Hugh studied the animal, wondered what was wrong with it. Ears drooping, it looked desperately unhappy. As he watched, he saw it raise its head, stare hopefully at the door, as if expecting a summons.

Then, not hearing anything, it sighed and sank back down. Obviously, the dog was waiting for its master.

It might, thought Hugh, have a long wait.

"Here are the clothes you wanted," Tretar was saying. "We took them off one of the slaves."

"What about my weapons?" asked Hugh. He examined the leather breeches, soft-soled boots, patched shirt, and worn cloak. Nodding in satisfaction, he began to dress.

Tretar regarded him with a disdainful air, his nose wrinkled at the smell.

"Your weapons wait for you in company with the dragon."

Hugh was careful to seem casual, at ease, hide his disappointment. It had been a fleeting hope, a half-formed plan, made before he gave in to exhaustion. He hadn't really expected the elves to give him the weapons. If they had . . .

But, they hadn't.

He shrugged the hope off. One way out, he told himself. Be thankful you have that.

He lifted his pipe from the table by the couch on which he'd slept. He'd persuaded the elves to bring him some stregno, enjoyed a pipe before bed. He tucked the pipe into his belt, indicated he was ready.

"Something to eat?" Tretar offered, gesturing to honey cakes and fruit.

Hugh glanced at it, shook his head. "What you elves eat isn't eating." Truth told, his stomach was clenched so tight he didn't think he could keep anything down.

"Are we finally going now?" Bane demanded grumpily. He tugged at the dog. The animal clambered reluctantly to its feet, stood looking woeful. "Cheer up," the boy ordered, giving the animal a playful smack on the nose.

"How's your mother this morning?" Hugh asked.

"Fine," Bane answered, looking at him with a sweet smile. He toyed with the feather he wore around his neck, held it up for Hugh to see. "She's sleeping."

"You'd tell me that, with that same look on your face, if she was dead," Hugh said. "But I'll know if anything happens to her. I'll know, you little bastard."

Bane's smile froze, twitched at the corners. Then he tossed his curls. "You shouldn't call me that," he said slyly. "You insult my mother."

"No, I don't," Hugh replied. "You're no child of hers. You are your father's creation." He walked past Bane, out the door.

At the count's command, three elven guards, heavily armed, surrounded Hugh the Hand, escorted him down the hall. Bane and Tretar followed, walking side by side.

"You must see to it, Your Highness, that he's publicly charged with the murders, executed before he can talk," Tretar said in an undertone. "The humans must not suspect that we elves have had anything to do with this."

"They won't, my lord," said Bane, two bright red spots burning in his pale cheeks. "Once I have no more use for the assassin, I'll have him executed. And this time, I'll see to it that he *stays* dead. He couldn't come back to life once his body's been cut apart, do you think?"

Tretar had no idea what Bane was talking about, but he didn't suppose it mattered. Looking down at the prince, who was gazing up at the count with limpid eyes and a curve of the rose-tinted lips, Tretar almost found it in his heart to pity the wretches who would so shortly be Bane's subjects.

Count Tretar's own personal dragonship was to carry Hugh and Bane up into the mountains, where the dragon was being held in thrall.

In the Imperial Harbor, another dragonship—one of the large ones that made the journey through the Maelstrom into Drevlin— was being hurriedly made ready to sail.

Human slaves, stumbling over their chains, were herded aboard. Elven mariners swarmed over the ship, testing lines, raising and lowering the sails. The captain ran on board, clutching together the flapping folds of his hastily put-on uniform. A ship's wizard, rubbing sleep from his eyes, dashed on board after.

Tretar's own small dragonship spread its wings, prepared to take to the air. Hugh watched the bustle on board the larger ship until he grew bored, was turning away when his attention was caught by a familiar figure.

Two familiar figures, Hugh amended, startled. The first he recognized as Sang-drax. The second, walking along beside the elf, was—of all things—a female dwarf.

"Jarre," said Hugh, coming up with the name, after some thought. "That girlfriend of Limbeck's. I wonder what the devil she's doing, mixed up in all this?"

His wonder was brief and it passed swiftly, for Hugh wasn't much interested in the dwarf. He stared hard at Sang-drax, however, wished that he might be granted the time to settle his score with the treacherous elf. But that wasn't going to be possible.

The count's ship sailed into the air, headed for the mountain peaks. Tretar was taking no chances with Hugh. An elven soldier stood with his sword at the Hand's throat during the entire short journey, just in case the human might have some desperate plan to seize control of the ship.

The elves needn't have troubled. Any attempt to escape would be futile, endanger Iridal's life, and all for nothing. Hugh realized that now, should have realized it during the night when he was concocting foolhardy, desperate schemes.

There was only one way, one way to alert Stephen to his danger, deliver Bane alive into the king's hands, keep him alive so that the elves wouldn't harm Iridal. The last was chancy, but Hugh had to take the risk. Iridal would want him to take the risk.

Most important, this would open her eyes to the truth.

Hugh had formed his plan. It was firm in his mind. He was confident it would work. He relaxed, at peace with himself for the first time in a long time.

He was looking forward to the night.

To what would be, for him, endless night.

CHAPTER ♦ 37

THE DUNGEONS

OF THE UNSEEN

MID REALM

♦

Haplo closed the circle of his being, gathered his remaining strength, healed himself. This time would be the last, though. He couldn't fight any longer, didn't want to fight any longer. He hurt, he was tired. The battle was futile. No matter what he did, they would defeat him at last. He lay in the darkness, waiting for them to come.

They didn't.

And then the darkness changed to light.

Haplo opened his eyes, remembered he didn't have any eyes. He put his hands to the bleeding sockets, *saw* his hands, and realized he had eyes to see. He sat up, stared at his body. He was whole, unharmed, except for a throbbing pain at the base of his skull and a dizzy sensation brought on by his too-swift movement.

"Are you all right?" came a voice.

Haplo tensed, blinked rapidly to clear his vision.

"Don't be afraid. We are not those who harmed you. They have gone."

Haplo had only to look down at his arm to know the voice spoke the truth. The sigla were dark. He was in no immediate danger. He lay back, closed his eyes.

Iridal walked in a terrible world, a world distorted, where every object was just a little beyond her reach, a world where people talked a language whose words she understood, yet they made no sense. She watched the world happen around her without being able to affect it, control it. The feeling was horrifying, that of existing in a waking dream.

And then all was darkness—that and the knowledge that she was imprisoned and they'd taken her child away from her. She tried to use her magic to free herself, but the words to the spell were hidden by the darkness. She couldn't see them, and she couldn't remember them.

And then the darkness grew light. Strong hands took hold of hers and guided her to stability, to reality. She heard voices and understood the words. She reached out, hesitantly, to touch the person who leaned over her and her hand closed over thin, fragile-feeling bone. Iridal gasped in relief, could have wept.

"Be at peace, Lady," said the Kenkari, "all is well. Rest. Relax. Let the antidote take effect."

Iridal did as she was told, too weak and still too disoriented to do anything else, for the moment, though her first and foremost thought was rescuing Bane. That much had been real, she knew. They had stolen him away from her. But with the Kenkari's help, she would get him back.

Struggling to clear the burning mists from her mind, she heard voices close by—one voice that sounded familiar. Chillingly familiar. Iridal leaned forward to hear better, putting aside irritably the restraining hand of the Kenkari.

"Who are you?" the voice was asking.

"I am the Keeper of the Soul, a Kenkari. This is my assistant, the Keeper of the Door. Though I fear these titles mean nothing to you."

"What happened to the ser—I mean the . . . uh . . . elves who took me prisoner?"

"They are gone. What did they do to you? We thought you were dead. Should you be moving around like this?"

Iridal sucked in a breath. Haplo! The Patryn! The man who had taken her son from her the first time.

"Help me get away!" Iridal said to the Kenkari. "I must . . . He mustn't find me . . ." She tried to stand, but her legs were weak and she fell back.

The Kenkari was perplexed, anxious. "No, Lady, you are not fully recovered . . ."

"Never mind what they did to me," Haplo was saying harshly. "What did you do to them? How did you fight them?"

"We confronted them," replied the Soul gravely. "We faced them without fear. Our weapons are courage, honor, the determination to defend what is right. Discovered late, perhaps," he added with a sigh, "but true to us when we needed them."

Iridal flung the Kenkari aside. She could stand now, weak, but she wouldn't fall. Whatever drug the elves had given her was wearing off rapidly, burned out of her blood by her fear of Haplo's finding her . . . and finding Bane. She reached the cell door and looked out. Almost immediately, she moved back, keeping herself hidden in the shadows.

Haplo was on his feet, leaning against a wall, not four paces from where she stood. He looked haggard, pale, as if he had endured some terrible torment. But Iridal remembered his magical power, knew it was far stronger than her own. She dared not let him find her.

"Thanks for . . . whatever," he was saying to the elves grudgingly. "How long have I been unconscious?"

"It is morning," answered Door.

The Patryn cursed. "You didn't by any chance see an elf and a dwarf, did you? An elf soldier, a captain. And he'd have with him a dwarf, a female."

"We know of whom you speak, but we did not see them. Count Tretar's weesham has informed us. They have taken a dragonship to Drevlin. They left at dawn."

Haplo cursed again. Muttering some excuse, he started to walk around the mensch. He was leaving, chasing after some dwarf and an elf captain. He hadn't said a word about Bane. Iridal held her breath, almost limp with relief.

Go! she urged him silently. Let him go, she urged the elves silently. But, to her dismay, one of the elves put a slender hand on Haplo's shoulder. The other Kenkari blocked Haplo's path.

"How will you go after them?" the Soul said.

"That's my concern," the Patryn returned impatiently. "Look, you elves may not care, but they're going to murder that dwarf, unless I—"

"You reproach us," said the Soul, closing his eyes, bowing his head. "We accept your rebuke. We know the wrong we have done and we seek only to make amends, if that is possible. But relax. You have time, time to heal your injury, for I believe such things are possible for you. Rest now. We must free the mysteriarch."

"Mysteriarch?" Haplo had been going to shove his way past. He stopped. "What mysteriarch?"

Iridal began to call upon the magic, to crumble the stone down around them. She did not want to hurt the Kenkari, after all they had done for her, but they were going to reveal her presence to Haplo and that was something she could not allow . . .

A hand closed over hers. "No, Lady," said the Book, her voice gentle and sad. "We cannot permit it. Wait."

"The Lady Iridal," said Soul, and looked directly at her.

"Bane . . . Bane's mother. She's here?" Haplo followed the Kenkari's gaze.

"Book," called Soul. "Is the Lady Iridal well enough to travel?"

Iridal cast a furious glance at the Kenkari, jerked her hand from the woman's grasp. "What is this—a trap? You Kenkari said you would help me rescue my son! And I find you with this man —a Patryn—one who carried Bane off! I will not—"

"Yes, you will." Haplo came up to her, stood in front of her. "You're right, this is a trap, but you're the one who fell into it. And that son of yours set it."

"I don't believe you!" Iridal clasped her hand over the feather amulet.

The Kenkari stood by, exchanging eloquent glances among themselves, but doing nothing, saying nothing.

"Of course, the amulet," said Haplo grimly. "Just like the one he used to wear when he communicated with Sinistrad. That's how Bane found out you were coming. You told him. You told him you were bringing Hugh the Hand. Bane arranged the capture, set the trap. Right now, he and the assassin are on their way to murder King Stephen and his queen. Hugh's been coerced into going along with the plot because he thinks they'll kill you if he doesn't."

Iridal held onto the feather amulet tightly.

"Bane, my child," she called. She would prove Haplo lied. "Can you hear me? Are you safe? Have they hurt you?"

"Mother? No, I'm fine, Mother. Truly."

"Are they holding you prisoner? I'll free you. How can I find you?"

"*I'm* not a prisoner. Don't worry about me, Mother. I'm with Hugh the Hand. We're riding on a dragon. The dog, too! Though I had quite a bit of trouble getting the dog to jump on. I don't think he likes dragons. But I love them. I'm going to have one of my very own someday." A moment's pause, then the childish voice, slightly altered. "What did you mean about finding me, Mother? Where are you?"

Haplo was watching her. He couldn't possibly hear what Bane was saying; her child's words came to her mind magically through the amulet. But the Patryn knew.

"Don't tell him you're coming!" Haplo said to her softly.

If Haplo is right, then this is all my fault, Iridal realized. Again, my fault. She shut her eyes, blotting out Haplo, blotting out the sympathetic faces of the Kenkari. But she took Haplo's advice, though she loathed herself for doing so.

"I'm . . . I'm in a prison cell, Bane. The elves have locked me in here and . . . they're . . . giving me a drug . . ."

"Don't worry, Mother." Bane sounded cheerful again. "They won't hurt you. No one will. We'll be together soon. It's all right if I keep the dog, isn't it, Mother?"

Iridal removed her hand from the feather amulet, smoothed it out with her fingers. Then she glanced around, took in her surroundings, saw herself, standing in a prison cell.

Her hand began to tremble; tears shimmered, dimmed the defiance in her eyes. Slowly, her fingers released the feather.

"What is it you want me to do?" she said in a low voice, not looking at Haplo, staring at her cell door.

"Go after them. Stop Hugh. If he knows you're free, knows you're safe, he won't murder the king."

"I'll find Hugh *and* my son," she said, her voice shaking, "but only to prove you wrong! Bane has been deceived. Evil men, men like you—"

"I don't care *why* you go, Lady," Haplo interrupted, exasperated. "Just go. Maybe these elves"—he glanced at the Kenkari—"can help you."

Iridal glared at him, hating him. She turned to the Kenkari, regarded them with equal bitterness. "You'll help me. Of course you'll help me. You want Hugh's soul. If I save him, he'll come back to you!"

"That will be his decision," said the Keeper. "Yes, we can help you. We can help both of you."

Haplo shook his head. "I don't need help from—" He paused.

"Mensch?" finished the Soul, smiling. "You will need a means of reaching the dragonship that is carrying the dwarf to her death. Can your magic provide it?"

Haplo looked grim. "Can yours?" he countered.

"I believe so. But first, we must return to the cathedral. Door, you will lead."

Haplo hesitated. "What about the guards?"

"They will not trouble us. We hold their souls in thrall, you see. Come with us. Listen to our plan. You must at least take time to heal yourself completely. Then, if you choose to go on your own, you will be strong enough to face your enemies."

"All right, all right!" snapped Haplo. "I'll go. Stop wasting time."

They entered a dark tunnel, lit only by the iridescent glow of the strange robes worn by the Kenkari. Iridal paid little attention to her surroundings, allowed herself to be led along, neither seeing nor caring. She didn't want to believe Haplo, couldn't believe him. There must be some other explanation.

There had to be.

Haplo kept close watch on Iridal. She did not speak a word to him when they arrived at the cathedral. She did not look at him or acknowledge his presence. She was cold, withdrawn into herself. She answered the Kenkari when they spoke to her, but only in polite monosyllables, saying as little as possible.

Has she learned the truth? Was Bane smug enough to tell her or is the child continuing the deception? Is Iridal continuing to deceive herself? Haplo eyed her, couldn't guess the answers.

She hated him, that much was obvious. Hated him for taking her child from her, hated him for making her doubt her son.

And she'll hate me far more if I'm right, Haplo thought. Not that I blame her. Who knows how Bane would have turned out, if I'd left him with her? Who knows what he would have been like without the influence of his "Grandfather"? But then, we would have never found out about the Kicksey-winsey, discovered the automaton. Funny how things work out.

And it might not have mattered anyway. Bane will always be Sinistrad's son. And Iridal's son, too. Yes, you had a hand in his upbringing, Lady, if only by withholding your hand. You could have stopped your husband. You could have taken the baby back. But you know that now, don't you. And, maybe, after all, there wasn't anything you could have done. Maybe you were too scared.

Scared like I'm scared, scared of going back into the Labyrinth, too frightened to help my own child . . .

"I guess we're not much different, you and I, Lady Iridal," he told her silently. "Go ahead and hate me, if it makes you feel better. Hating me is a hell of a lot easier than hating yourself."

"What is this place?" he asked aloud. "Where are we?"

"We are in the Cathedral of the Albedo," answered the Keeper.

They had emerged from the tunnel, entered what looked to be a library. Haplo cast a curious glance at several volumes bearing what he recognized as Sartan runes. That made him think of Alfred and he recalled another question he wanted to ask Lady Iridal. But it would have to wait until later, if and when they were ever alone. If and when she would speak to him.

"The Cathedral of the Albedo," Haplo repeated, musing, trying to recall where he'd heard that before. Then he remembered. The taking of the elven ship on Drevlin; the dying captain; a wizard holding a box to the captain's lips. The trapping of a soul. Now more of what the Kenkari had said was making sense. Or maybe it was the fact that the pain in his head was subsiding.

"This is where you elves keep the souls of your dead," Haplo said. "You believe it strengthens your magic."

"Yes, that is what we believe."

They had passed through the lower parts of the cathedral, come to the crystal walls that faced out over the sunlit courtyard. All was peaceful, serene, quiet. Other Kenkari padded by on slippered feet, making graceful reverences to the three Keepers as they passed.

"Speaking of souls," said the Keeper. "Where is yours?"

"Where's my *what*?" Haplo couldn't believe he'd heard right.

"Your soul. We know you have one," the Keeper added, mistaking Haplo's incredulous look for one of indignation. "But it is not with you."

"Yeah? Well, you know more than I do," Haplo muttered.

He massaged his aching head. Nothing at all was making sense. The strange mensch—and these were undoubtedly the strangest mensch he'd ever come across—were right. He was definitely going to have to take time to heal himself.

Then, somehow or other, he'd steal a ship . . .

"Here, you may rest."

The Kenkari led the way into a quiet room that appeared to be a small chapel. A window opened onto a beautiful, lush garden. Haplo glanced at it without interest, impatient to complete his healing and be gone.

The Kenkari indicated chairs with a polite and graceful gesture. "Is there anything we can bring you? Food? Drink?"

"Yeah. A dragonship," muttered Haplo.

Iridal slumped into a chair, closed her eyes, shook her head.

"We must leave you now. We have preparations to make," said the Kenkari. "We will return. If you need anything, ring the tongueless bell."

How can I save Jarre? There *has* to be a way. Stealing a ship will take too long. She'll be dead by the time I reach her. Haplo began to pace the small room. Absorbed in his thoughts, he forgot Iridal's presence, was startled when she spoke. He was even more startled when he realized she was answering his thoughts.

"You have remarkable magical powers, as I recall," she said. "You carried my son by magic from the ruined castle. You could do the same here, I suppose. Why don't you just leave on your own, let your magic take you where you want?"

"I could," said Haplo, turning to face her. "If I had a fixed location in my mind—somewhere I knew, somewhere I'd been before. It's hard to explain, but I could conjure up the possibility that I'm there—not here. I could travel to Drevlin, because I've been to Drevlin. I could take us both back to the Imperanon. But I can't take myself to a strange dragonship flying somewhere between here and Drevlin. And I can't take you to your son, if that's what you're hoping for, Lady."

Iridal regarded him coldly. "Then it appears we must rely on these elves. Your head wound has reopened. It has started to bleed again. If you can truly heal yourself, Patryn, I suggest it might be wise to do so."

Haplo had to admit she was right. He was wearing himself out, accomplishing nothing. Sitting down in a chair, he laid his hand upon the injured part of his skull, established the circle of his being, let the warmth of his magic close the crack in the bone, banish the memory of the ripping talons, the tearing beaks . . .

He had drifted into a healing sleep when he was jolted awake by a voice.

Iridal had risen to her feet, was staring at him in awe and fear. Haplo, confused, couldn't think what he'd done to upset her. Then he looked at his skin, saw the blue glow of the runes just starting to fade. He'd forgotten. The mensch on this world weren't used to such sights.

"You *are* a god!" Iridal whispered, awed.

"I used to think so," Haplo said dryly, experimentally rubbing his skull, feeling it whole and undamaged beneath his fingers. "But not anymore. Forces stronger than mine and those of my people exist in this universe."

"I don't understand . . ." Iridal murmured.

Haplo shrugged. "That's the point."

She regarded him thoughtfully. "You've changed from what you were. When you first came, you were confident, in control."

"I thought I *was* in control. I've learned a lot, since then."

"Now, you are more like us—'mensch,' I believe Alfred said is the term you use. You seem . . ." She hesitated.

"Frightened?" Haplo offered grimly.

"Yes," she said. "Frightened."

A small door opened. One of the Kenkari entered, bowed. "All is ready. You may enter the Aviary."

His hand indicated the garden. Haplo was about to protest irritably that this was no time for tea and cookies on the lawn when he caught a glimpse of Iridal. She was staring at the lush green foliage with a kind of horror, shrinking away from it.

"We must go in there?" she asked.

"All is well," said the Kenkari. "They understand. They want to help. You are welcome."

"Who?" Haplo asked the Kenkari. "Who understands? Who's going to help?"

"The dead," answered the Keeper.

Haplo was reminded of the second world he'd visited—
Pryan. Its lush jungles might have been uprooted and dropped
into this crystal dome. Then he saw that this foliage was arranged to look wild. In reality, it was carefully tended, lovingly
nurtured.

He was amazed at the vastness of the dome. The Aviary had
not looked this big seen through the chapel window. A dragonship—two dragonships—could have flown side by side in the
widest part. But what amazed him more, when he stopped to
think about it, was the greenery. Trees and ferns and plants such
as these did not grow in the arid Mid Realm.

"Why," said Iridal, staring around her, "these trees are like
those in the High Realms. Or rather, those that used to be in the
High Realms." She reached out to touch a soft and feathery fern.
"Nothing like this grows there now. All died, long ago."

"Not all. These are from the High Realms," said the Keeper of
the Soul. "Our people brought them to this Realm when they left,
long ago. Some of these trees are so old, I feel young around them.
And the ferns—"

"Forget the damn ferns! Let's get on with this, whatever it is,"
said Haplo impatiently. He was beginning to feel uncomfortable.
When they had first entered, the Aviary had seemed a haven of
peace and tranquillity. Now he sensed anger and turmoil and
fear. Hot winds touched his cheek, stirred his clothing. His skin
crawled and itched, as if soft wings were brushing against
him.

Souls of the dead, kept in here like caged birds.

Well, I've seen stranger things, Haplo reminded himself. I've
seen the dead walk. He'd give these mensch one chance to prove
their usefulness, then he'd take matters into his own hands.

The Kenkari lifted their eyes to the heavens, began to
pray.

"Krenka-Anris, we call to you," said the Keeper of the Soul.
"Holy Priestess, who first knew the wonder of this magic, hear
our prayer and give us counsel. Thus we pray:

Krenka-Anris,
Holy Priestess.

Three sons, most beloved, you sent to battle;
around their necks, lockets, boxes of magic,
wrought by your hand.
The dragon Krishach, breathing fire and poison,
slew your three sons, most beloved.
Their souls departed. The lockets opened.
Each soul was captured. Each silent voice called to you.

Krenka-Anris,
Holy Priestess,
Give us counsel in this, our trying hour,
A force for evil, dark and unholy,
Has entered our world.
It came at our behest. We brought it, we created it,
in the name of fear and hatred.
Now we do penance.
Now we must try to drive evil away.
And we are not strong.
Grant us your help,
Krenka-Anris,
Holy Priestess,
We beseech you.

The hot winds began to blow harder, fiercer, strengthening to an angry gale. The trees swayed and moaned, as if lamenting, branches snapped, leaves rustled in agitation. Haplo imagined he could hear voices, thousands of silent voices, adding their prayers to those spoken aloud by the Kenkari. The voices rose to the top of the Aviary, rose above the trees and greenery.

Iridal gasped and clutched at his arm. Her head was raised, her gaze fixed on the top of the Aviary dome.

"Look!" she breathed.

Strange clouds began to form, to coalesce, clouds woven from the whispering cacophony.

They began to take the form and shape of a dragon.

A nice bit of magic. Haplo was moderately impressed, though he wondered irritably just how the mensch thought a cloud shaped like a dragon was going to help anybody. He was *again* about to ask, about to interrupt, when the sigla on his skin burned in warning.

"The dragon Krishach," said Soul.

"Come to save us," said Book.

"Blessed Krenka-Anris," said Door.

"But it's not real!" Haplo protested, admonishing his own instincts as much as anything else. The sigla on his skin glowed blue, prepared to defend him.

And then he saw that it was real.

The dragon was a creature of cloud and of shadow; insubstantial, yet granted a terrible substance. Its flesh was a pale, translucent white, the white of a long-dead corpse. The dragon's skeleton was visible through the flaccid skin, which hung loosely over the bones. The eye sockets were empty, dark, except for a smoldering flame that gleamed bright one instant, then faded, then shone again, like dying embers being blown to life.

The phantom dragon soared in circles, floating on the breath of the dead souls. Then, suddenly, it swooped down.

Haplo crouched, instinctively, put his hands together to activate the rune-magic.

The Keeper of the Soul turned, regarded him with the large, dark eyes. "Krishach will not harm you. Only your enemies need fear him."

"You expect me to believe that?"

"Krenka-Anris has heard your plea, offers her help in your need."

The phantom dragon landed on the ground near them. It was not still, but remained in constant, restless motion—wings lifting, tail thrashing. The skeletal head wrapped in its cold, dead flesh turned constantly, keeping all in view of its empty, hollow eyes.

"I'm supposed to ride . . . that," said Haplo.

"This could be a trick, to lure me to my death." Iridal's lips were ashen, trembling. "You elves are my enemies!"

The Kenkari nodded. "Yes, you are right, Magicka. But somewhere, sometime, someone must trust enough to reach out his hand to an enemy, though he knows it means that hand could be cut off at the wrist."

The Keeper reached into the voluminous sleeves of his robes, withdrew from them a small, thin, nondescript-looking book. "When you reach Drevlin," he said, offering the book to Haplo, "give this to our brothers, the dwarves. Ask them to forgive us, if they can. We know it will not be easy. We will not be able to easily forgive ourselves."

Haplo took the book, opened it, flipped through it impatiently. It appeared to be of Sartan make, but it was written in the mensch languages. He pretended to study it. In reality, he was plotting his next move. He—

He stared at the book, looked up at the Kenkari.

"Do you know what this is?"

"Yes," the Keeper admitted. "I believe it is what the Evil Ones were searching for when they entered our library. They were looking in the wrong place, however. They assumed it must be among the works of the Sartan, guarded and protected by Sartan runes. But the Sartan wrote it for us, you see. They left it for us."

"How long have you known about it?"

"A long time," said the Keeper sadly. "To our shame, a long time."

"It could give the dwarves, the humans—anyone—tremendous power over you and your people."

"We know that, too," said the Keeper.

Haplo thrust the book into his belt. "It's not a trap, Lady Iridal. I'll explain on the way, if you'll explain a few things to me, such as how Hugh the Hand managed to get himself resurrected."

Iridal looked from the elves to the terrifying phantom to the Patryn who had taken away her son. Haplo's magical defenses had begun to fade as he fought down his own fear and repugnance. The blue glow that illuminated the sigla dimmed and died.

Smiling his quiet smile, he held out his hand to Iridal.

Slowly, hesitantly, she took it.

CHAPTER 38

DEEPSKY

MID REALM

♦

Seven fields, located on the floating continent of Ulyndia, was the subject of legend and song—particularly song, for it was a song that had, in reality, won the famous Battle of Seven Fields for the humans. Eleven years ago, by human time, the elven prince Rees'ahn and his followers heard the song that changed their lives, brought memories of an era when the Paxar elves had built a great kingdom, founded on peace.

Agah'ran—king at the time of the Battle of Seven Fields, now self-proclaimed emperor—had termed Rees'ahn a traitor, driven his son into exile, tried several times to have him killed. The attempts failed. Rees'ahn grew stronger, as the years passed. More and more elves—either swayed by the song or swayed by their own sense of outrage at the atrocities performed in the name of the Tribus empire—gathered around the prince's standard.

The rebellion of the dwarves on Drevlin had proved "a gift of the ancestors" for the rebels, as the elves term it. Songs of thanksgiving had been offered in Prince Rees'ahn's newly built fortress on Kirikari. The emperor had been forced to split his army, fight a war on two fronts. The rebels had immediately redoubled their attacks, and now their holdings extended far beyond the borders of the Kirikari Outlands.

King Stephen and Queen Anne were glad to see the Tribus elves pushed back, but were somewhat nervous to note the rebel elves moving closer to human lands. An elf was an elf, as the saying goes, and who knew but that these sweet-tongued rebels might start singing a different tune?

King Stephen had opened negotiations with Prince Rees'ahn and had, so far, been extremely pleased with what he heard. Rees'ahn not only promised to respect human sovereignty over the lands they already possessed, but offered to open up other continents in the Mid Realm to human occupation. Rees'ahn promised to stop the practice of using human slaves to power his elven dragonships. Humans would be hired to serve on these ships that made the vital water run to Drevlin. As part of the crew, the humans would receive their fair share of the water and be permitted to sell it in the markets of Volkaran and Ulyndia.

Stephen, in turn, agreed to end his own piratical attacks on elven shipping, promised to send armies, wizards, and dragons to fight with the rebels. Together, they would bring about the downfall of the Tribus empire.

Matters had reached this stage in the negotiations when it was decided that the principals should meet face to face, hammer out the final terms and details. If a concerted push was going to be made against the imperial army, it had better come now. Cracks had been discovered in the seemingly impregnable fortress that was the Tribus empire. These cracks, so rumor had it, were spreading, widening. The defection of the Kenkari was the battering ram that would allow Rees'ahn to break down the gates and storm the Imperanon.

Human assistance was vital to the prince's plans. Only by joining together could the two races hope to defeat the strength of the imperial armies. Rees'ahn knew this; so did King Stephen and Queen Anne. They were prepared to agree to terms. Unfortunately, there were powerful factions among the humans who were deeply mistrustful of the elves. These barons were arguing publicly against Stephen's proposed alliance, bringing up old injuries, reminding the humans of how they had suffered under elven rule.

Elves are sneaky and cunning, said the barons. This is all a trick. King Stephen's not *selling* us to the elves. He's *giving* us away!

Bane was explaining the political situation—as the child had heard it from Count Tretar—to a grimly silent and disinterested Hugh.

"The meeting between Rees'ahn and my father, the king, is an extremely critical one. Quite delicate," said Bane. "If anything—the least, little thing—should go wrong, the entire alliance would collapse."

"The king's *not* your father," Hugh said, the first words he'd spoken, almost since their journey had begun.

"I know that," said Bane, with his sweet smile. "But I should get used to calling him that. So I won't slip up, make a mistake. Count Tretar advised it. And I'm to cry at the funeral—not too much, or people won't think I'm brave. But a few tears will be expected of me, don't you think?"

Hugh did not answer. The boy sat in front of him, perched securely on the pommel of the dragon saddle, enjoying the excitement of the ride from the elven lands of Aristagon into the human-occupied territory of Ulyndia. Hugh could not help recalling that the last time he'd made this journey, Iridal—Bane's mother—sat in the very same place, cradled securely in his arms. It was the thought of her that kept him from snatching up Bane and tossing the boy into the open skies.

Bane must have known this, for every once in a while, the boy would twist around, twiddle the feather amulet he wore in Hugh's face.

"Mother sends her love," he would say slyly.

The one drawback to Hugh's plan was that the elves might take out their anger at him on their prisoner, on Iridal. Though now the Kenkari knew she was alive—at least Hugh hoped they knew—perhaps they could save her.

He had the dog to thank for that.

The moment they'd come within sight and smell of the dragon, the dog, yelping wildly, took one look at the beast, tucked its tail between its legs, and fled.

Count Tretar suggested letting the dog go, but Bane had thrown a red-in-the-face, feet-kicking tantrum, screamed he wouldn't go anywhere without the dog. Tretar sent his men in pursuit.

The Hand had taken advantage of the diversion to whisper a few words to Tretar's ever-present weesham. If the weesham was more loyal to the Kenkari than to the count, the Kenkari now knew that Iridal had been taken prisoner.

The weesham had said nothing, but the man had given Hugh

a significant look that seemed to promise he would carry the message to his masters.

It had taken some time for the elves to capture the dog. Muzzling it, they had been forced to wrap its head up in a cloak before they could wrestle it onto the dragon, lash it securely onto the back of the saddle among the packs and bundles.

The dog spent the first half of the flight howling dismally, then—exhausted—it had fallen asleep, for which Hugh was devoutly grateful.

"What's that down there?" Bane asked excitedly, pointing to a land mass floating in the clouds below.

"Ulyndia," said Hugh.

"We're almost there?"

"Yes, Your Highness"—spoken with a sneer—"we're almost there."

"Hugh," said Bane, after a moment of intense thought, to judge by his expression, "when you've done this job for me, when I'm king, I want to hire you to do another."

"I'm flattered, Your Highness," said Hugh. "Who else do you want me to assassinate? How about the elven emperor? Then you'd rule the world."

Bane blithely ignored the sarcasm. "I want to hire you to kill Haplo."

Hugh grunted. "He's probably already dead. The elves must've killed him by now."

"No, I doubt it. The elves couldn't kill him. Haplo's too clever for them. But I think you could. Especially if I told you all his secret powers. Will you, Hugh? I'll pay you well." Bane turned, looked at him directly. "Will you kill Haplo?"

A chill hand twisted Hugh's gut. He'd been hired by all manner of men, to kill all manner of men, for all manner of reasons. But he'd never seen such malevolence, such bitter, jealous hatred in any man's eyes as he now saw in the child's beautiful blue ones.

Hugh couldn't, for a moment, respond.

"There's just one thing you must do," Bane continued, his gaze straying to the slumbering dog. "You must tell Haplo, when he's dying, that Xar is the one who wants him dead. Will you remember that name? Xar is the one who says that Haplo must die."

"Sure," said Hugh, shrugging. "Anything for the customer."

"You'll take the contract, then?" Bane brightened.

"Yeah, I'll take it," Hugh agreed. He'd agree to anything to shut the kid up.

Hugh sent the dragon into a descending spiral, flying slowly, taking his time, allowing himself to be seen by the pickets he knew would be posted.

"There're more dragons coming," Bane announced, peering ahead through the clouds.

Hugh said nothing.

Bane watched for a while, then he turned, frowning, to look suspiciously at the assassin. "They're flying this way. Who are they?"

"Outriders. His Majesty's guard. They'll stop us, question us. You remember what you're supposed to do, don't you? Keep that hood over your head. Some of these soldiers might recognize you."

"Oh, yes," said Bane. "I know."

At least, thought Hugh, I don't have to worry about the kid giving us away. Deceit's his birthright.

Far below, Hugh could see the shoreline of Ulyndia, the plains known as Seven Fields. Usually empty and desolate, the vast expanse of coralite was alive with the movement of men and beasts. Neat rows of small tents formed lines across the fields—the elven army on one side, the human army on the other.

Two large, brightly colored tents stood in the center. One flew the elven flag of Prince Rees'ahn—bearing the emblem of a raven, a lily, and a lark rising, in honor of the human woman, Ravenslark, who had wrought the miracle of song among the elves. The other tent flew King Stephen's flag—the Winged Eye. Hugh marked this tent, noted the deployment of troops around it, calculated his best way in.

He wouldn't have to worry about a way out.

Elven dragonships floated at anchor off the coastline. The humans' dragons were penned further inland, upwind of the elven ships, which used the skins and scales of dead dragons in their making. A live dragon, catching a whiff, would become so enraged that it might overthrow its enchantment, create a damnable row.

The King's Own, Stephen's personal guard, was flying picket detail. Two of the giant battle dragons, each with its own contingent of troops riding on its back, were keeping watch over the ground. The smaller, swift-flying, two-man dragons scanned the skies. It was two of these that had spotted Hugh, were bearing down on him.

Hugh checked his dragon's descent, commanded it to hover in the air, wings barely moving, drifting up and down on the thermals rising from the land beneath it. The dog, waking up, lifted its head and started howling.

Though Hugh's action in drawing up his mount was a sign of peaceful intent, the King's Own was taking no chances. The two soldiers on the lead dragon had bows out, arrows nocked and aimed—one at Hugh, one at the dragon. The soldier riding the second dragon approached only when he was certain that the other guards had Hugh well covered. But Hugh noted a smile cross the man's stern face when he saw—and heard—the dog.

Hugh hunkered down, touched his hand to his forehead in a show of humble respect.

"What is your business?" the soldier demanded. "What do you want?"

"I am a simple peddler, Your Generalship." Hugh shouted to be heard over the dog's howling and the flap of dragon wings. He gestured to the bundles behind him. "My son and I have come to bring wondrous things of much value to Your Generalship's most illustrious and courageous soldiers."

"You've come to fleece them out of their pay with your shoddy merchandise, is what you mean to say."

Hugh was indignant. "No, General, sir, I assure you. My merchandise is of the finest—pots and pans to be used for cooking, trinkets to brighten the pretty eyes of those who wept when you left."

"Take your pots and pans, your son, your dog, and your glib tongue elsewhere, peddler. This is not a market. And I am not a general," the soldier added.

"I know this is not a market," said Hugh meekly. "And if you are not a general it is only because those of authority do not esteem you properly, as they should. But I see the tents of many of my comrades already set up down below. Surely King Stephen would not begrudge an honest man such as myself, with a small son to support and twelve more like him at home, to say nothing of two daughters, the chance to earn an honest living."

The King's Own might have doubted the existence of the twelve sons and two daughters, but he knew he'd lost this round. He'd known it before he started. The news of the peaceful meeting of two armies on the plains of Seven Fields was like the sweet smell of rotting pua fruit—it had drawn every conceivable sort of fly. Whores, gamblers, peddlers, weapons makers, water vendors —all flew to suck up their share. The king could either attempt to drive them away, which would mean bloodshed and bitter feelings among the populace, or he could put up with them, keep an eye on them.

"Very well," said the soldier, waving his hand. "You can land. Report to the overseer's tent with a sample of your wares and twenty barls for your seller's license."

"Twenty barls! An outrage," growled Hugh.

"What did you say, peddler?"

"I said I am most appreciative of your great kindness, General. My son adds his respects. Add your respects to the great general, my son."

Bane, blushing prettily, bowed his head, brought his small hands to his face, as was proper for a peasant child in the presence of illustrious nobility. The soldier was charmed. Waving off the bowmen, he steered his dragon away, went off in pursuit of still another rider, who looked to be a tinker, just approaching.

Hugh released the dragon from its hovering position. They began to descend.

"We did it!" cried Bane gleefully, yanking off his hood.

"There was never much doubt," Hugh muttered. "And put that back on. From now on, you wear it until I tell you to take it off. All we need is for someone to recognize you before we're ready to move."

Bane glowered at him, rebellious blue eyes cold. But the boy was intelligent, he knew what Hugh said made sense. Sullenly, he drew the hood of his shabby cloak up over his head and face. Turning his back, he sat stiff and rigid, chin on his hands, watching the panorama spread out below.

"Probably sitting there imagining all the ways he'll have me tortured," Hugh said to himself. "Well, Your Highness, my last pleasure in this life will be in disappointing you."

He was granted another pleasure, too. The dog had howled itself hoarse and could now only utter a pathetic croak.

Far below the Mid Realm, flying on a different track, the phantom dragon sped swiftly toward its destination—almost too swiftly for the comfort of its passengers. Since neither was concerned with comfort, only with speed, Haplo and Iridal bowed their heads before the wind that whistled shrilly past them, held on tightly to the dragon and to each other, and fought to see for the wind-induced tears that blinded their eyes.

Krishach needed no guidance, or perhaps it obtained its guidance from the minds of its passengers. There was no saddle, no reins. Once the two had reluctantly and cringingly mounted, the phantom dragon leapt into the air and soared through the crystal walls of the Aviary. The walls had not parted, but had melted into a glistening curtain of water, allowing them to pass through with ease. Haplo, looking back, saw the crystal harden again behind them, as if touched by an icy breath.

Krishach flew over the Imperanon. Elven soldiers stared up at them in astonishment and terror, but before any could raise his bow, the phantom dragon had swept past, soared into the open skies.

Haplo and Iridal, leaning close together to be heard, discussed their destination. Iridal wanted to fly immediately to Seven Fields.

Haplo intended to fly to the dragonship.

"The dwarf's life is in the most immediate danger. Hugh plans to kill the king tonight. You'll have time to set me down on Sang-drax's ship, then you can fly to Seven Fields. Besides, I don't want to be left by myself with this demon beast."

"I don't think either of us will be left with it," Iridal said, with a shudder. It took all her nerve and resolve to hold onto the folds of chill, dead flesh, to withstand the dread cold, so horribly different from the warmth of living dragons. "When we no longer need him, Krishach will be more than eager to return to his rest."

Iridal was silent a moment, then looked back at Haplo. Her eyes were softer, sadder. "If I find Bane and take him with me to the High Realms, will you come after him?"

"No," said Haplo quietly. "I don't need him any longer."

"Why not?"

"The book the Kenkari gave me."

"What's in it?" she asked.

Haplo told her.

Iridal listened, first amazed, then perplexed, then disbelieving. "They've known, all this time . . . and done nothing. Why? How could they?"

"Like they said—hate, fear."

Iridal was thoughtful, eyes on the empty sky around them. "And that lord of yours. What will *he* do, when he comes to Arianus? He will come, won't he? Will he want Bane back?"

"I don't know," said Haplo shortly, not liking to think about it. "I don't know what my lord intends. He doesn't tell me his plans. He expects me to obey his orders."

Iridal looked back at him. "But you're not, are you?"

No, I'm not, Haplo admitted, but he admitted it only to himself, saw no reason to discuss it with a mensch. Xar will understand. He'll have to understand.

"My turn to ask questions," Haplo said, changing the subject. "Hugh the Hand looked extremely dead when I saw him last. How'd he manage to come back to life? You mysteriarchs find a way?"

"You know better than that. We are only 'mensch.' " Iridal smiled faintly. "It was Alfred."

I thought as much, Haplo said to himself. Alfred brought the assassin back from the dead. This from the Sartan who swore he would never be caught dead practicing the black art of necromancy. "Did he tell you why he resurrected Hugh?" he asked aloud.

"No, but I'm certain it was because of me." Iridal sighed, shook her head. "Alfred refused to speak of it. He denied he'd done it, in fact."

"Yeah, I can imagine. He's good at denial. 'For every person brought back to life, another dies untimely.' That's what the Sartan believe. And Hugh's restored life means King Stephen's untimely death, unless you can reach him and stop him, stop your son."

"I will," said Iridal. "I have hope now."

They fell silent, the strain of shouting over the noise of the wind was too exhausting. The dragon had flown out of sight of land. Haplo soon lost any point of reference. All he could see was empty blue sky—above them, below, around them. A cloudy haze obscured the sparkle of the Firmament, and they were yet too far away to sight the swirling gray-black clouds of the Maelstrom.

Iridal was absorbed in her own thoughts, her plans and hopes for her son. Haplo remained alert, scanning the skies, keeping constant watch. He was the first to see the black speck beneath them. He focused on it, noted that Krishach turned its empty eye sockets that direction.

"I think we've found them," he said, at last able to make out the curved head, broad wingspan of a dragonship.

Iridal looked down. The phantom dragon's speed had slowed; Krishach began descending in large and lazy spirals.

"Yes, that's a dragonship," Iridal agreed, studying it. "But how will you know if it's the right one or not?"

"I'll know," said Haplo grimly, with a glance at the sigla tattooed on his skin. "Can they see us, do you think?"

"I doubt it. Even if they did, we would appear, from this distance, to be riding an ordinary dragon. And a ship that size wouldn't be alarmed by a single dragon."

The dragonship didn't appear to be alarmed, nor did it look to be in any hurry. It was traveling at a leisurely pace, the broad wings catching and riding the strengthening air currents. Far below, the darkening of the sky presaged the Maelstrom.

He could make out details of the dragonship—see the carving on the head, the painted wings. Tiny figures moved on the deck. And there was an insignia on the ship's hull.

"The imperial crest," Iridal said. "I think this is the ship you seek."

Haplo's skin had begun to itch and burn. The sigla were starting to glow a faint, soft blue.

"It is," he said.

Iridal, hearing the conviction in his voice, glanced at him, wondering how he could be so certain. Her eyes widened at the sight of his glowing skin, but she said nothing, turned back to watch the dragonship.

Surely they must see us now, Haplo thought. And if I know Sang-drax is down there, then he knows I'm up here.

It might have been Haplo's imagination, but he could almost

swear he saw the brightly dressed form of the serpent-elf, standing below, staring up at him. Haplo thought he could hear faint screams, too; cries of someone in terrible pain.

"How close can we get?" Haplo asked.

"Flying an ordinary dragon—not very," Iridal answered. "The wind currents would be too dangerous, to say nothing of the fact that they will soon start firing arrows and perhaps magic at us. But with Krishach. . . ?" She shrugged helplessly. "I doubt if either wind currents, arrows, or magic will have much effect on Krishach."

"Take me as close as possible then," said Haplo. "I'll jump for it."

Iridal nodded, though it was the phantom dragon who responded. Haplo was near enough now that he could see elves pointing upward, some racing to grab weapons or alter course. One elf stood alone, unmoving in the middle of the turmoil. Haplo's skin shone a bright blue, streaked with red.

"It was this evil I sense that made the Kenkari give up the book, wasn't it?" said Iridal suddenly, shuddering. "This is what they encountered in the dungeons."

Krishach was clearly visible to the elves by now. They must have seen that they were not facing an ordinary, living dragon. Many began to cry out in terror. Those who held bows dropped them. Several broke ranks and ran for the hatches.

"But what is this evil?" Iridal cried above the rushing wind, the flap of the dragonship's sails, the horrified shouts of the crew. "What do I see?"

"What we all must see, eventually, if we have the courage to look into the darkness," answered Haplo, tense, ready to jump. "Ourselves."

CHAPTER 39

DEEPSKY

ARIANUS

♦

THE PHANTOM DRAGON SWOOPED CLOSE TO THE ELVEN VESSEL, FAR TOO CLOSE. Krishach's wing clipped one of the guide ropes attached to the sails. The rope snapped, the starboard wing sagged like the broken wing of an injured bird. The elves, stricken with terror at the sight of the monstrous apparition, ran before it. Krishach appeared to be about to smash headlong into the frail ship. Haplo, balancing precariously on the dragon's back, made a convulsive leap for the deck.

His magic cushioned his fall. He hit, rolled, and was on his feet, dreading to hear the crack of the main mast, see the phantom dragon destroy the ship. He ducked involuntarily as the huge, corpse-white belly passed overhead. A chill blast of air, stirred by the pale wings, billowed the remaining sail, sent the ship into a perilous descent. Staring upward, Haplo saw the awful flames burning in the dead skull and, above that, Iridal's terrified face. Krishach, with a hollow roar, swooped overhead.

"Fly on!" Haplo shouted to Iridal. "Go! Quickly."

He didn't see Sang-drax; the serpent-elf had probably gone below decks, to Jarre.

Iridal seemed reluctant to leave him; Krishach hovered in the air near the crippled vessel. But Haplo was in no immediate danger—the elves on deck had either fled below decks or, driven mad with fear, leapt overboard.

Haplo shouted to Iridal, waved his arm. "There's nothing more you can do here! Go find Bane!"

Iridal raised her hand in farewell, turned her face upward. Krishach flapped his wings, and the phantom dragon soared swiftly away to his next destination.

Haplo glanced about. The few elves remaining on the top deck were paralyzed with fear, their minds and bodies numb with shock. The Patryn's flesh glowed, he had arrived on the wings of the dead. Haplo surged across the deck, grabbed one by the throat.

"Where's the dwarf? Where's Sang-drax?"

The elf's eyes rolled, he went limp in Haplo's grip. But the Patryn could hear, below decks, the dwarf's high-pitched, pain-filled screams. Flinging aside the useless mensch, Haplo dashed over to one of the hatch covers, tried to pull it open.

The cover was shut tight, probably being held from below by the panicked crew. Someone down there was shouting orders. Haplo listened, wondering if it was Sang-drax. But he didn't recognize the voice, decided it must be the captain or one of his officers, attempting to restore order.

Haplo kicked at the hatch. He could use his magic to blow it open, but then he'd be faced with fighting his way through a mass of desperate mensch who, by this time, were probably nerving themselves up to do battle. And he didn't have time to fight. He could no longer hear Jarre's cries. And where was Sang-drax? Lying in wait, in ambush . . .

Swearing beneath his breath, Haplo looked around for another way below decks. He was familiar with dragonships, having flown one to the other worlds he'd visited. The ship was beginning to list, the weight of its broken wing dragging it down. Only the magic of the ship's wizard was keeping it afloat.

A gust of wind hit the vessel, sent it lurching. A shudder ran through the ship. It had fallen too close to the Maelstrom, was caught in the stormy coils. The captain must have realized what was happening; his shouts turned to bellows.

"Get those slaves back to work on the port side. Use the lash, if you have to! What do you mean, they've bolted the door to the cable room? Somebody find the ship's wizard. Break down the damn door. The rest of you, get back to your stations or by the ancestors you'll be posted to duty on Drevlin! Where the devil is that blasted wizard?"

The port-side wing had ceased to move, the cable controlling it had gone slack. Maybe the galley slaves were too fear-crazed to perform their tasks. They could, after all, have seen the phantom from out the hawse-hole, located in the hull, through which the cable passed.

The hawse-hole . . .

Haplo ran to the port side, peered over the edge. The Maelstrom was still far below, though much closer than when he'd first boarded the ship. He climbed over the railing, scrambled, slipped, and slid the rest of the way down the side of the hull, catching himself on the cable that guided the port wing.

Clinging to the thick rope, he wrapped his legs around it and crawled forward toward the hawse-hole that gaped in the ship's side. Startled faces—human faces—stared out at him. Haplo kept his gaze fixed on them, not on the drop beneath him. He doubted if even his magic would save him from a fall into the Maelstrom.

Walk the dragon's wing, Hugh the Hand had termed this maneuver, a term that had become synonymous in Arianus with any daring, dangerous feat.

"What is he?" demanded a voice.

"Dunno. Human, from the looks of 'im."

"With blue skin?"

"All I know is he don't have slanty eyes and pointy ears and that makes 'im good enough for me," said a human, in the firm tones of an acknowledged leader. "Some of you men, give him a hand."

Haplo reached the hawse-hole, grasped hold of the strong arms that caught him, pulled him inside. Now he could see why the port-side wing had ceased to function. The human galley slaves had taken advantage of the confusion to slip their bonds, overwhelm their guards. They were armed with swords and knives. One was holding a dagger to the throat of a young elf, dressed in wizard's garb.

"Who are you? Where'd you come from? You was riding the back of that fiend . . ." The humans gathered around him, suspicious, frightened, half-threatening.

"I'm a mysteriarch," said Haplo.

Fear changed to awe, then hope. "You've come to save us?" said one, lowering his sword.

"Yeah, sure," said Haplo. "And I'm here to save a friend of mine—a dwarf. Will you help me?"

"Dwarf?" The suspicion returned.

The man who was their leader shoved his way forward through the pack. He was older than the rest, tall and muscular, with the huge shoulders and biceps of those who spend their lives in harness, working the giant wings of the dragonships.

"What's a damn dwarf to us?" he demanded, facing Haplo. "And what the hell is a mysteriarch doing here?"

Great. All Haplo needed now was mensch logic. Blows were thundering against the door. Wood splintered. The head of an ax sliced through, was jerked free, cracked through again.

"What's *your* plan?" Haplo retorted. "What do you intend to do now that you've seized control?"

The answer was one he might have expected.

"Kill elves."

"Yeah. And while you're doing that, the ship's being sucked into the Maelstrom."

The vessel shuddered, the deck listed precariously. The humans slid and fell, tumbling into the walls and each other.

"Can you fly it?" Haplo shouted, grabbing hold of an overhead beam for support.

The humans looked doubtfully at each other. Their leader's expression grew dark, grim.

"So we die. We'll send their souls to their precious emperor first."

Sang-drax. This was Sang-drax's doing. Haplo had a good idea now how the humans had managed to come by their weapons. Chaos, discord, violent death—meat and drink to the serpent-elf.

Unfortunately, now was not the time for Haplo to try to explain to the humans that they'd been duped by a player in a cosmic game, nor could he very well launch into an exhortation to love those who had inflicted the raw and bleeding lash marks he could see on their backs.

It's too late! Sang-drax's mocking voice whispered in Haplo's brain. *It's too late, Patryn. The dwarf is dead; I killed her. Now the humans will kill the elves, the elves will slay the humans. And the doomed ship hurtles downward, carrying them all to destruction. So it will be with their world, Patryn. So it will be with yours.*

"Face me, Sang-drax!" Haplo cried in anger, clenching his fists. "Fight me, damn it!"

You are no different from these mensch, are you, Patryn? I grow fat on your fear. We will meet—you and I—but in my time.

The voice was gone. Sang-drax was gone. Haplo felt the itch and burn of the runes on his skin start to ease. And there was nothing he could do. He was helpless, as the serpent-elf had said.

The door gave way, burst open. Elves charged inside. The humans jumped to meet them. The man holding the ship's wizard hostage started to draw his knife across the young elf's throat.

"I lied!" Haplo snarled, grabbing hold of the first mensch that came within his grasp. "I'm not a mysteriarch!"

Blue and red sigla from the Patryn's arm flared, enveloped the human's body in dancing runes. The sigla flashed around the terrified man like a whirlwind and, with the speed of lightning, arced from him to the elf he was battling. The jolt sizzled from that elf to a human fighting behind him. Faster than any of them could let go an indrawn breath, the runes jolted through the bodies of every elf and human inside the cable room, sped from there throughout the ship.

There was sudden, frozen silence.

"I'm a god," Haplo announced grimly.

The spell held the mensch immobile, muscles locked in place, movement suspended, killing strokes arrested, blows halted. The knife drew blood from the wizard's cut skin, but the hand that held the blade could not stab it home. Only the eyes of each man remained free to move.

At the sound of Haplo's pronouncement, the eyes of the mensch shifted in their frozen heads, stared at him in mute and helpless fear.

"Don't go anywhere until I get back," he told them, and walked around the unmoving bodies, which glowed with a faint, blue light.

He stalked through the shattered door. Everywhere he went, throughout the ship, the awed eyes of the spell-enthralled mensch followed him.

A god? Well, why not. Limbeck had mistaken Haplo for a god when they'd first met.

The god who wasn't, Limbeck had called him. How appropriate.

Haplo hurried through the eerily quiet ship, which was canting and rocking and shivering as if in terror itself of the black clouds swirling beneath it. He shoved open doors, kicked in doors, peered into rooms, until he found what he was searching for. Jarre, lying in a crumpled, bloody heap on the blood-soaked deck.

"Jarre. Jarre," he whispered, coming to stand by the dwarf. "Don't do this to me." Gently, carefully, he turned her faceup. Her face was battered, bruised, her eyes swollen shut. But he noticed, when he examined her, that her lashes fluttered slightly. Her skin was warm.

Haplo couldn't find a pulse, but, laying his head on her chest, he heard the faint beating of her heart. Sang-drax had lied. She wasn't dead.

"Good girl," he said to her softly, gathering her up in his arms. "Just hang on a little longer."

He couldn't help her now. He couldn't expend the energy needed to heal her and maintain his hold over the mensch on this ship at the same time. He would have to transport her somewhere quiet, somewhere safe.

Haplo emerged from the room, carrying the unconscious, tormented body of the dwarf in his arms. He made his way slowly through the ship. The eyes stared at him, shifted to the pitiful sight of the tortured dwarf maid.

"You heard her screams?" Haplo asked the mensch. "What'd you do, laugh? Can you still hear them? Good. I hope you hear them a long, long time. Not that you've got much time. Your ship is falling into the Maelstrom.

"And what will you do about it, Captain?" he asked the elf who was frozen in midstride, caught dashing off the bridge. "Kill the humans who are the only ones who can work the wings? Yeah, that sounds like a sensible idea to me.

"And you fools," he said to the humans, immobile in the port cable room. "Go ahead, murder the elf wizard, whose magic is the only thing keeping you afloat."

Holding Jarre in his arms, the Patryn began to chant the runes. The spell reversed, the blue glow surrounding the mensch slid off them like water. Flowing through the ship, the magic began to gather around Haplo. The fiery runes formed a circle of flame that encompassed him and the dying dwarf. The flames were blinding, forced the mensch standing near to back away, squint their eyes against the radiant light.

"I'm leaving," he told them. "Feel free to take up where you left off."

CHAPTER ♦ 40

SEVEN FIELDS

MID REALM

♦

THE LORDS OF NIGHT SPREAD THEIR CLOAKS, THE SPARKLE OF THE FIRMAMENT dimmed and died. The soft, shimmering glow of the coralite was lost in the brighter light of hundreds of campfires. Smoke rose, filling the air with a haze that had in it the scents of stews and roasting meat, carried the sounds of laughter and shouting and snatches of song. It was an historic occasion, a night of celebration.

Prince Rees'ahn and King Stephen had just this day announced agreement on the terms of the alliance. Each had expressed heartfelt satisfaction in forging a bond between two races who had, for centuries, been grappling for each other's throats.

There remained now only the formalities—the drawing up of the documents (clerks were working feverishly by the light of glowlamps) and the signing of the documents to make all legal and official. The signing ceremony was to take place one cycle after next, when both sides had taken time to read the documents and King Stephen and Queen Anne had presented them to the barons for consideration.

Their Majesties had no doubt that the barons would vote in favor of signing, though a few malcontents might agree grudgingly, with grumbling and black looks of distrust at the elven side of the camp. Each baron felt the iron grip of either King Stephen or Queen Anne at his throat. Each baron had only to look outside his tent to see the King's Own—strong and powerful and unfailingly loyal—to imagine that very army flying over his barony.

The barons would make no protest aloud but, that night, while the majority celebrated, a few skulked in their tents and muttered to themselves of what would happen should that iron grip ever go slack.

Stephen and Anne knew the names of the dissidents; they had been brought here on purpose. King and queen meant to force the recalcitrant barons to state their "ayes" in public, in full view of their own personal guard and in full view of each other. Their Majesties were aware—or soon would be—of the whisperings going on in camp that night, for the wizard Trian was not present among those celebrating in the royal tent. Had the rebellious barons peered closely into the shadows of their own tents, they would have received a nasty shock.

The King's Own did not relax their vigilance either, though Stephen and Anne had bid their soldiers drink their health and provided wine for the occasion. Those on duty—standing guard around the royal tent—could only look forward to the pleasure.

But those off duty were glad to obey Their Majesties' command. The camp was, therefore, a merry one, with much joyful confusion. Soldiers gathered around the fires, boasting of exploits, exchanging tales of heroism. The vendors were doing a brisk business.

"Jewels, elven jewels, from Aristagon itself," called Hugh the Hand, moving from campfire to campfire.

"You there! Over here!" cried a boisterous voice.

Hugh obeyed, stepped into the firelight.

The soldiers, wine cups in hand, left off their bragging and gathered around the peddler.

"Let's see what you've got."

"Certainly, most honored sirs," said Hugh with a flourishing bow. "Boy, show them."

The peddler's son stepped into the firelight, exhibiting a large tray he held in his hands. The child's face was grimy with dirt and partially obscured by an overlarge hood that hung down over his forehead. The soldiers didn't so much as glance at the boy; what interest did they have in a peddler's son? Their gaze was fixed on the brilliant, glittering baubles.

The dog sat down, scratched and yawned and looked hungrily at a string of sizzling sausages, roasting over a fire.

Hugh played his role well; he'd acted this part before, and he haggled over prices with an ardor and skill that would have made him a fortune had he been a true dealer. As he argued, his gaze darted about the camp, judging his distance from the royal tent, deciding where he would move next.

Hugh closed the deal, dispensed the jewels, pocketed the barls, was loud in his laments that he'd been outbargained.

"Come along, my son," he said grumpily, laying a hand on Bane's shoulder.

The child snapped the box shut and obediently traipsed after. The dog, after one final, wistful glance at the sausages, followed.

The royal tent stood in the center of the camp, in the middle of a large open area. A wide swath of coralite separated it from the tents of the King's Own. The royal tent was large, square-shaped, with a canopy extending out in front. Four guards were posted round the tent itself—one at each corner. Two guards, under the command of a sergeant, stood at the front entrance. And, as luck would have it, the captain of the guard was there also, discussing the day's events with the sergeant in a low voice.

"Come here, boy. Let me see what we've left," Hugh said gruffly for the benefit of any who might have been listening. He chose a shadowed spot, outside of the direct light of any of the camp fires, directly opposite the royal tent's entrance.

Bane opened the box. Hugh bent over it, muttering to himself. He looked intently at Bane, at the child's face that was a white glimmer in the light of the campfires. Hugh searched for any sign of weakness, fear, nervousness.

The assassin might, he realized, with a sudden shock, have been looking in a mirror.

The boy's blue eyes were cold, hard, bright with purpose, empty of expression and feeling, though he was about to witness the brutal murder of two people who had been mother and father to him for ten years. Raising his gaze to Hugh's, the child's sweet lips curved, smiled.

"What do we do now?" he asked, in a breathless whisper of excitement.

It took Hugh a moment to find the words to answer. The feather amulet hanging around the boy's neck was all that prevented the assassin from carrying out the contract he'd made so long ago. For Iridal's sake, her son would live.

"Is the king in the tent?"

"Anne and Stephen are both in there. I know. The royal body-guard wouldn't be posted outside if the king and queen weren't inside. The bodyguard always goes where the king goes."

"Look at the guards standing in front of the royal tent," said Hugh harshly. "Do you know any of them?"

Bane's gaze shifted, eyes narrowed. "Yes," he said after a moment. "I know that one man—the captain. I think I know the sergeant, too."

"Would either of them know you?"

"Oh, yes. Both were in and out of the palace a lot. The captain made me a toy spear once."

Hugh felt the rightness of things, experienced the exhilarating warmth and strange calmness that sometimes came over him when he knew with absolute certainty that fate was working with him, that nothing could go wrong, not now.

Not ever.

"Good," he said. "Perfect. Hold still."

Taking the child's head in his hand, Hugh tilted the face to the light and began to scrub off the dirt and grime he'd smeared over it as a disguise. Hugh wasn't gentle; there wasn't time. Bane winced, but kept quiet.

Work complete, Hugh studied the face—the cheeks pink with the rubbing and excitement, the golden curls falling in a rumpled mass over the forehead.

"Now they should know you." Hugh grunted. "You remember what you're supposed to say, what you're supposed to do."

"Of course! We've been over it twenty times already. Just you do your part," Bane added, with a cold and hostile stare, "and I'll do mine."

"Oh, I'll do my part, Your Highness," Hugh the Hand said softly. "Let's get going, before that captain of yours decides to leave."

He started forward and almost fell over the dog, who had taken advantage of the lull in the action to flop down and rest. The animal leapt back with a muffled yelp. Hugh had stepped on its paw.

"Drat the beast! Shut up!" Hugh told it, glowering. "Tell the damn dog to stay here."

"I won't," cried Bane petulantly, catching hold of the ruff around the dog's neck and hugging it. The dog was exhibiting its hurt paw with a woeful air. "He's mine now. He'll protect me, if I need him. You never know. Something might happen to you, and then I'd be all alone."

Hugh eyed the boy. Bane stared back.

It wasn't worth the argument.

"Come on then," the Hand said, and they started for the royal tent.

Hurt forgotten, the dog trotted along behind.

Inside the tent, Stephen and Anne were taking advantage of the few moments of privacy permitted them on this journey, as they both prepared for a well-earned night's rest. They had just returned from dining with Prince Rees'ahn in the elven camp.

"A remarkable man, Rees'ahn," said Stephen, starting to remove the armor he'd worn for both security and ceremony.

He raised his arms, permitting his wife to unfasten the leather straps that held on the breastplate. Ordinarily, in a military encampment, the king's manservant would have performed the task, but all attendants had been dismissed this night, as they were every night when Stephen and Anne traveled together.

Rumor had it that the servants were dismissed so that the king and queen could battle in private. On more than one occasion, Anne had stormed out of the tent, and many nights, Stephen had done the same. All for show, a show that was about to end. Any disgruntled barons hoping for discord on this night would be sadly disappointed.

Anne unfastened the buckles and untied the ties with expert swiftness, helped Stephen ease the heavy breastplate from his chest and back. The queen came from a clan that had won its fortunes by beating its rivals into submission. She had ridden on her share of campaigns, spent many nights in tents not nearly as fine or comfortable as this one. That had been in her youth, however, before her marriage. She was enjoying this outing immensely, the only drawback being the fact that she'd had to leave her precious baby behind, under the care of the nurse.

"You're right about Rees'ahn, my dear. Not many men—human or elven—would have fought on against the odds he faced," said Anne. She stood with his night robes in her arms, waiting for him to complete his undressing. "Hunted like an animal, half starving, friends turning traitor, his own father sending assassins to murder him. Look, my dear, here's a link broken. You must have it mended."

Stephen lifted the chain mail from his shoulders, tossed it carelessly into a corner of the tent. Turning, he accepted her assistance in dressing for the night (it was not true, again as rumor had it, that the king slept in his armor!). Then he took his wife in his arms.

"But you didn't even look at it," Anne protested, glancing at the chain mail that lay draped on the floor.

"I will in the morning," he said, regarding her with a playful smile. "Or perhaps not. Who knows? I may not put it on. I may not put it on tomorrow, or the day after, or the day after that. Perhaps I shall take the armor and toss it off the edge of Ulyndia. We stand on the brink of peace, my dearest wife. My queen."

Reaching out his hand, he loosened her long coil of hair, fluffed it to fall around her shoulders. "What would you say to a world where no man or woman would ever again wear the accoutrements of war?"

"I would not believe it," she said, shaking her head with a sigh. "Ah, my husband, we are a long way from such a world, even now. Agah'ran may be weakened, desperate, as Rees'ahn assures us. But the elven emperor is cunning and surrounded by loyal fanatics. The battle against the Tribus empire will be long and bloody. And the factions among our own people—"

"Nay, not tonight!" Stephen stopped her words with his lips. "Not tonight. Tonight we will speak only of peace, of a world we may not live to see, but one which we will bequeath our daughter."

"Yes, I'd like that," said Anne, resting her head on her husband's broad chest. "*She* will not be forced to wear chain mail under her wedding dress."

Stephen threw back his head and laughed. "What a shock! I will never get over it. I embraced my bride and thought I was hugging one of my own sergeants! How long was it before you left off sleeping with a dagger beneath your pillow?"

"About as long as you had a taster sample any food I cooked before you ate it," Anne said briskly.

"Our lovemaking had a strange excitement. I was never quite certain I'd live through it."

"Do you know when I first knew I loved you?" Anne said,

suddenly serious. "It was the morning our baby, our little boy, disappeared. We woke to find the changeling in his place."

"Hush, don't speak of such things," said Stephen, holding his wife fast. "No words of ill omen. All that is past, gone."

"No, it isn't. We've heard no word . . ."

"How can we expect to? From elven lands? To ease your mind, I will have Trian make discreet inquiries."

"Yes, please." Anne looked relieved. "And now, Your Majesty, if you will let loose of me, I will brew mulled wine, to keep off the chill."

"Forget the wine," Stephen murmured, nuzzling her neck. "We will relive our wedding night."

"With the soldiers standing right outside?" Anne was scandalized.

"That didn't bother us then, my dear."

"Nor did the fact that you brought the tent down on top of us and my uncle thought you'd murdered me and nearly ran you through with his sword before I stopped him. We're a staid old married couple now. Have your wine and go to bed."

Stephen, laughing, let her go, watched her fondly as she stirred the spices into the warm wine. He came over, sat beside her, lifted a lock of her long hair and kissed it.

"I wager I could still bring the tent down," he said, teasing.

"I know you could," she replied, handing him his wine, looking at him with a smile.

CHAPTER 41

SEVEN FIELDS

MID REALM

♦

"HALT!" CRIED THE KING'S OWN, BRINGING THEIR SPEARS UP, HOLDING THEM in front of two muffled and heavily cloaked strangers—one tall and one short—who had approached too near the ring of steel that surrounded Their Majesties. "Turn aside. You have no business here."

"Yes, I do," a shrill voice cried. Bane dragged off the hood that covered his head, stepped into the light of the sentry fires. "Captain Miklovich! It's me! The prince. I've come back! Don't you recognize me?"

The child poked his head beneath the crossed spears. The captain, at the sound of the voice, turned in frowning astonishment. Both he and the sergeant peered into the night. The firelight reflected off steel swords, spear points, and polished armor, cast strange shadows that made it difficult to see. Two guards started to lay their hands on the squirming child, but—at Bane's words—they hesitated, looked at each other, then glanced back over their shoulders at their captain.

Miklovich came forward, his expression hard and disbelieving. "I don't know what your game is, urchin, but you . . ." The rest of the words vanished in a whistling breath of astonishment.

"I'll be damned," the captain said, studying the child intently. "Could it—? Come closer, boy. Let me get a look at you in the light. Guards, let him pass."

Bane caught hold of Hugh's hand, started to drag the man along with him. The guards brought their spears up, blocking the way. No one was watching the dog, who slipped between the soldiers' legs, stood watching everyone with tongue-lolling interest.

"This man saved my life!" Bane cried. "He found me. I was lost, near starving to death. He took care of me, even though he didn't believe I was really the prince."

"Is it true, Your Worship?" asked Hugh, with the groveling manner and the thick accent of some uneducated peasant. "Forgive me if I did not believe him. I thought he was mad. The village wisewoman said the only way to cure the madness was to bring him here and make him see—"

"But I'm not mad! I am the prince!" Bane glittered with excitement, with beauty and charm. The golden curls glistened, the blue eyes sparkled. The lost child had returned home. "Tell him, Captain Miklovich. Tell him who I am. I promised I'd reward him. He's been very kind to me."

"By the ancestors!" the captain breathed, staring at Bane. "It *is* His Highness!"

"It is?" Hugh gaped in befuddled wonder. Snatching off his cap, he began to twist it in his hands, all the while edging his way inside the steel ring. "I didn't know, Your Worship. Forgive me. I truly thought the boy was mad."

"Forgive you!" the captain repeated, grinning. "You've just made your fortune. You'll be the richest peasant in Volkaran."

"What is going on out there?" King Stephen's voice sounded from inside the tent. "An alarm?"

"A joyous one, Your Majesty!" the captain called. "Come and see!"

The King's Own turned to watch the reunion. They were relaxed, grinning, hands slack on their weapons. Bane had followed Hugh's instructions perfectly, pulled the assassin in with him. Now the child let go of Hugh's sword arm, skipped nimbly to one side, out of the assassin's way. No one was watching the "peasant." All eyes were on the golden-haired prince and on the tent flap. They could hear Stephen and Anne inside, moving hastily toward the entrance. Parents and child would soon be reunited.

The captain walked a little ahead of Hugh—to the assassin's right—a step or two behind Bane, who was dancing toward the tent. The dog trotted along after, unnoticed in the excitement.

The sergeant opened the tent flap wide, began tying it back. He was on Hugh's left.

Excellent, Hugh thought. His hand, beneath the cover of his cloak and loose-fitting peddler's rags, was stealing to his belt, fingers closing around the hilt of a short sword—a poor choice of weapon for an assassin. The wide flat blade would catch the light.

Stephen appeared in the entrance, his eyes blinking, trying to adjust to the glow of the sentry fires. Behind him, clutching her robes around her, Anne stared out over his shoulder.

"What is it—?"

Bane dashed forward, flung out his arms. "Mother! Father!" he cried with a joyous yell.

Stephen paled, a look of horror crossed his face. He staggered backward.

Bane behaved flawlessly. At this point, he was to turn, reach out for Hugh, draw the assassin forward. Then the child was to fling himself out of the way of the Hand's killing stroke. This was how they had rehearsed it.

But Hugh muffed his part.

He was going to die. His life was measured in two, maybe three breaths. At least death would come swiftly this time. A sword through his throat or chest. The guards would not take chances with a man about to murder their king.

"This is the man who saved my life, Father," Bane shrilled. He turned, reached out for the assassin.

Hugh drew his blade, slowly, clumsily. He lifted it high, let the firelight catch it, gave out an attention-getting roar. Then he launched himself at Stephen.

The King's Own reacted swiftly, instinctively. Seeing the flashing blade, hearing the assassin's shout, they dropped their spears and leapt to throttle him from behind. The captain knocked Hugh's sword from his hand, drew his own sword, and was about to grant Hugh the swift death he sought when a huge, furry shape struck him.

Ears up, eyes bright, the dog had been watching the proceedings with interest, enjoying the excitement. Sudden movement, shouting, and confusion startled the animal. Men smelled of fear and tension and danger. The dog was jostled, stepped on. And then it saw the captain lunge at Hugh, about to harm a man the dog knew as a friend.

Jaws closed on the captain's sword arm. The animal dragged the man to the ground. The two tumbled over each other; the dog growling and snarling, the captain trying to fend off the animal's vicious attack.

The King's Own had firm grasp of Hugh. The sergeant, sword in hand, dashed over to deal with the assassin.

"Hold!" Stephen bellowed. He'd recovered from his first shock, recognized Hugh.

The sergeant halted, looked back at his king. The captain rolled on the ground, the dog worrying him like a rat. Stephen, perplexed, arrested by the expression on the assassin's face, came forward.

"What—?"

No one, except Hugh, was paying any attention to Bane.

The child had picked up Hugh's sword from the ground, was advancing on the king, coming up on him from behind.

"Your Majesty—" Hugh cried, struggled to free himself.

The sergeant struck him a blow to the head, with the flat of his sword. Dazed, Hugh slumped in his captor's arms. But he'd drawn Anne's attention. She saw the danger, but was too far away to act.

"Stephen!" she screamed.

Bane gripped the hilt of the sword in both small hands.

"I will be king!" he shouted in fury, and plunged the sword with all his strength into Stephen's back.

The king cried out in pain, staggered forward. He reached his hand around in disbelief, felt his own blood run over his fingers. Bane wrenched the blade free. Stumbling, Stephen fell to the ground. Anne ran from the tent.

The sergeant, stupefied, unable to believe what he'd seen, stared at the child, whose small hands were wet with blood. Bane aimed another stroke, a killing stroke. Anne flung her own body over that of her wounded husband.

Sword raised, Bane rushed at her.

The child's body jerked, his eyes widened. He dropped the sword, clutched at his throat with his hands. He seemed unable to breathe, was gasping for air. Slowly, fearfully, he turned around.

"Mother?" He was strangling, lacked the voice to speak, his lips formed the word.

Iridal stepped out of the darkness. Her face was pale, fixed, and resolute. She moved with a terrible calm, a terrible purpose. A strange whispering sound, as if the night was sucking in its breath, hissed through the night.

"Mother!" Bane choked, sank to his knees, extended a pleading hand. "Mother, don't . . ."

"I'm sorry, my son," she said. "Forgive me. I cannot save you. You have doomed yourself. I do what I have to do."

She raised her hand.

Bane glared at her in impotent fury, then his eyes rolled, he slumped to the ground. The small body shuddered and then lay still.

No one spoke, no one moved. Minds tried to assimilate what had happened, what even now seemed impossible to believe. The dog, sensing the danger had ended, left off its attack. Padding over to Iridal, the dog nudged her cold hand.

"I shut my eyes to what his father was," said Iridal in a quiet voice, terrible to hear. "I shut my eyes to what Bane had become. I'm sorry. I never meant for this to happen. Is he . . . is he . . . dead?"

A soldier, standing near, knelt down beside the child, laid a hand upon Bane's chest. Looking up at Iridal, the soldier nodded wordlessly.

"It is fitting. That was how your own child died, Your Majesty," said Iridal, sighing, her gaze on Bane, her words for Anne. "The baby could not breathe the rarefied air of the High Realm. I did what I could, but the poor thing choked to death."

Anne gave a gasping sob, averted her head, covered her face with her hands. Stephen, struggling to his knees, put his arms around her. He stared in horror and shock at the small body lying on the ground.

"Release this man," said Iridal, her empty-eyed gaze going to Hugh. "He had no intention of killing the king."

The King's Own appeared dubious, glowered at Hugh darkly. The assassin's head was lowered. He did not look up. He had no care for his fate, one way or the other.

"Hugh made a deliberately clumsy attempt at murder," Iridal told them. "An attempt that was meant to reveal my son's treachery to you . . . and to me. He succeeded," she added softly.

The captain, on his feet, dirty and disheveled but otherwise unharmed, cast a questioning glance at the king.

"Do as she says, Captain," Stephen ordered, rising painfully, gasping in agony. His breath came short. His wife had her arms around him, assisting him. "Release this man. The moment he raised his sword, I knew . . ." The king tried to walk, almost fell.

"Help me!" Queen Anne cried, supporting him. "Send for Trian! Where is Trian? The king is grievously hurt!"

"Nothing so terrible as all that, my dear," said Stephen, making an attempt to smile. "I've . . . taken worse than this . . ." His head lolled, he sagged in his wife's arms.

The captain ran to support his fainting king, but halted and turned in alarm when he heard the sentry's voice ring out. A shadow moved against the firelight. Steel clashed. The nervous King's Own snapped to action. Captain and sergeant raised their swords, stepped in front of Their Majesties. Stephen had fallen to the ground, Anne crouched protectively over him.

"Be at peace, it is I, Trian," said the young wizard, materializing out of the darkness.

A glance at Hugh, at the dead child, and at the dead child's mother was sufficient to apprise the wizard of the situation. He did not waste time in questions, but nodded once, took charge.

"Make haste. Carry His Majesty into his tent, shut the flap. Quickly, before anyone else sees!"

The captain, looking vastly relieved, barked orders. Guards carried the king inside. The sergeant lowered the tent flap, stood guard himself outside it. The young wizard took a few moments to speak a few brief words of reassurance to Anne, then sent her into the tent to prepare hot water and bandages.

"You men," Trian said, turning to the King's Own. "Not a word of this to anyone, on your lives."

The soldiers nodded, saluted.

"Should we double the guard, Magicka?" asked the ashen-faced sergeant.

"Absolutely not," Trian snapped. "All must seem as normal, do you understand? The wolf attacks when it smells blood." He glanced at Iridal, standing motionless over the body of her son. "You men, douse that fire. Cover the corpse. No one is to leave this area until I return. Gently, men," he advised, glancing again at Iridal.

Anne appeared at the tent flap, searching anxiously for him. "Trian . . ." she began.

"I'm coming, Your Majesty. Hush, go back inside. All will be well." The wizard hastened into the royal tent.

"One of you, come with me." The sergeant and a guard moved to obey Trian's commands, cover the small corpse. "Bring a cloak."

Hugh raised his head.

"I'll take care of it," he said.

The sergeant looked at the man's haggard face, gray, caked and streaked with blood, oozing from a deep slash that had nearly laid bare his cheekbone. His eyes were almost invisible beneath the jutting, furrowed brow; two tiny points of flame, reflecting from the watch fires, flickered deep within the darkness. He moved to block the sergeant's way.

"Stand aside," the sergeant ordered angrily.

"I said I'll go."

The sergeant looked at the wizardess—pale and unmoving. He looked at the small body lying at her feet, then at the assassin, dark and grim.

"Go ahead then," said the sergeant, perhaps relieved. The less he had to do with any of these fey people, the better. "Is there . . . anything you need?"

Hugh shook his head. Turning, he walked over to Iridal. The dog sat quietly by her side. Its tail wagged gently at Hugh's approach.

Behind him, the soldiers tossed water onto the campfire. There came a hissing sound, a shower of sparks flew into the air. Darkness shrouded them. The sergeant and his men moved nearer the royal tent.

The faint pearl glow of the coralite illuminated Bane's face. His eyes closed—the light of unnatural ambition and hatred doused—he looked like any small boy, fast asleep, dreaming of a day of ordinary mischief. Only the bloodstained hands belied the illusion.

Hugh drew off his own tattered cloak, spread it over Bane. He did not speak. Iridal did not move. The soldiers took up their positions, closed the ring of steel as if nothing had happened. Beyond, they could hear snatches of song; the celebrating continued.

Trian emerged from the tent. Hands folded together, he walked swiftly to where Hugh and Iridal stood, alone, with the dead.

"His Majesty will live," said the wizard.

Hugh grunted, pressed the back of his hand to his bleeding cheek. Iridal shivered all over, lifted her eyes to the wizard.

"The wound is not serious," Trian continued. "The blade missed the vital organs, glanced along the ribs. The king has lost considerable blood, but he is conscious and resting comfortably. He will attend the signing ceremony tomorrow. A night of revelry and elven wine will excuse his pallor and slowness of movement. I need not tell you that this must be kept secret."

The wizard looked from one to the other, moistened his lips. He glanced once, then avoided looking at, the cloak-covered form on the ground.

"Their Majesties ask me to express their gratitude . . . and their sympathy. Words cannot express—"

"Then shut up," Hugh said.

Trian flushed, but he kept quiet.

"May I take my son away with me?" Iridal asked, pale and cold.

"Yes, Lady Iridal," Trian replied gently. "That would be best. If I might ask where—"

"To the High Realms. I will build his funeral pyre there. No one will know."

"And you, Hugh the Hand?" Trian turned his eyes upon the assassin, studied him intently. "Will you go with her?"

Hugh seemed undecided whether to answer or not. He put his hand again to his cheek, brought it back wet with blood. He stared at the blood a moment, unseeing, then slowly wiped the hand across his shirt.

"No," he said at last. "I have another contract to fulfill."

Iridal stirred, looked at him. He did not look at her. She sighed softly.

Trian smiled, thin-lipped. "Of course, another contract. Which reminds me, you were not paid for this one. I think His Majesty will agree that you earned it. Where shall I send the money?"

Hugh bent down, lifted Bane's body, covered with the cloak, in his arms. One small hand, stained with blood, fell limply from beneath the crude shroud. Iridal caught hold of the hand, kissed it, laid it gently back to rest on the child's breast.

"Tell Stephen," Hugh said, "to give the money to his daughter. My gift, for her dowry."

CHAPTER 42

WOMBE, DREVLIN

LOW REALM

♦

Limbeck took off his spectacles for the twentieth time in almost as many minutes and rubbed his eyes. He tossed the spectacles on the table in front of him, plopped down in a chair, and glared at them. He had made them himself. He was proud of them. For the first time in his life, with these spectacles on, he could see clearly —everything sharp and in focus, no fuzzy blobs, no vague and blurry outlines. Limbeck stared at the spectacles, admiring them (what he could now see of them) and loathing them.

He hated them, detested them. And he dared not move without them. They had begun to give him frightful headaches that started in back of his eyeballs, shot what felt like little 'lectric zingers into his head. The 'lectric zingers fired up a giant whumping whammer that marked time by banging against his skull.

But now he could see his people clearly, could see their faces pinched with hunger, drawn with the fear that grew worse every day that passed, every day the Kicksey-winsey refused to move, remained shut down, shut off, silent. And when Limbeck looked at this people through the spectacles, when he saw their despair, he hated.

He hated the elves, who had done this to them. He hated the elves who had dragged off Jarre and were now threatening to kill her. He hated the elves or whatever it was that had killed the Kicksey-winsey. And when he hated, his stomach muscles twisted and lurched up and wrapped around his lungs, and he couldn't breathe for the tightness.

Then he planned grand and glorious wars, and he made very fine and impassioned speeches to his people. And for a while, they hated, too, and they forgot about being cold and hungry and afraid of the terrifying silence. But eventually Limbeck would have to fall silent, and then the dwarves would return to their homes and be forced to listen to their children cry.

Then the pain would be so bad it sometimes made him throw up. When he was finished throwing up, he'd feel his insides slide back into their proper places. He'd remember how life used to be, before the revolution, before he'd asked why, before he'd found the god who wasn't a god, who turned out to be Haplo. Limbeck would remember Jarre and how much he missed her, missed her calling him a "druz" and yanking on his beard.

He knew that the why had been a good question. But maybe his answer to the why hadn't been such a great answer.

"There are too many why's," he muttered, talking to himself (the only person he had to talk to now, most of the other dwarves not liking to be around him much, for which he didn't blame them, since he didn't like to be around himself much either). "And there are no answers. It was stupid of me to ask. I know better now. I know things like: That's mine!, Hands off!, Give me that or I'll split your skull open, and Oh, yeah? Well, you're another!"

He'd come a long way from being a druz.

Limbeck laid his head down on the table, stared morosely through the wrong end of the spectacles, which had the interesting and rather comforting effect of making everything seem far away and small. He'd been a lot happier, being a druz.

He sighed. It was all Jarre's fault. Why did she have to run off and get herself captured by elves? If she hadn't, he wouldn't be in this predicament. He'd be threatening to destroy the Kicksey-winsey . . .

"Which I couldn't do, anyway," he muttered. "These Gegs would never hurt their precious machine. The elves know that. They're not taking my threat seriously. I—" Limbeck stopped in horror.

Gegs. He'd called his people Gegs. His own people. And it was as if he were seeing them through the wrong end of the spectacles—distant, far away, small.

"Oh, Jarre!" Limbeck moaned, "I wish I *was* a druz!"

Reaching up, he gave his own beard a hard and painful yank, but it just didn't have the same effect. Jarre put love into her beard-yanking. She'd loved him when he was a druz.

Limbeck snatched up the spectacles, hurled them on the table, hoping they'd break. They didn't. Peering around nearsightedly, he went on a grim and frantic search for a hammer. He had just picked up what he'd thought was a hammer but which turned out to be a feather duster when a furious pounding and loud, panicked shouting exploded outside his door.

"Limbeck, Limbeck," howled a voice he recognized as belonging to Lof.

Bumbling into the table, Limbeck groped about for the spectacles, stuck them, slightly askew, on his face, and—feather duster in hand—flung the door open.

"Well? What is it? Can't you see I'm busy?" he said in an Important Voice, which is how he generally got rid of people these days.

Lof didn't notice. He was in a pitiable state, his beard sticking out wildly in all directions, his hair standing on end, his clothes every which way. He was wringing his hands, and when a dwarf wrings his hands, matters are desperate. For long moments, he couldn't talk, but could only shake his head, wring his hands, and whimper.

Limbeck's spectacles were hanging from one ear. He took them off, stuffed them in a vest pocket, and patted Lof kindly on the shoulder. "Steady, old man. What's happened?"

Encouraged, Lof gulped and drew a shuddering breath. "Jarre," he managed. "It's Jarre. She's dead. The elves killed her. I . . . I s-s-saw her, Limbeck!" Dropping his head to his hands, Lof gave a harsh sob and began to weep.

It was quiet. The quiet came from Limbeck, bounced off the walls, returned to him. He couldn't even hear Lof crying anymore. He couldn't hear anything. The Kicksey-winsey had long been silent. Now Jarre was silent, forever. It was all so very, very quiet.

"Where is she?" he asked, and he knew he asked the question, though he couldn't hear the sound of his own voice.

"In . . . in the Factree," Lof burbled. "Haplo's with her. He . . . he says she's not dead . . . but I know . . . I saw . . ."

Limbeck saw Lof's mouth moving, forming words. Limbeck understood one—"Factree."

Taking out his spectacles, placing them firmly on his nose and over his ears, Limbeck grabbed hold of Lof. Dragging him along, Limbeck headed for the secret tunnels that led to the Factree.

As he went, he rallied every dwarf he found. "Come with me," he told them. "We're going to kill elves."

Haplo's magic transported him to the Factree, the only place on Drevlin—other than his ship—that he could picture clearly in his mind. He had considered his ship. Once there, he could save Jarre's life, return her to her people, then he could return to his people. He would sail to Abarrach and try, once again, to persuade his lord that the serpents were using him, using them all.

The idea of his ship was in his mind only briefly, before he abandoned it. Sang-drax and the serpents were plotting something—something major, something dire. Their plans for Arianus were going awry. They hadn't expected Haplo or Iridal to escape, they hadn't taken the Kenkari into consideration. They would have to make a move to counter whatever good effect Iridal might be able to achieve in the Mid Realm. Haplo had a good idea what the serpents next move was going to be.

He materialized inside the Factree, near the statue of the Manger. Haplo laid Jarre down gently on the base of the statue and took a swift look around. His skin glowed a faint blue, a residue of the magic expended to bring himself and the dwarf here, but also a warning. The serpents were near. Down below, he guessed, down in their secret caverns.

As for more immediate danger, he was prepared to face the elven soldiers, who were bivouacked in the Factree, prepared to deal instantly with any who might be standing guard duty around the statue. They would be astounded to see him materializing out of nowhere. In that moment of shock, he would subdue them.

But there was no one there. The statue's base had been shut again, covering the tunnel beneath. Elves still moved about the Factree, but they were all gathered at the front of the huge building, as far from the statue as they could get.

The glimmerglamps were dark, this part of the Factree was left to darkness.

Haplo looked up at the benign face of the statue, reflected in the blue light radiating from the Patryn's skin. He saw, in the face, Alfred. "This fear of your people would grieve you, wouldn't it, my bumbling friend?" the Patryn asked. Then the shadows moved, and Haplo saw Samah's stern face beneath the statue's hood. "But *you'd* think their fear a fitting tribute."

Jarre moaned and stirred. Haplo knelt by her side. The statue shielded them from the sight of the elves. Should any happen to look this direction—a possibility he didn't consider likely—they would see only a blue glow, soft and faint, so soft and faint that they would probably think their eyes were deceiving them and discount it.

But other eyes were watching, eyes Haplo hadn't counted on.

"J-Jarre!" gasped a horrified voice.

"Damn!" Haplo swore, and turned.

Two figures crept out of the darkness, emerging from the hole in the floor that led to the dwarves' secret tunnels.

Of course, Haplo realized, Limbeck would have posted spies to keep an eye on the elves. The dwarves could sneak up the ladder, sit in the darkness, watch the elves' movements without running serious risk. The only drawback would be the feeling of fear that flowed from beneath the statue, from the serpents below.

Haplo noted that the dwarves appeared hesitant to approach the statue, were drawn to it by their shock and their worry over Jarre.

"She's all right," Haplo told them, trying to sound reassuring, hoping to prevent panic. One bellow and it was all over. He'd have the entire elven army to cope with. "She looks bad now, but I'm going to—"

"She's dead!" gasped the dwarf, staring. "The elves killed her."

"Limbeck!" said his companion. "Must tell . . . Limbeck."

Before Haplo could say another word, the two had turned and dashed off, trundling across the Factree floor toward the tunnel entrance. He heard their heavy boots clumping down the ladder; they'd forgotten to shut the metal cover.

Fine. Just fine. If he knew Limbeck, Haplo would soon have half the dwarves in Drevlin up here. Well, he'd deal with that when it happened.

Leaning over Jarre, he took both her hands in his, extended

the circle of his being, made her a part of it. The sigla's glow
brightened, traveled from Haplo's right hand to Jarre's left. His
health and strength flowed into her, her pain and torment flowed
into him.

He'd known the pain was coming, was braced to receive it.
He'd experienced the same thing, healing the elf lad, Devon, in
Chelestra. But this was more terrible, the pain was far worse, and
—as if the serpents knew it would reach him eventually—the torment took him back to the Labyrinth.

Again the cruel birds with their razor talons and tearing beaks
gorged on his flesh, tore at his vitals, beat at him with their leath-
ery wings. Haplo grit his teeth, closed his eyes, told himself over
and over it was not real, and held fast to Jarre.

And some of her strength—the strength and courage that had
kept her alive—flowed to him.

Haplo gasped and shuddered, wanted desperately to die, the
pain and fear were so bad. But firm, strong hands held his and a
voice was saying, "It's all right. They're gone. I'm here."

The voice was a woman's, a Patryn's. He knew it. It was *her*
voice! She'd come back to him. Here, in the Labyrinth, she'd
found him at last. She'd driven away the serpents. He was safe,
with her, for the time being.

But the serpents would come back, and there was the child to
protect . . . their child.

"Our child?" he asked her. "Where is our child?"

"Haplo?" said the voice, now sounding puzzled. "Haplo,
don't you see me? It's me, Jarre . . ."

Haplo sat up, caught his breath. Level with his face was the
frightened and anxious face—and quivering side whiskers—of a
female dwarf. His disappointment was almost as terrible to bear
as the pain. He closed his eyes, shoulders slumped. It was all
hopeless. How could he go on? Why should he? He'd failed,
failed her, their child, failed his people, failed Jarre's people . . .

"Haplo!" Jarre's voice was stern. "Don't be a druz. Snap out
of it."

He opened his eyes, looked up at her, standing near him. Her
hands twitched; he had the impression that if he'd had a beard,
she'd be yanking it—her usual remedy for restoring Limbeck to
sense.

Haplo smiled his quiet smile, rose to his feet. "Sorry," he said.

"Where was I? What did you do to me?" Jarre demanded, eyeing him suspiciously. Her face paled, she looked frightened. "The . . . the elf . . . he hurt me." Her expression grew puzzled. "Only he wasn't an elf. He was a horrible monster, with red eyes . . ."

"I know," said Haplo.

"Is he gone? He is gone, isn't he?" she said, brightening with hope. "You drove him away."

Haplo regarded her in silence.

She shook her head, hope dimming. "He's not?"

"No, he's here. Down below. And there's more of them. Many more. The elf, Sang-drax, was only one of them. They're able to enter your world the same way I enter it."

"But how—" she wailed.

"Hush!" Haplo raised his hand.

The sound of feet, many feet, heavily booted feet, pounded down below—in the dwarves' secret entrance. Deep voices, shouting and clamoring in anger, echoed through the tunnels. The heavily booted feet began climbing up the ladder that led into the Factree.

The noise was like the rumble of the storms that swept Drevlin, swelling from beneath the Factree floor. Haplo cast a swift glance toward the elves, even as he raced over to the dwarves. The elven soldiers were on their feet, grabbing for weapons, their officers shouting orders. The expected dwarven attack was underway. The elves were prepared.

Haplo reached the tunnel entrance and was nearly bowled over by a surge of dwarves, leaping out at him. The elves were hastily overturning cots, throwing up barricades. The Factree doors flew open, a gust of rain-laden wind blew inside. Lightning flashed and the crack of thunder nearly drowned out the shouting dwarves. Someone cried in elven that the entire dwarven community was in arms. An officer yelled back that this was what he'd been waiting for, now they could exterminate the little "Gegs."

Limbeck charged past Haplo. At least Haplo assumed it was Limbeck. The dwarf's face was contorted with hatred and fury and the lust to kill. Haplo would not have recognized the dwarf had it not been for the spectacles, planted firmly on his nose and tied around his head with a long piece of string. He was carrying a wicked-looking battle-ax in one hand and, unaccountably, a feather duster in the other.

Limbeck dashed past Haplo, leading his fellow dwarves in a mad, frenzied dash that would take them headlong into the advancing ranks of the disciplined elves.

"Avenge Jarre!" shouted Limbeck.

"Avenge Jarre!" answered the dwarves in a single, rumbling, dire voice.

"I don't need avenging!" Jarre yelled shrilly, from where she stood at the base of the statue of the Manger. "It wasn't the elves! Limbeck!" she howled, wringing her hands. "Don't be a druz!"

Well, it worked once before, Haplo thought, and was extending his arm to unleash the spell that would freeze everyone in his or her place. But the chant died on his lips. He looked at his arm, saw the runes flare a brilliant, vibrant blue, saw it intertwined with red, felt his skin flame with warning.

The statue of the Manger came to life, began to move.

Jarre screamed, lost her balance on the swiveling base, and tumbled down the dais on which the statue stood. Limbeck had not heard her shout, but he heard her scream. He stopped in midrush, turned toward the sound, saw Jarre, scrambling to her feet, and the statue of the Manger, opening slowly.

The fear and terror and horror that flowed out of the tunnel ahead of the serpents acted more effectively than any of Haplo's spells to stop the dwarven advance. The dwarves stumbled to a halt, stared fearfully at the hole. Defiance and fury seeped out of them, leaving them cold and shivering husks. The elves, farther away from the tunnel entrance, couldn't see precisely what was going on, but they could see the giant statue moving on its base, could hear the rumble it made. And they, too, could feel the fear. They crouched behind their barricades, gripped their weapons, looked questioningly and nervously at their officers, who were grim and uneasy themselves.

"It won't work, Sang-drax," Haplo shouted. Through the dog's ears, Haplo could hear Hugh's voice, talking to Trian. He could hear the words of Iridal's bitter sorrow. "You're defeated! Bane's dead. The alliance will hold. Peace will come. There's nothing you can do now!"

Oh, yes there is, said Sang-drax, whispering inside Haplo's head. *Watch!*

Jarre half stumbled, half ran to Limbeck.

"We've got to escape!" she shrieked, plummeting into him, nearly knocking him flat. "Tell everyone. We have to leave. A . . . a horrible monster is coming. It lives down there! Haplo said—"

Limbeck knew a horrible monster was coming, something dark and evil and hideous. He knew he should run, knew he should order everyone to run for their lives, but he couldn't manage to get the words out. He was too frightened. And he couldn't see clearly. His spectacles had misted over from the sweat dripping down his brow. And he couldn't take them off. The string was knotted around his head and he didn't dare let loose of the battle-ax he was holding to unknot the string.

Dark shapes, dreadful beings, poured up out of the hole.

It was . . . They were . . .

Limbeck blinked, rubbed at his spectacles with his shirtsleeves.

"What . . . what is it, Jarre?" he demanded.

"Oh, Limbeck!" She drew in a shivering breath. "Limbeck . . . it's *us!*"

CHAPTER 43

WOMBE, DREVLIN

LOW REALM

◆

AN ARMY OF DWARVES MARCHED UP OUT OF THE TUNNEL BENEATH THE STATUE.

"Not bad, Sang-drax," Haplo muttered in grudging admiration. "Not bad at all. Confuse the hell out of everyone."

The serpents resembled the dwarves of Drevlin in every aspect—in clothes, in appearance, in the weapons they carried. They were shouting their hatred of the elves, urging their fellows to launch the attack. The true dwarves were beginning to waver. They were afraid of the newcomers, but their fear was starting to merge with their fear of the elves and soon they wouldn't be able to tell one fear from the other.

And they wouldn't be able to tell one dwarf from another.

Haplo could. He could see the red-eyed glint that gave away the serpents, but how could he explain all this to the true dwarves, how could he warn them, convince them? The two dwarven armies were about to join together. They would attack the elves, defeat them, drive them from Drevlin. And then the serpents, disguised as dwarves, would attack the machine, the Kicksey-winsey, on which the lives of all of the races on Arianus depended.

A brilliant stroke. So what if the humans and elves allied? So what if Rees'ahn and Stephen overthrew the Tribus empire? Word would come to them that the dwarves were wrecking the Kickseywinsey, about to deprive the Mid Realm of water. The humans and elves would have no choice but to fight the dwarves to save it. . . .

Chaos. Endless conflict. The serpents would grow powerful, invincible.

"Don't believe them! They're not us!" Jarre cried shrilly. "They're not dwarves. And they're not elves, either. They're the ones who hurt me! Look at them, Limbeck. Look at them!"

Limbeck tried to wipe the mist from his spectacles.

Frustrated, Jarre grabbed hold of the spectacles, gave them a tug that broke the string. Snatching them off Limbeck's nose, she threw them on the floor.

"What have you done?" Limbeck roared in anger.

"Now you can see, you druz! Look at them! Look!"

Limbeck peered myopically ahead. The army of dwarves was now only a dark blur, congealed together into a long, flowing mass. The mass heaved and writhed and glared at him from countless pairs of gleaming red eyes.

"A giant snake!" Limbeck shouted, raising his battle-ax. "We're being attacked by a giant snake!"

"We are?" Lof asked confusedly, looking up and down and in front and behind him. "Where?"

"Here," said Haplo.

Drawing the elven sword, stolen from the Imperanon, the Patryn lunged at the red-eyed dwarf standing nearest him. The runes etched on the sword flared, the metal glowed. A cascade of blue and red flame flowed from the blade toward the dwarf's head.

Except that it was no longer a dwarf.

A massive, flat, and snakelike body—ancient and awful— reared upward, expanding out of the dwarf's body like a monstrous plant bursting out of a seed pod. The serpent took shape and form faster than the eye could follow. Its tail lashed out, struck the sword, sent it flying. The weapon's rune-magic began to fall apart, the sigla shattered, crumbled in midair—links of a chain broken and scattered.

Haplo sprang back, out of the way of the lashing tail, watched for an opportunity to recover his weapon. He'd expected this—his attack had been too swift, too random. He hadn't had time to concentrate on his magic. But he had achieved his goal. Killing, even wounding the serpent, was not his objective. He'd meant to force it to show its true form, disrupt *its* magic. At least now the dwarves would see the serpent for what it was.

"Very clever of *you*, Patryn," said Sang-drax. The graceful form of the serpent-elf walked slowly out of the ranks of red-eyed dwarves. "But what have you accomplished—except their deaths?"

The dwarves gasped in shock, fell over themselves and each other in an effort to escape the hideous creature that now loomed over them.

Haplo darted beneath the serpent's whipping tail, snatched up his sword. Falling back, he faced Sang-drax. A few dwarves, shamed by the cowardice of their fellows, came to the Patryn's side. The other dwarves rallied around him, gripping pipes, battle-axes, whatever weapons they had been able to find.

But their courage was short-lived. The rest of the serpents began abandoning their mensch bodies. The darkness was filled with their hissing and the foul odor of decay and corruption that clung to them. The fire of the red eyes flared. A head dove down, a tail struck out. Massive jaws picked up a dwarf, lifted him to the Factree roof far above, dropped him to a screaming death. Another serpent crushed a dwarf with its tail. The serpents' best weapon—fear—swept through the ranks of dwarves like an ague.

Dwarves bellowed in panic, dropped their weapons. Those nearest the serpents scrambled to retreat down the hole, but ran up against a wall of their brethren, who could not get out of the way fast enough. The serpents leisurely picked off a dwarf here and there, making certain that they died loudly, horribly.

The dwarves fell back toward the front of the Factree, only to encounter the elven barricades. Elven reinforcements had begun arriving, but they were meeting—by the sounds of it—dwarven resistance outside the Factree. Elves and dwarves were fighting each other among the wheels and gears of the Kicksey-winsey, while inside the Factree itself, chaos reigned.

The elves cried that the serpents had been built by the dwarves. The dwarves shrieked that the snakes were a magical trick of the elves. The two turned on each other, and the serpents drove them on, inciting them to the slaughter.

Sang-drax alone had not altered his form. He stood in front of Haplo, a smile on the delicate elven features.

"You don't want them to die," said Haplo, keeping his sword raised, watching his opponent closely, trying to guess his next move. "Because if they die, you die."

"True," said Sang-drax, drawing a sword, advancing on Haplo. "We have no intention of killing them, not *all* of them, at any rate. But you, Patryn. You no longer provide sustenance. You have become a drain, a liability, a threat."

Haplo risked a swift glance around. He couldn't see either Limbeck or Jarre, presumed that they had been caught up in the panicked tide, swept away.

He stood alone now, near the statue of the Manger, who stared out unseeing on the bloodshed, an expression of stern and absurdly foolish compassion frozen on the metal face.

"It is all hopeless, my friend," said Sang-drax. "Look at them. This is a preview of the chaos that will rule the universe. On and on. Everlasting. Think of it, as you die . . ."

Sang-drax lashed out with his sword. The metal gleamed with the sullen, reddish light of the serpent's magic. He could not immediately penetrate the magical shield of the Patryn's sigla, but he would try to weaken it, batter it down.

Haplo parried the blow, steel clanging against steel. An electrical jolt ran from the serpent's blade to Haplo's, surged through the hilt, passed into his palms—the part unprotected by the runes—and from there up his arms. His magic was shaken. He fought to hold on to the blade, but another jolt burned the flesh on his hand, set the muscles and nerves in his arm twitching and dancing spasmodically. His hand no longer functioned. He dropped the sword, fell back against the statue, grasping his useless arm.

Sang-drax closed in. Haplo's body-magic reacted instinctively to protect him, but the serpent's blade easily penetrated the weakening shield, slashed across Haplo's chest.

The sword cut the heart-rune, the central sigil, from which Haplo drew his strength, out of which sprang the circle of his being.

The wound was deep. The blade sliced through flesh, laid bare the breastbone. To an ordinary man, to a mensch, it would not have been mortal. But Haplo knew it for a death blow. Sang-drax's magical blade had cut open more than flesh. It had severed Haplo's own magic, left him vulnerable, defenseless. Unless he could take time to rest, to heal himself, to restructure the runes, the serpent's next attack would finish him.

"And I'll die at the feet of a Sartan," Haplo muttered dazedly to himself, glancing up at the statue.

Blood flowed freely, soaked his shirt front, ran down his hands, his arms. The blue light of his sigla was fading, dwindling. He sank to his knees, too tired to fight, too . . . despairing. Sang-drax was right. It was hopeless.

"Get on with it. Finish me," Haplo snarled. "What are you waiting for?"

"You know full well, Patryn," said Sang-drax in his gentle voice. "I want your fear!"

The elven form began to alter, the limbs merged horribly, coalesced into a slack-skinned, slime-coated body. A red light glared down on Haplo, growing brighter. He had no need to look up to know that the giant snake head loomed above him, prepared to tear at his flesh, crush his bones, destroy him.

He was reminded of the Labyrinth, of the time he'd been mortally wounded there. Of how he'd laid down to die, too tired, too hurt . . .

"No," said Haplo.

Reaching out his hand, he grasped the hilt of the sword. Lifting it awkwardly in his left hand, he staggered slowly to his feet. No runes shone on the blade. He'd lost the power of the magic. The sword was plain, unadorned mensch steel, notched and battered. He was angry, not afraid. And if he ran to meet death, he could, perhaps, outrun his fear.

Haplo ran at Sang-drax, lifting the blade in a blow he knew he would never live to strike.

At the start of the battle, Limbeck Bolttightner was on his hands and knees on the floor, trying to find his spectacles.

Dropping his battle-ax, he paid no attention to the shouts and frightful yells of his people. He paid no attention to the hissing and slithering of the serpents (they were only shadowy blobs to him anyway). He paid no attention to the fighting raging around him, no attention to Lof, who was rooted to the spot with terror. Limbeck paid absolutely no attention to Jarre, who was standing over him, beating him on the head with the feather duster.

"Limbeck! Please! Do something! Our people are dying! The elves are dying! The world is dying! Do something!"

"I will, damn it!" Limbeck yelled at her viciously, hands pawing desperately over the floor. "But first I have to be able to see!"

"You could never see before!" Jarre shrieked at him. "That's what I loved about you!"

Two panes of glass shone red in the reflected light of the serpent's eyes. Limbeck made a grab for them, only to have them shoot out from under his very fingers.

Lof, jolted free from his paralyzing fear by Jarre's shout, turned to run away and accidentally kicked the spectacles, sent them skittering across the floor.

Limbeck dove after them, sliding on his rotund belly. He scrabbled under one dwarf's legs, reached around another's ankles. The spectacles seemed to have become a live thing, perversely keeping just beyond his grasp. Booted feet crunched on his groping fingers. Heels jabbed into his side. Lof toppled to the floor with a panic-stricken yell, his rump missing smashing the spectacles by inches. Limbeck clambered over the prostrate Lof, stuck a knee in the unfortunate dwarf's face, made a wild, stabbing grab.

Intent on the spectacles, Limbeck didn't see what had terrified Lof. Admittedly, Limbeck wouldn't have seen much anyway, nothing but a large gray, scaly mass descending on him. His fingertips were actually touching the wire frame of his spectacles when he was suddenly grabbed roughly from behind. Strong hands took hold of his collar, sent him flying through the air.

Jarre had run after Limbeck, trying to reach him through the milling crowd of frightened dwarves. She lost sight of him for an instant, found him again—lying on top of Lof, both of them about to be crushed by the body of one of the horrible serpents.

Dashing forward, Jarre caught hold of Limbeck's collar, yanked him up, and flung him out of danger. He was saved, but not the spectacles. The snake's body crashed down. The floor shook, glass crunched. Within instants, the serpent reared up again, red eyes searching for its victims.

Limbeck lay on his stomach, gulping for breath and not having much luck finding it. Jarre had only one thought—to keep the red eyes of the serpent off them. Again, she took hold of Limbeck by the collar and began to drag him (she couldn't lift him) over to the statue of the Manger.

Once, long ago, during another fight in the Factree, Jarre had taken refuge inside this statue. She'd do it again. But she hadn't counted on Limbeck.

"My spectacles!" he screamed with the first breath he was able to suck into his lungs.

He lunged forward, pulled himself free of Jarre's grasp . . . and was almost beheaded by the backswing of Sang-drax's sword.

Limbeck saw only a blur of red fire, but he heard the blade whistle past him, felt the rush of air on his cheek. He stumbled backward, into Jarre, who caught hold of him, pulled him down beside her at the statue's base.

"Haplo!" she started to cry, then hastily swallowed her shout. The Patryn's attention was fixed on his enemy; her yell might only distract him.

Intent on each other, neither Haplo nor his foe noticed the two dwarves, crouching at the statue's base, afraid to move.

Limbeck had only the vaguest idea of what was going on. To him, it was all a blur of light and motion and confusing impression. Haplo was fighting an elf, and then it seemed that the elf swallowed a snake, or perhaps it was the other way around.

"Sang-drax!" Jarre breathed, and Limbeck heard the horror and fear in her voice.

She shrank back against him. "Oh, Limbeck," she whispered unhappily. "Haplo's finished. He's dying, Limbeck."

"Where?" shouted Limbeck in frustration. "I can't see!"

And the next thing he knew, Jarre was leaving his side.

"Haplo saved me. I'm going to save him."

The serpent's tail lashed out, smashed into Haplo, knocked the sword from his hand, battered him to the floor. He lay dazed and hurting, weak from loss of blood, no breath left in his body. He waited for the end, for the next blow. But it didn't come.

A dwarf-maid stood over him protectively. Defiant, fearless, side whiskers quivering, a battle-ax in both hands, Jarre glared at the serpent.

"Go away," she said. "Go away and leave us alone."

The serpent ignored the dwarf. Sang-drax's gaze and attention were concentrated on the Patryn.

Jarre jumped forward, swung the ax at the snake's putrid flesh. The blade bit deep. A foul ooze flowed from the wound.

Haplo struggled to regain his feet. The serpent, wounded and in pain, struck at Jarre, intending to rid itself of a pest, then deal with the Patryn.

The snake's head dove at the dwarf. Jarre stood her ground, waited until the head was level with her blade. The serpent's toothless jaws opened wide. Jarre sprang clumsily to one side, swinging her ax. The sharp blade struck the snake's lower jaw, the force of the blow buried the head of the ax deep in the serpent's flesh.

Sang-drax howled in pain and fury, tried to shake the ax loose, but Jarre clung to the handle tenaciously. Sang-drax reared his head, intending to slam the dwarf's body into the floor.

Haplo grasped his sword, raised it.

"Jarre!" he cried. "Stop it! Let go!"

The dwarf released her hold on the ax handle, tumbled to the ground.

Sang-drax shook the ax loose. Infuriated at this insignificant creature who had inflicted such terrible pain on him, the serpent lashed out, jaws open to snap Jarre in two.

Haplo thrust the blade into the serpent's gleaming red eye.

Blood spurted. Half blind, mad with pain and outrage, no longer able to draw on the fear of its foe for strength, the serpent thrashed about in murderous fury.

Haplo staggered, nearly fell. "Jarre! Down the stairs!" he gasped.

"No!" she shrieked. "I've got to save Limbeck!" and she was gone.

Haplo started to go after her. His foot slipped on the serpent's blood. He fell, slid painfully down the stairs, too weak to catch himself.

It seemed he fell for a long, long time.

Oblivious to the fighting, searching for Jarre, Limbeck groped his way around the statue of the Manger and nearly tumbled into the hole that gaped suddenly at his feet. He stood gazing down into it. He could see blood and darkness and the tunnel that led to his unraveled sock, to the automaton, to the turning on of the wondrous machine. And down there, too, was that room, the mysterious room where he'd seen elves and dwarves and humans coming together in harmony. He peered around him and saw on the floor elves and dwarves lying together, dead.

A frustrated "why" was on his lips, but it was never spoken. For the first time in his life, Limbeck saw clearly. He saw what he had to do.

Fumbling in his pocket, Limbeck dragged out the white cloth he used to clean his spectacles and began to wave it in the air. "Stop," he shouted, his voice loud and strong in the silence. "Stop the fighting. We surrender."

CHAPTER 44

THE FACTREE

LOWER REALM

◆

ELVES AND DWARVES STOPPED LONG ENOUGH TO STARE AT LIMBECK. SOME WERE puzzled, some frowning, most suspicious, all astounded. Taking advantage of the general stupefaction, Limbeck climbed atop the statue's base.

"Are you all blind?" he shouted. "Can't you see where this will end? Death for us all. Death for the world, unless we stop it." He held out his hands toward the elves. "I'm High Froman. My word is law. We'll talk, negotiate. You elves can have the Kicksey-winsey. And I'll prove I mean what I say. There's a room down there." He pointed to the tunnel. "A room where you elves can turn the machine on. I'll show—"

Jarre screamed. Limbeck had a sudden impression of a huge mass rearing above him, a noxious hissing breath blowing over him, like the wind of the Maelstrom.

"It is too late!" roared Sang-drax. "There will be no peace for this world. Only chaos and terror, as you fight for survival. On Arianus, you will be forced to drink blood instead of water! Destroy the machine!"

The serpent's head swept over the startled dwarf and smashed into the statue of the Manger.

A resounding clang, deep and shuddering, rang through the Factree. The statue of the Manger, the stern and silent form of the Sartan that had stood for centuries, worshiped and adored by countless dwarves, shuddered, rocked on its base. The snake, lashing about in fury, struck at it again. The Manger let out another resounding clang, shook, shivered, and toppled to the floor.

The booming echo of its fall tolled like a knell of doom through the Factree.

All over Drevlin, the serpents began smashing the 'lectric zingers and ripping off the whistle-toots and battering into bits of metal the wondrous machine. The dwarves halted their retreat, picked up their weapons, turned to face the serpents.

The elves saw what was happening, had a sudden vision of their water-ships, sailing up to the realms above—empty. They began to fire their magical arrows at the serpents' red eyes. Inside the Factree and out, drawn together by the terrible sight of the serpents attacking the machine, dwarves and elves fought side by side to protect the Kicksey-winsey.

They were aided by the timely arrival of a crippled dragonship that had managed, by the combined efforts of its human and elven crew, to make its way safely through the Maelstrom. A group of burly humans, acting under the command of an elven captain, carrying weapons enchanted by the spells of an elven wizard, joined the dwarves.

It was the first time, in all the history of Arianus, that humans and elves and dwarves fought together, *not* against each other.

The sight would have made the leader of WUPP proud, but unfortunately he couldn't see it. Limbeck had disappeared, lay buried beneath the broken statue of the Manger.

Jarre, half blinded by tears, lifted her battle-ax and prepared to fight the serpent whose bloodied head was weaving over the statue, perhaps seeking Haplo, perhaps Limbeck. Jarre ran forward, shrieking defiance, swinging the ax . . . and couldn't find the enemy.

The serpent had vanished.

Jarre stumbled, unable to stop the momentum of her violent swing. The ax flew from her blood-slick hands. She fell to her hands and knees.

"Limbeck?" she cried desperately, feverishly, and crawled toward the broken statue.

A hand appeared, waved feebly. "Here I am. I . . . I think . . ."

"Limbeck!" Jarre dove for the hand, caught hold of it, kissed it, and then began to tug on it.

"Ouch! Wait! I'm stuck! Ooof! My arm! Don't—"

Ignoring Limbeck's protests, not having time to pamper him, Jarre clasped his pudgy hand, planted her foot against the statue, and pulled. After a brief but invigorating struggle, she managed to free him.

The august leader of WUPP emerged from underneath the statue of the Manger, rumpled and disheveled, shaken and confused, all his buttons missing, and with the overall impression of having been stomped on and squashed, but otherwise unhurt.

"What . . . what happened?" he asked, squinting, trying to see.

"We're fighting to save the Kicksey-winsey," said Jarre, giving him a swift hug. Then she grabbed up the bloody battle-ax and prepared to launch herself into the fray.

"Wait, I'll come with you!" Limbeck cried, clenching his fists and looking fierce.

"Don't be a druz," Jarre said fondly. Reaching out, she yanked on his beard. "You can't see a thing. You'd only hurt yourself. You stay here."

"But . . . what can I do?" Limbeck cried, disappointed. "I must do something."

Jarre could have told him (and would, later on, when they were alone together) that he'd done everything. That he was the hero of the War, responsible for saving the Kicksey-winsey and the lives of not only his people but of everyone on Arianus. She didn't have time for all that now, however.

"Why don't you make a speech?" she suggested hastily. "Yes, I think one of your speeches would be just the thing."

Limbeck considered. It *had* been a long time since he'd made a speech. Not counting the surrender speech, which had been rather rudely interrupted. He couldn't quite recall where that one had been headed, however.

"But . . . I don't have one ready . . ."

"Yes, you do, my dear. Here."

Jarre reached into one of Limbeck's baggy pockets, pulled out a sheaf of ink-stained paper, and, removing the sandwich, handed the speech to Limbeck.

Resting his hand on the fallen statue of the Manger, Limbeck held the papers up to his nose and began to thunder, "Workers of Drevlin! Untie and throw off your freckles . . . No, that can't be right. Workers of Drevlin! Unite and throw off your mackerels!"

And so the dwarves marched into what would later go down in history as the Battle of the Kicksey-winsey, with the occasionally confused but always inspiring words of the leader of WUPP, soon to be world hero, Limbeck Bolttightner, ringing in their ears.

CHAPTER 45

WOMBE, DREVLIN

LOW REALM

◆

HAPLO SAT ON THE STAIRS LEADING DOWN FROM THE BASE OF THE FALLEN statue into the secret tunnels of the Sartan. Above him, Limbeck harangued, the mensch battled the serpents to save their world, and the Kicksey-winsey stood silent, unmoving. Haplo leaned against the wall, weak and light-headed from shock and loss of blood.

The dog was with him, gazing at him anxiously. Haplo didn't know when it had come back, was too tired to think about it or what its return portended. And he could do nothing to help the mensch; he could barely help himself.

"It doesn't sound as if they need any help, though," he said to the dog.

He had closed the terrible wound in his chest, but he needed time, a long time, to completely heal himself. The heart rune, the very center of his being, was torn.

He leaned against the wall, shut his eyes, grateful for the darkness. His mind drifted. He was holding the small book, the one given him by the Kenkari. He would have to remember to turn the book over to Limbeck. He was looking at it again . . . he had to be careful . . . didn't want to smear blood . . . on the pages. . . . The drawings . . . diagrams . . . instructions.

"The Sartan didn't abandon the worlds," he was telling Limbeck . . . or the dog . . . who kept changing into Limbeck. "Those on this one foresaw their own demise. Alfred's people. They knew they would not be able to complete their grand scheme for uniting the worlds, for providing air to the world of stone, water to the world of air, fire to the world of water. They wrote it all down, wrote it down for those they knew they would have to leave behind.

"It's all here, in this small book. The words that will start the automaton upon its tasks, start the Kicksey-winsey operating, align the continents, bring them all life-giving water. The words that will send a signal through Death's Gate to all the other worlds.

"It is all in this book, written down in four languages: Sartan, elven, dwarven, human.

"Alfred would be pleased," Haplo told Limbeck . . . who kept changing into the dog. "He can quit apologizing."

But the plan had gone awry.

The Sartan who were supposed to awaken and use the book had not. Alfred, the one Sartan who did wake up, either didn't know about the book or had searched for it and couldn't find it. It was the Kenkari elves who had found the book. Found it, suppressed it, hidden it away.

"And if it hadn't been the elves," Haplo said, "it would have been the humans, or the dwarves. All of them, too filled with hate and distrust to come together . . ."

"Workers of the world!" Limbeck was winding up. "Unite!"

And this time, he got it right.

"Maybe this time, they *will* get it right," Haplo said tiredly, smiling. He sighed. The dog whimpered, crowded close to its master and sniffed worriedly—flesh twitching—at the blood on his hands and arms.

"I could take the book," came a voice. "Take it from your dead body, Patryn."

The dog whimpered, pressed its nose into his hand.

Haplo's eyes flared open. Fear snapped him to full, alert wakefulness.

Sang-drax stood at the bottom of the stairs. The serpent had resumed his elf form, looked much the same as before, except that he was wan and pale and only one red eye gleamed. The other eye socket was a dark and empty hole, as if the serpent had plucked out the injured orb and tossed it away.

Haplo, hearing the dwarves shout triumphantly from above, understood.

"They're winning. Courage, unity—the pain's more bitter than a sword's thrust inside you, isn't it, Sang-drax? Go on, get out. You're as weak as I am. You can't hurt me now."

"Oh, I could. But I won't. We have new 'orders.' " Sang-drax smiled, his voice lingered over the last word as if he found it amusing. "You're to live, after all, it seems. Or perhaps I should rephrase that. *I'm* not the one destined to kill you."

Haplo bowed his head, closed his eyes, leaned back against the wall. He was tired, so very tired . . .

"As for your mensch friends," continued Sang-drax, "they haven't managed to turn the machine on yet. It may prove to be a 'jolting' experience. For them . . . and for all the other worlds. Read the book, Patryn. Read it carefully."

The serpent's elven form began to waver, started to lose consistency and shape. He was visible, for an instant, in his hideous snakelike body, but that transformation, too, was difficult for him to maintain. He was, as Haplo had said, growing weak. Soon, only his words were left, and the faint flicker of the gleaming red eye in the darkness of the Sartan tunnels.

"You are doomed, Patryn. Your battle can never be won. Unless you defeat yourself."

THE CATHEDRAL

OF THE ALBEDO

ARISTAGON, MID REALM

♦

THE DOORS TO THE CATHEDRAL OF THE ALBEDO REMAINED CLOSED. THE Kenkari continued to turn away the weesham, who occasionally came to stand forlornly, staring at the ornate grillwork until the Keeper of the Door emerged.

"You must go," he would tell them. "The time is not right."

"But what do we do?" they cried, clutching the lapis boxes. "When do we return?"

"Wait," was all he said.

The weesham found no comfort in that, but they could do nothing except return to the Imperanon or to their dukedoms or principalities and wait. Everyone on Paxaria was waiting.

Waiting for their doom.

News of the alliance forged between the rebel elves and the humans had spread rapidly. The Unseen brought back reports that human and elven forces were massing for the final assault. Imperial elven troops began to withdraw from towns on the perimeter of Volkaran, falling back to encircle and defend Aristagon. Towns and cities on the perimeter immediately made plans to surrender to Prince Rees'ahn, on condition that human armies would not be permitted to occupy them. (The elves recalled their own tyrannical occupation of human lands and feared retribution. Their fears were undoubtedly justified. Some wondered if centuries-old, festering wounds would ever heal.)

At one point, a strange report, whose source was later traced to Count Tretar, went round the Imperanon. Agah'ran had announced publicly, during luncheon, that King Stephen had been assassinated. The human barons were reportedly in revolt against Queen Anne. Prince Rees'ahn had fled for his life. The alliance was about to crumble.

Parties were held in celebration. When the emperor sobered up, however, he discovered that the report was not true. The Unseen assured Agah'ran that King Stephen was alive and well, though it was observed that the king walked somewhat stiffly and haltingly—the result of a fall suffered during a drinking bout.

Count Tretar was no longer seen at court.

But Agah'ran was confident. He gave more parties, one or two each night, each more glittering, more frantic than the last. The elves who attended (and there were fewer of them each night) laughed at certain other members of the royal family who had purportedly abandoned their homes, gathered up what wealth they could carry, and headed for the frontiers.

"Let the rebels and the human scum come. We will see how they fight against a real army," said Agah'ran.

In the meantime, he and the other princes and princesses and counts and earls and dukes danced and drank and ate sumptuously.

Their weesham sat silently in the corners and waited.

The silver gong rang. The Keeper of the Door sighed, rose to his feet. Peering through the grillwork, expecting another geir, he gave a small gasp. He opened the door with trembling hands.

"Come in, sir. Come in," he said in low and solemn tones.

Hugh the Hand entered the cathedral.

The Hand wore, once again, the robes of a Kir monk, though in this instance he didn't wear them to disguise himself for travel through enemy lands. A Kenkari elf accompanied Hugh. The Kenkari had been assigned to escort him from the camp of Prince Rees'ahn in Ulyndia, back to the cathedral in Aristagon. Needless to say, no elf had dared stop them.

Hugh stepped across the threshold. He did not look back, did not take a final glance at a world he would soon be leaving forever. He'd seen enough of that world. It held no joy for him. He was leaving it without regret.

"I will take over from here," said the Door in a low voice to
Hugh's escort. "My assistant will show you to your quarters."

Hugh stood apart, silent, aloof, staring straight ahead. The
Kenkari who had accompanied him whispered a few words of
blessing, pressed long, delicate-boned fingers into Hugh's arm.
The Hand acknowledged the blessing with a flicker of the deeply
sunken eyes, a slight inclination of the head.

"We will go to the Aviary now," said Door, when they were
alone. "If that is what you wish."

"The sooner I get this over with, the better," Hugh said.

They walked down the crystal corridor that led to the Aviary
and the small chapel room just outside.

"How do you do it?" Hugh asked.

The Door flinched, startled. He'd been absorbed in his own
thoughts. "Do what, sir?"

"Execute people," said the Hand. "You'll excuse the question,
but I have a rather personal interest in this."

The Door went exceedingly pale. "Forgive me. I . . . . I cannot
answer. The Keeper of the Soul . . ." He stammered and fell silent.

Hugh shrugged. After all, what did it matter? The worst part
was the journey, the wrenching agony of the soul, unwilling to
leave the body. When all ties were severed, he'd be welcomed
back home.

They entered the chapel without ceremony, without knocking.
Obviously, they were expected. The Keeper of the Book stood
behind her desk, the Book open. The Keeper of the Soul stood
before the altar.

The Kenkari shut the door, placed his back to it.

"Hugh the Hand, approach the altar," said the Keeper of the
Soul.

Hugh stepped forward. Behind the altar, through the window, he could see the Aviary. The green leaves were very still,
this day; no motion, no disturbance. The dead souls, too, were
waiting.

In moments, Hugh would join them.

"Make this quick," said Hugh. "No praying, no singing. Just
get on with it."

"It shall be as you desire, sir," said the Keeper of the Soul,
gently. He raised his arms, the butterfly wings shimmered, falling

in folds about him. "Hugh the Hand, you agreed to give your soul to us in return for our assistance to you and the Lady Iridal. Such assistance was granted. Your quest to save the child was successful."

"Yes," said Hugh, voice gruff, soft. "He is safe, now." As I'll be safe, he thought. Safe in death.

The Keeper of the Soul flicked a glance at Book and Door, then turned his complete attention back.

"And you, Hugh the Hand, now come forward to fulfill your contract with us. You give us your soul."

"I do," said Hugh, kneeling down. "Take it." He braced himself, clasped his hands before him, drew a deep breath, as if he guessed it must be his last.

"I would," said the Keeper, frowning. "But your soul is not yours to give."

"What?" Hugh let out his breath, glowered at the Keeper. "What do you mean? I've come here to you. I kept my part—"

"Yes, but you do not come to us free of mortal bonds. You have taken on another contract. You agreed to kill a man."

Hugh was growing angry. "What tricks are you elves up to? What man did I agree to kill?"

"The man called Haplo."

"Haplo?" Hugh gaped, uncomprehending. He honestly had no idea what the elf was talking about.

And then . . .

There's just one thing you must do. You must tell Haplo, when he's dying, that Xar is the one who wants him dead. Will you remember that name? Xar is the one who says that Haplo must die.

The Keeper of the Soul watched Hugh's face, nodded when the man looked up at him in stunned and baffled realization. "You promised the child Bane. You took his contract."

"But . . . I never meant . . ."

"You never meant to live long enough to fulfill it. Yet you are alive. And you took the contract."

"And Bane is dead!" Hugh said harshly.

"Would that make a difference to the Brotherhood? The contract is sacred . . ."

His expression dark and grim, Hugh rose, stood facing the Keeper. "Sacred!" He gave a bitter laugh. "Yeah, it's sacred. Apparently it's the only thing sacred in this accursed life. I thought you Kenkari were different. I thought at last I'd found something I could believe in, something . . .

"But what do you care? Pah!" Hugh spit on the floor at the Keeper's feet. "You're no better than all the rest."

Book gasped. Door averted his face. Inside the Aviary, the leaves of the trees whispered, sighed. The Keeper regarded Hugh in silence.

At length, the Keeper said, quietly, calmly, "You owe us a life. Instead of yours, we choose his."

Book caught her breath, stared, horrified, at the Keeper of the Soul. Door opened his mouth, about to do the unthinkable—about to speak, about to protest. The Keeper cast the other Kenkari a swift, stern gaze and both bowed their heads, fell silent.

"Why? What'd he do to you?" Hugh demanded.

"We have our reasons. Do you find this arrangement acceptable?"

Hugh folded his arms across his chest, tugged thoughtfully at his twisted beard. "This pays for all?"

The Keeper smiled gently. "Perhaps not all. But it will come close."

Hugh considered, eyed the Kenkari suspiciously. Then he shrugged. "Very well. Where do I find Haplo?"

"On the isle of Drevlin. He has been grievously wounded and is weak." The Keeper lowered his eyes, his face was flushed. "You should have no difficulty—"

Book made a choking sound, covered her mouth with her hands.

Hugh glanced at her, sneered. "Squeamish? Don't worry, I'll spare you the gory details. Unless you want to hear how he died, of course. I'll throw that part in free. Describe his death throes . . ."

Book turned away, leaned weakly on her desk. Door was livid, his frail body shook and trembled. The Keeper of the Soul stood silent, unmoving.

Hugh turned on his heel, walked toward the door. The Keeper glanced questioningly at the Soul.

"Accompany him," the Kenkari commanded his fellow. "Make whatever arrangements he deems necessary for his transportation to Drevlin. And provide whatever . . . weapons . . ."

Door blanched. "Yes, Keeper," he murmured, barely able to

walk. He glanced back, pleadingly, as if he would beg the Keeper to reconsider. Soul remained firm, implacable. Sighing, Door prepared to escort the assassin out.

"Hugh the Hand," the Soul called.

Pausing on the threshold, Hugh turned. "Now what?"

"Remember to fulfill the condition you promised. Tell Haplo that Xar is the one who wants him dead. You will be certain to do that? It is most important."

"Yeah, I'll tell him. Anything for the customer." Hugh gave a mocking bow. Then he turned to Door. "The only thing I'll need is a knife, with a good, sharp blade."

The Keeper shrank into himself. Pallid and wan, he cast a final glance back at Soul. Receiving no reprieve, he accompanied Hugh out and shut the door behind them.

"Keeper, what have you done?" cried Book, unable to contain herself. "Never, in all the centuries of our existence, have we taken a life! Any life! Now our hands will be stained with blood. Why? For what reason?"

The Keeper stood staring after the assassin. "I do not know," he said in a hollow voice. "I was not told. I did only as I was commanded." He looked behind the altar, through the crystal window, into the Aviary.

The leaves of the trees rustled quietly, in satisfaction.

APPENDIX ♦ I

THE BROTHERHOOD

OF THE HAND

♦

ORIGINS AND HISTORY

No one is certain when the Assassins' Guild was first established or who established it. It was in existence before the Sartan left Arianus, to judge by writings left behind that lament the guild's activities and ponder ways to put a stop to it. Sartan scholars speculate that the Brotherhood's origins date from the rise of guilds in general, during the prosperous rule of the Paxar elves. The Paxar encouraged free trade, thus allowing the development of a strong merchant class.

Thus, while the more peace-minded citizens of the Mid Realm were forming Silversmiths' guilds and Brewers' guilds, it was perhaps natural that the darker elements of society should think of forming their own guild. The Brotherhood may have, at first, been formed in mockery of the legitimate guilds, but members soon saw the advantages of banding together: self-protection, self-regulation, and the ability to set and control prices.

Probably founded by elves, with only elven members, the Brotherhood soon extended its membership to include humans. The guild would have added dwarves to its ranks, as well, for the Brotherhood's credo is that the color of every man's money is the same, just as is the color of his blood. But most of the dwarves had, by this time, been shipped off to Drevlin and, therefore, were out of the realm of the Brotherhood's interest and jurisdiction.

Shifting winds of change and war wreaked havoc on nations and people of the Mid Realm, but these gales only served to strengthen the power of the Brotherhood. A series of strong, intelligent, ruthless, and cold-blooded leaders, culminating in Ciang, herself, not only held the ranks of the Brotherhood together, but increased its stature and wealth.

Shortly after the fall of the Paxar and the rise of the Tribus elves, the Brotherhood took control of the island of Skurvash, built its fortress there, and has continued to exert a powerful influence on all underworld operations in the Mid Realm since.

CURRENT STATUS

The power of the Brotherhood during this particular period of Arianus's history is enormous. War and rebellion serve as an ideal cover for its operations. Although not directly involved in the smuggling operations of Skurvash (just as they are not "directly involved" in other illegal activities), the Brotherhood levies a "tax" on smuggled or stolen merchandise, in return for providing protection to those who sell it. This "tax" and the income derived from membership dues make the Brotherhood the wealthiest guild in existence. Such wealth and influence is undoubtedly due to the genius of Ciang, the Brotherhood's current leader.

CIANG THE ARM

Ciang's word is law. She is highly respected (almost worshiped) by all the members. The cruelest, most heartless murderer has been known to cower like a small, naughty child under Ciang's rebuke. Nothing is known about her youth, except that she was reputed to be one of the most beautiful elven women ever born and that, from hints she herself has dropped, she is a member of elven royalty. She is quite charming, amoral, and totally ruthless. She is the only one of the Brotherhood who can make the final decision to "send round the knife" and has done so on numerous occasions. Although a fellow member may call for such an action, Ciang herself must initiate the order.

SENDING ROUND THE KNIFE

"Sending round the knife" is the term used for the most-feared ritual in the Brotherhood of the Hand. Violation of certain laws in the Brotherhood is punishable by death, and, as might be expected, the members themselves police their own organization. If a member is deemed to have broken one of the laws and the death sentence is passed, Ciang orders that wooden knives carved with the offender's name be circulated among the members. The knives are passed one to the other, as members encounter each other, until the word goes around (which it does with alarming speed). Any member who meets the offender is required to carry out the death sentence or face a similar punishment. It does not matter that the member under sentence may be friend, lover, spouse, sibling, or parent. Loyalty to the Brotherhood takes precedence over all other loyalties and vows.

MEMBERSHIP DUES

Originally membership dues were low, intended to cover the guild's expenses and not much more. It was Ciang who determined that the dues be raised to their extraordinarily high level, forcing out many of the "stew-plate" variety of assassin (one who would kill a man for a plate of stew). The move was quite controversial at the time, many members arguing (but not in Ciang's presence) that it would prove the death of the guild. Ciang's wisdom soon became apparent, however.

Assassins were at first required to pay a percentage of their contracts, but this proved too difficult to monitor. Ciang ordered that this practice cease. All members are now required to pay yearly dues that vary in amount, based on rank; the assumption being that a skilled assassin is a rich assassin.

Any assassin who has fallen on hard times and can't afford the dues has only himself or herself to blame. The Brotherhood wants only skilled, disciplined members and can afford to rid itself of drunks, gamblers, or any other person whose personal failings make him or her a failure at the craft.

Payment of annual dues is excused only for those injured in the line of duty. Wounded members may come to the fortress on Skurvash and avail themselves of the fine-quality (perhaps the finest available in the Mid Realm) medical treatment. During their recovery period, dues are waived.

THE BROTHERHOOD'S INFIRMARY

Strict rules pertain to the admittance of injured members into the Infirmary. The injury must have been obtained while on a job. The wounds must be honorable in nature and must be honorably obtained. (Being struck over the head from behind by a chair during a barroom brawl, for example, would not qualify. Nor would being knifed by a jealous lover.) If a contract is unfulfilled due to an injury obtained while attempting to fulfill it, the assassin must return the money he or she was paid for the job and complete the contract on personal time, for personal honor.

DEFINITION OF VARIOUS TERMS

"Scars Are Still Fresh."

This pertains to the rite of investiture and refers to the fact that the person has not been a member of the Brotherhood long. Ciang uses this term in reference to Ernst Twist.

Note: Hugh the Hand described his meeting with Twist to Haplo, to whom we are indebted for the story. Haplo recognized Twist as a serpent from Hugh's description of the peculiar red cast to the man's eyes, as well as the connection between Twist and Sang-drax.

Given the fact that the serpents could not have been long in coming to Arianus, Haplo found it remarkable that Twist had risen this far in the membership in so short a time. He reasons that the serpents, having seen the vast potential of the guild in terms of furthering their own ambitions for plunging the world into chaos, must have gone out of their way to join.

Haplo adds a certain rumor (probably obtained from Hugh the Hand), that an attempt to assassinate Ciang was deliberately staged by the serpents, in order for one of their own to "save" her life and emerge a hero. If this did indeed occur, no record of it exists. Ciang herself would have been far too proud to have publicized it. The fact remains, however, that Ernst Twist rose rapidly in the ranks and is, according to all reports, still rising.

"Sheath to Tip . . . Make Blade . . ."

These terms refer to the various stages of rank of those who join the Brotherhood. A new member—one "whose wound bleeds"—is said to be a "sheath," for, just as a sword remains sheathed, the new assassin's potential is still untried. From "sheath" one moves to "tip"—newly blooded—and then up to "blade," "crossguard," "hilt." Such advancements may take years. How they are determined is kept highly secret, but Ciang presumably has final word. Hugh's rank, "the hand," is highest, next to Ciang's own. She is known as "the arm."

SPONSORS

Except under certain circumstances, all current applicants to the Brotherhood must have a sponsor. The sponsor is a person who is willing to literally bet his or her life on the new member, for if any of the Brotherhood's rules are broken by the novice, retribution is swift and fatal and falls not only on the newcomer, but also on the one who sponsored him or her.

One might imagine that such a rule would discourage old members from sponsoring new ones, but a very handsome bonus is paid to those who bring in "fresh blood."

In the event that the knife is "sent round" on one member of such a team, the other may claim first right to enact the penalty of death. Such an act may not serve to save the surviving member's life, but he or she will at least be considered by the Brotherhood to have died with honor redeemed.

Teams often work together but are not required to do so. Some may take separate paths and rarely see each other again.

Occasionally, individuals of rare skill and talent are invited by the Brotherhood to join. Hugh the Hand was one of these. A loner by nature, Hugh would never have sought admittance to the Brotherhood on his own. Some say that Ciang herself acted as his sponsor. Others say it was the man known only as the Ancient. Hugh never speaks of it.

THE FUTURE OF THE BROTHERHOOD OF THE HAND

A peaceful Arianus will no doubt bring changes to the Assassins' Guild. But the guild's demise is not foreseen. The evil serpents' plot against Arianus has been thwarted for the time being, but not the serpents themselves.

As Sang-drax reminds us, their influence has been felt since the beginning of time and will continue to be felt until time's end. And, until that time, the Brotherhood of the Hand will flourish.

APPENDIX ♦ II

DEATH GATE

SINGULARITIES

♦

**A report compiled by Haplo
for his lord. Never delivered.**

The Jrandin Rheus, as the Sartan called it, took unified creation and sundered it into independent yet interdependent realms. Most Patryns familiar with the Sartan diagrams of the Sundering and the Sundered Realms, however, seem to be led to a false image of the final nature of that structure—that is, as some series of globes neatly connected by arrows and lines floating in nebulous space. It is not surprising. The Sartan loved symmetry and linearity above all and took comfort in picturing their Jrandin Rheus as some beautifully ordered and balanced thing. The details are a great deal more complex and messy, as we well know.

In fact, all of the Sundered Realms exist in the same place. Viewed in terms of the Probability Wave of Patryn Magic, the unified creation that existed before the Jrandin Rheus was harmonically shifted into several different realities. These harmonic realities manifest themselves into the various partitioned realities that we perceive as fire, water, earth, and sky, as well as such special subrealities we know as the Nexus and the Labyrinth.

However, the harmonics of these realities are not entirely separate. The original harmonics that set up the Sundering continue to reverberate between the worlds. Through these harmonics, each of the realms touches the others in special ways that are manifest in our understanding as harmonic paths. These paths take two forms: conduits and Death Gates.

Conduits and Death Gates are quite similar in basic structure but radically different in their form. The basic structure of each is formed by a rotating singularity—a spinning mass of such high gravity that all laws of time, space, and existence have no meaning. It is a place where nothing exists and everything exists. It is a place where perfect chaos and order exist simultaneously in the same space. The contradictions themselves that allow these singularities to essentially be in both disparate existences of different realms at the same time.

The spin of such singularities determines their form (Death Gate or conduit) and their state (barred, open, or stopped).

FORM

The form of the harmonic path is determined by the direction and complexity of the spin of the singularity relative to the probability boundary between the two realms. This spin compresses the event horizon surrounding the singularity and gives direction to the Death Gate or conduit.

Death Gates were given a single, simple rotation direction (Figure 1). This configuration from the original magic produced a flattened disk that, as rotation increased, developed a depression on both sides (Figure 3). It was the development of this symmetrical event horizon that gave the Death Gates a stable axis of direction and, eventually, would allow passage from one realm to the next. Due to this symmetry, the Death Gates are stable in both directions of passage. This made the Death Gates ideal for Sartan and mensch to travel between the realms once the Death Gates were open at the Jran-kri.[1]

Conduits, however, are created when a singularity is given, or develops on its own, a complex motion relative to the probability boundary between realms. When more than one axis of rotation is involved (Figure 2), the complex event horizon in fast-rotating singularities creates a field allowing one-way passage between realms but offers no way of returning through the same singular-

---

[1] A Sartan phrase meaning the third phase of the Sartan plan.

ity. Conduits were to be utilized to transport raw materials, power, light, and water between the realms at the Jran-kri. It found other uses as well, apparently, for I suspect that one such conduit was used to send our people to the Labyrinth—as well as those Sartan who disagreed with the council under Samah.

STATE

In addition to their form, each harmonic path also has a state. This state is determined by the speed of its rotation. The higher the speed of the rotation, the more flattened the event horizon of the singularity. The thinner the event horizon at the point of passage, the more defined the direction of travel and the easier the trip.

There are three states mentioned in the Jrandin Rheus, though only the first two are explained.

Barred

The first state is called barred. This state is created when a singularity rotates "slowly." This rotation rate is quite high compared to the turning of a mill wheel, for example, but is slow compared to the open state. As a Barred Gate, the rotation of the singularity forms a disk with a depression on each side (Figure 3). Through this depression—the thinnest part of the disk—a traveler can pass from one realm to the next. Such passage, however, comes at tremendous personal cost. I, of course, have transited the Death Gate while it was barred. It was not an experience I would care to repeat, for it brings one uncomfortably close to knowledge that one would just as soon forget.

Conduits rotating in the barred state can allow the passage of some people and materials in one direction, as I have stated, but are subject to the same difficulties as the Death Gates. Until these conduits were brought to a full and open state, it would be impossible for the realms to function together.

Open

At the Jran-kri, the gates and conduits were "open." This means that the relative rotation of the gates and conduits was vastly increased. This resulted in the event horizon of the harmonic paths forming a torus shape with the event horizon surrounding a clear hole of reality bridging the realms (Figure 4). In the region of this bridging reality, all the realms could be linked and traveled. The thoughts of the individual at the time of transition are critical to the transition to the desired destination being properly made. Concentration is vital for a successful passage.

With the conduits open, the interaction of the worlds is set in motion. The conduits widen and allow vastly greater amounts of all kinds of power and materials to move into the next realm. The circuitous design of the realms, as originally planned by the Sartan, allows for the smooth flow of goods and materials. Within a few months, the realms should be productive and functioning well. It is ironic that the Sartan abandoned their experiment before they could taste its fruits.

Stopped

There is a third state mentioned in the text, a state where the singularities stop rotating altogether (Figure 5). Such a state would, of course, prevent any passage from realm to realm of either personnel or goods.

Deathgate Singularity Rotation
(Single Directional Rotation)

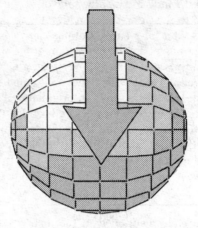

Figure 1

Conduit Singularity Rotation
(Multidirectional Rotation)

Figure 2

Deathgate Singularity States

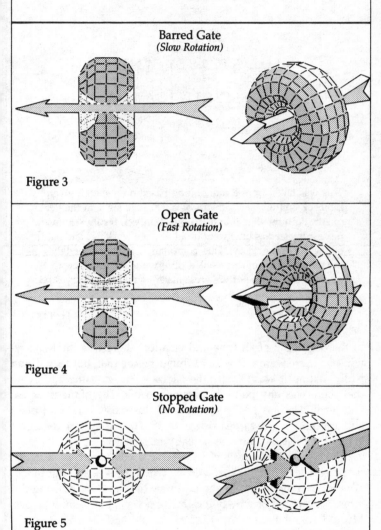

Barred Gate
(Slow Rotation)

Figure 3

Open Gate
(Fast Rotation)

Figure 4

Stopped Gate
(No Rotation)

Figure 5

THE KICKSEY-WINSEY

DEMYSTIFICATED

✦

This was taken from a monograph based on a speech given by Limbeck Bolttightner, a dwarf of my acquaintance in the Realm of Air. Both intelligent and curious, Limbeck became more and more interested as time went on in the true workings and nature of the Kicksey-winsey. This compilation is almost certainly a mixture of the Kenkari book's observations coupled with the intimate knowledge of the great machine that the dwarves possess.

—HAPLO

In the beginning of all time and creation, there was the Kicksey-winsey. There were also a lot of things before that, but they didn't really matter. It wasn't until the Kicksey-winsey came into being that there was any point or purpose to life. The Mangers, great and terrible beings of the sky, created this most wonderful place and brought we dwarves down to it. Then they left us alone. When they left us alone, they really messed up.

From that time until now, we have continued to struggle, work, and serve the Kicksey-winsey with our lives and our blood. We didn't know why. No one told us what the lever twisting did when we twisted or why bolt tightening was of any consequence. My old friend Balin Purgeflusher—a fine and dedicated dwarf until his untimely accident—had no concept of what he was flushing when he purged.

You, my fellow dwarves, have been born in an age of enlightenment—when we are no longer slaves to the elves nor to the humans nor even to the Mangers who dumped us here like so much garbage. We no longer grovel. We no longer live off the scraps tossed to us by others. Today, we have lifted up our heads and stand tall—as tall as we can in such circumstances—with our elven and human neighbors.

One of the great benefits of this age of enlightenment is that we now have a better understanding of the Kicksey-winsey and its overall purpose. Dwarves from every scrift often ask me, "What is the Kicksey-winsey?" and "Where did it come from?" and "What do all the parts do?" and "When do we eat?" They should be asking, "*Why* do we have a Kicksey-winsey?" but since I just asked that question, I'll answer all of them—even the one you didn't think to ask.

WHAT IS THE KICKSEY-WINSEY?

The Kicksey-winsey is a *masheen*. A *masheen* is a collection of wheels and turn-knobbies and lever-bangers and tube-zoomers that, when all put together, DO SOMETHING! That is a *masheen*. When you turn your turny-wheelie, you are helping the *masheen* to do something.

Just what you are doing is highly dependent upon what part of the Kicksey-winsey you are serving. The diagrammatic map of the Kicksey-winsey—drawn by myself and reproduced here for the first time—should serve to demystificate the mystifying *masheen*. If you will pay attention and follow along on my map, you will recognize parts of the Kicksey-winsey that you and your family have served for generations.

At its very simplest, a *masheen* takes stuff called *matrels* and turns it into *poduct-goodys*. *Matrels* are, by themselves, pretty useless stuff. An example of *matrels* would be the ore brought up by the dig claws from below. To date, the dig claws have been the primary source of *matrels* for the Kicksey-winsey. However, in a startling revelation, we now know that this ore was only intended to be used for the building of the Kicksey-winsey itself—not for the actual creation of *poduct-goodys*! The primary source of *matrels* was to be a location that we know as Wombe. Wombe has traditionally been the home of the Scrift Heads and the High Froman. Perhaps many of you, too, have told jokes about the Froman and how they never really worked and served the Kicksey-winsey. This is because his tasks—the collection of *matrels* from the Lexax[1] through mystical processes understood only vaguely by the Froman through tradition—was not possible to perform until the Alignment of the World. With the lands of all creation[2] now brought into harmony, the intended work of the Froman has begun, and at last, all the people of our government are honestly employed.

From Wombe, these *matrels* are then distributed via a number of different means to various cities of our acquaintance through a system called *Conveyer*. Everything from whoosh-wagons, sucker tubes, rip-roads, flushers, and zoomers is utilized to distribute these *matrels* to their destination. Throughout our history, this movement of raw *matrels* about the Kicksey-winsey has, of course, been noted but never clearly understood. Various theories regarding its meaning have been forwarded. Groth Staredial's theory, popularly called Blood-winsey,[3] though crude, was not far from the truth. The late Throtin Pushpuller's competing theory that the *Conveyer* was intended to be an alternate transportation system was tragically disproved by his own tests near the Erm Melty-vat only last year. Though too late for Throtin, we now understand this *Conveyer* as a distribution system for *matrels*, never intended to transport live dwarves.

At the same time that the Fromen at Wombe are sending out *matrels* for each of the scrifts, a second system with the magical and mystical name of *trami-sond* is at work. This was not always

---

[1] The dwarves' spiritual concepts are limited to the realm of Arianus. They have little conception of an "outside" reality or of other spheres of existence beyond a vague and often self-contradictory mythology of a place called Lexax—a possible derivation from the word Nexus. In trying to convey the notion of importing raw materials from the other realms of existence, this was the only framework in which the dwarves could understand the concept.

[2] Again, the dwarves' understanding of their universe is limited to their own realm.

[3] Staredial's theory involved the notion that the movement of raw materials through the Kicksey-winsey was like the movement of dwarf blood through their veins. Limbeck, an early supporter of Staredial's theory, has a hard time giving it up.

so. In the beginning, the Kicksey-winsey created its own *powher* with a device called a *spinnerator* that put water into large *holdings*. The amount of *powher* that the *spinnerator* made, however, was not enough to fulfill the destiny of the Kicksey-winsey. Now, with the Alignment of the Worlds, *powher* comes from a different source. Through processes unknown to us, an *enput* device gathers a mystic force called *Powher* from the realm of Lexax. This wonderful force is then channeled into a secret place, known only to the Mangers, called the Room of Trol.

(I must interject, for our young audience, that the Room of Trol has no connection to actual trolls. No trolls exist in the Kicksey-winsey, although I have been told that there may be some in remote locations in the Mid Realms. There is no need to panic!)

The Room of Trol then takes the *powher* and sends it as a *tramis* down the *tramis-sond* system. The form of this *powher* varies from the gas that lights your lamps to the driving force that wheels your wheels in the Kicksey-winsey. Whatever form it takes, *powher* is the stuff that makes everything in our world work.

When enough *matrel* and enough *powher* are brought together in the different scrifts, then the Kicksey-winsey creates—through our help and efforts—a variety of *poduct-goodys*. *Poduct-goodys* are riches beyond need. They are everything from tunics and trousers to lamps and forks. They are everything from pillows to hammers. They are chairs, tools, weapons, food, and water. Everything that one could think of that one would want—and a great number you haven't thought of—are *poduct-goodys* of the Kicksey-winsey.

However, do not be led to the false conclusion that this wealth comes without a price! "Everything has a price, some just hide it better than others."[4] There are others who live in the Lexax who exact payment for the *matrels* and *powher* that they send to us through *enput*. They call this tribute that they demand *esport*. Once the *poduct-goodys* are finished, we select that which we need and then send the rest—an enormous surplus—through the *esport* just outside of Het back as tribute to those who are now sending us *matrels* and *powher* in such abundance.

---

[4] A dwarf aphorism that is used far too much and heeded far too little.

Why should we send *esport*, you ask? Well, you probably didn't ask why, but I will. Why should we send *esport*, I ask? Because, I answer, if we don't send *esport*, they'll stop sending *emport* and *powher*, and we no longer would get to have new *poduct-goodys* instead of the garbage the elves used to give us.

The Kicksey-winsey does many other things such as sending water from the *holdings* to the other realms above us through the Liftalofts and keeping the various continents in line with a series of *masheens* called *linners*.[5] I will not be describing them here. They are complex subjects and are probably better dealt with another time.[6]

WHERE DID IT COME FROM?

Just before the beginning, the Kicksey-winsey was started by the Mangers. The first dwarves, led by the legendary Dunk Pullstarter, were brought to Drevlin by the Mangers and established here. The Kicksey-winsey was started.

The common misconception is that the Kicksey-winsey was always as large as it is now. This is simply not true. In the beginning, the Kicksey-winsey was quite small—some say no larger than a single scrift section—and did nothing but work to increase itself. This was natural. The first part of the purpose for the Kicksey-winsey was to establish and protect itself so that it could eventually fulfill its second, and more important purpose, of serving the dwarves, elves, and humans as well as those who exist in the Lexax.

WHAT DO ALL THE PARTS DO?

I have no idea. Neither do you.

The reason we have no idea is that the Kicksey-winsey is so

[5] While some of the terminology used by the dwarf is modeled after more common words, some of his names have no discernible source other than his own imagination.

[6] The truth is that I could never make Limbeck understand runic alignment theory nor even the notion that water—so common a commodity on his own continent—could be of such importance to the upper realms. This is just his way of dodging the issue.

unfathomably huge, so titanically complex, and has been so out of control for so long that it has grown beyond our ability to understand it. Without Mangers and Trollers to direct it, the Kickseywinsey itself has been taking whatever steps were required for its own brainless survival.

WHY DO WE HAVE THE KICKSEY-WINSEY?

We serve the Kicksey-winsey so that it may serve us. This is the second purpose of the great *masheen* that we have directed for so many years without any knowledge of why. If we take care of the Kicksey-winsey it will take care of us and that should be enough purpose for any dwarf. It certainly is enough for me.

WHEN DO WE EAT?

Now that the Kicksey-winsey is operating as it was always meant to—whenever we want. That concludes my talk and begins our lunch.

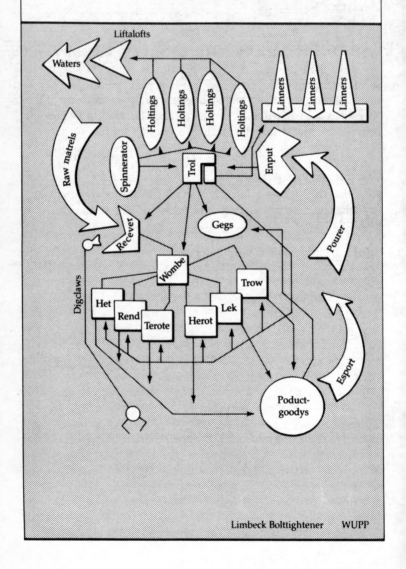

Kicksey - winsey
Demystificated

Liftalofts

Waters

Linners   Linners   Linners

Holtings   Holtings   Holtings   Holtings   Holtings

Raw matrels

Spinnerator   Trol   Enput

Recevet   Gegs   Pourer

Digclaws

Wombe   Trow

Het   Rend   Terote   Herot   Lek

Poduct-goodys   Esport

Limbeck Bolttightener   WUPP

Prayer

by Janet Pack

Repeat as needed for length of chant

For A. Neal Deaver, my father
Love, Janet